GAME—OR REALITY?

"Well, [illegible] is going to poison the [illegible]

"I su[illegible]e is."

"And then I have to kill Randolph, right? Because the King was my father? And I'm the new King?"

"Yes, what about it?"

"Ruth, I don't want Randolph to poison the King."

"Of course you don't," said Laura, relieved to hear someone say something she could understand. "The King is a good, kind man, but he's been corrupted, and he's old, and—"

"You don't know that," said Ted. "I met him, and he *is* a good, kind man. And I met Randolph, and I don't want to kill him, either."

"Well, of course not, that's the point," said Ellen, "he's your best friend, but you kill him for his honor and yours because—"

"Ellen!" Ted shrieked, and startled them all. He stood up and threw his stick into the fire. "You don't know anything, none of you do."

"I made up as much as you did!" said Ellen.

"That's not what he means," said Ruth. "Sit down, Ted."

"I have a good mind to quit right now," said Ted, not moving. "What *do* I mean, if you're so smart?"

"It's real, that's what you mean."

"But I tell you, it isn't," broke in Patrick. "It can't be. There's no such thing as magic."

✖ ✖ ✖

FIREBIRD
WHERE FANTASY TAKES FLIGHT™

THE
SECRET COUNTRY

PAMELA DEAN

FIREBIRD

AN IMPRINT OF PENGUIN GROUP (USA) INC.

FIREBIRD

Published by Penguin Group

Penguin Group (USA) Inc., 345 Hudson Street, New York, New York 10014, U.S.A.

Penguin Books Ltd, 80 Strand, London WC2R ORL, England

Penguin Books Australia Ltd, 250 Camberwell Road,
Camberwell, Victoria 3124, Australia

Penguin Books Canada Ltd, 10 Alcorn Avenue,
Toronto, Ontario, Canada M4V 3B2

Penguin Books (N.Z.) Ltd, 182-190 Wairau Road, Auckland 10, New Zealand

First published in the United States of America by Ace Fantasy Books,
The Berkley Publishing Group, 1985
Published by Firebird, an imprint of Penguin Group (USA) Inc., 2003

7 9 10 8

ISBN 0-14-250153-0

Printed in the United States of America

For my mother,
Mary Ann Dean,
who let me read
when I should have been
outside playing softball

ACKNOWLEDGMENTS

This book took a long time to write. I am grateful to the following people, without whose aid it would not be written yet:

Brian Davies, Kathy Etter, Betsy Mitchell, Ellen Trumbull, and David Weiner, who gave me my earliest encouragement;

Nick O'Donohoe, who gave me notebooks that the story might not languish in my head;

Gerri Balter, Judy Cilcain, Joyce Odum, Laramie Sasseville, Joyce Scrivner, and Mike Smith, who prevented its languishing in the notebooks;

Nate Bucklin, Steven Brust, Emma Bull, Kara Dalkey, Will Shetterly, and Pat Wrede, whose stern advice and kindly nagging transformed what had come out of the notebooks;

David Dyer-Bennet and Scott Robinson, who rescued the transformed book from the wrong computers;

and David Dyer-Bennet, who cheerfully married the book along with its author.

PROLOGUE

EDWARD Fairchild, Prince of the Enchanted Forest, Lord of the Desert's Edge, Friend to the Unicorns, and King of the Secret Country, wished he were somewhere else. Pretending his foot was asleep, he slid closer to the door.

"My lord," said Randolph, his chief counselor, "I beg you—"

"I do more than beg!" said Fence the Wizard. "Edward, keep thy place."

Edward looked at him. "I will not hear these things," he said.

"Thou wilt if I say thou wilt."

"I am king here."

"And I am above kings. I am not thy servant."

"Hey!" said a page.

"Be still!" said Fence. The page scowled.

"Very well, then," said Randolph, "as I was saying. Could vintners or merchants distill this poison? Could butlers, cooks, pages"—the page looked up, pleased—"know its secret? Thou," he said to Fence, "taught me the use of my wits. Now where are thine?"

Fence stood up, and as the folds of his robe fell into place he seemed suddenly to dwarf the room. "If mine are addled," he said, "I must needs make do with thine. Make thine work for me." He fixed Randolph with piercing blue eyes, and the counselor looked suddenly blank.

"I know the truth," whispered the page.

"Silence, varlet!" said Edward, and was pleased to see the page's eyes widen.

"I know the truth," said Randolph. "I do not need my wits to discover it. And knowing it already, how can I tell thee in what way thou shouldst work thy wits to discover it thyself?"

"Tell me this truth, then," said Fence.

The page tugged at the King's sleeve and whispered, "Your crown's slipping." Edward pushed the crown farther back on his sweaty head. Was it so hot in the room?

"No, indeed I shall not," said Randolph. "I would not betray thy teaching thus. How many times, knowing the truth thyself, hast thou made me dig it out for myself? Can I do less for thee?"

"Do you know," said Fence to Randolph, "why I did thus?"

"I do," said Randolph. "It was that I might believe the truth when I saw it. For truth hath shapes strange and terrible."

"And this truth," said Fence, "a most terrible one."

"Say it," said Randolph.

"Randolph," said Fence, "you have betrayed all I ever taught you; you have betrayed your liege lord and your solemn word; you have done this besides with the lowest and cruelest of all weapons, a weapon of cowards. You poisoned King William."

"I have said I will not listen to this!" shouted Edward.

"Well done," said Randolph to Fence.

"What?" said Edward.

"Will you set a trial, my lord," said Randolph, "or—"

"A trial is a coward's weapon also," said Edward, loosening his sword in its sheath.

"My lord, have a mind for your cloak," said the page. Edward unfastened it, and the page took it from his shoulders and folded it.

Randolph took off his own and dropped it onto the floor. He and Fence looked at each other. "You can do no good here," said Randolph.

The wizard nodded and turned to go.

"What about his ring?" demanded the page.

"Be quiet!" said Edward.

"But he forgot—"

In the distance a bell rang.

"Hell!" said Randolph. "That's lunch."

"You forgot to take his ring of sorcery and kick him out of the guild of wizards!" said the page fiercely.

"Ellen," said Randolph, "no matter what anybody forgets, you shut up. You're only a page and we can hang you for mouthing off, okay?"

"You try it!" said Ellen. She pulled off her velvet cap and shook out her cloud of black hair. In the hat she had looked very like a page. Without it, thought Edward, she looked like someone who would grow up to be a witch.

"I'd love to," said Fence, struggling out of his robe. "But we'd be late for lunch."

"This is it, then, isn't it?" said Edward. "The plane leaves at two-thirty." He pulled at his crown, which came damply apart in his hands.

"And you still didn't get it right," said Ellen. "You ought to let Ted do Fence, Patrick, and you be Prince Edward."

"I *am* Prince Edward, and I want to be him in this part," said Ted. "Especially in this part."

"Oh, all right."

"So this is it," said Patrick, cramming Fence's robe under his arm.

"And you still didn't get it right," said Ellen. "And neither did Ruth. Randolph is supposed to be resigned, Ruthie, and you just sounded bored. And Ted, Edward is much more shocked than that; you just sounded like somebody's put a frog in your bed, not like—"

"Ellie, stop that, please," said Ruth, picking up Randolph's cloak again. Being fifteen to Ellen's twelve, and having the same wild hair and green eyes, she looked like a witch already, no matter how inspired a Randolph she could do. "When you're grown up and directing plays," she told Ellen, like a sorcerer lecturing her apprentice, "you can fuss at people like that. Until then, cut it out."

The bell rang again.

"Next summer," said Patrick, "we should—"

Laura stuck her head into the doorway of the barn. Ted looked at his sister in despair. Her braids were coming undone. She would never look like a witch.

"Will you guys come on?" she said. She looked at what Patrick had under his arm and added, "Your mother just started wondering what happened to that sheet."

"Took her long enough," said Ellen.

"Next summer," said Patrick to Laura, "*you* can be a page. She talks too much."

"Hey!" said Ellen.

"Well," said Laura, "it might be better than being a dead king. Lying there waiting for the worms to come."

"Laurie, for goodness' sake, you don't have to wait for the worms to come," said Ruth. "Dead people don't, you know."

"How do you know?" demanded Ellen. "You ever been dead?"

4

"We could embalm you," said Patrick to Laura. "They'd leave you alone then."

"Embalming's barbaric," said Ruth. "The Secret Country is more civilized than that."

"Civilized!" said Patrick. "They don't even have machines!"

"I don't want to be embalmed," said Laura hastily. "I'd rather wait for the worms."

"I don't think you'd make a good page," said Ellen. "I like to be impudent, so I make a good page, but you only like to be a mouse, which is better for a dead king, really."

"On the other hand," said Patrick, "it'd be good for her to be impudent once in a while. Next summer—"

Laura seemed to feel that she was on Ellen's side and that she did not want to hear any more about this. She asked Ellen, "How'd it go?"

"They messed it up," said Ellen. "They forgot that we decided that Fence *is* Edward's servant, and they forgot to take Randolph's ring away, and—"

"Next summer," said Ruth.

"Let's eat," said Laura.

"Shut up, brat," said Ted, throwing the remains of Edward's crown at her.

"I'm hungry!"

"Me too," said Ellen.

"Next summer," said Ruth, giving in and turning for the door, "we'll do it right."

CHAPTER 1

Who's done what now?"

"Laura. In the two weeks that that child has been here—"

"Eight days."

"In the eight days that seem like two weeks that that child has been here, she has broken four cereal bowls, two mugs, three plates, a mirror, a Waterford bowl, two pots with plants, three pots without plants—"

Their voices came clearly through the closed door of the study. Laura crouched further behind the Japanese screen they kept in the hall. Three cereal bowls, she thought.

"—and, just now, the stained-glass window in the bathroom."

"Where is she?" asked her uncle.

"I don't know."

"Did she run? Poor kid."

"Poor kid?" Her aunt's voice rose to a squeak in the way her mother's would when you said something silly. But her mother would not think that her uncle was being silly.

"She's also cut herself picking up all the pieces," said her uncle. "And fallen down the front stairs twice. Not to mention cracking her head on—"

"And she won't let me cut her hair."

Maddeningly, at this most important point, her uncle lowered his voice to answer. Laura, wondering if she dared to stand right at the door and listen, put her head around the edge of the screen and saw her older brother standing in the middle of the hall. He looked disgusted.

"Ted!" she hissed. To her great satisfaction, he jumped and looked around in the wrong direction before he spotted her on the floor. He came and leaned against the wall next to her.

"Jen's up crying in the bathroom," he said, just above a whisper. "She liked that window."

"It was an ugly window," whispered Laura, who had liked it too.

"How did you break it when it's up so high?"

"There was a wasp."

"I told you, you want something killed, come and get me."

"I can kill my own wasps!"

"They'll kill *you*," said Ted, pointing at the door of the study, "if you break anything else. They'll put you in an orphanage for the summer."

"I'm not an orphan."

"You are for the summer."

"So are you! If I go you're coming with me!"

"You don't have to go if you'd just—"

"They'll hear you," said Laura.

"They're talking too loud themselves," said Ted. They listened again.

"I know her parents are in Australia, I know she misses them, I know she's shy, I know she doesn't get along with our kids. Does that mean she can turn the whole house into a wreck and kill herself—and probably us—in the process?"

"All I'm trying to say—"

"She wants to cut my hair," said Laura, watching Ted try to catch what her uncle was saying. Her uncle had lowered his voice again.

"What good would that do?" said Ted absently, his eyes on the study door.

"She says it makes me look like a waif."

"Be quiet a minute," said Ted.

"It's her own fault. She can't braid hair," said Laura. Ted squinted at the door. "What's a waif?" she asked him.

"A beggar child. You've been one in the Secret, don't you remember?" said Ted, still looking at the door.

"I don't look like a waif."

Ted finally looked at her. "It wouldn't hurt you to cut it," he said. "Jen says it takes you forever to wash it."

Laura was stung. "Whose side are you on anyway?"

"I'm not on anybody's side, I just talked to Jen. We have to live here, you know. Jen's all right; she asks us to play tag."

So what, thought Laura. "I hate tag."

"So do I, dimwit. That's not the point."

"Yes it is. It's a stupid game. All their games are stupid."

"Why don't you let them cut your hair?" said Ted. "It'll grow again."

"I'm a princess," said Laura, who had never had her hair cut and was not about to entrust the process to people who talked about her the way her aunt and uncle did.

"Not this summer you're not a princess. Come on, Laurie."

"No." Laura forgot to whisper.

"Shut up," said Ted.

They both shut up, but the voices in the study went on.

Ted sat down on the floor and scowled at Laura, who scowled back.

"You've got to do something. They're really mad."

"I can't help it if I break things."

"But you can cut your hair. Then they'll see you want to be nice."

"I don't want to be nice. I don't like them and I want to go home."

"Well, so do I. You'll just make it worse if you don't like them. Come on. Let's go in the study and tell them you'll cut your hair. Then they won't be so mad about the window." He studied her with a look she had not seen since last summer, and his voice became formal. "You could do it for a penance."

That was too much. You did penance for things like murder not for breaking a window when you hadn't meant to. Laura jumped to her feet, crying "Leave me alone!" and bumped her elbow on the screen, which tilted dangerously. She put her hands out to catch it. Ted, who was quicker, had already caught the screen, but he pushed it right into them. The taut paper gave suddenly with a horrible popping tear; the screen, trailing shreds, crashed past a shocked Ted to the floor of the hall, and their aunt flung the study door open and caught them in the wreckage.

The problem was that they were staying with the wrong cousins. Ted and Laura had been spending summers with the Carroll cousins for as long as they could remember, and probably, said Laura, longer. They had never stayed with the Barretts before and they didn't want to.

The worst of it was that there was really nothing wrong with the Barretts. Tommy was too little to bother anybody.

Jennifer was almost Laura's age and delighted in letting guests have their way. David wouldn't talk to them, but he wouldn't talk to anybody else either, and he let Ted read his books. Katie was seventeen and presumably too old to bother with cousins of fourteen and eleven, but she had some of the best books they had ever read, and she didn't care who read them as long as they were given back in one piece. Aunt Kathy and Uncle Jim, as other people's parents went, were bearable.

The Barretts were very good people with whom to spend a nice, ordinary summer playing tag and hide-and-seek and red light, green light and watching television. But Ted and Laura had never spent a summer like that in their lives, and hadn't wanted to, and didn't like it. The Secret had grown every year with Ruth and Ellen and Patrick, and after a whole winter of deprivation, they wanted to get back to it.

Besides, Jennifer and David were never very enthusiastic about playing anything, even when they suggested it themselves. Worse yet, they objected to snide remarks about the television shows they watched. Ted and Laura came from a family in which a television show that could wring fifteen minutes of silence from its audience was rare and valuable. The reverent attitude of Jennifer and David bewildered them.

But they were stuck with Jennifer and David, because the right cousins had moved to Australia and Ted and Laura's parents had gone to visit them for the summer. It cost too much to let Ted and Laura go too.

Ted and Laura did not even have the solace of letters from their cousins. They had tried to write to them. Laura had suggested doing it in the alphabet of the Secret Country. They excitedly got out their key sheet, which contained not only English and Secret Country alphabets, but the Sorcerous Letters and the Runes of the Eight Ghostly Kings. They tackled the date and "Dear Ruth, Ellen, and Patrick," with great satisfaction. But then they looked blankly at each other. What was there to say? They felt that the Secret was not a subject to be trusted to the mails, and they had nothing else to say that was of any interest to their cousins, or indeed to themselves. So they ceremoniously burned the unfinished letter, which gave them a melancholy sort of pleasure and got them into trouble with their aunt, and gloomed through the long days, which gave them no pleasure at all.

And now this. Laura had broken things all the eleven years of her life, but nobody had ever been so upset about it as the Barretts were.

Their upset this time extended only to sending Laura to the room she shared with Jennifer, and Ted to the one he had to himself. Laura, feeling certain that this was only a method of getting her and Ted out of the way until a suitable punishment could be devised, became reckless and sneaked along to Ted's room as soon as her aunt's footsteps went away down the stairs.

"What's the good of having things if they break?" she demanded of her brother.

Ted was reading, as usual. He turned a page, and Laura sighed.

"Mom doesn't scream when I break something."

"You've never broken so many things before."

"Well," said Laura, putting her hand flat down in the middle of his book, "I can't help it."

"You could be more careful," said Ted, pulling his book out from under her hand.

"I am careful!"

"So how come you break so many things?" Ted asked the book.

"They're always in the way," said Laura sullenly. She did not know how she broke so many things. It was much more as if they broke themselves.

"So are you," said Ted. "Always."

"Well, I don't have anything to do!" said Laura, furious.

"Read," said Ted, and went on doing so.

"I've read all the ones I can. The words in the rest of them are too hard."

"Laurie!" yelled Jennifer from downstairs. "Mom says you can come play tag."

"I'm too hot!" shrieked Laura.

The back door banged.

"Would you read to me?" said Laura.

"I'm in the middle of the book. You wouldn't understand anything. You don't like the way I read anyway." He did not say, "Go away and leave me alone," but Laura knew he wanted to.

"Tag is a penance," she said.

"So go play."

Laura went resignedly downstairs and outside. It was very hot and bright and stuffy.

There was no one in the backyard, so she started around to the front. There were lilac bushes all along one side of the house, in which they were not supposed to play. The bushes would have made a fine Green Caves for the Secret, but here it didn't matter. As Laura came around the corner of the house, she heard people talking among the bushes.

"What did she say?"

"There are spies among us."

Laura pushed her hair away from her ears. Something in their voices was familiar to her.

"Who are they?"

"This place is probably bugged." Laura moved guiltily away, but only a few steps. It was Jennifer and David talking, but she had never heard them sound like this.

"So speak crookedly," said Jennifer.

"They are those who eat and sleep with us and share our bathing place."

"Where are they from?"

"I fear the Imperium."

"Well, then, let's tell the captain."

"She may be one of them."

"Nonsense!" said Jennifer, in her own voice.

"She's shown them documents," said David.

"She'd never betray us," said Jennifer; once more her voice had the quality Laura had found familiar. Now she recognized it. Ted had just used it to suggest she do a penance. They were playing: not this business of running around and hiding for no reason, but a real play, with parts.

"The documents had red covers," said David.

"Oh, no!" said Jennifer. "Not the plans for the black-hole gun!"

Laura went tearing into the house and back up to Ted's room, banging doors. She skidded on a braided rug in the upstairs hall, but caught herself on the edge of Ted's door.

"Ted!"

"What's wrong?"

"They've got a secret too!"

Ted put his book down. "Quit yelling. How do you know?"

Laura told him. Ted shrugged. "Probably just some s-f show they saw on TV." Laura hauled him down to the side of the house.

"The crew all love her," said Jennifer earnestly, out of the bushes. "If we put it to the vote she will go free and the spies will be able to work their will unchecked."

"No doubt," said David, "we can think of—we can devise other means to rid ourselves of this—this—maggot."

"We could hire—" began Jennifer.

"Hirelings talk," said David. "We'll have to do it ourselves."

Laura looked at Ted's face and was satisfied. There was a note in David's voice that told her a scene had just ended. Ted had heard it too. They crept around the house, eased themselves up the creaky steps of the porch, and went back to Ted's room.

"How can they have a secret?" demanded Laura.

"All that tag was just for us," said Ted. Laura looked at him and was alarmed as well as puzzled. She had not seen Ted look so worried since two summers ago, when they lost Ellen in the Thorn Forest during the Secret. They had almost had to ask their parents for help, and they would never have been able to explain what they were up to.

"We shouldn't be here," said Ted now.

"What?"

"We couldn't work our Secret with a lot of strange kids around."

Laura was horrified. "No, we couldn't."

"We'll have to keep out of their way," said Ted.

Laura showed her teeth at him. "It's not fair. It's bad enough we have to be in this place all summer and not have any Secret, without having to keep out of the way and have any fun, either." That was more horrifying than interfering with somebody's secret.

"You don't like tag anyway."

"But if *they* don't like tag we could—"

"Would you let them in our Secret?"

"No!"

"Well, then."

"It's not fair. Tag's better than nothing."

"Laurie," said Ted in a way he had.

Laura looked at the rug.

"It won't be so bad," said Ted, as comfortingly as he could. "It didn't sound like a really good Secret, you know." Laura was not comforted. Ted hardly ever tried to comfort her, so he was no good at it; anyway, she could tell that he could not see anything to be comforting about.

She looked at him, trying to decide whether to hit him or to start crying.

"Look," said Ted desperately. "Do you want to go to the library? We could find some more books you could read."

"All summer?"

"We'll think of something for all summer, okay? Right now we need something to do while we're thinking, that'll get us out of Dave and Jen's way."

"Oh, all right."

They found Katie and told her what they wanted to do. She gave them a shrewd look. "Mom wanted to know if you wanted to go horseback riding this afternoon."

Laura shuddered.

"Laurie's afraid of horses," said Ted, "and we would really rather read."

Katie told them where they could find the library, and where in it they could find the sort of books they wanted. She gave them Jennifer's card, Jennifer having lost Katie's.

The library was an old building with many steps and

many small rooms. Ted and Laura came in by a door nowhere near the checkout desk, to which they eventually had to ask directions. Then they were so excited about the books they had found that they went out the nearest door and walked several blocks, reading first paragraphs aloud to each other. Ted, as was his exasperating habit, became absorbed and began to mumble. Laura, knowing that to read while walking was a good way to fall down, put her books under her arm and surveyed the neighborhood.

"Look at that house!" she said, pulling her brother's arm. "It's a secret house!"

It was an enormous gray stone house, bigger than the library, and it had had pieces added onto it here and there, some of brick, some of wood, and some of a different gray stone than the original. It had mullioned windows. It had two towers with round windows and peaked red roofs. Around its yard was an overgrown viny hedge with a brick arch and an iron gate in it. Weeds, some as tall as Laura, and violets and dandelions grew in the yard. There were dark pines, and cedars, two hoary oaks and many maples. The sunlight falling through their leaves was dusty. The flagstone walk leading to the front door was covered with dry brown maple seeds. It was a very secret house. Laura looked at Ted, expecting him to be pleased, but he was alarmed.

"Where are we?" he said. "We didn't go by here on the way to the library; we'd remember."

A cardinal whistled somewhere in the trees. Laura felt a shock of delight. Here was a secret house, and there was the most secret of all the secret birds. All members of the Secret, even those in exile, must pay heed to cardinals, she decided.

"It's the Call!" she yelled at her brother, and dived into the hedge. She caught her foot in a twist of root, came down on her knees, and felt a pain in one of them that made her shriek.

She struggled through the hedge into the tall grass on the other side, and stared at her knee. It was covered with blood. She was too impressed to shriek again.

"Watch out," she said to the cracking and rustling that was Ted trying to get through the hedge. "I fell on something sharp."

Ted wormed his way through. "Are you all right?"

"It's awfully bloody," said Laura.

"If I tie my handkerchief around it it'll stick," said Ted, with the certainty of experience.

"Give it to me," said Laura. She wiped the blood off. "Ech!" she said. "That's a cut! Look at that!"

"What did you fall on?"

"It was in the hedge," said Laura, busy with the handkerchief.

Ted ducked back into the hedge. "I can see something shiny in here," he said. "At least you won't get tetanus." He rustled about in the dead maple leaves. The cardinal sang suddenly overhead.

"What is it, a broken bottle?" asked Laura, obliterating the last clean spot on Ted's handkerchief.

Ted did not answer her.

"Hey," said Laura.

Ted backed out of the hedge, holding a small sword. There was no dirt on it. The hilt was black and set with blue stones. Neither Ted nor Laura knew anything about jewels, but they both agreed that the stones did not look like sapphires. Lines they could not quite make out ran down the blade. It caught a stray sunbeam and dazzled their eyes.

"It doesn't have any blood on it," said Laura.

"It's the only thing under there."

"It's so little," said Laura. "Secret size, for a sword."

"Maybe it belongs to the people who live here. We should ask."

"Nobody lives here," said Laura, who was afraid of strangers and wanted the sword. She put her hand out for it.

"They could," said Ted, pulling it out of her reach and standing up. He started for the door, which opened. A tall woman with a broom came out onto the path.

"How came you here?" she demanded, and her voice made the fine hairs stand up on the backs of their necks. Ted dropped the sword and hauled his sister to her feet, trying to push her through the hedge. Laura, surprising herself, shoved him, and he fell through it himself.

Laura grabbed the sword and scrambled through after him. Instead of ending up on the sidewalk, she fell into cold water, sword and all.

CHAPTER 2

Laura stood up in the stream. Its gravelly bottom had taken some skin off an elbow, but at least she had not fallen on the sword. She wiped her wet hair out of her face and shook water from the sword. The sun struck the swinging blade, making a flash that brought tears to her eyes.

She put the sword behind her and looked at where she was. The house was still there, but there was no woman at the door. There were no Ted, no street, and no other houses. The stream went down a hill and vanished into a forest, and everywhere else were green fields. It was very hot and bright, but not stuffy. Laura looked at the pattern the oak and maple leaves made against the sharp sky, and felt something poke at the back of her mind—nothing so clear as an apprehension nor so definite as a memory, but something. The leaves looked right. So, in this desolate setting, did the house. She frowned at the house. She felt, somehow, that she ought to be afraid of it.

Laura floundered to the sandy edge of the stream and climbed up onto the grass below the hedge, dripping.

"Ted!" she yelled through the hedge.

No one answered.

Laura screamed at the top of her lungs. "Ted!"

No one answered. Laura drew in her breath to call again, and changed her mind. The hot still air made her feel as if she were shouting into a pillow. If Ted was not in the yard, he was probably not where he could hear her, and who knew what *was* where it could hear her?

Thinking about that made her remember the sword. She did not think being wet could be good for it. She lifted it out of the stream, holding it at arm's length, and stared up at the house. There were lace curtains at the windows, and she was trying to remember if there had been curtains there before, when she heard voices.

She turned and looked across the stream. Three figures, one tall and two not, were just coming down a long slope. When they got to the bottom, there would be only a narrow flat space before they came to the stream. If they looked up from their conversation they would see her.

Laura was under the hedge in one bound, dragging the sword with her. The thought of the woman with the broom kept her sitting in the middle of the hedge instead of going all the way into the yard. But when it seemed clear from their gestures that the three people were interested in the house, and coming to the house, she panicked and rolled into the yard, still clutching the sword.

"Laurie!" It was Ted's voice, from the other side of the hedge, back on the sidewalk. A shadow fell over Laura and the prickling voice of the woman said, "Stay!" Laura plunged through the hedge again, caught the sword in a tangle of branches, and wrenched at it. "Stay, in the name—" said the voice. Laura abandoned the sword and flung herself onto the sidewalk, skinning both knees. Ted picked her up and grabbed her by the hand, and they ran.

After three blocks and a corner they stopped.

"You idiot!" said Ted. "Is your leg all right?"

"Yes, listen—"

"It doesn't look like it. What were you doing in there?"

"I found a secret country!" Excitement poured into her, although while she had been in the other place she had felt only a sort of exploratory wariness.

What she had said took much explanation before Ted so much as understood it, and before he believed it, Laura had to sit down on the curb and say passionately, "As I am a Bearer of the Secret, I am telling you the truth."

It helped that she was very wet, although it had not rained for three weeks and the yard of the secret house had been as dry and dusty as everywhere else. But they were left with many problems. If she really had found a secret country, they should certainly go back and see if it was their Secret Country or if it belonged to someone else. It had looked, to Laura, immensely Secret but, though right, not familiar. It could have been anybody's, even, they supposed reluctantly, Jennifer and David's. But there was the problem of just how to get in, and there was the woman with the broom.

"She didn't just want to sweep the sidewalk," said Laura, shivering as much from the voice as from her wet clothes.

"No," said Ted. "While you were off falling in streams she beat the hedge with the broom and yelled."

"What did she say?"

" 'The devil damn thee black,' " said Ted, not without relish, "and things like that. Never mind her. Why did you push me?"

"You wanted to leave the sword there, and I wanted to take it."

"Dishonest child."

Laura was furious. "I bet it wasn't hers at all!"

"Then why was she after us with the broom?"

"Well, it is her yard," said Laura. She was possessed of a vague feeling that nobody could defend something so vehemently unless he had no right to it, but she could not explain this to Ted. "Anyway, if the sword is hers why does she keep it under the hedge? Why doesn't she lock it up?"

"Well, where is it now?"

"I dropped it under the hedge," said Laura.

"You would," said Ted. Then he opened his eyes so wide that Laura forgot she wanted to hit him. "Exactly when did you have the sword and when didn't you?"

Laura considered this. "I had it when I went through the hedge the first time and then when I saw people I brought it back into the yard."

"You had it with you," said Ted, "and you crawled under the hedge and fell in the stream."

"Yes," said Laura, "and you and that lady weren't there. And—"

"And you crawled back under the hedge with it and then the lady and I were here?"

"Yes," said Laura. "And I came back this way without it and you and the lady were still here."

"It's the sword," said Ted. "I thought there was something about it. That's how we get to the other country. You dummy, why did you leave it under the hedge?"

"You wouldn't have tried to take it at all!"

"Well, I didn't know what it did!"

"It got stuck," said Laura, "and she was coming."

"Laura."

"What's the matter with you now?"

"We left the library books back there."

"And Jen's card."

"And you're wet."

"And we don't know where we are."

They did some sneaking about, which under other circumstances would have been fun, and recovered their books.

The house was shuttered and silent. Laura wondered about the curtains behind those shutters. Ted peered and squinted and managed to read the house's address. Complex letters over the porch said, ONE TRUMPET STREET. They had just begun to think about trying for the sword again when the front door opened, and they took off. They got safely out of sight by becoming even more lost than they had been, and stood looking at one another.

"Why don't you just run up to that door there," said Ted to Laura, "and ask how to get to Mercer Street?"

"Why don't you shut your fat mouth?" said Laura bitterly.

"Come on, it's good for you. Mom says so."

"I don't care."

"Well, then, we'll just stand here all day."

"That's fine with me," said Laura.

"What's the matter with you? They don't bite."

"Will you shut up!" shouted Laura, and punched him in the stomach. He was not supposed to hit her, but nobody had told her not to hit him.

"You are a coward," said Ted, doubled over and glaring at her. "How can you deserve a secret country?"

Laura burst into tears.

Ted asked the woman who came to the door of the brick house on the corner how to get to Mercer Street, and she told him, and they went home. Laura squelched and sniffled.

"Aunt Kathy'll wonder what happened to you," Ted told her.

"I'm not going to tell her."

"She has to take care of your knee."

"You do it."

"No."

"I'll tell her you hit me."

Ted smuggled her into the downstairs bathroom. They investigated the medicine cabinet, and derived some comfort from the fascinating behavior of hydrogen peroxide.

"Can we go back this afternoon?" said Laura, regarding her foaming knee with satisfaction.

"I think," said Ted, trying to stick a bandage onto her knee, "that we should give that lady a chance to calm down. She was madder than Aunt Kathy was when you broke the window."

"Well," said Laura.

"We've got books to read. They'll think it's funny if we go back to the library so soon. We can go back tomorrow. Hold still. I think this bandage'll work."

"But if she was mad because I took the sword—" began Laura.

"She didn't say what she was mad at. Hold still."

"But if she was mad because I took the sword, won't she put it where we can't get it?"

"Well, maybe. But she'll do that right away, so it won't hurt to wait to find out."

"But—"

"Hold still!"

"Ow!"

"That'll stay."

"That was a sharp sword," said Laura, sadly.

There was a pounding on the bathroom door. "Hurry up!" yelled Jennifer. They shrugged at each other and went out.

"You're wet," said Jennifer to Laura.

Laura regarded her with distaste. Grown-ups with nothing better to think about kept saying that Jennifer and Laura looked like sisters. It was true that they both had straight light brown hair and blue eyes. But Jennifer's short hair fit-ted her head like Ellen's velvet cap, and her eyes were almost as piercing as Patrick's. Laura thought her own eyes always looked as if she wanted to be somewhere else. She hated to look at Jennifer's and remember this.

"What happened to your knee?" asked Jennifer.

"She tripped on somebody's sprinkler," said Ted, while Laura stood dreamily imagining how Jen would look if she should say, "Somebody shot me with a black-hole gun."

"Figures," said Jennifer, and shut the bathroom door.

"Jerk," said Laura, bitterly, to the door.

"You did trip."

"We wouldn't have found the sword if I hadn't!"

Between then and supper Ted read his books and Laura pestered him to stop reading and go back to the secret house. After supper she pestered him to help her spy on Jennifer and David, who were in the backyard doing something which involved Tommy and the largest soup kettle.

"I think the people in their secret must be cannibals," said Laura, hunched up on Ted's windowsill.

"On a spaceship?"

"I think they're on a planet now. I think they're going to betray their captain to the cannibals."

"Heh," said Ted, turning a page. "At least when Lord Randolph decided to kill the King, he did his own dirty work."

"I miss Lord Randolph," said Laura.

"I miss Princess Laura," said Ted. "She was too busy with her music to bother anybody."

Laura sighed. Ted turned a page. Laura went back to the window, and watched David and Jennifer as they danced around the soup kettle, waving lilac branches and singing.

The next day Ted made Laura wait until after lunch to leave, so he could finish his book, and he made her read one of hers. Once again they borrowed Jennifer's card from Katie, who looked at them pityingly and asked them if they wouldn't like to go roller skating. They said they would not, and she told them to try E. Nesbit if they could stand a little stickiness.

They returned their books. They did not bother to get any more, asking instead for directions to Trumpet Street. They found their way to the secret house, and stood on the sidewalk and looked at it. It seemed the same. The front door was shut.

"Do you want to go first?" asked Ted.

"No," said Laura, hoping he would cut his knee on the sword.

Ted crawled under the hedge. "It's still here," he said, sounding nonplussed. Laura grinned to herself. No wonder he had been in no hurry.

"Well," said Ted, "neither of us can go first, or the other one can't come at all."

Laura squeezed in next to him and put her hand on the hilt of the sword above his. They knee-walked awkwardly out of the hedge and stood up in the yard. It looked greener than the yard on the other side had looked. Laura felt the same waiting quiet all around them. The cracked bluish flagstones of the front walk pricked at the back of her mind; they looked as they ought to.

"It doesn't look any different to me," said Ted, looking at the house.

"Let's go through the gate," said Laura.

This turned out to be locked, but looking through it was enough to convince Ted that they were indeed somewhere else. He leaned on it for a long time, staring out over the long empty plain while the stream mumbled along over its rocks and the wind lifted Laura's damp hair off her neck and the delicate leaves and flowers of the black wrought-iron gate suddenly fell into place like the right piece of a jig-saw puzzle. If Laura had been able to explain what she meant, she would have asked him if anything here affected him in the same way. As it was, she kept quiet and let him stare as long as he liked.

"Well," he said finally, "is there a way across the stream?"

"It isn't deep," said Laura, who was hot.

"Actually," said Ted, "the first thing is to get through the hedge. How did you get home again?"

"Dropped the sword in the middle."

"So if we *don't* drop the sword in the middle we should come out in the right spot?"

"I guess."

They held the sword again and squirmed through the hedge. Laura was getting tired of the hedge. Ted thrust his arm in front of her in time to keep her from falling into the water, let go of the sword, and stood up. "Now about this stream," he said, and stopped.

Laura looked where he was looking. Over the same hill came what looked like the same three figures, one tall and two not, gesturing at the house.

"I bet they're the same people I saw yesterday," said Laura, and took a step backward into the hedge. Ted caught her as she ducked to go through it.

"Only one of them is bigger than I am, and we've got the sword."

"You take it, then," said Laura, holding it out to him. It was making her hand prickle; she thought it must be too heavy for her.

"Wait a minute," said Ted, squinting across the water.

The three people were coming down the long slope before the stream.

"The tall one looks like Ruth," said Laura.

Ted squinted again. "It is Ruth," he said.

Laura looked at him, suspecting him of teasing her, and saw that he was so stunned that he had no energy left to sound surprised. She looked at the tall person again.

"It is?"

"Sure. Look at her hair."

"Then that's Ellen—and Patrick!"

"It is our Secret Country!"

"Ruth!" yelled Laura. "Ellen! Patrick!"

The tall person jerked its head up. One smaller person stopped. The second small person bumped into the first, said "Hell!" quite audibly, and then gaped at Ted and Laura. They all stood there.

"Hey!" shouted Ellen, the small one who had bumped the other. She always found her voice first and had often gotten them out of trouble. "Have you got a sword?"

Patrick held one up, and Laura waved theirs back at him. "Is this house in Australia?" she yelled.

Ellen and Ruth and Patrick came down the hill and across the flat space in a sudden bound, all talking at once.

"We've been here for weeks—"

"We found the sword under a bottle tree, and—"

"Where have you been?"

"How do we cross the stream?" demanded Ted.

"There's a bridge in the woods," said Patrick. He began hurrying his sisters, who were involved in complicated explanations of enormous gardens and too many prickly pears and the essential oddness of Australia downstream. Ted and Laura hurried along on the other side of the water. Its banks grew steeper as it went into the woods, and Laura slid down one of them suddenly and found one foot in the water and the other in mud.

Ted pulled her out. "Give me the sword," he said. "You'll kill yourself."

Laura let him take it. As she scrambled to her feet, she looked across the stream and caught Patrick giving her a look of great concentration, as if he or Ted or Ruth or Ellen had not been pulling her out of pools, streams, ditches, swamps, and patches of mud ever since she could walk. She wondered what was the matter with him.

Just when the thickening trees were beginning to crowd and poke them uncomfortably close to the edges of the stream, they came to the bridge. It was an unassuming bridge of wooden planks, with one handrail. Ted and Laura bolted across it. Laura tripped on the last plank and fell flat. Ellen picked her up, and Patrick gave her that look again.

"How did you get here?" asked Laura, pointedly addressing Ellen.

"I was throwing a ball for the dog," said Patrick. He did not look like his sisters. They had black hair, but he had pale brown hair and blue eyes, like Ted and Laura. He seemed never to blink, and he could stare anyone down. "And the ball went smack into the middle of this clump of bottle trees. And I went crawling after it, and I put my hand down on something sharp, and sliced it good. So I was almost to the other side of the clump anyway, so I just grabbed the thing, and slithered on through, so I could look at it better. And then I was here. The house and the dog and Ellen were all gone, and it was dark. So I took the thing back through with me and crawled out the side I had come in, and I was still here. So I went *back* under the trees and left the sword, because it was a nuisance and I couldn't see it anyway and I only had one good hand. I came out again, and I was back in Australia, and it was day again. So I told Ruth and Ellen, and we all came."

He sat down on a stump, looking satisfied.

Ted told him about what had happened to himself and Laura.

"So," said Ellen to Laura, "we've been wandering around for days looking for you."

"Living in the woods?" said Ted. "Or have you met anybody who—"

"No," said Ellen, "we had to go home."

This isn't a very good secret country," said Patrick. "Time is the same. If you spend three hours here, it's three gone at home too."

"That's stupid," said Ted, outraged.

"That's not all," said Patrick. "You know what's even worse? The time zones. With us in Australia and you in the States. I figured it out last night." Laura thought that he did not sound very happy about it, which was unusual for something he had figured out. "It's spooky. You're on central daylight, right? Well, that's twelve hours from us. When it's midnight for you, it's noon for us."

"It's two in the morning in Australia?" said Ted.

"That's nothing," said Patrick. "It's three in the afternoon here. We're on eastern daylight here."

"How do you know?" demanded Ted.

"There's a clock in that house," said Ruth, shivering.

"Did you get in?" said Laura.

"No," said Ruth, "and I don't want to. You can hear the clock from out here. You can hear it from a long way away and it sounds—each stroke sounds like somebody's head being chopped off."

"How do you know?" said Ellen. "Have you ever heard anybody's head being—"

"She can start with yours if you don't shut up," said Patrick. He addressed Ted. "We're on eastern daylight here," he said again.

"Just like Pennsylvania; just like on the farm," said Ted slowly.

"But daylight savings time isn't real," said Laura.

"Darn right it isn't," said Patrick.

"It might make sense," said Ted. "Maybe we couldn't have found out about the Secret Country if we hadn't been spending all those summers in a place that has the same time as it does. I mean, eastern daylight isn't real time for Pennsylvania, but it is for somewhere out in the Atlantic, so—"

"You think this is somewhere out in the Atlantic," said Patrick.

"No," said Ted, irritated. "Obviously it isn't."

Patrick looked very much as if he were going to say something unpleasant, but he didn't. Laura knew what he had wanted to say. He had wanted to say that they had not found out about the Secret Country, they had made it up. But he knew better than anyone, having been shouted at for it so often, that the one thing you did not do during a game was to so much as hint that it was one.

There was a wary silence; they all knew that look.

When Ellen was sure that Patrick was not going to say anything after all, she said, "Do you want to see the well?"

"Sure," said Ted, formally.

"It's back over the hill," said Ellen. She let Ruth and Ted and Patrick go on before her, and waited for Laura.

"Is it really the well?" said Laura eagerly.

"Well," said Ellen, "I suppose. I thought it ought to have

a roof, instead of a stone lid, and Ruth wanted it to be more mossy, and Pat said the tree by it ought to be hollow. But it looks right somehow."

"Is it an oak tree?"

"Yes," said Ellen. "And a very good one."

"Do the acorns fall into the water?"

"Well," said Ellen, "they would if you left the lid off."

"Heh," said Laura. "Are the stones white?"

"No," said Ellen. "Pink."

"Pink?"

"Well, spotted. Patrick says they're granite."

"But—"

"I know," said Ellen. They came out from the shade of the trees, blinking in the sudden heat. They were across from the house again. Ted and Ruth and Patrick, talking and waving their arms, turned to go up the long slope, and Laura and Ellen followed them.

"So is it our Secret Country or not?" asked Laura.

"Patrick," said Ellen, "was happy that it didn't look the way we wanted it to, and said of course it wouldn't. He became very superior," she said, burying both hands in her mop of hair in a way she had, "and wouldn't tell us why it shouldn't look the way we thought it should. He has ideas about this place."

Laura, who liked Patrick but did not trust him, and who knew about his ideas, had a brief but vivid desire to have gone roller skating this afternoon. She did not say anything because they had caught up with the other three.

"Now look," said Patrick, pointing before them, "and tell me what you think this is, Ted and Laura."

Down at the bottom of the hill was a round stone well beside a warped oak tree. Laura knew immediately what Ellen had meant by calling the tree a good one. It, like the pattern

32

of leaves and the flagstone and the iron gate, was right. The well was far from right; it looked even worse than Ellen had said it did. A road began at the foot of the tree and ran straight away from them to the horizon through a flat grassy plain. Here and there beside the road were a few more warped oaks. It was blazing hot and the air wavered like water.

"The Great Plain," said Ted, "and the road to Fence's Country." He sounded as if he were reciting a poem he liked very much but was not sure he remembered.

"And the Well of the White Witch and the Sorcerer's Tree," said Laura. She felt strange. She did not recognize these things; she did not remember having seen them; it was more like looking at something you had read a lot about, but never seen a picture of. Parts were right and parts were not. She wasn't sure which disturbed her more.

She and Ted looked at one another. Ted observed that Laura's hair was full of leaves from the hedge, and Laura that Ted was very red in the face; they both looked back at the dry plain and the sinister trees and felt that perhaps those things were truly there after all.

"But the well ought to have brambles around it," said Ted.

"It should be white," said Laura. "Like the witch."

"But we all know what it is," said Patrick.

"What else have you found?" asked Ted. He shifted his sweaty grip on the hilt of the sword. Laura wondered if it might be too heavy for him too.

"This is all," said Ruth. "Remember we all agreed that it was ten leagues to Fence's Country? It really must be. A whole afternoon walking along that road got us nowhere."

"Oh, fine," said Ted. "Wonderful. And four leagues to High Castle . . . which way?"

"East from the well," said Ruth, "but which way is that? Does the sun rise in the east?"

"Yes," said Patrick, "or we couldn't tell stories of how the unicorns came out of it. Let me see—the house is south of the well, so High Castle is that way, to our right. Because we're facing north. I told you people we shouldn't make the distances so large."

"We didn't make them," said Ellen impatiently, "they were already here."

"And don't sound so smug," said Ruth to Patrick, "you didn't know this would happen; you're just picky."

"But that's why I'm picky, because things might happen, and if you're picky you have a better chance—"

"Besides," said Ellen, "it didn't matter so much. We had horses. What happened to them? Were they spirited away from us in the night by the—"

"Well, not really we didn't have them," said Patrick.

"We said we had them," said Ellen, scowling ferociously, "and—"

"Let's get a drink," said Laura, hoping to stop a fight, or at least get away from it, and she lay down in the grass and rolled down the hill. It was a hard and prickly roll, as it had always been at the farm, and the grass smelled hot and brown, as it always had. But she was not used to having a real well at the bottom the hill, and before she realized how close it was it hit her in the back, which hurt. Complaining might make Patrick give her that look again, so she rubbed her back in silence and lay waiting for the others.

Ellen came running down the hill, flung herself over the stone lid of the well, and shrieked, "I won!"

Ted and Ruth panted up behind her. "You didn't put your foot in a gopher hole," said Ruth.

"It's a good thing Laurie didn't try running down that hill; she'd have broken her neck," said Ted.

Patrick came placidly up beside Ruth, carrying both swords. "Get up, Laurie, and help us get the lid off the well. This was your idea; get to work."

Patrick laid the swords in the grass. "There are grooves to put your hands under," he said. "If Ellen would remove herself from the lid, she could take the third groove."

With some scraping of both stone and hands they managed to lean the lid against the side of the well nearest the hill. The wooden bucket was in a niche in the inside wall of the well, and the rope tied to its handle was fastened at the other end of an iron ring in the niche. They leaned over the edge of the well, and a damp green air smote their hot faces.

Ted reached for the bucket and stopped. "Milady Ruth," he said, and bowed, and stood aside.

"I'd almost forgotten," said Laura to Ellen, "only a sorcerer of the Green Caves may draw water from this well."

"And remember what happens if anybody else tries it."

"Do you suppose it really would?"

"I don't want to find out."

"Shut up," said Patrick.

Ruth took a ring from her finger and dropped it into the well.

"That's not a good ring?" whispered Laura.

"No, no, just the one we always used."

"Shut up," said Patrick.

"We are travelers in great need," said Ruth. "I am a maiden of One We Do Not Name. We beg your aid." She lowered the bucket. Ted had to help her raise it again, which was something they had not thought about at home. They had used a plastic bucket, not a wooden one, and Ruth had

35

not had very far to lift it. But the well did not seem to object.

"Remember the gift of the ring!" said Ruth, and cupped up some water in her hands and drank.

"She always picked the bucket up before," said Laura.

"Too heavy," said Ellen. "Real water. She'd dump it all down her front."

"Will you two shut up!" said Ted. They glared at him, but they shut up. Here, he was the Prince.

Ruth stood staring at her dripping hands. A look of surprise stole over her face, and she cupped up a little more water and drank that. "That," she said, passing the bucket to Patrick, "is very good water."

"I should hope so," said Patrick austerely, but after he drank he looked back at her and said, "Yes, it certainly is." He held the bucket for Laura while she scooped up water.

"It's weird," said Laura, who was a fussy eater, "but it's better than faucet water." She caught with her tongue a drop running down her chin and suddenly scooped up another handful. It was much better than faucet water. She took one more handful, and almost choked on it. As the smell of summer savory always brought back to her all her memories of Thanksgiving, the taste of the water suddenly filled her mind with bits and pieces that seemed right but were not familiar to her.

"Don't kill yourself," said Ted, and took the bucket away from her.

Ellen was the last to drink. "You guys didn't leave much," she said, tipping the bucket. "Hey, there's something in there."

"Drink first!" said Ruth sharply. "Refuse at your peril."

"You'll be sorry if I choke to death," snapped Ellen, but she drank. Ruth was after all a sorcerer of the Green Caves.

"Well," said Ellen, "no wonder you didn't leave much." She scrabbled with her hand in the bottom of the bucket and found what she had seen. It was silver, with a blue stone. It was not Ruth's ring, but it looked like the kind of ring Ruth had always said Lady Ruth had.

"What's that supposed to mean?" said Patrick.

Ellen held it out to Ruth, who put it on her finger.

"It was never a real gift, was it?" said Patrick.

"Yes, it was," said Ruth. "But I never used this ring. I mean, we used the same ring for everything we did, but we always said that the rings we gave to the well were just ordinary rings. But this is my Ring of Sorcery."

"It's no more that than it is any other if we said—" began Patrick.

"It is now," said Ruth. "This is a real silver ring, not the thing from the dime store I put in there; it's my Ring of Sorcery. It feels like the sword did when we picked it up."

"Oh," said Laura, "does yours do that too?"

"Here," said Ted, holding out their sword with its winking blue stones. "These are the same kind of stones as the one in the ring."

"That's reasonable," said Ruth. "The swords are certainly magic. But will someone kindly explain how I put in a fake ring made of plastic and got back a real one made of silver with a magic stone in it?"

"It's a magic well," said Ted, hopefully.

"It never did things like that before."

"How do you know?" said Ted. "You put rings in all the time and they never came back, so how do you know?"

"Listen," said Patrick, "she has never put a ring in that well before, and—"

"This is my well," said Ruth to Ted, "and I know what it's supposed to do, and it's not supposed to do this."

"What do we do now?" asked Laura, who saw another fight trying to start.

"Well, we can't go anywhere," said Ellen.

"What about the house?" asked Ted.

"It's locked," said Patrick, "everywhere. And curtains over all the windows. You can't see a thing."

"Ellen!" said Laura. "That must be the house you and I were born in!"

Ellen and Laura were sisters, in the Secret Country. Ted and Patrick were brothers, and they were cousins to Ellen and Laura. Ruth had been born their sister, but now she was no one's sister and no one's child. She was a sorcerer of the Green Caves.

"Then why won't it let us in?" said Ellen.

"Patrick," said Ruth, "what did you mean, I never put—"

"I hear something," said Ellen.

"I don't," said Ted, "and what did you mean, Patrick?"

"You're right," said Patrick to Ellen. "It's horses."

"Where?" said Ted.

"From the east," said Ellen.

Laura laughed. "It's Benjamin from High Castle out looking for us!"

"We never did that," said Ted.

"Well, we talked about it."

"It is Benjamin, I bet," said Ellen, squinting across the plain. In the Secret Country she had excellent eyesight. In fact she had been told she needed glasses, but she would not wear them. "He has a black horse," she added. "Isn't that Ebony?"

"He has a red cape; Benjamin always wears a red cape," said Ted, who really did have good eyes, although Prince Edward did not because he read too much. "And a beard, I think. Criminy," said Ted. He looked at the sword, and Laura saw him shiver. "We're here," he said.

"Who's on the other horses?" asked Ellen.

"Nobody," said Ted.

"Ellen," said Laura, who had stopped laughing, "he's bringing five empty horses—"

"Horses aren't empty," said Ted, snorting. "Empty saddles."

"And there are two white," said Laura, "and two bay and—"

"One black pony," said Ellen. She and Laura looked at each other.

"But we didn't really have horses," said Laura.

Patrick laughed.

"We do now," said Ted.

"What'll we do?"

"Ride them," said Ted.

"You can talk," said Laura. "You can ride."

"I was afraid of this," said Patrick.

"You already knew it," said Laura.

"Don't you remember," Patrick said to her, stooping for his sword, "that Princess Laura of High Castle can ride better than any of the others even though she's the youngest? And she's remarkably light of foot, don't you remember?"

"I want to go home," said Laura.

"Give me that sword," said Patrick to Ted. "I don't think we're supposed to have swords."

"Sure we—"

"Anyway, we aren't supposed to be carrying them around *naked*."

"There's nowhere to hide them."

"The well would protect them," said Ellen.

"Maybe behind the cover," said Patrick.

Laura watched him and Ted slide the swords between the wall of the well and the cover that still leaned against it. Patrick busily brushed the long grasses back up against the cover. Laura marveled at his calm. She herself was fighting an urge to run up the hill and hide in the hedge. She wanted nothing to do with this.

"He's getting closer," said Ellen, so Laura looked at her. She wore the face of pleased expectation that Laura was accustomed to seeing on her face on the morning of her birthday, which fell in August. Wasn't anybody else afraid at all?

"He's seen us," said Ruth, and waved.

"Oh, don't," said Laura. That seemed to show how Ruth felt.

"How else can we get to High Castle before suppertime?" said Ted. And that seemed to show how Ted felt.

"We won't be able to get back here by then and here's where we have to be to get home!" wailed Laura, before she could stop herself. All of them were true adventurers, and she was the coward.

"Be quiet," said Ruth, "it's unseemly to argue before him. Besides, if he heard what we were saying he'd think we were crazy." She was playing. That was Lady Ruth's voice.

"Aren't we?" said Patrick. He wasn't playing, but he wasn't scared, either.

Laura saw Ted look at him sharply, but there was no time to ask what he meant. The man under discussion had drawn up his horse and dismounted so neatly that Laura hoped he had done it by magic, which he could teach her. He was very angry, and strode toward them scolding vigorously. They could not quite tell what he was saying, but the tone of his voice made them gather themselves into a bunch against the well. That everybody else seemed alarmed now did not comfort Laura.

The man stopped before them and looked them over one by one, grimly. When they talked about it later, Ruth thought that his hands should have been bigger, and Ted that he should not wear brown beneath his red cape, and Patrick that his mouth was wrong somehow, and Ellen that his hair had too much gray in it. Laura was astounded at how big he was. But no one doubted that he was Benjamin, Royal Groom, whose father was a cobbler in Fence's Country, and under whose care, for some reason they had never decided, the children of High Castle came when they had grown too old to have a nurse. No one doubted, either, that Benjamin's temper was just as they had imagined it.

"Not only truant," said Benjamin, "not only negligent, not only disobedient, late, shoddily attired, and cowering, but treacherous."

He addressed this last epithet, with a particularly grim emphasis, to Ted and Ruth, who seemed at a loss, when Laura looked at them, to account for being singled out.

"We are not," said Ellen.

"It's a ceremony of the Green Caves," said Ruth, surreptitiously patting Ellen's shoulder. "We could not choose our garb or our companions; we were sent for."

Benjamin was dumbstruck. He was usually what Ellen, when writing down descriptions of the main characters, had been pleased to call "of a ruddy complexion," but he looked quite white when he had heard what Ruth had to say. He stood perfectly still and stared at her for so long that she could think of what to say next.

"It was a hasty summons," she told him happily, "in the dead of night. I was reading in my chamber, and a white bird fluttered through the window and flew three times around my candle and made great shadows on the wall." Laura began to feel a little better. "And it spoke with a voice like the Green Witch's, and it said to me—"

"Ruth," said Patrick, "don't."

" 'There is great peril from across the sea,' " said Ted with alacrity, " 'and by the oaths ye swore when Shan the first wizard delivered you from—' "

"Angels and ministers of grace defend us!" shouted Benjamin. He was once more of a ruddy complexion. Laura's stomach clenched itself tight. Ruth looked appalled.

"Why are thy tongues not black in thy conniving heads!"

"I knew it!" said Patrick, not appalled at all, but extremely angry at Ruth.

"And where," Benjamin demanded of him, "were thy wits that thou still dangled after, if thou knewest so much?"

Patrick had nothing to say. Laura did not think this as funny as she might have expected.

Benjamin flung his hands out in a gesture that rejected all of them. "I've no words for you," he said. "I must take you all home and you shall go to bed without supper; when I myself have supped and can, perhaps, bear the sight of you again, we shall see what's to be said and done." He turned away from them, and Ted and Ruth followed him to the horses, which had been munching grass all the while.

"What'd we do?" whispered Laura to Ellen.

"Ted and Ruth," said Patrick quietly on her other side, "are Romeo and Juliet. We are all the old nurse."

"I went to bed early when they read us that one," said Ellen. "I hate love stories. When did we act this out, anyway?"

"You and Laurie had the mumps," said Patrick. "Summer before last. The King had Ruth betrothed to Lord Randolph when she was just a baby, but Ted and Ruth want to marry each other."

"How boring," said Ellen.

"Benjamin doesn't think so," said Patrick. "He thinks we are all scheming, and he thinks Ruth lied to him about the ceremony of the Green Caves so she could—"

"Come your ways!" called Benjamin, and they hurried over to the horses.

Laura stood and watched Ellen and Patrick struggle onto their horses. Their difficulties did nothing for Benjamin's temper. He scowled at them and then looked down at Laura.

"Well?" he said.

Laura, who did not like the way the horses smelled, the way they moved sideways as if they wanted to go somewhere very fast, or the way they eyed her, looked straight up at Benjamin and was speechless.

"I'll have none of your big blue eyes," said Benjamin sharply, and he picked her up as if she were a much smaller child than she was, and put her on the black pony.

After she had fallen off it for the fifth time, he hauled her up by an elbow with considerably less care than he had exhibited the first four times, and boosted her up in front of Ruth, who was almost unseated herself by this sudden maneuver. Benjamin looked at her for a moment as if this were more than he was prepared to manage, then turned and busied himself with Laura's pony.

"You okay?" whispered Ruth.

"Sure," said Laura; it was, after all, no worse than mistiming a jump from a swing in the school playground. Of course, she had never misjumped four times in a row. But the first grateful moment of stillness, when you were lying on a piece of ground that wasn't going anywhere, was almost worth the pain of the bruises.

Laura settled herself as securely as she could in Ruth's trembling grip and took her first good look at where they were heading. She was too outraged to speak, which was no doubt just as well. High Castle—if it was High Castle—looked like a piece of peppermint candy, concentric rings of pink and white. It was supposed to be a square white—or maybe gray—fortress with towers at its corners and a moat around it. Laura drew in a breath to protest to Ruth, and let it out again suddenly as the horses began to move. Benjamin set a much slower pace than he had tried earlier, but it was still far from comfortable.

The flat plain was not really flat, but full of small rises and falls of ground. As they came down the rise from which Laura had first seen High Castle, it lost its aspect of peppermint and became simply a line of pink barring the way before them. Behind it the land rose again in long slopes of dark green forest, and beyond those were misty humps that Laura at first took for clouds on the horizon. It was not until Ruth said in her ear, "The Mountains of Dusk" that she realized what they were. She had never seen mountains, and these did not look as they ought to. She had imagined sharp dark triangles standing up out of a flat green plain like something in a pop-up book. She squinted at the betraying cloudy masses, and thought she saw hints of blue and purple in them, and an underlying solidity not owned by clouds; she was not comforted.

That first pink wall of High Castle turned out to be immense, six stories tall or more. Most of the stones that made it were longer than Laura was tall. They were smooth and sharp edged, and looked very new. The wall had a tower on each corner and three more along its length, and two smaller ones flanking its gate. The gate was open, which confounded Laura almost as much as the color of the walls. They passed into a short, wide tunnel lit from above and paved in the pink granite, with another gate at its far end, which was also open. There were, at least, two guards at this gate, and they even had long spears. They did not, however, leap up and bar the way with these spears. On second reflection, Laura was just as glad that they had not.

They did stand up, looking remarkably as if they were trying not to laugh, and bowed briefly. Benjamin got down from his horse. So did Ted and Ellen. Ruth gave Laura a small shove, so Laura slid down haphazardly and sat down hard on the cold stone. Ted picked her up quickly. Patrick dismounted with a show of ease that made Laura want to hit him. A number of young men who had appeared through the gate took the horses away. Benjamin marched between the guards as if he were daring them to say a word, and the five children followed him onto a wide space of short grass.

This looked a little more like High Castle. There was the moat, just as it ought to be, sailed on by white swans and cluttered with lily pads, and holding upside-down a perfect glassy image of the white walls and towers on its far side. The drawbridge was directly before them; it was down. Patrick muttered something about this, but nobody cared to answer him with Benjamin so close. There were still too many towers in the white wall, and it was circular, not square.

They went over the drawbridge, past two more amused and easy guards, and were confronted by yet another pink wall. The stones of this one were rough and pitted, but the wall itself was, at least, properly square, and had towers only at its corners. Between it and the previous white wall was a huge and somewhat untidy rose garden, on the left, and on the right a herb and vegetable garden that looked as if it had been laid out on a gigantic piece of graph paper.

Laura wondered if the respective gardeners glared at one another over the pink marble path that separated their domains. As far as she knew, High Castle had only one gardener, a dour and silent man named Timothy. But one look at the vast stretch of these gardens told her that there must be more than one person to care for them. Even in the rose garden, the grass had been mowed and most of the weeds hacked from around the white stone seats. Laura craned her neck longingly after the rose garden, with its mossy paths and mysterious nooks, but the thought of being lost in this enormous and unfamiliar labyrinth of castle walls made her hurry after the others.

They went through the open gate in the pink wall and into a small paved yard. And there before them, finally, was the High Castle of Laura's mind, white towers and red roofs and bright banners flying.

"Page!" shouted Benjamin, at the top of his considerable voice.

Laura saw Ellen leap forward, then stop and look furious. Benjamin had not noticed her. A yellow-haired boy perhaps a few years younger than Laura came hurrying across the yard to them, and bowed to Benjamin.

"Fetch me Agatha," said Benjamin, much more kindly than he had spoken to any of the five of them.

"My lord," said the page, and went away again.

There followed a very uncomfortable interval. Benjamin had turned his back on them, but was far too close to permit the kind of outraged conversation they needed to have. Laura occupied herself with staring at High Castle, and almost forgot to worry. Aside from the moat's being two walls back, everything was perfect. She admired the narrow windows, the moss growing between the cobbles of the yard they stood in, and even the distant blue of the mountains still visible over the wall. The lake that fed the moat was on the other side of the castle, and so was the room shared by the princesses Laura and Ellen. Ted and Patrick's room, though, should look out on this very courtyard, and Ruth's—

"Suffering, deception, and mercy!" said a vigorous voice behind them.

Laura jumped, bumping Ruth, who took no notice of her. They all turned around, and there, larger than life and half as natural, stood Agatha. There was nothing right about her except her voice and her gray dress. She was plump where she should have been bony, young where she should have been old, pretty where she should have been dignified, and she had a great deal of straight, smooth black hair that ought to have been white.

"You may well say so," said Benjamin to Agatha, over their five heads. "Take you these four, and I'll manage His Highness."

"Come then, my lords and ladies," said Agatha, in a tone of faint mockery. And she ushered Ruth, Patrick, Ellen, and Laura into High Castle, leaving Ted to stand with Benjamin in the courtyard.

CHAPTER 3

B Y the time Benjamin got the five of them back to High
Castle, Ted was too battered to be exasperated and too
tired to be thoughtful. He was beginning to be afraid instead. Benjamin was too big, the horse was too big, High
Castle itself was too big, too high, and too grim. Benjamin
had said they were all treacherous, and he had sounded as if
he meant it. Ted kept remembering that this was a country
in which a page could be hanged for mouthing off. Nobody
had mouthed off to Benjamin on the way back, but Benjamin had looked at Laura every time she fell off that pony
as if he would have liked to hang her for that. And as
Agatha led the other four off into High Castle, Benjamin
stood looking at Ted as if he would still like to hang somebody.

"I'd give thee worse than bed without supper," he said,
"hadst thou chosen thy time differently."

"What?" said Ted. Benjamin's face took on an expression
common to grown-ups everywhere, and Ted added, "Sir."

"What is the date, then?" Benjamin asked him.

"I think—I think it's June the fourteenth. Sir."

"Think!" said Benjamin. "If thinking made things so,
things would be otherwise."

Ted, trying to remember what date it was and why it
should matter, only looked at him, and wished he would

back away a little. He was taller than Ted's father, who was not a small man.

"Has that child bewitched all of you?" demanded Benjamin.

"What?" asked Ted, giving up.

Benjamin flung up his hands. "The King thy father," he said, "was to hold a council at midday today, and thou wast summoned to't."

Already, thought Ted. We've missed the whole beginning of the game. While Laurie and I were playing tag and everybody else was running around looking for us, they started the game. That doesn't make any sense; how could they start it without us? It is us. "Heh," he said.

"Didst remember, then?"

"No! I mean—"

"She hath bewitched thee."

"Who has?"

"Thy spitfire cousin!"

Who's my cousin here? he thought. Laura and Ellen. My spitfire cousin. Does he mean Ellen? Ruth's the only one who can bewitch anybody, but she's not my cousin. Minions of the Green Caves have no family save the leaves.

Benjamin, in a tempestuous motion like that of a startled man trying to catch a falling vase, came to his knees in front of Ted and took him by the shoulders. "Look at me," he said.

Ted blinked at him.

Benjamin stared him in the eyes for much too long. Eyes like Benjamin's could find out anything. Ted tried to back into the cold stone of the wall, and a cardinal whistled the first three notes of its call somewhere over his head. Ted jumped; Benjamin let go of him, but did not get up. Ted looked gratefully at Benjamin's shirt lacings.

"I never thought to say so," said Benjamin, still too close for comfort, "but I would Fence were here. I have sorcery in my blood and my bones, but none in my learning; I will not come between the cardinal and its charges. If thou art one. If thou art." He put a hand under Ted's chin and made Ted look at him again. "Edward—"

"Benjamin," said Ted, who understood none of this and was not sure he wanted to, "you're getting all muddy."

"I am fresh laundered next to thee," said Benjamin, "and the King's council is in a quarter of an hour. Come away."

He let go of Ted and stood up, and they started across the yard.

"I thought it was this morning?" said Ted, too bewildered to be cautious.

"It was planned so," said Benjamin, "till I found thee gone. I contrived to change the time and came ahunting thee. Thy father knows nothing of this, yet."

"Oh," said Ted.

"I would not trouble him with more troubles than he hath withal," said Benjamin.

"Oh."

"But I can deal with thee myself if the occasion warrants."

"I don't think it warrants nearly as much as you think it does," said Ted.

"No doubt," said Benjamin, dryly.

"Ruth hasn't bewitched me," said Ted, "and I don't want to marry her."

"Oh, excellent," said Benjamin. " 'Twill do thee no great hurt to forgo her company, then."

Ted was furious, and speechless. He was afraid to say too much. Benjamin might ask just what the five of them had been doing out by the Well of the White Witch, if they had not been arranging a secret meeting between Ted and Ruth.

They came through the last set of doors, past yet two more unconcerned guards, and into a high dim drafty hall strewn with what Ted supposed were rushes. Three dogs lay by the fire, and Ted almost tripped over a cat, but there were no people there, and almost no furniture. It felt like a place where you waited.

"Well," said Benjamin, "go dress thyself as well as thou canst, and I will do likewise."

Ted froze. He had only a vague idea of where his room was, or wherever it was he should go to dress himself. Nor was he sure what he should dress himself in. He looked at Benjamin hopelessly, and Benjamin scowled at him.

"Now, Edward, what's the matter?"

"Well."

"Last time," said Benjamin, "'twas stuffing it up the chimney to stop the draft. And the time before that 'twas using it as a lake for thy sister's dolls to play at swimming in. What is it now?"

"What?" said Ted.

"Plague take thee!" said Benjamin, and catching his arm, hustled him through the hall into an even draftier stair. "I thought as much! An it were not my ears as well as thine would ring with thy father's wrath, I'd leave thee to it."

"But what are you going to do?" said Ted feebly.

"Hide thy scrapes, as always," said Benjamin; he sounded cross, but not actually furious anymore. "Thou shalt wear one of the robes i' the West Tower, and drown in it, and look a fool, and serve thee right."

"The dolls didn't drown," said Ted, tentatively.

Benjamin cuffed the side of his head, and Ted shut up.

The blow did not feel unfriendly, but it did hurt. He began to wonder whether, when Benjamin had said their ears would ring with the King's wrath, Benjamin meant more than that the King would yell at them.

"While I have thine ear," said Benjamin over his shoulder, "how didst thou come by that outlandish garb, and what perversity led thee to wear and not burn it?"

Ted produced the reason which explained more sins than any other. "We were playing a game," he said, "about people who wear outlandish garb."

" 'Twas sweet and commendable in thee," said Benjamin, in a tone Ted did not like, "to find time to play with thy cousins."

"Thank you," said Ted, trying not to grin.

"The devil damn thee black," said Benjamin. He said it mildly, about in the tone Ted's mother might have used to say "You are a nuisance," but Ted was shocked into stopping. This was what the lady with the broom had said, back at the secret house.

"What?" he said.

"I do not want," said Benjamin, stopping, turning, and taking hold of Ted's T-shirt as if it were a dead spider, "to see any of these garments again."

"Yes, sir." Wonderful. We can go back home in whatever they give us to wear here. And *they* may not tell us they never want to see those garments again, but they'll sure want to know where they came from. Or we can—

"Tell thy brother and thy cousins likewise."

"Even Ruth?" said Ted, daring.

"The Lady Ruth is not dressed so. The Lady Ruth," said Benjamin grimly, "knoweth better than to irk me in small matters."

"She doesn't mean to irk you in large ones," said Ted.

Benjamin snorted. "Do not tell me," he said, "that any minion of the Green Caves doth what he meaneth not."

Ted decided that anything he said would make things worse.

Benjamin hurried him down several windy passages, up a winding staircase, and into a high room which even in the dim dregs of the sunset glowed with color. It was hung and draped and piled with clothes. Ted could see a sleeve here or a collar there, but for the most part nothing looked like anything he had ever worn or seen worn or imagined wearing. The room smelled of cloves and dust. Ted sneezed.

Benjamin turned his back on him and began burrowing in a mound of blue. He shook out several massive robes of velvet, scowled at them, and flung them down again. Finally he thrust one at Ted, who pulled it over his head, sneezed again, and sat down on the floor, the weight of the material having upset his balance. He sat there in the stuffy spicy dark, feeling the cold of the stone floor seep through his jeans, and wished he were playing tag.

"One would think," grumbled Benjamin's voice above him, "that thou hadst never worn a robe in thy life. Up with thee." He parted the material and briskly thrust it down over Ted's shoulders, and Ted blinked at him and stood up, staggering a little. "Thank you," he said.

Benjamin jerked and tugged at the heavy folds of the garment, straightening it on Ted's shoulders and turning up the sleeves for him. Ted stood meekly, trying not to sneeze again as Benjamin stirred up more dust from the velvet, and feeling as if he were Laura's age and being dressed for Halloween. If only that were all it was.

"This was Lord Justin's robe," said Benjamin, shaking a sleeve, "and even when thou hast thy full growth, 'twill be too large for thee."

Ted scowled. Who had Lord Justin been? He could not remember. Maybe Ellen would. She was the one who had written down all the history.

He watched Benjamin pull a robe over his own head. Why would Benjamin keep his robe up here in the dust, even if people didn't sneeze here?

"Hey," said Ted. "Where's your robe?"

"Lord Randolph hath the loan of it," said Benjamin shortly.

"And where's his?"

Benjamin did not smile. "He hath lent it to thy cousins—"

"For their dolls to play at swimming in?"

"E'en so."

Benjamin still did not smile. Ted tried not to. He was delighted and afraid at once. He had gotten the better of Benjamin. But this was no scene he had ever played in the nine summers of the Secret. He had never thought of Lord Randolph, brilliant counselor, apprentice wizard, King's man, and murderer, as the sort of person who would lend his counselor's robe to anybody to play dolls with. Ted felt that things were getting away from him.

"Why can't he have one of these old dusty ones, then, and you wear your own?"

"What will pass muster in me and thee, my young lord, will not so in Randolph. Come away; by now the council stays for us."

Outside it was dark now, and although Ted saw sockets for torches set in the walls every few feet, most of them were empty. Benjamin strode along as if he were in broad daylight, his robe floating behind him, and Ted stumbled in his wake, clutching handsful of his own heavy velvet, and fuming. The floors and steps near the tower room were rough, and invited one to trip. As they came back to the central part of the castle, the floors, worn with greater use, became smooth, and invited one to slip. Ted began to feel like Laura.

They came up one last flight of stairs. There was a door at the top of it, and a man-at-arms before the door. There was a torch above his head and a short sword in his hand. His shadow, in the pulsing light of the torch, clawed at the ceiling. Ted gaped at him under Benjamin's elbow. He had never seen a man-at-arms—the casual guards at the gates did not count—and he wished the light were better.

"Good even," said Benjamin to the man-at-arms. "Is the King before us?"

"No, my lord," said the man, "you're safe. Neither the King nor Lord Randolph is there yet." He did not speak as Benjamin did, which Ted found a relief. Benjamin was hard to keep up with; if everyone talked like that, things here would be even harder than they already were.

The guard pushed the heavy door open for them, standing aside to let them through. Light and a clamor of voices poured down the stairs and engulfed them. It was much warmer in this hall, and torches blazed from every socket. Ted noticed for the first time that they smelled like turpentine.

He and Benjamin went down the hall toward the voices and light that spilled from a wide doorway. Ted would have liked to inspect the carving of the double doors, which had been his idea and which he had even drawn in pen and ink, with great care, for Ellen's history. But Benjamin hustled him on into the room. Like everything else, it was too big.

So were the people in it. They all knew him, and he recognized none of them. He looked up, grinned, and murmured, "My lord, good even, my lord," at a series of faces, some bearded and some smooth, mostly young, and thanked his stars that Prince Edward was shy and scholarly and not good for much. He had not started out that way, but Ted and the others had soon discovered that there were not enough of them to play more than a few interesting characters. Ted had had to play the King, until the King was poisoned. Then Prince Edward could be dragged out of his library and become interesting, but right now he was of little account.

As soon as he and Benjamin had greeted everyone, the clamor began to settle, as noise in a classroom subsides just before the bell rings. People began to take their places. Ted, backed against a tapestry he had not had time to look at, felt his stomach lurch as he realized that he could not remember where he should sit. He had played the King in this scene. When Patrick or Ruth got tired of being counselors, he had played himself so one of them could play the King. He had also played Lord Andrew, the Secret Country's villain. He could not remember, in this room that could hold a table big enough for six games of hopscotch, swimming with torchlight, where any of them was supposed to sit.

He scowled. King William always sat at one end of the table, with Lord Randolph on his right and Benjamin on his left. Prince Edward sat at the other end of the table. If only Benjamin or Randolph would sit down. But Benjamin, across the table, was talking to a thin man with an elegant moustache, who might be Lord Andrew, although Ted would not have wanted to bet on it. And the man-at-arms had said Randolph was not here yet.

The man with the elegant moustache was trying to convince Benjamin of something, and it was clear to Ted that Benjamin did not want to talk to him at all, let alone be convinced by him. The moustached man began to look a little tight around the mouth, and over Benjamin's face settled the lowering anger that had been there when he found the five children at the well.

Get mad and sit down, Ted begged him silently. Benjamin went on getting angry, but he did not sit down. Ted became aware, in the quieting room, that he was not the only one watching them. Ted was reasonably sure by now that the moustached man was in fact Andrew. The man did not look like Andrew, but he acted like him. His voice was becoming steadily more unpleasant. Head after head turned in his direction, and voice after voice petered out, until Ted could hear him clearly.

"No evidence," he was saying, "neither in action nor in reason nor in philosophy."

My God, thought Ted, he sounds just like Patrick.

"Nor in magic?"

Andrew snorted.

"So," said Benjamin, in a tone that stilled the last murmurs, "now we come to't."

Ted, who did not remember this scene, struggled to make sense of it. Andrew, he knew, did not believe in magic. Patrick had fought bitterly against this, maintaining that, in the Secret Country, not believing in magic was about as sensible as not believing in the law of gravity. Ellen informed him that she did not, in fact, believe in the law of gravity. Patrick said that he had hoped for a villain who was smarter than his sister, Ruth made him shut up, and Andrew had continued to disbelieve in magic.

Ted wondered if Benjamin was just now finding this out. Even if he was, should he be so upset? What had he said in the courtyard? I have magic in my blood and my bones, but not in my learning . . . I will not come between the cardinal and his charges. Oh, of course. Benjamin came from Fence's Country, where, instead of keeping little kids from falling into puddles, you had to keep them from summoning thunderstorms. He, too, would probably think that disbelieving in magic was about as sensible as disbelieving in the law of gravity. Although, come to think of it, he probably didn't even know about the law of gravity.

Ted was lost in this swamp of thought, and Benjamin and Andrew were still looking at each other like two cats deciding whether to fight, when the double doors opened, sending in a draft that slanted every flame, made Ted abandon his thoughts, and caused Andrew and Benjamin to jump guiltily.

Two men came into the room. The first was clearly the King. He did not look much as Ted had imagined him, perhaps because the torchlight did strange things to people's faces. But he was old and he wore a crown. Ted was reminded, by something about his eyebrows, and the way he fixed Benjamin and Andrew with his stare, and the way he held his head, of Patrick.

Well, he *is* Patrick's father, thought Ted. I guess he should look like him. He's my father too; I wonder if he looks like me. He's awfully old to be either of our fathers. I wonder how old *we* are? I forget.

Finding this direction of thought unsettling, he looked from the King to the second man, and could not breathe. This was Lord Randolph. He was taller and thinner than Ted thought he should be, and he resembled Ruth and Ellen to an alarming degree, much more strongly than the King resembled Patrick. But Ted was certain that this was Lord Randolph, and something in the look of him almost stopped Ted's heart. He was smiling, and everyone in the room except Andrew smiled back at him. Even Benjamin, whose furious scowl had smoothed to a sort of blank inquiry when the King came in, smiled at Randolph.

"So here be our truants," said Benjamin.

Randolph made him a bow, a very brief and tidy one, and Ted blinked. That bow meant things, among them that Randolph liked Benjamin very much, that he had no intention of telling Benjamin why he and the King were late, and that he was tired. He reminded Ted of an actor, whose every move meant something.

And how do you know what that bow means? he demanded inwardly. Have you ever seen any other bow that you thought meant anything at all?

"My lord," said Benjamin to the King, "allow me." He assisted the King into the end chair nearest the door. Ted, shaking off the paralysis with which the sight of Randolph had afflicted him, made a beeline for the chair at the other end, and was arrested by Benjamin's voice.

"What dost thou think on so deep, my young lord, that thou canst not greet thy father?"

Ted, his face hot, turned slowly so as not to trip on Lord Justin's robe, and made his way past amused and sympathetic faces to stand by the King's chair. Benjamin looked the way Ted felt when Laura broke something: He was tired of it, but he was used to it. Ted, once more grateful for Prince Edward's being an impractical daydreamer, bowed to the King.

"Sir," he said, groping for his lines. This scene he had played, though it was not one of their favorites. He caught with the corner of his eye the expression on Andrew's face. Andrew looked both pleased and pained. Ted had once seen a similar expression on his mother's face when the child of a neighbor she disliked had spilled grape juice on a white velvet chair. She was unhappy that the chair was ruined, she said later, but it was almost worth it to see the consternation of the neighbor. The hell with you, thought Ted at Andrew, you won't see my consternation.

"How does your honor for this many a day?" he asked the King.

"I thank thee, well," said the King. His voice was a little husky, but it was not old. "And thou?"

"Very well, sir," said Ted.

"How fare thy studies?"

"Some well, my lord, and some indifferent."

"And which indifferent?"

Ted's next line dealt with his inability to learn to handle a sword, but he balked. He did not want to admit to incompetence before Andrew. He looked involuntarily at Randolph, who was his fencing master.

Randolph surprised him by giving him a companionable wink and speaking. "Sire," he said.

The King turned to him. Ted looked at them looking at one another, and shivered. They had known each other for a long time and they were fond of one another; Randolph was going to kill the King, and Randolph knew it now.

"His Highness thinks," said Randolph, "because I have told him so, that he is but an indifferent swordsman. He grows smug when praised, my lord, and while a smug scholar is a fool, a smug swordsman is a dead man. But it were shameful for him to say before your council that he is an indifferent swordsman, and since it is not true, he shall not say it. He does very well, my lord. The blood of King John shows in him."

The King, who had appeared pleased during most of this speech, scowled suddenly at the name of King John. Randolph raised an eyebrow at the King, and Ted recognized the gesture as a challenge.

"It delights my heart to hear thee say so," said the King to Randolph, a little stiffly. Randolph nodded at him. The King turned back to Ted. "This likes me well," he said, "that thou art skillful outside thy books. A bookish king is a shaky fortress."

Ted, who had no lines for this scene because he had never played it, bowed again. From the corner of his eye he had seen Randolph wince at what the King said.

The King nodded at Ted in what Ted took for a gesture of dismissal, so he turned and made his velvet-encumbered way to the other end of the table. Andrew and Benjamin, finally, moved for their seats. Ted saw that Benjamin seemed taken aback, and that on Andrew's face was a sort of outraged bewilderment, which made Ted want to laugh.

He dragged out his heavy wooden chair with a horrible scraping on the stone floor, and crammed himself and his robe into it.

Everyone he knew was at the other end of the table. On his right he had a lean young man, clean shaven, with a mass of red hair and a sardonic eye. If Ted had not heard the moustached man and Benjamin, he would have thought that this was Andrew. The young man grinned at him. Ted smiled back, not very well, and looked at the man on his left. This was a large, older man with very little hair on his head and a vast black beard. He, too, looked like Ruth and Ellen. Ted, struggling with his memory, produced triumphantly the knowledge that this was Conrad, Laura and Ellen's father and, he thought, Randolph's brother. That would explain, at least, why Randolph looked like Ellen.

King William, fifteen feet away, rang a bell, and everyone was instantly quiet.

"My lords," said the King. His voice carried clearly down the long table; Ted might have been sitting next to him.

"We are met with ye this fourteenth day of June, in the forty-sixth year of our reign, the four hundred and ninetieth year since King John vanquished the Dragon King, that we may impart to ye such matters as ye may aid us in the resolution of."

Ted, puzzled by a scratching sound at his elbow, looked around and saw that the young man on his right was scribbling with a quill pen on some thick stuff. Ted knew then who he was: Matthew, the King's scribe. He was in fact much more like a secretary, but Ruth and Ellen had objected to this term, so he was called the Scribe. Ted, who had thought Matthew would take his notes on wax tablets and commit them to parchment only for presentation to the King's library, felt chagrined, and wondered how he could keep Patrick from saying I-told-you-so.

"We have spoken to our scouts," said the King, "those who returned at month's end; their tale is all of disquiet. Keeping watch in their accustomed places, where from year's end to year's end only the sheep have walked, they have seen the very stones rise and hurl themselves through the air; they have discerned wisdom in the eye of the sparrow, malice in the call of the dove, cunning in the step of the hare."

Ted sat with his eyes widening. Nobody he knew had written this speech. They had decided that the Dragon King had sent his shape-changers as harmless animals to spy out the southern reaches of the Secret Country, but they had never said it like this.

Conrad saw him staring, and leaned and spoke to him. "A speaketh as one in thy books, eh, lad?"

Ted grinned. That much was true. "Aye, my lord," he said. From clear down the table he felt Benjamin's glare, and he looked quickly back at the King.

"They say sorcery stalks our southern lands, as has not been since King John rode out to quell the Dragon King," said King William.

"They say that the rivers stand in their beds or run up-hill, that the very trees walk so that a man may wake of a dawn and find his cornfield a forest. They say the fish speak and the children are dumb." The King stopped to clear his throat. The room was still except for the scratch of Matthew's pen and the hiss of the torches. "They say there are plagues of man and dog and crop, and they say the people beg our aid."

He stopped, and Andrew put out his hand palm up in the middle of the table.

"Our Lord Andrew," said the King.

"Saving Your Majesty," said Andrew. He said this less pleasantly than he might have, and Ted saw Randolph's brows draw together. "If these tales did come at last month's end, why a fortnight's delay in the telling of them?"

"They also say," said the King, quite pleasantly, "that Fence cometh, with better report and fuller. I have sent physicians to the ailing, but this bodes some strange eruption to our state, more than a plague of nature. We needs must conclude what mean these things and how we shall meet them."

Andrew's hand was still palm up on the table, and the King nodded to him.

"Sire," said Andrew, "have our scouts seen these things themselves, or do they but repeat the tales of the wild, the ignorant, or the mad? I know well how the work of our guardians has turned to rumormongering in these fat and pursy times."

Randolph flung his hand down upon the table with a crack that must have hurt his knuckles.

"Our Lord Randolph," said the King.

"I," said Randolph, with great precision, "have spoken to

the scouts. Among them are Morgan, Gregory, and Suzanne. I think, my lord, you will allow that these are neither wild, nor mad, nor ignorant?"

Andrew nodded.

"They did indeed begin by hearing rumors," said Randolph, "but they ended by being themselves besieged. Fence delivered them, or we might have no report at all. These are no idle tales, my lord. Our own men have seen these things, and some nearly died of it."

Andrew took his hand from the table. He did not seem distressed. Randolph left his where it was, and the King nodded to him.

"Sire," said Randolph. "Since I spoke with the scouts I have been studying the Book of King John. I have shown some part of it to the more trustworthy of the scouts. My lords," he said, looking up and down the table with an economical movement that made every one of them sit forward, "the scouts agree with me that the things they have seen are precisely the warnings, in the Book of King John, of another rising of the Dragon King. His agents are among us, and we must prepare for battle."

Conrad put his hand down.

"Our Lord Conrad," said the King.

"My lords," said Conrad, "I do not doubt these tidings, but I doubt their import. There has ever been grave doubt that indeed King John's book is history and not fable. Nature does not teach us of such things as he has written. But she teaches much of sham and trickery. The only spells anyone has witnessed for a generation have been spells of illusion. Methinks these are none other than such."

"And what then," said Randolph, "is their import?"

"No doubt, my lord," said Conrad, leaning across his neighbors so that he could see Randolph, "that some power in the south sends spies to us, and doth indeed contemplate an invasion. But how to meet that power is what we must contend. To meet these signs with King John's tactics is to meet our end."

Matthew's hand came down on the table, still holding his pen, and startling Ted. Randolph quickly took his away, and Conrad's stayed where it was.

"Our lord Matthew," said the King.

"Two points," said Matthew. "First, King John's book is not the only record of his battle. Worthy generals filled pages with their wonder that he had won with such outlandish strategies. They quarreled with him bitterly about his battle plans, using just such speeches as we hear from Lord Conrad, and when they went to battle 'twas with the certainty that they but trailed a madman to his death and theirs."

"Those documents," said Conrad, "are but doubtful."

"So are all documents," said Matthew. "We can but use what we are given."

He looked as if he would say more, but Ted, quaking, put his hand down on the table.

"Your Highness," said the King.

"My lords," said Ted. His voice cracked, and he cleared his throat. Speech class would be nothing after this. "My lords, I have made a study of these documents. The men who seemed to doubt them were not scholars. They were renegade wizards who wished to make all men disbelieve in magic, that in secret their power might be greater. Nothing they say is to be trusted." He took his hand away and wiped sweat from it onto Lord Justin's robe.

Matthew and Conrad's hands remained on the table, and both lords looked at the King.

"Your second point," said the King to Matthew.

65

"Just this matter of wizards," said Matthew, inclining his head to Ted. "I grant, my lord Conrad, that indeed there are spells of illusion which can deceive an ordinary man. But which of them can deceive Fence? If he says these things are real, then they are real."

Conrad snatched his hand from the table as Andrew slapped his down again.

"Andrew," said the King.

"Your pardon," said Andrew, "but our young scribe is perhaps too honest in his own mind to perceive the crookedness of others."

Ted stole a glance at Matthew, who was taking down Andrew's words in a series of vicious stabs which could not have been good for the pen but which Ted was entirely in sympathy with.

"Prince Edward has spoken of renegade wizards," said Andrew. "I submit, my lords, that those of whom he spoke were not villains, but honest men endeavoring to show forth the trickery of their fellows. I submit that all wizardry is but trickery, and all spells but illusion. That Fence says the signs reported by the scouts are real, means nothing unless Fence is to be trusted. My lords, no wizard is to be trusted." Randolph's hand came down on the table, very gently. Andrew went on. "They are no man's servants; they pursue their own ends. The wizards of Fence's Country were ever ready to aid our enemies. Shan himself served the Dragon King for a score of years. My lords, Fence is a traitor, using the ignorance of our ancestors as a trap to catch us in."

Even in the uncertain and ruddy light of the torches, Ted could see that Randolph had turned red. The King looked toward Randolph and began to nod, but Benjamin put a hand on Randolph's wrist, and Matthew put his own hand down quickly. The King surveyed them all for a moment. "Randolph?" he said.

"I yield to Matthew," said Randolph, with no particular emphasis, but Ted shivered.

"Shan did not serve the Dragon King in his wars against us," said Matthew, "and, even were Shan a blacker traitor than Melanie, that says nothing of Fence. Wizards go their own ways, they have no common goals, they are not a force, together. They cannot work together, and they dislike one another's company."

"So," said Andrew, without permission, "they would have us believe."

"Cease," said the King. Andrew was silent, but only, Ted knew, because he had no more to say. "Matthew," said the King, "write not that remark."

"Sire," said Matthew, "I would prefer to let it remain. I yield to Andrew, that he may have said it."

"As you will," said the King. Matthew's pen scratched on. Benjamin lifted his hand from Randolph's wrist, and Randolph moved the hand a little further out onto the table. "Randolph," said the King with a trace of resignation.

"Andrew," said Randolph. "With regard to Shan's serving our enemies, may I remind you that he left the service of the Dragon King and aided King John in the battle against him, and that he later worked for us the Border Magic. He did these things because it was in plans to attack us that the Dragon King first revealed his true purposes and his madness."

"So Shan said," said Andrew, one hand under his chin and the other in his lap.

"Cease," said the King, more sharply this time.

Andrew bowed his head. "Your pardon, Sire," he said; he did not sound sorry.

"Matthew, write not that remark," said the King. "Randolph, pray continue."

"Sire, I would prefer to let it remain," said Randolph, "and I yield to Andrew that he may have said it."

"As you will, then," said the King. "This courtesy among my counselors is more strange than Fence's reports, I think. I prithee, say on."

"Sire, I cannot see that there is anything more to say," said Randolph. "If there is a conspiracy of wizards against us, then whatever we say, Andrew will but answer 'so say they.' To prove him wrong, we have history, which may be lies; eyewitnesses, who may have been deceived by illusion; and Fence, who may be a traitor. I would follow Fence to war with a child's hoop for my weapon, if he told me 'twould serve me best. He is my master and my friend, and I think that, were he treacherous, it must have shown itself to me in some way in the years we have worked together. But unless you trust my judgment, Sire, which Andrew will say may be overturned by spells of illusion, nought that I say can help you. Andrew has no proof except to say, if things are as he says they are, then indeed there would be no proof. We have no proof of which he cannot say 'this is illusion.' If we march to meet the Dragon King with the weapons and strategies which will vanquish men, we will have our proof when we are vanquished by monsters. And that will be too late." He took his hand from the table, in a motion so final that Ted shivered again.

Matthew put his hand down.

"Matthew," said the King.

"My lord Andrew," said Matthew, "granted that your view of the nature of wizards answers all our arguments, what reason do you have for such a view? Why should there be such a conspiracy? What would it profit them? Why have none discovered it earlier? Can you at least show that what you say is probable?"

"Andrew?" said the King.

"My lords," said Andrew, "it is more probable than the opposite view. It is more probable than the existence of magic."

Benjamin, Randolph, Matthew, Ted, and someone Ted did not recognize and who had not spoken, all put their hands down at once. The King sat still, studying them.

"My lords," he said, "this is not a conference of philosophers. We do not see the profit in wrangling, and that is what it would come to should we let ye speak. I will ponder what has been said here. Any of ye who yet hath arguments to make, when the blood hath cooled a trifle, speak to Lord Matthew, and he will see that ye have audience with me. I thank ye for your aid."

He stood and bowed to them. With a tremendous scraping of chairs, they stood and bowed back to him. He gestured to Benjamin, shook his head at Randolph, and swept from the room. Ted, even in his consternation, wished he could manage his own robe like that.

The room erupted into babble. Matthew turned to Ted. "I thank you for your help," he said. "I had not known that anyone had doubted the generals' writings, let alone who or why."

"I'm afraid Andrew turned the information to his own ends," said Ted; he was much too angry to be worried about what he said.

"That is the way of Andrew," said Randolph, behind Ted. Ted nearly jumped. Randolph edged himself between Ted and Matthew, dropping a hand on Ted's shoulder. Ted did jump.

"I cry you mercy," said Randolph, letting go of him. "So

you are nervy after all. How many times have I sat in council, knowing what you knew well enough to see it should be
said, but not well enough to say it; how often have you
avoided my eye? When you spoke today, I thought my
praise of your fencing had suddenly made you fearless."

"Not that," said Ted. "I didn't even know whether to believe you. It was Andrew; he made me angry."

"He makes me angry thrice a day," said Randolph, dryly,
"but it does not start me from my accustomed way."

"Don't tell me," said Ted, rendered reckless by a desire to
impress Randolph, "that you always let Benjamin keep you
from speaking in council."

Matthew, who had been gathering up his writing para-
phernalia, laughed. "A hit, Randolph, a very palpable hit."

Randolph eyed Ted with a curiosity that made him uncomfortable. "It's true enough," said Randolph, "I do not."

"Randolph," said Matthew, serious again, "does he believe
what he says, think you, or is it he who is the traitor?"

"Mind your tongue," said Randolph. "I do not know, but
you should not make that accusation lightly."

"Andrew accused Fence!" said Ted. This had not happened
in their play, and he was both dismayed and furious.

"He may well pay for it," said Randolph.

"Not 'he will'?" asked Matthew. He looked over his armful of paper and pen and ink at Randolph, and Ted saw that
they understood each other and that they were afraid.

"My prince," said Benjamin from across the room.

"Sir?"

"A word with you."

"Please excuse me," said Ted to Randolph and Matthew,
his Secret language having deserted him. He went to Benjamin. Everyone else had gone.

"I fear thou must share the fate of thy brother and thy cousins," said Benjamin. "To bed with thee; may thy hunger sharpen thy wits for the future."

"But—"

"I have gi'en thee as much aid as I have stomach for; away wi' thee."

Ted, remembering suddenly that he and his companions had to get home before their other set of grown-ups was as angry as Benjamin had been at the well, nodded. He hoped that all the royal children were, in fact, quartered in the east wing (where the game had put them). He bowed to Benjamin and again to Matthew and Randolph. Benjamin scowled. Matthew and Randolph bowed back. Ted went away quickly.

CHAPTER 4

ELLEN and Laura sat in the room they shared. Exploring it had occupied them for some time. It was as large and as green carpeted and as hung with tapestries as it ought to have been. They had delved into large cedar and oaken chests and pulled out odd underwear packed with sweet herbs, and thick woolen blankets, and quilts worked with dragons and unicorns and foxes and flutes and stars. They had opened the enormous oak wardrobe and stared half in delight and half in horror at the far-too-many, far-too-lacy dresses and the velvet cloaks and feathered hats. They had subjected the tapestries to a historical scrutiny that left Ellen with very little to complain about. Laura objected to one tapestry because it was full of white horses, but Ellen reminded her that the Princess Laura loved horses, and Laura had to shut up.

They had found a bone flute, a wooden lap harp, three daggers, about two dozen rag-and-china dolls, and a pile of sloppy-looking embroidery spotted with what Ellen said were Princess Ellen's bloodstains, Princess Ellen having little use for the domestic arts. They had bounced on the feather bed and discovered that it had no springs, but that the feather pillows worked far better in a pillow fight than foam or Dacron polyester. They had crawled over their green carpet, admiring the blue birds and curlicues it was worked with. They had found their bathing room, which had a tub about the size of a normal bathroom, with all its bronze fixtures in the shape of dragons. Laura was taken aback by the realization that this really was a bathroom, nothing more nor less, but then Ellen found its other half, lavishly done in some carved golden wood. Ellen announced with considerable delight that this was a garderobe. It was slightly smelly but a considerable improvement over the latrines at Girl Scout camp, and therefore not to be complained of. On a shelf in the garderobe they had found a black cat that refused to wake up and pay attention to them.

But they were not happy now. They had been sent to bed—where they had not gone, except for the pillow fight—without any dinner. Laura was hungry. Ellen was hungry and sleepy both, because dinnertime in the Secret Country was breakfast time in Australia and she had, by her reckoning, been up all night. She was nervous because soon her mother would be coming to wake her and she wouldn't be there. Laura sat envisioning the Barretts' frantic search of the library, and nursed her bruises. Only the dolls surprised her; she did in fact feel at home in this room. But she had too many things to worry about to enjoy the feeling.

They were locked in, and even if they had not been, they had no idea where any of the others were. They were especially worried about Ted, because Benjamin had kept him in the courtyard.

"We have to get out of here!" said Ellen.

Laura rattled the heavy door for the fourth time, and then went over to the window and knelt on the cushioned seat. This time she spared no notice for the red fox worked on the blue cushion, but just opened the shutters. They opened outward; there was no glass in the window. It was tall, deep and narrow, and narrower at the outside than at the inside.

"Ellen!" said Laura, staring. "Come look."

Ellen uncurled herself from the enormous bed and stalked over to the window, pushing handsful of hair out of her eyes. "What?"

Laura pointed. "Down by the lake."

"It's a horse," said Ellen. "Drinking. So what?"

"That isn't a stupid *horse*. Wait till it's finished."

"I thought you meant the view at first," said Ellen, obligingly fixing her eyes on the animal. "It's pretty."

"I've never seen real mountains before," said Laura.

She was still not sure she liked them. They floated over their reflections in the glassy lake like drifts of snow, as if they might melt by morning and flood the castle. Their trees were as tiny as the little curly weeds that grow between cracks in the sidewalk and look like forests seen from a long way up. Laura did not recognize them at all.

"This must be the famous view the famous artist came to paint, and we had to go live in Ruth's room," said Ellen. They giggled.

The animal drinking at the lake raised its head. Its long horn was red in the light of sunset.

"Oh," said Ellen. Then she frowned. "I thought they lived in the Enchanted Forest. What's it doing in our backyard?"

"That *is* the Enchanted Forest, where the mountains turn west," said Laura. "This was Princess Margaret's room, remember, and she looked out at the Enchanted Forest all day and wrote songs about it, because her father—"

"I still don't think it belongs in our backyard."

"Well, if you can call that a backyard—"

"I bet it Means Something," said Ellen.

"I hope not," said Laura, her pleasure in the animal considerably diminished.

The door clanked and rattled and scraped, and they jumped. The door opened, and Ruth and Patrick came in. Patrick wore a leather belt with a scabbard on it around his waist. The scabbard was empty, but he seemed to have trouble walking with it.

"You could have knocked," said Ellen. "We might have been timid ladies-in-waiting or spies plotting or anything, for all you knew."

"Where's Ted?" said Laura.

"He's attending a council," said Patrick. "It was supposed to be this afternoon, but of course they couldn't find Ted."

"Which was why Benjamin was angry even before he thought that Ted and I were plotting to elope," said Ruth, sourly.

"And we did too know it was you in here," said Patrick, "because in my room there's a historical map of High Castle. I know your room used to be Princess Margaret's chamber, and Ruthie's was where Mad John hanged himself after—"

"I can't imagine," said Ruth hastily, "what made me think it would be fun to live in a haunted room."

"You don't like it," said Patrick, "but Lady Ruth of the Green Caves loves it."

"Lady Ruth of the Green Caves is a weird person."

"Well, you'd better start acting weird, then."

Laura wished she had only to be a weird person, instead of an expert horsewoman and the best dancer in six kingdoms.

"Are you and Ted planning to elope?" said Ellen to Ruth.

"No," said Ruth, "and I ought to slap your face for even asking."

Laura looked at her with admiration. She had always liked

Ruth's sorceress voice, as long as the Lady Ruth and Princess Laura were on the same side.

Ellen gaped at her sister, who had never hit anybody in her life. But she recovered quickly. "You touch me, milady," she said, "and I'll speak to my undergardener about that hemlock."

"Cut it out," said Patrick, earning himself three scandalized looks. "We have to decide how to escape. Ted's coming here when the council's over—or I hope he is. I left him a note in our room."

"How'd you get out?" said Ellen.

"I got him out," said Ruth, sitting in their rocking chair. "Lady Ruth has a set of all the keys in High Castle. She's trusted."

"If she's so trusted," said Patrick, maneuvering himself and his scabbard onto the bed, "how come Benjamin can send her to bed without dinner?"

"I think Benjamin might have overstepped himself," said Ruth; she sounded smug. "I have a lady-in-waiting, or a chambermaid, or something—not Agatha, somebody else—and when I told her what he'd done, first she thought I was joking and then she was shocked. She was the one who mentioned the keys." Ruth patted the waistband of her skirt, which jingled.

"If you'd wear pants like a normal person," said Ellen, "you could just keep the keys in your pocket."

"Don't start that," said Patrick. "How are we going to get out of here?"

"Yes," said Ellen, "we must finish our interrupted ceremony before the Spirit of the Green Caves blights all our—"

"Cut it out," said Patrick. "This is serious. Good grief, we're stuck in a magical country and we have to sneak past the best guards in it and ride four leagues in the dark and then sneak back into our houses—isn't that enough? Do you have to play too?"

Ellen and Ruth looked at Patrick. Laura looked at the floor.

"Which door," said Ruth at last, "is the least guarded?"

And they argued about escaping. Ted did not come for several hours, so it was quite an argument. The main problem was that Ruth or Ellen would say, "Let's say Benjamin had too much wine and fell asleep," or "Let's say they left that little window open in the stable and . . ." and Patrick, nastily, would remind them that no matter what they said, Benjamin would remain sober and the window would remain locked. Then he would add, thoughtfully, that they didn't even know if there *was* a little window in the stable.

About halfway through the discussion, Laura asked, "But what about all those extra walls?"

"The outer one isn't on the map in my room," said Patrick. "But there are lots of little doors and gates in the other ones. They've got really rotten security around here."

"Well, of course they have," said Ruth patiently. "Only the two innermost castles were ever used as a fortress. The rest were built after we got the Border Magic."

"It's still too easy for prisoners to escape," said Patrick. "Anyway, Laurie, I think there are lots of ways for people to get to the gardens and the lake. We just have to worry about stealing the horses."

The sun had been almost down when Ruth and Patrick came in. Eventually they had to light the lamps. This diverted one argument and began another. Ted walked into the middle of it. He wore a long blue robe and an unhappy expression. Laura, who had not been arguing, looked at him and giggled.

"You shut up," he said heavily, and sat upon the bed. He

scowled lengthily at Laura and Ellen and Patrick, and then he looked at Ruth. "Oh, I see," he said to her. "You're lucky you're wearing that."

"What?" said Ellen, looking at her sister's long skirt and lacy blouse.

"On top of everything else," said Ted, "I got a lecture on proper attire which I was told to pass to you all. Benjamin never wants to see any of these garments again."

"What's wrong with us?" said Ellen belligerently.

"You," said Ted, "are wearing very dirty blue jeans with holes in both knees, and a blouse I guess is Ruth's, because it sure is too big for you. Also it has chocolate stains on it. Your brother has red paint all over his jeans."

Laura stared at him. This was not like Ted, who didn't care what anyone wore, and it was not like Prince Edward, who did care but was much too shy to say anything about it.

"Laurie," said Ted, staring back at her, "is wearing one of David's T-shirts that David slid down the dirt slide in yesterday and there are gravy stains on her shorts. Under this stuff"—he plucked at the shining folds of his robe—"I have this T-shirt my mother hates because it's only got one sleeve, and old patched blue jeans. Benjamin wants to know where in the world we found this stuff and how we could possibly want to wear it."

"What did you tell him?" asked Laura, fascinated.

"We have to get home," said Patrick.

"I've been thinking about that," said Ted. "We were here before we were here, if you know what I mean. So maybe we're back home too, doing just what we're supposed to do, and nobody is worried."

"The only way to find out is to go home and see," said

Patrick, "and if you're wrong then the sooner we get home the better."

"But we have to have a conference," said Ted. "That council—" He shook himself a little.

"Was it like the well?" said Ellen. "Not quite right?"

"Worse," said Ted, thoughtfully; "some of it was too right."

"Let's have our conference tomorrow, then," said Patrick.

"Oh, all right." Ted stood up and clambered out of his robe. "I found a sheath for the sword," he said, patting it.

"Me too," said Patrick. "Come on."

"You do look grubby in those other clothes," said Ellen to Ted. "How'd you get Benjamin to let you keep them?"

"You should talk. He was in a hurry."

Patrick stood up. "Let's go."

"Go how?" said Ellen.

"Just come on," said Patrick. They trailed him out of the room, muttering at one another.

They had trouble finding their way out of the castle. They were acquainted with its floor plan, but they were used to certain landmarks which did not exist here, such as the rose trellis, the doghouse, and the hammock, and they were not used to having things be as big as they had said the things were.

Laura, whose legs were the shortest, scrambled behind the other four, tripping only occasionally and wondering how it could be so cold in here when it was so hot outside. This was better than the Barretts' stuffy house, but there was no time to enjoy it. Laura tried to decide whether she preferred the Barretts without horses or the Secret Country with the horses, tripped on a spot where a paving stone was missing, and gave up trying to think.

It was very dim in the passages; torches burned in brackets on the walls, but not many and not bright. Finally they found the door that would take them down to the south side of High Castle. It creaked. It was supposed to, so that the vigilant guards of the Crown might discover Lord Randolph as he tried to sneak through it. It had never occurred to any of them that they might one day need to sneak through it themselves.

"I hate this," said Ellen.

"Shut up!" said Patrick, patiently easing the door open and drawing its squeaks out so long that they were hardly noticeable.

"You don't have to open it all the way," said Laura, who by now was in a fever to be gone. "We can squeeze through."

"No we can't," said Patrick. "We don't want somebody falling down the stairs." Laura knew whom he meant by "somebody."

"We need a flashlight," said Ted.

"Be quiet," said Ruth.

They huddled against the wall and let Patrick finish opening the door. Laura wanted to ask Ellen whose idea it had been to make the halls so drafty. She thought of the vast spaces of High Castle above them, and wondered where all the guards had gone, and kept still.

"All right," said Patrick finally. Colder air came out of the open doorway at them. The stairs were not lit at all.

"Keep close to the walls," said Ted.

"And not too close together," said Patrick.

"Ted," said Ruth, "you should go first and I last."

Nobody contradicted this, so Ted put a foot out and felt cautiously for the first step. Laura cringed, expecting it to creak as the door had. Then she remembered that the steps were stone, and felt foolish. Ted meanwhile had felt his way down two more steps.

"All right," he said, his voice a little hollow in the stairwell, "first Laurie, and then Patrick, and then Ellen."

Laura heard Patrick grumbling under his breath as she started after Ted, and she wished he were not behind her. She started cautiously down the stairs. There was no banister or handrail, and the wall was cold. When the wall stopped she knew she was at the bottom. The lower hall was not lit either. She took two more steps so she would be out of Patrick's way when he got there, and bumped into Ted.

"Dammit, you made me blink!"

"You'd better watch your language," said Laura automatically.

"Oh, shut up. Look—do you see light?"

"No."

"Look. Here. Patrick, don't bump into her," said Ted over her head. "Turn and look down the hall to the right."

"Yes!" said Patrick immediately, in Laura's ear. "It must be moonlight through the crack in the door."

"What crack?" demanded Laura.

"That's the Great South Door," said Patrick, "and the crack is where the Dragon King hit it with his battering ram. He had a bet with King Conrad, you know, which is why they never mended the door and why it's not guarded— ow!"

"Well," said Ellen, "your foot was where my foot had to go next."

"Be *quiet*," said Ruth, behind Ellen.

They blundered down the hall toward the faint splinter of light until Laura found the door by hitting her head on it.

She was glad it was a plain door, not carved. Ted moved her out of the way and fumbled with the bolts. "How many of these are there?" he asked.

"Three," said Ellen.

Ted drew the first two back with nothing worse than a little rattling, but the third one screamed. They all froze. This was the worst noise yet. Nothing happened. Ted finally pushed the door open to a rush of pale warm air and the smells of mud and herbs.

"Careful down the steps," he said.

They stumbled down the steps and stood in the shadow of the castle wall. A wide path, probably pink by day, but pleasantly pearly in the moonlight, ran from the south door to an open gate in the far wall of the garden. Through the gate they saw the shift and glint of moonlight on the water of the moat, with the shadow of the next wall black at its far side.

"The stables should be through there, across the moat, and to the left," said Patrick.

"Stay on the path," said Ted. "There are snares for rabbits in there."

"Rabbit snares?" said Ellen.

"They eat everything," said Ted patiently, and began to lead the way along the path. The moon was lopsided, not quite full, but it gave more light than was comfortable. Laura felt like a strayed hamster in a flashlight beam. She took hold of Ellen's blouse and was towed along in her wake as Ellen, crowding behind Ted and stepping on his heels, demanded, "Did you put those rabbit snares in that garden?"

"The gardener did, dummy . . . what's his name, anyway?"

"Timothy," said Ellen. "You know what I mean. Did you

put those rabbit snares in that garden? Because that is my garden and if I want rabbits kept out, I will—"

"Ellen," said Patrick wearily, "we don't even know for sure if there are rabbit snares. We'd just rather be safe than sorry."

They crowded through the open gate and stared across a little lawn at the broad waters of the moat.

"Laurie can't swim," said Ted.

"Conrad's Bridge," said Patrick, herding them all to the left along the outside of the garden wall. "It should be right before the moat empties into the lake."

They followed the wall as it curved around to form the eastern boundary of the garden. Something splashed in the moat, and Laura was grateful she could not swim. Then again, walking wasn't pleasant either; she had stumbled over every stone and stick for the past ten yards.

"How long is this wall?" she asked.

Ted stopped, letting Ellen bump into him and Laura into Ellen. Patrick and Ruth managed to stop without bumping.

"Do you people suppose you could possibly be just a little bit quieter?" said Ruth.

"Yes," said Patrick, quietly enough. "Where are the great skilled catlike guards that are supposed to be lurking all over the place?"

"So how long is this wall?" whispered Laura.

Ted pointed along the white lumpy line of the wall to a bright patch about twenty yards ahead of them. "That is the lake. Now come on and be quiet."

They came on, being quiet. There had been a path of sorts when they started, but it kept getting rockier and weedier, and they had not gotten very much farther when it turned into wet knee-high grass.

"Oh, criminy," said Ted, in a startled tone.

"Shhh!" said Laura, stepping into the grass behind him. A cold and wet and horribly close sensation overtook her, as if she were in a slimy cave. She shook her head and looked up, and shrieked.

Of what really happened next she missed almost all. Of what she thought happened next she remembered almost all and wished she did not. Discussing it later, they found that Patrick, Ted, and Ellen were in similar straits. Only Ruth knew what had really happened, and this is what she said it was.

"What's the matter!" bellowed Ellen.

"Shut up!" hissed Patrick, but it was too late. Right above them torches flared upon the moon-silvered battlements of High Castle. Ellen shoved Patrick, who stepped into the grass.

"Run!" cried Ellen.

"Not that way!" shouted Patrick. Ruth watched him swing his sword at the empty air, duck away from nothing, and deliver to Ellen a push in the stomach that knocked the breath out of her and sent her right into Ruth.

"Will you move!" said Ruth, pushing her back the other way.

Ellen fell flat on her stomach into the grass, and then she yelled. Ruth picked her up and ascertained that she was not bleeding or dead. Ellen went on yelling. Ruth looked over her shoulder. More torches were coming to light on the walls, and people were shouting up there now. Ruth looked for the rest of them. Ted and Laura were running, but not very well. Ted was flailing his arms around his head as if to keep off flying things, and Laura kept screaming "Go away!" to the moonlit air. Ellen suddenly kicked Ruth in the shin, and Ruth dropped her. Ellen screamed again.

Ruth took two steps into the grass, which twined itself around her ankles with blades as sharp as swords and began climbing up her legs. Ruth flung herself backward out of the grass, landing painfully on several inconvenient stones. She looked at her legs, and felt them for blood, and stood up, looking across the grass at the others. None of them seemed to be afflicted with climbing plants, although they were certainly afflicted with something.

"Oh," said Ruth. She had remembered a piece of the Secret Country's history that might account for all this. Then she heard the grate of wood on stone as the Great South Door was opened, and the clank of mail as men-at-arms came out of it.

Ruth caught Ellen, who was wrestling on the ground with nothing in particular, by the collar of her blouse, and dragged her into the grass. The grass sank itself into her legs again, and every time she took a step she felt as if it were cutting her legs to ribbons. But she went on being able to walk on them long after they should have been hacked to mincemeat, and after a few strides she was able to ignore the feeling. A more serious problem was Ellen, who was kicking and scratching and seemed inclined to bite as well. Ruth clutched her harder, which produced a lull, and grabbed Patrick with her free hand. He was dangerous; he had the sword.

"Patrick," said Ruth urgently, "cut it out. It's me. You know what this is, you idiot, this was part of your coming-of-age, stop it!"

Patrick immediately closed his eyes. "You're right," he said. "Come on." He took one of Ellen's arms, and he and Ruth dragged her along.

"What's it doing to *you?*" asked Ruth, who thought that fighting a sturdy twelve-year-old was hard enough without being aided only by someone who refused to open his eyes. "Can't you look where we're going?"

"Never mind," said Patrick.

They caught up with Ted and Laura. Ted had his sword out now. Laura was engaged in a vicious battle with her own hair. Patrick looked behind and saw the guards, the great skulking catlike guards, reach the edge of the grass.

He clamped his arms around Ellen as Ruth let go of her, and was rewarded by being bitten in the shoulder. He pushed her away.

"Ellie, if you don't cut it out I'll trample your broccoli when we get home. I swear it. Close your eyes!"

Ellen did so. "Oh," she said. "They aren't roaring after all."

"Ted," said Ruth, catching at Ted's sword arm, "you made this up, it's not real, stop it! Close your eyes," she added hopefully.

Ted closed his eyes, and opened them again immediately. "It's worse that way," he said, "but now that you mention it, it's not so bad." He collared his sister. "Shut your eyes!" he commanded.

"They are!"

"Well, open them, then! This isn't real!"

Laura did as she was told. "Are you sure? *Watch out, it's coming at you!*"

The guards stepped into the grass and roared.

All five children ran.

"Keep your eyes closed!" hollered Patrick as he stumbled out of the grass and tripped over something at the edge of the lake. Laura fell over him and began beating on him with both fists.

Ruth stepped into the cold water of the lake and involuntarily opened her eyes. Ted came up beside her and attempted to deal with Laura. "That's Patrick," he told Laura, "leave him alone." He tried to pick her up, and she hit him in the eye.

Ellen staggered up in time to help Ruth prevent Ted from hitting Laura back.

"It's you?" said Laura. "Your bones aren't coming out?"

"Not yet," said Ted, trying to get his eye open.

They all stared at one another for a moment, panting. The guards were yelling and cursing on the other side of the field.

"Here's the bridge!" called Patrick.

They pounded across the bridge, slithered through a muddy space covered inadequately with straw, and leaned on the back wall of the stables, gasping. The noise of the guards did not seem to be coming any closer.

"What was that?" said Laura, wrapping her arms around herself and shivering.

"Why are you cold?" demanded Ellen. "It was like a volcano and the grasses burned our feet."

"It was wet," said Laura, "and I don't want to talk about it."

"How do we deal with Benjamin?" said Patrick.

"And all the undergrooms and stable boys and all that," added Ellen.

"I'll bet you they've gone to see what all the noise is about," said Laura, more hopefully than firmly. She could not break the habit of deciding what would happen according to the necessity of the moment.

They went to find out, and Benjamin and everyone else had done just that, leaving the stable door wide open.

"He's not supposed to do that," said Ellen as they struggled with saddling the horses, which did not like the noise from outside and were not inclined to be forgiving of incompetence. Only Patrick had been taught to saddle a horse, and he was not forgiving either.

"Maybe he recognized our voices," said Laura, who was standing as far away from the horses as she could get. "He always comes if we're in trouble."

"He ought to be right here, then," said Ellen. "Where does this go?"

"Never mind the saddles, there isn't time," said Patrick. "Just do the bridles. Here, Ellie, like this."

"It's all slobbery!" said Ellen.

From outside came three splashes and renewed cursing. It sounded much too near. Laura considered hiding in an empty stall.

"Hurry *up*," said Ruth.

Patrick got four horses bridled, and Laura watched the other four manage to get themselves onto the horses. Then Ted had to dismount and boost Laura, whom everybody had forgotten, up behind Patrick, who was the only one among them with any real claim to horsemanship. They clattered and jingled and creaked out of the stable. The noise from the guards was still going on, but it came from the garden now.

"I bet there *were* rabbit snares in that garden," said Ted. "Listen to them swear!"

Feet pounded across the stableyard. They took their horses out the southern door of the stable and stopped, staring at the outermost walls that still towered above them.

"There's a postern at the southeast corner," said Patrick, neatly turning his horse in that direction. Laura suspected that the other horses followed him because they felt sociable rather than because anybody else knew how to tell a horse what to do. She was already having difficulty staying on the horse, and felt that being caught, even by furious guards, would be more a relief than otherwise.

Patrick's postern was right where he had said it was. It was bolted on the inside and not very large, but Patrick dismounted and got it unbolted and they all got the horses through it without mishap. The horses needed no encouragement to gallop across the plain, and since Patrick had managed to head his in the right direction, they all went that way. They heard no new outcry behind them, and began to feel hopeful. After a few horrible jolting moments, Patrick even convinced his and Laura's horse to assume a smoother gait, and Laura thought she might manage not to fall off after all.

They did not really know the way from High Castle to the Well of the White Witch, but the horses did. It seemed a very long ride. Laura knew that four leagues was twelve miles, a distance one could travel in a car in about fifteen minutes. She did not know how fast horses could go.

She tried to look around her. The land was flat and dark. The moonlight laid a skin of silver over it that revealed nothing except an occasional stream or pond. Laura tried the sky instead. The stars were huge. It was hard to be sure with the jouncing of the horse, but she could not find any of the familiar constellations, and the whole of the heavens looked wrong somehow.

"Patrick," she said, "are the stars right?"

Patrick looked up, bumping her nose with the back of his head. "Heh," he said. "I don't think so. Those aren't the northern constellations. I haven't really learned the southern ones yet."

"Does the Secret Country have any constellations?"

"I didn't make any up," said Patrick.

Laura spent part of the rest of the trip trying to remember if anyone had, and another part trying not to fall asleep, and suddenly they were there. They slid off the horses and stood around uncertainly. The well glowed a faint pink, but no one seemed to have the strength to remark on this. Patrick pulled the two swords from their hiding place and gave one to Ted. Laura hoped it was the right one.

"What do we do with the horses?" asked Ellen.

"They know their way home," said Ted.

"How do we tell them that's what we want them to do?"

There was a brief argument which involved examples from most of the history of the Secret Country; finally Ruth agreed to say a spell over the horses which would make them go home. She whispered sorcerous words into their ears, and they plodded off in the direction of High Castle.

"They don't act very eager," said Ellen.

"We didn't give them any water," said Ted.

"They'll survive," said Patrick. "When and where do we meet again?"

"Here," said Ted, "but how do we know when we'll be able to get away?"

"Well, why don't we try to be here twice a day, at noon and midnight?" said Ruth. "If nobody's here, wait half an hour and then go home."

"All right," said Ted "and the first thing we do is have a conference."

"Good-bye," said everyone.

Ruth and Patrick and Ellen went toward the woods where their bottle trees must wait. Laura wondered how a bottle tree liked Pennsylvania weather. Feeling grateful that they did not have to go through the woods in the dark, she followed Ted up the hill to their stream.

"Why don't you put some water on your eye?" she suggested as they stepped into the stream. "It's cold enough," she added.

"Nothing but an ice bag will do any good," said Ted. "You really hit me, you little beast."

"Well," said Laura, "I thought you were a big beast."

"What did it look like?"

"What did yours?"

"Never mind," said Ted.

They climbed the other bank of the stream and Ted held out the sword to Laura. They held on to it together and got themselves through the hedge. After some discussion involving whether magic swords rusted, whether anyone would take this magic sword away, and how they could hide it if they took it to the Barretts', Ted left the sword, belt and all, under the hedge. They walked home slowly. They were so late that there was no use in hurrying.

"What are we going to tell them?" asked Ted.

Laura's empty stomach felt full of snowballs. "Oh."

"I don't suppose we can lie," said Ted.

"Who could think up a good enough story anyway?"

"I could," said Ted, stung.

"You don't know how to make up that kind of story."

"We're late and wet," said Ted. "And beat-up," he added. "We could say we got lost and were knocked around by some high school kids and had to hitchhike home." He considered this. "They took us to their clubhouse in the woods and we had to struggle through fields and streams before we found a road."

"Wouldn't the people who gave us a ride come in with us and talk to Aunt Kathy and Uncle Jim?"

"Well, maybe," said Ted, discouraged. "They might call the police too, I guess."

"I'm not lying to any policeman!"

"Okay, okay."

There was a terrible scene when they got home. Their aunt, even without tales of high school bullies, had been about to call the police, their three older cousins were combing the neighborhood for the third time, and their uncle was driving around town searching theaters and roller-skating rinks and swimming pools.

All of them descended upon Ted and Laura with the fury of relief, and demanded explanations. Ted told his aunt that he and Laura could not tell her where they had been, and she would just have to take his word for it that it had not been perfidious mischief, and they could not help being late and battered. This line of argument had been known to work with his mother. It did not work with Aunt Kathy. Having been cleaned, dried, and bandaged where necessary, they were sent to bed without supper a second time, which made them even hungrier. They were also grounded for two days. Neither of them knew what that meant. Laura asked Jennifer, who had followed her upstairs to the room they shared and hung around, looking intrigued, while Laura changed into her nightgown.

"It means you have to stay in the house."

"That's barbaric!"

"Mom says *we're* barbaric."

"Heh," said Laura.

"Where were you?"

"I can't tell you."

"Mom sure was mad," said Jennifer.

Laura shrugged.

"If you do it again she'll probably write your parents."

"Oh."

Jennifer glared at her. "We could try some different games."

"It's not your fault," said Laura, relenting. "We had something we had to do, that's all. And we hate games, truly."

Jennifer went away to brush her teeth, slamming the bathroom door, and Laura went to tell Ted what being grounded meant.

"We can't wait two days!" said Ted. "Benjamin'll kill us!"

"*They'll* kill us if we don't wait two days," said Laura.

"Maybe we could sneak out at midnight," said Ted. "Ruth and Ellen and Patrick are more likely to be there then; that's daytime for them."

"If we get caught they'll write Mother and Dad."

"Benjamin will tell the King if we stay away two days."

That was clearly worse. "Oh, all right," said Laura.

They sat glumly.

"I don't think I like this," said Laura.

"I know I don't," said Ted, with such emphasis that Laura looked at him.

"You look like Randolph," she observed.

"How the hell would you know?" demanded Ted.

"I only meant," said Laura, taken aback, "that you look like you do when you're playing him."

"Wonderful," said Ted. "That's just wonderful."

"What," demanded Laura in her turn, "are you trying to decide? That's Randolph's problem, trying to decide what to do about the King? So what are *you* trying—"

"Never you mind," said Ted, firmly; that was one of Randolph's lines to Princess Laura.

Laura looked at him a little fearfully. She was used to living with Ted, and she could manage with Prince Edward, but she was not sure she wanted to live with Randolph.

CHAPTER 5

LAURA had no trouble staying awake; she was hungry, and she ached. When Ted padded into her room, she sat up so quickly that Ted made a frightened hiss, and Jennifer turned over. Ted backed into the hall, and Laura seized her clothes and followed him.

"You get dressed," whispered Ted, "and I'll get some food."

He creaked off down the stairs, leaving Laura cringing. High Castle was less nerve-wracking than this. She put her clothes on, started down the stairs with her shoes in her hand, then remembered the flashlight under Ted's pillow. It was half hers, through one of their parents' infrequent departures from good sense. But since she and Jennifer were obliged to share a room, while Ted had his own, it had been decided that the flashlight would be safer under Ted's pillow. Laura left her shoes on the stairs, fetched the flashlight, started back down the stairs, and tripped over the shoes.

The kitchen was dark except for a patch of moonlight that made the refrigerator look like a polar bear. Laura did not care to turn the flashlight on it.

"Ted?"

The light went on, and the polar bear became a refrigerator with Ted standing to one side of it. "Was that you making all that noise?" he demanded.

"Where's the food?"

Ted looked unhappy. "We shouldn't take it. It isn't ours. We're just houseguests."

"It's our dinner!"

"Yes, but we got sent to bed without it. And deserved it, you know."

"Heh," said Laura. She sat on the floor and put her shoes on.

"Good, you brought the flashlight."

"Yes," said Laura, slowly, "but I think we should use a candle."

"Don't be silly," said Ted, and Laura shut up. She decided that she should not have laughed at him in High Castle.

They went out the side door, being careful to let it latch behind them. They did not want anyone to burgle the house because they had left the door unlocked.

They had not had much experience with flashlights, since it would have been cheating to use them in the Secret. After a few blocks, Laura began to hate the way uncomfortable sorts of things seemed to scurry out of the path of the light. She made Ted, who had thought himself very kind to let her carry it, carry it himself.

"It's just shadows," said her brother impatiently.

"Well, good, it won't bother you to hold the light, then."

The house, when they got to it, was thoroughly alarming. It had no porch light and no yard light, and the streetlight closest to it was broken. It leaned over them, crooked and black. The night was still and cloudy, but in the yard a little wind rattled the maple seeds on the sidewalk, as if they were being swept with a broom. Laura stopped dead and wished she had never noticed the house in the first place. Even Ted stared for a moment before he stooped under the hedge. He swore when Laura bumped into him; she had moved forward smartly to show herself that she wasn't really afraid.

Ted shone the flashlight about under the hedge for a moment, making all the sharp shadows of the leaves jump. Then he dragged the sword and scabbard out onto the sidewalk, and buckled the belt around himself. Laura saw him look up at the house, and then he turned the flashlight off. Laura put her hand on the piece of hilt he had left her, and they scrambled through. The hedge and the tall grass were sopping with dew, and both Ted and Laura acquired a layer of dirt and leaves on the way.

They stood up in the yard, and a great darkness engulfed them. On this side of the hedge, the night was clear and the huge stars steady. But the globes of the working streetlamps, the faint background glow of the city, all the lights of civilization were gone. They were in the deep country on a dark night.

"Let's get out of this yard," whispered Ted, and they slithered back through the hedge. A fine mist drifted along the surface of the stream.

"The flashlight will come in handy once we're in the woods, where she can't see it from the house," breathed Ted. "Can you get that far?"

"You can't use a flashlight here!" hissed Laura. "I told you we should have brought a candle."

"Why?"

"It's cheating."

"Laura," said Ted, "how can it be cheating if it's real?"

"But there aren't any flashlights in the Secret Country."

"There would be if I brought one."

Laura began to feel stubborn. "It won't work."

"Want to bet?"

"All right, I will. How much?"

"Five dollars."

He knew that was her whole week's allowance. She snorted at him.

"Well, you'll win, won't you?" said Ted.

"Oh, all right."

They crept carefully along the bank of the stream, hearing no noise but their own feet, and the small lap of the water. Except for the awful presence of the house behind them, this night was far less frightening than its equivalent in Illinois. Laura had just begun to be able to see properly when they moved under the shadows of the trees. She bumped into Ted, and heard the click as he turned the flashlight on.

There was a great flash of blue light from which the crowding trees seemed to retreat hastily. Laura also retreated, into a bush, and was prickled. Ted swore and dropped the flashlight; it rolled down the bank and splashed into the stream, where it hissed and fizzled in a whole spectrum of sparks, and then went out.

"What was *that?*" said Laura, trying to get herself out of the bush.

Ted knelt and sloshed his hand around in the water, mumbling. "Here it is. No—what?"

Laura peered over his shoulder.

"It's metal," said Ted, "all curled and twisted, and something in the middle." He stood up and knocked Laura over.

"God damn it!" said Laura, in a furious whisper. She was instantly surprised; she never swore at Ted. Perhaps she had done it because, although Laura Carroll was accustomed to being knocked over by larger people, nobody would ever dare do that to the Princess Laura—and they were on the Princess Laura's side of the hedge.

Ted, to whom this had apparently not occurred, laughed, but he did pick her up and brush sand from her back. "You'd better watch your language."

"Oh, shut up."

Ted held the object up in the air, trying to catch enough moonlight to see it.

"It looks like a lantern," said Laura, wishing she could feel better pleased. "That's a candle in the middle."

"It sure isn't the flashlight. Hell. Mom'll have a fit if I've lost it."

"You didn't lose it," said Laura, who had scraped an elbow when he knocked her down, and was not feeling kind. "It blew up. I told you it wouldn't work, and I want my money."

"You'll just get it wet."

"I want it now."

"And you haven't won the bet until I'm satisfied that the flashlight didn't just roll downstream, or something."

"You're never satisfied," said Laura, who had heard her mother tell him as much, "and I want my money."

"Will you give it back if you're wrong?"

Laura was incensed. "I can challenge you to a duel if you question my honor, Edward Bartholomew Carroll!"

"Yeah? You can't even throw a rock straight, what makes you think—"

"Ted?" came a voice from across the stream. Laura jumped.

"Patrick?"

"What are you guys trying to do? Shut up and come on."

"Ted's not being a gentleman!"

"Of course he isn't. Hurry up, will you? Ruthie has a flute lesson at two, and she hasn't practiced."

"What do you mean, of course?" demanded Ted. "She's being a brat, she doesn't deserve—"

"I," said Patrick, whom they could now see, faintly, against the strange stars of the Secret Country, "am going back to the fire before Ruth and Ellen eat all the marshmallows."

He trudged off along the bank of the stream in the direction of the bridge, and Ted started to parallel his course on their side, saying, "Come on."

"I want my money."

Ted made a strangled sound, pulled something out of his pocket, flung it to the ground, and started away.

"Pick it up and give it to me," said Laura, astounding herself. She did not like having been right. The transformation of the flashlight had made her feel that she was being laughed at—it had been like a fireworks display, or a stage magician's trick. She felt mockery in the very air, as someone will who walks into his third-grade classroom wearing the shirt his grandmother's friend gave him. Feeling all this, she was determined to get what little satisfaction she could out of her brother.

Ted hurled himself around, fists clenched. "What's the matter with you!"

"I'm a princess, aren't I?"

"And when I'm king I swear I'll cut your head off," said Ted, but he searched the ground for a moment, found the five-dollar bill, and handed it to her. Laura stuffed it into the pocket of her shorts and followed him at a safe distance, trying to giggle. What, after all, was the use of feeling like Princess Laura when, in far too many ways, she could not act like Princess Laura?

Princess Laura might not mind walking in the woods at night, but Princess Laura never fell down. It was dark in the woods, and rustly with small animals, and crossing the wooden bridge was not pleasant. Laura tripped where she had tripped the first time. The whole bridge shook and creaked, Ted tramped stolidly on, and a number of things leaped from the banks of the stream into the water with ominous ploppings. Laura ran to catch up with Ted, and was slapped in the face by all the branches he had pushed out of his way. She fingered the money in her pocket and kept her mouth shut.

It was better when they got out onto the grass where there was nothing in the way, and Laura could let Ted get ahead of her without fear of losing him. And when they had struggled up the hill and looked from its top over the vast dark plain, they saw a fire flickering beside the Well of the White Witch. The well itself cast no light this time.

Laura began by running down the hill and finished the journey sitting, and was picked up by Ruth and given a brief brushing and two marshmallows.

"Those were mine!" said Ellen. Laura sat down next to her, chewing.

"You've had twelve already," said Ruth austerely.

Ted came up in a dignified silence and accepted a stick and two raw marshmallows from Patrick.

"We were going to bring food too," he said, "but it's not really ours."

"That's right, you're guests," said Ruth. "We just told Mother we were having a picnic. And she wouldn't mind feeding you guys, she's done it for years."

"It's too bad you have to bring all the supplies," said Ted.

"This summer of all summers you have to be stuck in a house where you can't do anything," said Ellen.

"If they weren't stuck in that house we wouldn't be having this kind of summer," Patrick told her. "We'd be playing the Secret just as usual."

"What makes you say that?" demanded Ted.

"Well, I figure the Secret is so important to us that when we were separated and couldn't play it, our minds just managed things so we could play it anyway."

"You think our minds did this?" said Ted.

"Sure, why not?"

"But it's real," said Ellen.

"But what is real?" said Patrick, not jesting.

Laura had a swift intimation that the Princess Laura, in response to that question, would, faster than thought, have leaned over Ellen and hit him solidly in the stomach, saying, "That." She did not do it.

"Do you mean we're magic ourselves?" asked Ted.

"No, no, no. There's no such thing as magic. This is what's called mass hallucination. That means lots of people—us— see things that aren't there."

"How do they do that?" asked Laura, so skeptical that she challenged Patrick.

"Drugs," said Ted.

"What!"

"It doesn't have to be drugs," said Patrick. "It can be nervous tension."

"I thought that gave you headaches," said Laura.

"Patrick," said Ruth, "you're crazy."

"I am not. We were nervous because we couldn't play the Secret, you know we were."

"I get nervous about my flute lessons too," said Ruth, "but I don't look out the front window and see Mrs. Jordan get hit by a truck, do I? I don't see the dentist's office burning down before I go in for them to put a filling in, do I? I don't—"

"Be quiet. That's not nervous enough."

"I'm a lot more nervous about going to the dentist than I am about not having the Secret!"

"It's not just nervous, it's upset, or disappointed, or—or—unsettled. Like Macbeth, Ruthie, okay?"

"Oh."

"Just a minute," said Ted. "Who's imagining who, then?"

"What?" said Patrick as Ruth began laughing and Ellen and Laura looked at each other and made puzzled faces.

"Who," said Ted, "is imagining who? Is this your hallucination, so we're not really here, or is it ours, so you're not?"

Patrick was silent, Laura was sorry. Usually she would have liked Patrick to be wrong, but at the moment she preferred Ted to be wrong.

"Maybe it's telepathy, then," said Patrick at last.

"Besides," said Ted, "you don't go places when you have a hallucination. You stagger around like Macbeth and scare everybody half to death because you see things they don't. We weren't home last night, where were we if we weren't here?"

"Listen," said Laura, who had been thinking, "if it isn't real, shouldn't we still be able to change things?"

"We tried that," said Ruth.

"We did not," said Ellen. "We wanted to and Patrick told us it wouldn't work."

Patrick did not allow them so much as a triumphant pause. "I *said* it wouldn't work," he said, "but I thought it was too dangerous."

"Why?" said Ruth.

"Because it wouldn't come out exactly the way any of us expected it to, and then anything could have happened."

"You mean the way nothing else has been exactly the

way we expected it to be?" said Ted. "The well, and Benjamin, and—"

"Exactly," said Patrick.

Laura snitched three marshmallows from the bag next to Ellen and ate them without bothering to toast them.

"But how does that fit in with our having a hallucination?" asked Ruth.

"Well . . . I'm not sure," said Patrick, causing both of his sisters and Laura to stare at him, astonished. Patrick never said he wasn't sure. "I mean, I never read anything about this, but I thought maybe everybody's hallucinations are interfering with everybody else's, you know, like radio stations or something. What Ted thinks is making my hallucination look wrong, and what you think is messing up Laura's, and—I did say maybe it was telepathy too, you know."

"Patrick," said Ruth, "you're crazy."

"I am not. You explain it."

"I don't want to explain it, I want to know what to do about it."

"You can't unless you can explain it."

"Nonsense."

Patrick became inarticulate, and Ted said to Ruth, "What do you want to do about it?"

"I want to make it so we don't have to go back and forth all the time and get yelled at wherever we go, so we can settle down here and finish the story."

"Me too," said Ellen.

"You do," said Ted. Laura looked at him. She knew that tone. If she had told her mother that she wanted to paint her room in red and white stripes, she would have been answered in just that tone.

"Do you think this is in our heads?" Ted asked Ruth.

"What difference does that make?"

"It sure as hell makes a difference to me."

"Why?"

Ellen felt in the bag for marshmallows and discovered that Laura had eaten them all. "You pig," she said mildly.

"Shut up," said Ruth. "Why, Ted?"

"Well, look," said Ted. "Lord Randolph is going to poison the King, right?"

"I suppose. If this is our game, yes, he is."

"And then I have to kill Randolph, right? Because the King was my father? And I'm the new King?"

"Yes, what about it?"

"Ruth, I don't want Randolph to poison the King."

"Of course you don't," said Laura, relieved to hear someone say something she could understand. "The King is a good, kind man, but he's been corrupted, and he's old, and—"

"You don't know that," said Ted. "I met him, and he *is* a good, kind man. And I met Randolph, and I don't want to kill him, either."

"Well, of course not, that's the point," said Ellen, "he's your best friend, but you kill him for his honor and yours because—"

"Ellen!" Ted shrieked, and startled them all. He stood up and threw his stick into the fire. "You don't know anything, none of you do."

"I made up as much as you did!" said Ellen.

"That's not what he means," said Ruth. "Sit down, Ted."

"I have a good mind to quit right now," said Ted, not moving. "What *do* I mean, if you're so smart?"

"It's real, that's what you mean."

"But I tell you, it isn't," broke in Patrick. "It can't be. There's no such thing as magic."

"Shut up, Horatio," said Ted, scornfully.

"My philosophy's as good as yours!"

"But even if it is real," said Ruth, "how can you miss the Unicorn Hunt and the Banquet of Midsummer Eve, Ted, and Fence fighting the Dragon?"

"How can I miss watching the King die, and killing Randolph?" said Ted, still scornfully. "Not to mention dying myself and talking to a lot of ghosts and killing God knows what-all all over the battlefield and trying to run a kingdom when I hate politics?"

"Do you have to do all that?" asked Ellen.

"Yeah!" said Laura. "Can't we say Randolph doesn't poison the King? Then the rest would be fun, until the battle."

"And then what?" said Ted, less scornfully.

"We could go home," said Laura, dubiously.

"We could see what happens and decide later," said Ruth.

"Well," said Ted. "I tell you right now, no matter what happens, I won't kill Randolph."

"You'd better figure out how to stop him poisoning the King, then," said Patrick.

"I thought you thought changing things would be dangerous," said Ruth.

"Well," said Patrick, "it might not be so bad if we agreed very carefully on what we want to happen. And you're obviously going to try to change things no matter what I think, so you might as well change the right thing."

"I'm not sure that is the right thing," said Ted. "Randolph poisons the King because the King won't see sense about the battle strategy, and if the King won't, somebody had better poison him, or the dragons will get us all."

"So if we just persuade the King about the battle strategy," said Ruth, "everything will be all right."

"Probably," said Ted. "There's still the battle. I still have to die in the battle. Which I won't, I can tell you."

"Nonsense, of course you don't," said Ruth. "If we can change the King's mind, we can change anything; it doesn't have to go the way the game went unless we want it to."

"Don't get so cocky," said Patrick. "Wait until you see how hard it is to change things, and what happens when you try. It really could be dangerous, you know, if you think it's real."

"All right, we hear you," said Ted. "It can't be any more dangerous than dying in battle, can it?"

Patrick was silent.

"So how do we persuade the King?" asked Ellen.

"Why do you have to persuade him?" asked Laura. "Why can't we just say he decides to fight the battle right?"

"That's what I meant about agreeing carefully beforehand," said Patrick, approvingly. Laura was dumbstruck. "But we'll have to figure out all the details of who convinces him, if we don't convince him ourselves."

"We could try Laurie's way on something else first," said Ruth.

"The time!" said Patrick. "Let's try to change the time so we don't have to sneak around so much. We can tell right away if that's worked."

"How shall we change it?" said Ruth.

"Let's say," said Patrick, "that no matter how long we spend here it's only five minutes at home, and we'll be the same age when we get back even if we've been here long enough to grow up."

"I don't want to grow up twice!" said Laura.

"It doesn't hurt, Laurie," said Ruth.

"How would you know?" said Ellen. "You ever been grown up?"

"Shut up," said Patrick. "Laura, it would be worse the other way, you know. You wouldn't know how to be grown up in the real world, and if you were a grown-up they'd expect you to know."

"Maybe I wouldn't have to go home at all?"

"You sure as hell would," said Ted. "Do you know what kind of trouble I'd get in if I came home without you?"

"Oh, all right, I'll come home and grow up twice."

"It'll take you two tries to get it right anyway," said Ted.

Laura, abandoning herself to Princess Laura, opened her mouth.

"And *other* objections?" asked Patrick.

"Well," said Ruth, "all those ideas are just out of books."

"So's the rest of the game!" said Patrick, exasperated.

"All right," said Ruth.

"Do we all agree?" asked Patrick.

They all muttered and nodded.

"Now we have to check it," said Patrick. "Whatever time it was when we decided, it should still be then, or only five minutes later, when we get home." He looked at his wrist and yelped.

"What's wrong with you?" said Ruth.

"That's not my watch!"

"What?" said Ted.

"Look at that!" said Patrick furiously. Ellen, who was next to him, did so.

"Hey!" she said. "That's your old watch, Patrick, not the new one with the ugly numbers."

"Digital," said Patrick, in a tone that told Laura that Ellen knew perfectly well what the watch was called, and pretended to forget for the sole purpose of irritating Patrick. "And it is not my old watch, either."

"How can you tell in this light, anyway?" said Ruth. "Why don't you go home to check what time it is there, Patrick, and then you can look at the watch better."

"It hasn't been long enough," said Patrick, "we only just decided. It's one-thirty. If I leave here at two by this watch—assuming the lousy thing works—and it's still one-thirty when I get home, then we'll know we managed to change something."

"My watch says one-thirty too," said Ruth, "and it really is my watch and it does work. If they both say two at the same time we'll know yours is okay."

"What do we do in the meantime?" said Patrick.

"I'd better tell you about the council I went to yesterday," said Ted, "so you'll know what we're up against. Aren't there any more marshmallows?"

"Laurie ate them," said Ellen, righteously.

"You can buy me some more," said Ted to his sister, "since you're so rich."

Ellen stifled Laura's outraged exclamations, and Ted took up his tale.

CHAPTER 6

T HE beginning of his narrative was accorded a polite silence. Laura thought he was doing a good job. He could quote Benjamin and even imitate his voice. This was not like Ted, and not at all like Edward. Laura wondered who Ted was being. Fence was a good storyteller; perhaps Ted was being Fence.

"That was the West Tower," she said, when he told them about the room full of clothes. "First floor is old—"

"What in the hell," said Patrick, "are we supposed to do about clothes? If Benjamin says he doesn't want to see ours again, he means it."

"One of us," said Ellen, "must make a daring foray to the West Tower and find garments that will fit us withal."

Laura, judging by the standards of their game, found this idea good. Then she began to imagine the actual deed, and felt dismayed.

"Will you let me finish!" said Ted, sounding exactly like Ted. "You think this is bad, just wait."

They all shut up, and Ted went on. The further he got into the king's council, the more his hearers muttered and fidgeted. "And then," said Ted, "Andrew said Fence was a traitor."

"What!" said the other four.

"But that's wrong!" said Ellen. "He's just supposed to say that the Dragon King's men dressed themselves up to be the likeness of monsters, and that King John, when he came to write his book, being a man—"

"—of most piercing wit," said Laura, "did devise an allegory of plain fighting strategy—"

"Well, he didn't say that," said Ted, "and you'd better listen to what he did say."

They let him finish in peace.

"And the King didn't even defend Fence?" asked Laura. Princess Laura was Fence's particular favorite among the royal children, and the real Laura felt outraged on his behalf. Next to the Lady Ruth, Fence was her favorite character.

"And didn't let anyone else defend him either," said Patrick. "That was unfair. And I wonder—"

"Well, Randolph did get to say something, and the King did say they could come to him privately if they had anything to say," said Ted.

"That might be dangerous," said Patrick.

"That's what Randolph and Matthew seemed to think," said Ted, over Ellen's snort and Ruth's, "Patrick, you think everything's dangerous!"

"Everything is," said Patrick, placidly.

"No, but listen, Pat," said Ted. "Matthew said maybe Andrew was a traitor, and Randolph told him to mind his tongue. And Matthew didn't ask him why. They were scared about something."

"What's going on?" cried Ruth. "How can we do anything if it keeps changing all by itself?"

"That," said Ted, triumphantly, "is why I think it's real. Patrick, you see? None of us thought of what happened, but it still happened."

"Andrew's the one who's right," said Patrick. "I wish the King had let him argue longer."

"Andrew's the villain!" said Laura. "*He's* the traitor."

"Sure, in the story," said Patrick. "But really he's right. There's no such thing as magic." He threw another stick onto the fire. "I'm afraid this is my fault," he said.

"Oh?" said Ruth, dangerously, like Lady Ruth.

"Andrew's saying what I think, you see."

"That Fence is a traitor?" said Laura. "That's stupid! What kind of a game is it if Fence—"

"No, not exactly," said Patrick. "That there's no such thing as magic, I mean. But, you see, if there is no such thing as magic, then Fence has to be a traitor, or at least a quack and a villain."

"Go on," said Ruth, still dangerously.

"I must think so strongly that there's no such thing as magic that it's warping the whole hallucination."

"You think that your mind is stronger than all of ours put together?" said the sorcerer of the Green Caves.

"Well . . . ," said Patrick, "I think one thing, you know, strongly, and the rest of you don't really think anything one way or the other; you don't really believe in magic the way I don't believe in it."

"I believe in magic," said Laura.

"You're only a mouse," said Patrick, not unkindly. "You've got no strength of will."

This was so much in accord with what Laura thought of Laura, and so little in accord with what she thought of Princess Laura, that she was caught between sorrow and fury, and could say nothing.

"But the hallucination is magic," said Ted. "If you don't believe in magic, why did the swords work? Why are we here at all?"

"No," said Patrick, "the hallucination has magic in it. It's just a hallucination. There aren't any swords, really."

"Why swords, then?" said Ted. "We never said there were swords to get us from one world to another. Why should all of us think of the same thing to get us here?"

"That's where the telepathy comes in."

"Patrick," said Ruth, "you are crazy."

"We all are," said Patrick, "seeing things that aren't there and—"

"I keep asking you," said Ted, "where are we really while we are having this hallucination? Laura and I got in terrible trouble for being late yesterday; you're all worried because Ruth has a flute lesson at two—"

"Good grief," said Ruth, "it's five till now. I have to go."

"You can't," said Ted, "we—"

"Maybe the time changed," said Patrick. "Check it, Ruthie, when you go back."

"Well, if it didn't, I'm going to be packed off to my flute lesson—without having practiced—and I can't come back and tell you it didn't work."

"So if you don't come back we'll know."

"How will you know?" said Ellen. "She might have been hit by a car—"

"In the west forty?"

"—or gone through the trees into another place—"

"So go with her yourself and come back and tell us if the time didn't work."

"And hurry," said Ruth, leaping up and pulling Ellen to her feet. "Give me the sword, Patrick."

Patrick unbuckled the sword belt and held it out to Ruth, who gathered the whole thing up in her arms as if it were a bundle of laundry.

"And bring more marshmallows," said Ted.

"Pig," said Ellen to Laura, and she and Ruth trudged off into the dark.

Laura felt much less safe when they were gone.

"Well?" said Ted to Patrick.

"I don't know," said Patrick. Laura blinked; this was the second time in two days and the second time in her whole life she had heard Patrick say that. This time, though, he did not sound defeated; he sounded, rather, as if he meant to do something about it, immediately.

"I really have to meet some of these people; maybe that will tell me something," he said.

"It sure told me something," said Ted, "but you don't believe it."

"You know what we could do," said Laura, moved both by a genuine interest in her idea and by an impulse for mischief.

"What?" said Patrick.

"Me and Ted," said Laura, "could use our swords to meet you here, and then we could use your sword to get to Australia, and then we could just play, there, the way we always did."

"That's a terrible waste," said Patrick, "when we've got this whole wonderful hallucination to play with."

"Ted doesn't think it's so wonderful."

"Ted doesn't think it's a hallucination," said Patrick.

"Just wait," said Ted.

"Besides," said Patrick to Laura, "we don't know if that business with the swords would work anyway. Maybe your sword only works for you and Ted and ours only works for us."

He leaned over the fire to put another stick on it, and the

red light hollowed his eyes and made crevices in his face. Ted made the kind of noise you make, if you are not ticklish, when someone pokes you in the ribs.

"What?" said Patrick.

"You look like the King," said Ted. "You look just like the King."

"Did I ever play him?" asked Patrick.

"No," said Laura, "you said he was a dimwit and you wouldn't. Is he a dimwit, Ted?"

"No," said Ted.

"Ha," said Laura to Patrick.

"I wish he was," said Ted, "it would make things easier."

"And after all the trouble we went to to make them hard," said Patrick.

"That was a game."

"And so is this."

"You wait," said Ted.

"What's that?" demanded Patrick.

They all listened. Clearly, over the crackle of their fire, they heard a steady and ominous tramping, overlaid with the crack of twigs and the rustle of branches. Someone large was coming through the wood.

Ted struggled, muttered, stood up, and drew his sword. It blazed out blue, subduing the firelight. Laura saw flicker in the depths of the light faces and other bright blades and, dimly, a rearing shape like a horse, but snakier. Her eyes watered, and she looked away for a moment. The tramping grew quieter, but it did not stop.

"Laurie," said Ted, "hold one of those dry branches in the fire till it catches, for a weapon."

"Don't be silly, she'll burn herself," said Patrick. "Just take a good heavy piece of wood, Laura."

He took one himself and stood up. Laura looked up at their two figures, lit crazily by the light of the fire, and did not know whether to be reassured by their courage or frightened by their stupidity. Whatever was coming, could they really fight it with a little sword and a stick of wood?

With two sticks of wood, she amended, rummaging in their pile of branches. Most of them were small and light and tended to crumble when dragged out of the tangle. Maybe they should all run. Laura looked briefly out over the dark fields and, at the thought of running across them with something after her, felt cold. There was nowhere to go. She wished she were back at the Barretts'. Something was coming down the hill.

"What on earth are you doing?" said the tramper, crossly, and Ruth stepped into the firelight.

"Getting ready to hack you up," said Patrick. "You sounded like a large, dangerous—"

"I feel like one," said Ruth, and sat down with a flump.

"Well?"

"It didn't work," said Ruth. "We didn't change the time. I missed the bus to my flute lesson. Mom wouldn't drive me because I need to learn responsibility. So I asked if I could take a taxi and pay for it myself—that's responsible, isn't it?" Ruth hurled a stick into the fire. "So she said I needed to learn thrift too."

"Where's Ellen?" asked Patrick.

"Weeding the broccoli," said Ruth, with a sort of grim satisfaction. She sounded, thought Laura, exactly like Lady Ruth telling the unicorns what she thought of them.

"I don't suppose you brought the marshmallows," said Ted.

Ruth sighed. "I'm sorry, I forgot."

"I should hope you did," said Patrick. "Catastrophes falling on our heads, Ted, and you worry about marshmallows."

"You've eaten lately," said Ted.

"Put that sword away, for pity's sake," said Ruth, "and let's decide what we're going to do."

"I want mine back, please," said Patrick. Ruth gave it to him, and he put it back on.

"Without Ellen?" said Laura.

"She said she'd hurry. Let's talk about it, at least."

"What can we do?" said Ted, putting his sword away.

"Maybe you should leave the sword out," said Ruth. "It's better than a flashlight. Patrick, does ours do that?"

"Don't," said Laura. "It hurts my eyes."

"It does?" said Patrick.

"It's probably magic light," said Ruth, "and we shouldn't use it until we know what it means."

Patrick promptly pulled his sword out. It pulsed a green with too much yellow in it to be pleasant, but not enough to be ugly. Laura stared, but saw no shapes in the light or in the blade.

"Huh," said Patrick, interested, "they're not the same."

"That one hurts *my* eyes," said Ruth. "Put it away."

"Do you see things in it?" asked Laura.

"What?" said Ruth.

Patrick sheathed his sword and sat down. "Now. What are we going to do?"

"What can we do?" repeated Ted, still standing. The firelight lit up his face from below. Laura thought once again that he looked like Randolph, or as she imagined Randolph, but she kept her mouth shut.

"We should collect as much information as we can,"

said Patrick, "and see if we can manage to be in on all the action."

"We are all going to be out of action for the rest of the summer," said Ted, "if we disappear one more time and get any grown-ups anywhere any madder than they already are."

"I bet we could fix that somehow," said Patrick. "Let's figure out how the swords work and then we'll see."

"You can't take them apart like a stereo amplifier, Patrick," said Ruth.

"I don't mean that," said Patrick, "although I would like to see what's in these blades. And there could be lots of miniature circuitry in the hilts—"

"Patrick," said Ruth, awfully, "I forbid thee to meddle with those swords."

Patrick looked at her, and she looked back at him, and the fire crackled.

"The swords aren't real anyway, according to you," said Ted to Patrick, "so why be interested?"

"I have a new theory," said Patrick. No one asked him what it was. He went on. "Either we're having a hallucination, or what's happening can be explained scientifically. Maybe this could all happen without magic."

"I still forbid you," said Ruth.

"What did you mean about finding out how they work if you didn't mean taking them apart?" asked Laura.

"I want to run some tests," said Patrick, "and see who can go where with these things, and where you can get to from where else, and things like that."

"Do we have to do it in the dark?" asked Laura, who did not like the idea.

"I suppose you could sneak out at night, so it'd be light here," said Ted to the others.

"We'll have to once things get going," said Ruth. "Most of what happens is in the daytime, except the banquets and reviving Prince Edward."

"I don't expect to need reviving," said Ted, shortly.

"But we don't want to miss the banquets," said Ruth.

"Look," said Patrick. "Let's not waste the time we've got. We're already in trouble—you guys sneaked out, and Ruthie missed her flute lesson. Let's do something now that we're here."

"We do need a light, though," said Ruth.

"It was stupid not to bring a flashlight," said Patrick, "but I forgot it would be dark here."

"*We* brought one," said Laura.

"Where is it?"

"It turned into a lantern."

"What?" said Patrick.

"It did not," said Ted. "I dropped it in the stream, and we found a lantern in the stream."

"Listen," said Laura.

"You've got your money," said Ted. "You shut up."

"I will not," said Laura, incensed at the idea that he was paying her to lie. "It blew up and turned into a lantern."

"Like your watch!" said Ruth to Patrick.

"My watch didn't blow up," said Patrick skeptically.

"But it did change."

"Heh," said Patrick. "Well, where's this lantern?"

"Under the hedge," said Ted. "And the wick's wet."

"We've got a whole fire to light it with," said Patrick.

The lantern, when Ted fetched it back to the fire, submitted to being lighted, but it was not as good as a flashlight. There was no way to direct the light toward what you wanted to see, and if you moved the lantern too quickly, it went out. Even if it had been a flashlight, one would not have been enough for four people. One lantern was even less enough for four people who insisted on scrambling in the dark through the woods from hedge to bottle trees and back again.

Laura, who was always last, could tell by the light where the others were, but not how they had gotten there, and by the time they all collapsed beside their fire again, she had a collection of scratches and bruises. She was also sure that she had left half of her hair hanging from tree branches and tangled in bushes. Since she had steadfastly refused to do more than follow the rest of them around, she had not the remotest idea of what the rest of them had found out.

"This fire's almost out," said Patrick, cautiously putting a few twigs on the coals and blowing at them.

"That's better than burning up the plain," said Ruth, "which it could have done for all we knew. We'd better learn to be responsible."

"You're just mad about your flute lesson," said Patrick, "and—hey!"

"Well?" said Ruth.

"You didn't have to go to your flute lesson."

"I couldn't go," said Ruth, with irritation. She was sounding more like Lady Ruth all the time. Laura's eldest cousin had never snapped at anyone.

"Yes, exactly," said Patrick. "You get nervous about your flute lesson, so your mind creates a hallucination that makes you not have to go."

"Patrick," said Ruth, "stop it."

"But think about it."

"Just to avoid a flute lesson?" said Ted. "All of this, for that?"

"Stop it," said Ruth.

"I wish Ellen were here," said Patrick, peaceably. "She could write down what we've discovered about the swords."

"It's nothing useful," said Ruth. "We can't use our sword, or theirs, to get to America, and they can't use ours, or theirs, to get to Australia. And the only way to get to the Secret Country from home or to home from the Secret Country is to hold on to the sword; you can't hold on to someone who is holding on to the sword and get through that way. I still don't see how this helps at all."

"You just never know," said Patrick, "so you can't know too much."

"But what are we going to do?" said Ruth.

"What's happening next that we want to get in on?" asked Patrick.

"Fence comes back," said Laura.

"There are some things before that," said Ted. "The Banquet of Midsummer Eve is the next big thing, I think."

"Fence comes back in the middle of it," said Laura.

"When's Midsummer Eve, anyway?" asked Ted.

"Midsummer's Day is June the twenty-first," said Patrick, "so the Banquet is the twentieth."

"We're okay until next week, then?" said Ted.

"Nonsense," said Ruth, "if we're gone from here for a week they'll—"

"What's after the Banquet?" asked Patrick.

"Another big council," said Ted.

"And the Unicorn Hunt," said Laura, happily, "and the Riddle Game." She thought she would even be willing to put up with the horses if she could really go to the Unicorn Hunt.

"Now look," said Ruth. "We can't possibly manage that. We'd have to be gone for three days, one for each riddle. I keep telling you, this whole thing is hopeless unless we can change the time."

"Well," said Patrick, "we can't do anything outside the Secret Country. So what sources of power are there in the Secret Country?"

"Wizards," said Laura.

"Minions of the Green Caves," said Ruth.

"Could you change it?" Patrick asked her.

"I don't think so," said Ruth. "It's not my talent, and besides, I'm only a student. And I don't even know what I'm supposed to know, and even if I did know, I still wouldn't know it. I mean—"

"Could Fence do it, then?"

"Even if he could," said Ted, "why should he?"

"We'd have to explain everything, I guess," said Ruth. "I don't like the idea."

"He'd believe us, I bet," said Laura.

"Don't count on it. He's a grown-up," said Ted. "They always ask why and they never believe you."

"He's not a normal grown-up," protested Laura.

"How would you know? I suppose you think Benjamin and the King and Randolph aren't normal grown-ups, either? You just try sitting through a council with them."

"Unicorns?" said Laura, who had never liked the council scenes even in the game. "Unicorns never ask why."

"Could they do it?" asked Patrick.

"They can do anything, can't they?"

"If you can convince them," said Ruth. "They don't care why you want a thing done, but you have to show them how it will profit them."

"And they're sly," said Patrick. "It would be dangerous."

"Yeah," said Ted, "remember what happened to Shan.

He asked for a magic ring, but he couldn't tell them what good it would do them if they gave him one."

"So," said Laura, "being a young wizard still, and hasty—"

"—and too proud," said Ruth.

"—he told them," said Ted, "what harm it would do them if they didn't give him a ring—he said he'd curse them."

"So," said Laura, "they gave him a ring—"

"—and wouldn't tell him what it did, so what?" said Patrick. "This isn't helping."

"That's it!" cried Ruth. "That's it. The Riddle of Shan's Ring. How's it go—where's Ellen when we need her? 'I am a trinket in the world—sullen stone and—' No, that's not right. Bother!"

" 'Unvalued gold and sullen stone,' " said Ted.

"I've got it!" said Ruth.

" *'I am a trinket in the world,*
Unvalued gold and sullen stone;
But outside power is unfurled,
When outside Power I am hurled:
Then Time awry is blown.
What am I?' "

"The Ring of Shan," said Patrick, "and what good is that? The problem is what Shan's ring *does*."

"It's pretty bad poetry," said Ted. "It could mean anything."

"Oh, who cares!" said Ruth. "Can't you see? Shan's Ring will change the time for us if we take it outside the Secret Country, outside the Power, outside the magical place. There's certainly no Power in Australia or Illinois. If we take it outside the Power, then outside power—whatever that means—is unfurled, and time awry is blown, you see? I bet that's it."

"Do you have to hurl it?" said Laura dubiously.

"That was just for the rhyme," said Ted.

"Well, it still says you have to hurl it."

"I'll throw it up in the air and catch it again," said Ruth. "I bet that's it, though."

"It is if you think so," said Patrick.

"What can it hurt to try?" said Ruth.

"Where," said Patrick, "is Shan's Ring?"

CHAPTER 7

INTO the dumbfounded silence Laura said proudly, "In the West Tower, of course."

"How do you know?" said Patrick.

"I remember, that's how. First floor is old weapons, second floor is old books, third floor is old clothes, fourth floor is old jewelry." It was with some difficulty that she refrained from giggling. Patrick was so obviously irked that someone did in fact know.

"How do you remember all that?" he said crossly.

"I made it up just last summer," retorted Laura, and stopped.

"Even if the fourth floor is old jewelry," said Patrick, after a moment, "would it be there and not in some safe place with the royal treasures?"

"It's not a royal treasure," said Laura, exasperated.

"It's a royal embarrassment," added Ruth.

"Don't you remember anything?" asked Laura, grinning because she was fairly sure he would not be able to see her in the firelight. "Every year, just to remind us who's boss, the unicorns make us bring that Ring and ask that riddle—"

"Just so they can answer, 'I am the Ring of Shan,'" said Ruth, "—which is perfectly true and means nothing—and laugh."

"And Princess Laura gets to go and fetch it," said Laura.

"All right," said Patrick, "it's on the fourth floor of the West Tower. How do we get it out?"

"Let's not get caught again until after we've changed the time, if we can help it," said Ted. "Let's sneak up on High Castle, if we can, and—"

"You can't sneak up on High Castle," said Lady Ruth.

"Why, because of the guards?" said Ted. "I didn't think much of them, myself."

"No, fool, because of the grass!"

"Listen," said Ted, "you don't have to call names."

"What was that grass?" asked Laura, feeling the cold again.

"If you had learned your history properly," said Lady Ruth, to Laura's delight, "you would remember."

"History!" said Princess Laura. "History's nothing. It heals no wounds and gladdens no hearts. Now, music—"

"It would have kept you from yowling like a stepped-on cat and rousing the castle," said Lady Ruth.

"Listen," said Laura, "everybody else yelled too."

"As the Border Magic protects the Secret Country against invasion from without," said Ruth, "so the Nightmare Grass protects High Castle from treachery within the Secret Country. It's planted in all the possible sneaking-up places—"

"Why wasn't there any outside the postern, then?" said Ted.

"There probably was," said Patrick. "You could hardly expect it to work on horses."

"—and it makes you see whatever you're most afraid of."

"I wasn't afraid of it until I did see it," said Laura; "what I'm most afraid of is telephones." Perhaps she had seen what Princess Laura was most afraid of. Laura had been afraid of it herself, but she preferred that sort of fear, marrow-chilling though it had been, to the stomach-sinking dread of picking up the telephone and calling to find out when the library closed, or whether Roxanne thought it was her mother's turn to take everybody to the Girl Scout meeting.

"They don't have telephones here," said Ruth thoughtfully, and Patrick laughed.

"I wonder what would've happened," he said, "if nobody had remembered what the grass was?"

"We'd all still be running in circles and screaming," said Laura.

"Or maybe," said Patrick, "it never would have happened at all."

"Nonsense," said Ruth, "I remembered what it was after it started doing things to me."

"But your subconscious knew."

"So did your subconscious know," said Ruth, smugly. "You remembered as soon as I reminded you."

"Ruth," said Ted, "why didn't the guards know?"

Laura saw the firelight gleam in Ruth's eyes as she turned and stared at Ted.

"They couldn't have known," said Ted, "or they wouldn't have walked into the grass. If it's really a part of the defenses, why didn't the guards know about it?"

"Oh, my God," said Ruth.

"Don't swear," said Laura.

"The grass is a device of the Green Caves," said Ruth. "Remember all the feuds between the different kinds of magicians? Probably the ones of the Green Caves thought it would be funny not to tell the other kinds about the grass. It would do its job whether anybody knew about it or not, because people trying to sneak up would make a racket."

"I don't see why you should swear about that," said Ellen.

"I'm a sorcerer of the Green Caves. They'll think I lured the guards into it as some kind of joke."

"Don't knock it," said Ted. "That's better than their thinking you sneaked off with me."

"Well," said Patrick, "how do we get Shan's Ring?"

"We get caught again," said Ted, throwing a stick clear across the remains of the fire and narrowly missing Patrick, "and wait until the punishment is over, and then we get the ring and take it home, get caught again and punished again because we won't have changed the time yet. Then we change the time. That takes care of home; they won't notice we're gone. But then we come back here and we have to account for the time we spent at home, because they *will* notice here, if it works the way we think it does, because this will be our normal time. So we get clobbered again. And then we can settle down and enjoy treason, and murder, and not knowing what we're doing."

"Can't we get the magic to take care of all that too?" said Laura.

"Don't make things too complicated," said Ruth. "We don't have much to go on as it is."

"Let's get it over with, then," said Patrick, and stood up. "Let's start walking."

"In the dark?" said Laura.

"It's too far for Laurie," said Ted.

"It is not," said Laura automatically, "but we have to wait for Ellen."

"Benjamin found us here last time," said Ted. "Maybe he'll come back."

"He probably already did," said Patrick, "when we weren't here."

"Could he have found out anything from the horses?" asked Ted.

Patrick snorted.

"He can talk to them," said Ruth, "because he's from Fence's Country. But only to the ones that can talk. I mean, there's a special kind of horses with their own language—"

"Which the Unicorns gave Benjamin," said Laura.

"—and he can speak to them. But I don't think the ones we rode were that kind."

"So let's start walking," said Patrick.

"Listen," said Ted, "Laurie and I haven't had any supper or any sleep. And we have to be back by seven at the latest because they start getting up around then. And—"

"We ought to be back by six," said Patrick, "to eat dinner. But what I meant by getting it over was, let's go and do it, now, no matter how long it takes. The longer we're gone from High Castle, the worse we'll catch it, so let's show up as soon as we can."

"But the longer we're gone from home," said Ted, "the worse we'll catch it there."

"Have some sense," said Patrick, beginning to walk back and forth in his agitation. "Nothing they can do to us at home can possibly match what they'll do to us here. At home we're just irresponsible kids. Here we're somebody. They'll try you for treason and kick milady here out of her magic school if they think you two have sneaked off again. They'll probably get the rest of us for conspiracy."

"Are you sure you don't think this is real?" said Ruth.

"What's real?" said Patrick. "You all think it's real. You can certainly think yourselves to death, and maybe me too."

"Oh, you're hopeless," said Ruth.

"Anyway," said Patrick, "you do think it's real, so you ought to listen. Let's stay here for as long as it takes to get the Ring. Then let's go home, change the time, face the music, and come back—"

"And face the music," said Ruth, dolefully.

"I know what would be better," said Patrick, stopping in midpace. "Get the Ring, go home, change the time, come back here and face the music, but leave facing the music at home until we're done here."

"I don't like that at all," said Ruth, "leaving them all stuck like that at home the whole summer while we're here. I'd rather get it over with."

"Me too," said Laura.

"What's wrong with you?" said Patrick passionately. "I don't even believe this and I make more sense than you. They won't be stuck there from *their* viewpoint, and we can't afford to get in trouble with Benjamin again."

"Your marvelous plan *has* us getting in trouble with Benjamin again," said Ruth, in a tone Laura had never heard either from her cousin or from the sorcerer. "Because we can't get the Ring without running into Benjamin."

"So we should split you and Ted up," said Patrick, "so at least he won't think it's as bad as he thinks it was last time."

"Pat," said Ted, "if you and I went together we could say we'd dared each other into the Nightmare Grass—say I'd been irritating you with my learning and you told me you didn't believe in the stuff."

"Edward's learning wouldn't include the Nightmare Grass," said Ruth. "But you could say that I told Ellen about it and she told you, maybe."

"Huh," said Patrick, "and the grass so unsettled our wits that we fled off into the night."

"Having enough wit left to take five horses?" said Ruth.

"No," Patrick told her, "you must have done that."

"I know!" said Ruth. "I was planning to gather herbs by moonlight—and Laurie and Ellen had been pestering me to let them go too—you know, anything to postpone bedtime.

And we saddled two more horses for my attendants. I'm sure they wouldn't want three young girls riding around alone in the dark. But the noise you two made in that grass made the horses bolt with us, before the attendants got there. And the two extra horses just came along too."

"And we were carried far over the plain and lost!" exulted Laura.

"Why didn't you keep the horses?" asked Patrick. "Princess Laura wouldn't let a horse get out from under her, even if you and Ellie can't ride. And I think you both can. I mean, I think Princess Ellen and Lady Ruth can."

"We sent them for help," said Ruth.

"Well—"

"I'll polish it up before they find us. I'll say they didn't enchant right because they're not the talking horses."

"Last time you tried that Benjamin caught you."

"That was bad luck," said Ruth. "I think he just happens to keep track of when the ceremonies of the Green Caves are, so he knew there wasn't one. Benjamin can't know everything about what Lady Ruth can do."

"Well," said Patrick, "as long as you're not with Ted, I suppose it doesn't matter. So we should split up now."

"What about Ellen?" said Laura.

"I'll get her," said Ruth. "She must be sick of that broccoli by now. Please give me the sword." He did, and she tramped off into the darkness.

"There's one thing I don't like about this plan," said Ted. "Talk about three young girls riding around in the dark—"

"You can give me our sword," said Laura. "I found it anyway."

"None of you know how to use it."

"Neither do you!"

"She's right," said Patrick. "And Ruthie's bigger than me or you."

Laura grinned to herself. Ted's height was becoming a sore point with him as all his friends grew taller and he stayed stubbornly short. She hoped to be taller than he was someday, although her mother said it was unlikely.

"Well," said Ted, "there's probably nothing out there to hurt them anyway."

"Aren't there wolves?" asked Laura, who was determined to have the sword.

"Not this near to the well," said Ted. "It's a protection against normal dangers. It'd rather zap you itself."

"Who thought that up?" asked Patrick.

"Ellen, probably," said Ted. "All the really weird ideas about things that don't matter are hers."

"Some of them seem to matter now," said Patrick.

"I wish we hadn't been so thorough," lamented Ted.

"Mom says it's a virtue to be thorough," observed Laura.

"That's just to get you to clean your closet."

"Oh."

"It is a virtue when you're finding out about things," said Patrick. "But not when you're making them up."

"Sure it is," said Laura. "It makes it more fun."

"But it's not fun now."

They heard the ominous tramping again, and a cacophony of cracking twigs.

"Is that really only Ruth and Ellen?" said Patrick.

Ted pulled the sword out, and it blazed like the sun on a mirror, bright gold and hurtful. Laura's eyes squeezed themselves shut and overflowed.

"What are you doing now?" said Ruth's voice. Laura swiped at her eyes and made them open. The glow of the sword had steadied down to its kinder blue. Not even the runes she had seen before danced on the blade. Ruth and Ellen and Ted and Patrick were all standing up, and looking a little ghostly in the sword light. The fire had gone out.

"I'd swear there was something besides you two coming through those woods," said Patrick. "Unless there's some echo effect, and I don't see why there should be."

"I'm sure there's a lot you don't see," said Ellen. "Ted, why did your sword do that?"

"How should I know?" said Ted. "Laurie found it."

"And you can give it to me now," said Laura, "so the wolves don't get us."

Ellen snorted. "There aren't any wolves around here."

"Why should they get both the swords? And I found it."

"Why don't you give it to her, so we can get going?" said Patrick.

"You just don't want to give them yours," said Ted. "All right, but I want Ruth to carry it."

"I don't want it," said Ruth. "I don't like sharp pointed things."

"Some hero you are."

"I'm not a hero, I'm a sorcerer."

"Will you go on and give Laura the sword?" said Patrick.

"I get it next time," said Ted.

"Oh, all right," said Laura.

Ted unbuckled the belt and handed it to her with the sword and sheath. Laura stood up to put the belt around her waist and promptly dropped it into the ashes of the fire.

"You see?" said Ted.

"Shut up," said Laura.

Ruth had to help her put the belt on.

"You'd better practice walking with it or you'll kill your-self," said Patrick, kindly enough.

"You shut up too," said Laura, who was mortified to a degree she had never experienced before. It was all right to be clumsy back home, but here, and especially with the sword, it suddenly felt like a crime. She pondered this for a moment while Ruth tried to adjust the belt so it would stay on. Falling off the pony had not felt like a crime, even though Benjamin had certainly acted as if he thought it were one. But standing under the strange stars of the Se-cret Country with the belt too tight around her middle, and the sword's weight making her want to lean side-ways, and the smoky dust she had disturbed making her want to sneeze, she felt like her usual grubby self for the first time since she and Ted had sneaked out of the house.

And that was it. She had been Princess Laura all evening, until Laura the mouse dropped the sword in the ashes.

"This is hard!" she said.

"Standing up with the sword on?" said Ted. "You'd bet-ter give it back."

"No!" said Laura. She backed away from him, and fell down.

Patrick laughed, Ted groaned, Ellen told them to shut up, and Ruth came and picked Laura up.

"You'd better let me have that sword," said Ted, holding his hand out for it.

"I meant," said Laura, "it's hard being Princess Laura."

Ted's hand dropped. "You see?" he said. "See?"

"See what?"

"Why I might want to quit?"

"Oh," said Laura.

"Patrick," said Ted, turning away from her, "let's go if we're going."

"We'd better agree on a time and place to meet," said Patrick. "We could lose each other for days in High Castle. I don't think our lives overlap that much."

"What fun is that?" demanded Ellen.

"Tomorrow," said Ted. "Let's get it over with."

"Should we sneak out after bedtime," said Ruth, "or is there anything wrong with just going sometime during the day?"

"We don't know when we'll all be free," said Patrick, "so we'd better sneak. Besides, that will make it easier to get out of here right after we get the ring."

"Midnight, then," said Ted.

"The witching hour," said Ellen.

"Let's meet at the foot of the West Tower, then, if that's where the Ring is," said Ruth.

"I think," said Patrick, when everyone had agreed to this, "that Ted and I should go south and you guys go east."

They took their separate ways in the darkness, and Laura fell down the hill.

CHAPTER 8

LAURA and Ellen were late for the rendezvous at the West Tower. Ellen was comfortably sure which way was west, but it turned out not to be. They found themselves treading a long stretch of very dusty and cobwebby corridor lit by two torches that burned an unlikely and disconcerting purple. What should have been the door to the West Tower, flung hospitably open so that people could go up and rummage, was shut and bolted, and guarded by a grumpy beast the exact nature of which they did not stay to ascertain. It looked like the pool of light made by an imaginary sun shining through a round purple stained-glass window, and gurgled at them like a suddenly unclogged drain. They ran.

They were still running when they reached the rendezvous. If Laura had not tripped on the skirt of the dress Agatha had made her wear that day, they would probably have run right past their relations and ended up in Conrad's Close, which would have pleased neither of them. It was said (by Agatha, in the course of a long and impassioned lecture) to be haunted by the ghost of Conrad's bitterest enemy, who had actually died in the Nightmare Grass, and whose ghost therefore appeared to everybody it saw as what Conrad's enemy had feared most when alive.

As it was, Laura tripped, Ellen stopped and went back for

her, and they both blinked in a sudden blaze of green from Patrick's sword.

"You don't have to run yourselves to death even if you are late," said Ruth from behind her brother.

Laura, sitting on the cold stone floor and panting for breath, looked at her green-tinged face and would have run again if she had been standing.

"There was something," said Ellen, "some beast." She stopped to breathe.

"Where?" demanded Patrick. "Is it following you?"

"I didn't hear it," said Laura doubtfully.

Ellen pointed in the direction they had come. "We thought it was at the bottom of the West Tower, but—"

"South," said Patrick, disgustedly. "That's Fence's tower, you ninnies, and whatever he left to guard it wouldn't hurt you."

"It's probably just a handful of moonlight and six rhymes," said Ruth.

"Where's Ted?" asked Laura.

"He's guarding the way we came," said Patrick. "Some of the catlike guards might walk this way sometimes. I hope nobody heard you guys charging along."

"I don't think anybody except Fence uses that part of the castle," said Ruth.

"It didn't look like it," said Ellen. "All dusty."

"I'll get Ted," said Ruth. "Give me the sword, Patrick, please."

"Why didn't you bring a torch or a lantern?" asked Ellen. "We tried to get one but they wouldn't let us, and the candles just blew out. It's awfully windy in this place."

"Ted's got the lantern," said Ruth. "He didn't want to stand where the guards might come, holding this weird sword."

Patrick handed her the weird sword, and she went off down the hall in a halo of green. Laura leaned against the hospitably open door to the West Tower's stairs and tried to peer up them. There was a faint glow on the wall of the first turn.

"How was your first day at High Castle?" Patrick asked them.

"Benjamin said we couldn't have anything but bread and water," said Ellen, "but Agatha brought us pasties."

"They were awful," said Laura.

"They were not."

"Do you have any left?" asked Patrick. "Because Ted and I don't have any Agatha, and—"

"Ellen ate them all," said Laura.

"What happened to Ruthie?" asked Ellen.

"They turned her over to Meredith, who's the head sorcerer of the Green Caves at High Castle. They scolded her and turned her from a journeyman back into an apprentice. Don't ask her about it. She's furious."

Laura could well imagine. Ellen seemed unimpressed.

"*We* were actually lucky to be punished," said Ellen. "It meant no lessons. Whoever decided we should have lessons in the summer?"

"You think you're unhappy," said Patrick. "Ted and I have a fencing lesson with Randolph first thing tomorrow, and he thinks he's been teaching Ted for three years and me for one, and we don't know anything about it at all."

"Well," said Ellen, "we don't know anything about the history of the Outer Isles, either."

"The what?"

"The Outer Isles. I made them up one day when it rained and you guys were all playing cards."

"How many more things like that are we going to run into?" demanded Patrick. "If I'd had any idea you were all going around making things up on your own—"

"Weren't you?" asked Ellen.

"No!"

"You're weird."

Patrick's reply to this was forestalled by the return of Ted and Ruth, who came clattering down the corridor in a muddle of green light from Patrick's sword and yellow from Ted's lantern.

"Why are you so loud?" said Ellen.

"It's these boots," said Ted. "They're heavy. Don't you have any?"

Ellen stuck her foot into the circle of lantern light and showed him her soft leather shoe.

"That's much better for sneaking around in," said Ted.

"Lady Ruth has some of those," said Ruth, "but they're not warm enough for this place. They might fit you."

"What's Patrick got?" said Ellen.

"Boots," said Patrick. "But I know how to walk." He took his sword back from Ruth and sheathed it, and a new set of darker shadows sprang up around them.

"Where's my sword, Laurie?" said Ted.

"It's not yours," said Laura. Ellen's reminder that they were likely to get in trouble over their lessons, and the fact that Ted was no longer guarding against discovery by the guards, were making her feel frightened again. As a result, she felt uncompromising. "It's under the bed. I had to tell Benjamin it was a toy."

"Did he believe you?"

"No," said Ellen.

"Well, he let me keep it."

"He kept looking at those stones on the handle," said Ellen.

"Hilt," said Patrick. "Take care of that sword, you guys. We can't get you back if you lose it."

"Let's go," said Ted, holding the lantern up. They started up the narrow stairway, first Ted, then Ruth, then Patrick, then Ellen, and then Laura.

There was indeed a torch burning just beyond the first turn of the stairway, high up on the wall. There was also another beast. Laura could not see it, but she could hear it gurgle.

"Back up!" said Ted's voice, echoing a little in the stairwell. "Patrick, the sword—"

The sword rang as Patrick drew it, and the beast made a noise like a bucketful of water thrown into a patch of mud. All of this sounded hollow and horrible.

"What's it doing!" cried Laura, retreating back around the corner so that Ellen would not knock her over.

"I can't see, they're all in the way," said Ellen. She sounded like someone who has discovered that he has chosen a bad seat at the movies, and Laura, who wanted to take off down the stairs and find a bed to hide under, marveled at her.

"Give me the sword," said Ted's voice.

"You get out of the way," said Patrick's. "You believe in this stuff. It'll probably drown you."

The beast produced a remarkable imitation of a water balloon hitting a hot sidewalk from a long way up.

"Will you give it here!"

"Will you move!"

"Will you wait!" said Ruth's voice. Laura, two steps farther down than she had been when the water balloon hit, froze, looking up at their shadows on the wall.

"Does anybody remember anything like this?" said Ruth.

"No," said Ted. "Give me the sword."

"It sounds," said Ellen, "like the one we met at Fence's tower."

"Does it look like it?"

"You're in the way."

"Well, come on up."

Ellen disappeared around the corner and her shadow joined the tangle on the wall. The beast bubbled like a coffee percolator for a moment, slurped once, and stopped.

"Hey, Laurie!" called Ellen, reappearing around the bend. "Come and look at this."

Laura shook her head. "One's enough."

"I want you to see if you think it looks like the other one. It's not doing anything."

"It's gurgling!"

"Well, maybe we sound like that to it too. Come on."

Laura, feeling as if someone else had broken the bathroom window and she were going to get the blame, came slowly up the stairs she had sneaked down, and stood next to Ellen.

The beast, taking up three or four steps, sat in the torchlight, looking like a pool of water with a scum of purple fur. It had no eyes, no legs, no up or down, and no edges. There were spots that were clearly step, and spots that were clearly beast, and an odd zone between that was not clearly anything. It bubbled gently at Laura from somewhere inside itself.

"Yes," said Laura, and went back down a step.

"Handful of moonlight, huh?" said Ellen.

"Why should Fence care what happens to the West Tower?" wondered Patrick.

"Maybe it's not Fence's beast," said Ellen.

The beast made a sudden sucking noise and they all jumped.

"Are you Fence's beast?" Ellen asked it.

The beast was quiet.

"Whoever you are, we'd be obliged if you'd let us by."

The beast made precisely the same noise that the other beast had made at Laura and Ellen, folded and swirled in on itself like water going down a narrow space, and disappeared. Patrick leaned over and put his hand on the steps where it had been.

"Not wet," he said.

"Let's go," said Ted.

"I want to know whose fault that was."

Ted started up the steps, carrying the lantern with him. Ruth followed. Patrick stood between them and Ellen and Laura, still holding the sword and staring at the empty steps under the torch.

"Move, please," said Ellen.

"I bet you made this up."

"I did not. Move."

Patrick flattened himself against the wall, Ellen went by him after the rapidly diminishing glow of Ted's lantern, and Patrick looked at Laura. "Did you make this up? It's your tower."

"It's not my tower!" said Laura, feeling that the one thing worse than that oozy beast would be to be blamed for its existence. "I don't make up beasts. I don't like them. Can we go up?" she added, trying to behave like Princess Laura. "They'll find the ring, and it's my job to find the ring."

"You're all crazy," said Patrick, sheathing the sword, and he went ahead of her up the steps.

They went around and around, past the open doors of the rooms with old clothes and old weapons, up to the third landing. Laura wished for a quiet afternoon to rummage. It seemed unlikely that she would ever get one, if quiet meant not having to worry about some grown-up, somewhere, who would yell at her when she came back. There was a bench on the landing and another torch on the wall above the bench. Ellen was sitting on the bench, and Ted and Ruth were having an altercation about the door, which was shut.

"What's going on?" said Patrick. Laura sat down next to Ellen.

"Door won't open," said Ted. "There's no lock or handle on this side and it won't open."

"It's supposed to be open," said Laura.

"What do they need a beast for if the door won't open anyway?" said Ellen.

"Why is everything around here three times as hard to do as it should be?" said Ted, leaning on the door. Laura looked at his tired face in the torchlight and was still reminded of Randolph, whom she still had not met. She and Ellen had seen only Benjamin and Agatha, and a few amused guards, since they came to High Castle.

"Why don't you ask it to open?" she said to Ted. "The beast moved when Ellen asked it to."

Ted rolled his eyes at the ceiling, turned his face against the carved wooden surface of the door, and addressed it sarcastically. "I prithee open," he said.

And fell into the darkness of the West Tower's third room, dropping the lantern. The lantern rolled in crazy circles exactly as a dropped flashlight will do, went out, and clanged against the far wall. Laura and Ellen held each other, and Ellen laughed until the tower echoed, and Laura pretended that she had not been scared half out of her wits.

"Shut up," said Patrick, taking Ted by an arm and hauling him up again.

Ted shook himself free and advanced upon Laura menacingly. "Very funny, Laurie," he said. "You made this up, didn't you?"

"No," said Laura. "This isn't supposed to be a magical castle and I didn't make up any of this."

"Leave her alone," said Ruth.

"I thought you thought this was real," said Patrick, "so how can she have made it up anyway?"

Ted wheeled on him. "I do think it's real. I also think we made it up. It's real now. Somehow, things got out of hand. And once they did, then things could start happening that we *didn't* make up."

"And you say I have silly theories."

"We have a ring to find," said Ruth.

Ted turned away from Patrick as if Patrick were something he had decided not to buy. "Laurie, where's the ring supposed to be?"

"It's in a casket."

"What?"

"In a lead casket," said Laura, stubbornly.

"She means like in *Merchant of Venice*," said Ellen. "A box, is all."

"I wish we'd never heard of Shakespeare," growled Ted as he stamped into the tower room and retrieved the lantern. He stood on the bench, displacing Laura and Ellen rather roughly, lit the lantern from the torch, and handed the lantern down to Ruth. Then he took the torch from its socket. "Where is this casket?" he asked Laura.

"In a niche in the north wall."

Ted strode into the tower room, trailed by the others, and made a minute inspection of the north wall. It was empty except for three arrow slits.

"Are you sure it's north?"

"No."

Ted made for the west wall, muttering.

"Watch out, you'll set the tapestries on fire," said Ruth as the light of the torch showed up a crowd of colors and shapes.

"Give me the lantern," said Ted, thrusting the torch at her, and disappeared under the tapestries.

"Why's he so grumpy?" Ellen asked Laura.

"He's always grumpy."

"But Prince Edward is meek and gentle."

"Heh," said Laura.

They watched the disturbance under the tapestries that was Ted looking for the niche. It came around to the door, and Ted emerged, looking ruffled and indignant. "There's not a darn thing under there," he said. "You're crazy, Laurie."

"I am not." She was sure she had remembered properly. She felt indignant herself; somebody had tampered with her tower.

Ted crossed to the south wall, disappeared under the tapestries, and came out where they stopped for the east wall. "Not there either," he said. "Lead casket indeed."

Laura eyed him, but he did not seem disposed to come at her menacingly again.

"Now what do we do?" he said, sitting on the floor. Then he stopped. He held the lantern closer to the floor, and Laura saw something glitter faintly. Ted moved the lantern, and more glitters sprang up. "Oh, God," said Ted, in such heartfelt tones that no one reproved him.

"What?" said Ruth.

"Look at the floor," said Ted, tragically. " 'Unvalued Gold.' "

They all stooped and looked at it in the light of Ruth's

torch. Embedded in the smooth gray stone were rings, dully gleaming brass rings, hundreds and thousands and hundreds of thousands, patterning the floor in circles, in diamonds, in cloverleafs, in scallops and whorls.

"Whose idea was this?" said Patrick, and he sounded almost as terrible as Lady Ruth.

"I'm not sure it has to be anybody's," said Ruth.

"Of course it does," said Patrick. "They're just scared to admit it."

Everybody looked at Laura.

"It's not mine!" she said. "I told you mine, and it's all messed up." They all stood and glared at one another in the flaring light.

"Well," said Ted, "I guess we'd better start looking. Just hope it's good and loose, wherever it is." He took himself and his lantern back to the door, got down on his hands and knees, and began methodically sweeping his hands across the floor.

"Wait, wait, wait," said Patrick, arresting the other three in the act of joining Ted.

"Well?" said Ruth.

"This is clearly not a place for storing old jewelry," said Patrick. "There's none here. So if there's no old jewelry here, probably Shan's Ring isn't here either."

"The old clothes were in the right place," said Laura.

"And there are brass rings here," said Ruth, "and Shan's Ring is a brass ring."

"We might as well keep looking," said Ted. "We can't do anything else tonight."

He went back to his task. Ruth held the torch for Ellen and Laura, and they crawled doggedly across the floor, one on either side of her, picking at myriads of brass rings.

Laura, scraping her fingertips and acquiring little round imprints on her knees and the heels of her hands, began to feel put upon.

They had advanced about two feet across the floor in this fashion when Patrick, who had been standing and watching them, spoke again.

"Wait a minute," he said.

Laura stopped crawling and began rubbing her knees.

"What now?" said Ruth, without stopping.

"Assuming Shan's Ring is here," said Patrick, "there must be a pattern to this."

Ruth sighed audibly, and Patrick went on. "You always hide things with a pattern. You don't just dump them down somewhere and hope you remember where you put them."

"*You* don't," muttered Ruth, sitting back on her heels. But he had caught Ted's interest.

"What kind of pattern?" Ted asked him, still on the floor with his lantern.

"In the riddle," said Patrick, promptly. Laura, catching the pleased note in his voice, guessed that he had figured the whole thing out before he spoke. Just like Patrick, she thought.

"'I am a trinket in the world,'" quoted Ted. "Well?"

"Maybe it's an acrostic," said Patrick. "Or maybe it has a code in it. We should write it out and work on it."

"That could take weeks," said Ruth.

"Well," said Patrick, still with that pleased note in his voice, "maybe there's a clue in the riddle about where on this floor Shan's Ring is."

"Patrick," said Ruth, "did *you* make this up?"

"No, I did not."

"What are you so happy about, then?"

"I've been thinking," said Patrick, "and observing, not

grubbing around on the floor, and I think there's a connection between the riddle and the tapestries."

"I thought you didn't believe—" began Ruth, and was interrupted by Ted.

"What is it?" he said.

"There's a map of the Secret Country on that wall," said Patrick, waving at the south wall of the room. "I think that's for the first line, for the world."

"Why shouldn't it be a picture of a trinket?" said Ted, but he had straightened up on his knees and was regarding Patrick hopefully.

"Too vague," said Patrick.

"Just because you think—"

"Let him finish, Ruthie," said Ted. "What about 'unvalued gold and sullen stone'?"

"Well," said Patrick, wilting a little, "that one I couldn't figure out."

"Well, what's next, then?" said Ted. "'I am a trinket in the world, unvalued gold and sullen stone; but outside power is unfurled when outside Power I am hurled, and Time awry is blown.'"

"Well," said Patrick, "there's a dragon—I thought that could be the outside power being unfurled."

Ted stood up with the lantern. "Where?"

Patrick took him over to the middle of the north wall, stepping around Ruth and Ellen and Laura with a certain disdain, like a cat, thought Laura, walking on a wet floor. His shadow and Ted's blotted out what they were looking at.

"Huh," said Ted. "It's even unfolding its wings. 'Outside power is unfurled.' Okay. What next?"

"'When outside Power I am hurled,'" said Laura, who was becoming interested.

"I couldn't get that one either," said Patrick. "But over

here," and he led Ted and the lantern along the north wall to its western edge, "there's a tremendous storm, and it's overturned a sundial, see?"

" 'Time awry is blown!' " cried Laura, scrambling to her feet.

"That's only three lines," said Ruth, "and even if—"

"I couldn't see a lot of the things on the tapestries," said Patrick.

Ted handed him the lantern, and Ted and Laura hovered along behind him as he inspected the hangings. He had to tell them several times to get their shadows out of his way. Ruth and Ellen stayed where they were, murmuring to each other.

"Outside Power I am hurled," muttered Patrick, moving light along a dismaying wealth of pictures.

"The tapestries," Laura observed after a time, "go all the way up to the ceiling."

"They wouldn't put clues above eye level," said Patrick.

"Yes, but whose eye level?" said Ted. "They're all very tall."

"Ruth," said Patrick, "come over here, please. You're not Benjamin but you'll have to do."

"This is crazy," said Ruth, but she came over. Ted gave her the lantern, taking the torch from her and finding it a socket in the wall.

At the west corner of the north wall, she discovered a subsidiary tapestry, a long narrow one. It was hung over the main tapestry, which at that point was frayed and ragged. It contained nine panels, bordered with a design of climbing plants and an occasional animal of some indeterminate type between cat and rabbit. In the first panel, a young man in disheveled clothes, and with what Laura thought of as decided eyebrows, sat at the feet of an old man. The old man was clearly a wizard. He had beard, robe, staff, and an assortment of peculiar instruments that Patrick said were astrological but that looked to Laura like Patrick's own chemistry lab.

In succeeding panels, the young man changed his disheveled clothes for a wizard's robe and staff and began taming animals. In the third panel he enchanted a cat, in the fourth he and the cat collared a dog, in the fifth the three of them acquired a horse, in the sixth they subdued an eagle. In the seventh they spoke with a unicorn, but in the eighth the unicorn was not there. Man and animals stood around something which looked more like a hole in the tapestry than part of the weaving. This appearance may have been due to the light, which was wavering more than ever now because Ruth's arm hurt.

The man held his staff pointed at the hole, and red fire leaped from its tip. The cat's tail was fluffed, the eagle's beak opened in a scream. Every other animal had its ears flat to its head.

In the ninth panel, the man was gone, with a lightning bolt where he had been standing. All the animals were bounding away from the hole in the tapestry as hard as they could go.

"Think he was hurled outside power?" asked Patrick, after a long silence.

"Who is that?" said Ruth. "Does anybody remember that story?"

Nobody did. Even Shan had not come to such an end as that.

"For now," said Patrick, "that's one more clue. Good thinking, Ted."

"It was my idea," said Laura, who did not usually have them.

"Look," said Patrick, "before we forget what we're doing—"

"What are we doing?" asked Ruth.

"There are five lines," said Patrick, "so there are probably five clues. And luckily there are five of us. So I want somebody to stand in front of each of the clues we've found so far. Not you, Ruthie, you've got to hold the lantern up."

After a certain amount of shuffling and muttering, and one quarrel over where exactly a particular clue had been, they got Laura positioned in front of the map of the Secret Country, Ellen in front of the dragon unfurling its wings, Patrick in front of the tremendous storm, and Ted in front of the ninth panel of the wizard's story.

"Now," said Patrick, " 'unvalued gold and sullen stone.' "

Ruth went around and around the room, holding the lantern high and grumbling. Then she went around holding it at eye level and grumbling. Then she took Patrick's place in front of the tremendous storm, and made him go around holding the lantern at his eye level. He did not grumble, but he kept finding scenes he thought were perfect for the line in question. Since the others thought the scenes were nothing like it, the argument became heated.

Patrick was particularly obstinate about a scene, on the east end of the south wall, in which the sun was rising or setting behind a range of dark mountains. Patrick said the sun was setting, Ruth and Ellen that it was rising. This difference was due to Patrick's insistence that the mountains were the Dubious Hills, out of which came the stone which was set in Shan's Ring. That would be the sullen stone; he said the sun was the unvalued gold. Ruth and Ellen said that the mountains were the Dwarves' Chairs, a northern range which was full of jewel mines and therefore had no sullen stones. They also scorned his suggestion about the sun. They could recite more facts than he could, but he was more stubborn. Laura sat down on the floor and wished they were all in New England.

"Why don't we try my way?" said Patrick at last, setting the lantern down and startling Laura from a doze. "Then if it's wrong we'll look some more."

"What do you want to do?" asked Ruth.

"Everybody start moving into the middle of the room. Try to take the same-size steps."

"That's silly," said Ruth. "We'll just end *up* in the middle of the room."

"The room's not symmetrical," said Patrick, smugly.

"How do you know?"

"I looked at it. Besides, you can see even from the outside."

"Oh," said Laura, pleased. "Is this the lopsided tower?"

"Yes," said Patrick. "Now try to take the same-size steps."

"Laurie's the littlest," said Ted. "Get up, Laurie."

They watched her take a few steps and measured them by the stones in the floor. Then they did as Patrick asked. This eventually brought them into a huddle somewhat to the northeast of the room's middle, staring at their own shadows on the floor.

"Don't move," said Patrick, and fetched the lantern.

"There it is!" crowed Laura, bending over, and was hit in the head by Ted's elbow as he too reached for the ring.

"Ow!" she said.

Ted held the ring close to the lantern. The brass glittered a little. The round black stone reflected no light. It looked, Laura thought, unnervingly like the hole-in-the-tapestry that had blasted the magician. She wanted nothing to do with it, but it was no use saying so.

"Patrick," said Ruth, "are you sure you didn't make this up?"

"Yes!"

"I don't see how you could have figured it out."

"I've got a brain."

"I never thought so."

"Well, now you know."

"Come on," said Ted, "let's get out of here and get this over with."

Laura, who had been watching him as he tried the ring on all his fingers and discovered that it was too big for any of them, observed, "You'll lose it."

"First we have to decide who's going," said Patrick. He sounded faintly uneasy, and Laura wondered what he had done. He had sounded that way when, having spent a day being angry at the others, he had come back to inform them that he had turned Fence's robe into a sail and lost it in the pond.

"We can't all go," said Patrick, "because the swords don't work that way."

Laura found herself enormously pleased with this statement. She did not think she could take one more trip in the dark, especially on horseback. The others, however, did not look pleased, especially Ted.

"It was my idea," said Ruth.

"I've got the ring," said Ted.

"I can get it away from you," said Lady Ruth.

Laura wished she were elsewhere. Ted was clearly taken aback, but he rallied quickly. "You can not," he said, "and anyway it would make noise."

"So?" said Ruth.

"That's why I should do it!" cried Ted. "Nobody takes

this seriously but Pat, and he's only doing it to be obnoxious. I don't trust you guys."

"If you take it seriously," Patrick said to him, "you should let Ruth do it. She's the sorcerer."

"But she doesn't know anything."

"Neither do you," said Ruth, heatedly. "This was my idea and I want that ring. Besides, I can come and go as I please. You'll get in trouble if you do that. And you've got a fencing lesson tomorrow."

Ted sagged. "It won't take long to change the time," he said, without conviction. "We could get back before seven in the morning."

"Don't count on it," said Ruth. "Everything seems to go wrong around here."

"If you screw this up," said Ted, "I'll—"

"I promise you I won't," said Ruth, sounding more like herself and less like a haughty and impatient adult.

Ted sighed heavily and handed her the ring. She put it on, and it fit.

"Well, come on, Ellie," said Patrick.

"What makes you think you're going anywhere?" said Ted, rounding on him.

"Why shouldn't I?" said Patrick.

"You've got a fencing lesson tomorrow too."

Patrick looked blank. "But Ruth and Ellen can't go by themselves."

"Look," said Ruth, "I'm older than you, and I'm bigger than you, and there's nothing out there anyway. If we're going to have this argument every time I want to do something I'll just stay home when I get there."

"That's a very good idea," said Ted, but nobody seemed to pay any attention to him. Laura, who was feeling better because nobody had so much as mentioned horses to her to-day, thought she would wait a little longer before deciding to quit. Besides, she thought glumly, she could decide to quit, but that didn't mean they would let her. They hadn't let Ted the last time he suggested it.

Ruth recovered the torch and they went down the stairs. It was colder than it had been on the way up. The beast was nowhere to be seen.

CHAPTER 9

TED dreamed that night that he was fighting Randolph in the rose garden, by moonlight. He had not yet been in the rose garden, and the one in his dream did not look as he had expected it to. He had the moon in his eyes, and the grass was wet.

These were the only things that bothered him. He knew exactly what to do with the sword. It was both longer and lighter than the one Laura had found under the hedge, and it fit into his hand as one piece of a jigsaw puzzle fits into its neighbor.

He was fighting in the same way he tied his shoes or rode a bicycle: easily and without thought. Randolph was making motions with his sword, which seemed to one part of Ted to be incredibly tiny and frighteningly quick. But most of him knew how to counter them almost before the incredulous part had noticed them at all. Somewhere far in the back of his mind, almost like a voice outside, the names of Randolph's moves and of his own were flicking by, too quick and faint to catch. Their boots squeaked a little on the wet grass, and their light blades hissed more than clanged as they came together, and they breathed a little hard. And that was all the sound in the whole sweet silver garden.

Ted suddenly knew that he had Randolph. He did something with his wrist, ignoring the part of him that demanded to know what it was and refused to kill Randolph anyway. He lunged straight at Randolph with a force that should have put the sword through him. And froze, fully extended (whatever that meant, the incredulous part of him thought), his sword stretched foolishly in the empty air, three inches from Randolph.

Ted was momentarily outraged. He knew his reach was longer than that. Then he saw on Randolph's face not fear, nor relief, but a sort of sick disappointment; he knew that if Randolph went on standing there, he could still kill him. And then someone's hand clamped onto his shoulder from behind.

Ted flung himself around, swinging the sword as if it were a stick of wood, and found that he was in bed, and had caught Patrick across the face with the flat of his hand.

Patrick was too stunned to say anything, which gave Ted no reason not to apologize. "Sorry," he said. "I was dreaming."

Patrick touched his cheek carefully and pulled his hand away as if he expected to find blood on it. "I had bad dreams too," he said, "but I didn't hit you."

"Did you?" said Ted. "What about?"

"I don't remember," said Patrick. "I think you must have knocked them out of my head."

"They can't have been that bad, then."

"Well, they were weird, anyway. Something about the Crystal of Earth."

"The what?" said Ted, rubbing his eyes. It was barely gray outside, but Patrick had managed to light a lamp.

"I'm not sure what it is; I think Ruth and Ellen know. But it's dangerous. I think it's a kind of magical globe of this place, and if you break it, it's like blowing up the country. What'd you dream?"

"I dreamed I knew how to fence and was killing Randolph."

"Well, at least that makes sense," said Patrick.

"Why'd you wake me up so early?"

"I thought we should go down to our lesson early so we won't look as if we've never been there."

"They'll know soon enough we haven't," said Ted. "Unless I can remember enough of that dream."

"Well," said Patrick, "I was thinking, I bet they'd believe us if we acted like we'd been bewitched and lost our memories, or parts of them."

"Benjamin'd think Ruth did it," said Ted. "He's already asked me if she bewitched me. Ruth's in enough trouble already."

"They'll probably think we're bewitched whether we try to act like it or not," said Patrick, shrugging.

"Where are we supposed to go?"

"Outside," said Patrick. "And I think it's somewhere on the north side, where it's cooler."

"And what're we supposed to wear?"

"I thought we should wear our jeans," said Patrick, who already had his on. "Everything else I could find looked too good to get all hot and sweaty and cut up in."

Ted, gazing a little blearily around the room, realized that Patrick had emptied all six oak chests onto the floor. The princes seemed to have a lot of clothes, many in colors Ted would not have been caught dead in. He started to chide Patrick for making a mess, and then the last thing his cousin had said suddenly registered. "What makes you think," Ted demanded, "that we're going to get cut up?"

"Well, we don't know how to fight back."

"The swords aren't bated."

"What?"

"I mean they aren't sharp. This is just practice. You know, like fencing demonstrations at home. They have little red and blue plastic buttons on the tips."

"They don't have plastic here. I think we should wear our jeans."

"Benjamin'll kill us," said Ted.

"He won't be up."

"Heh. I bet he never sleeps."

"Huh," said Patrick, arrested in the act of putting his T-shirt on. "Maybe he doesn't. He is from Fence's Country."

"What?"

"Well, wizards don't sleep, do they? I mean, Thomas Edison hardly ever slept."

"Edison wasn't a wizard!" said Ted, wondering if Patrick had finally gone crazy.

"They called him one."

"It's not the same thing."

"You mean Fence isn't like Thomas Edison," said Patrick, the T-shirt falling from his hand to mingle with the velvet cloaks and linen shirts he had strewn on the floor.

"No! He's not a scientist; he doesn't invent things!"

"Well, what the hell good is he, then?"

"He's a magician," said Ted, exasperated almost beyond bearing. "He casts spells. He has power. He can do things."

"What things?"

Ted opened his mouth and shut it again. It had just seemed right to have a wizard on the King's council. This did not seem the time to rehearse the deeds of Shan, who had gotten himself into a great deal of trouble in his time. "Well," Ted said, "he can fight other magical things."

Patrick shrugged.

"He can tell whether things are real or illusion."

"I bet he can't tell us whether this is real or illusion."

"Shan," said Ted, goaded into desperation, "could call the winds and make floods and control dragons."

Patrick shrugged again.

"Well," said Ted, "I'm not wearing jeans."

Benjamin was, after all, far more formidable than Patrick. Ted sat down and sifted through strange soft fabrics, and finally found a sort of tunic, made of what he thought was linen, which had a minimum of embroidery. He found himself a belt and some sandals ("You could at least wear your tennis shoes," said Patrick), and ventured with the disapproving Patrick into High Castle.

People were astir already, pages and guards and servants. As Ted and Patrick made their way down and north, they began to smell food. It did not smell like breakfast particularly: no coffee, no toast, no bacon. But it smelled wonderful. Patrick wanted to stop and have breakfast, but Ted would not.

"How can we fight when we're faint with hunger?" demanded Patrick.

"We can't fight anyway."

"Well, I'd like to be able to dodge," said Patrick.

"You'll be lighter if you don't eat," said Ted, absently. He felt a little light in the head himself, but his feeling resembled the detachment of the dream he hoped to recapture when he faced Randolph. He did not want to do anything which might disturb the feeling. The dream seemed their only hope.

The place for fencing practice was just where Patrick had thought it was, and he was pleased enough to have been right that he stopped muttering about food. It was at the northeast corner of High Castle, between the second white wall and the second pink wall, and between the rose garden and the lake. It consisted of a large circle of sand surrounded by drystone walls, along which were ranged racks of weapons and masks and gloves. The sun was not up, and the air was a little chilly and very clear. The lake lapped lightly against the eastern wall, and over the western one trailed white and yellow roses. They looked very bright in the gray air. Ted firmly turned his back on them. He did not want to look at the rose garden.

They had only been in the practice area a few moments, and were examining the weapons with some dismay, when Ted experienced a creeping feeling on the back of his neck, and looked up.

"Here he comes," said Ted.

"How can you tell?" said Patrick, squinting at the advancing figure.

Ted did not answer him. He had not seen Randolph since the King's council, but he knew, as he had known then, that this was Randolph.

"He's too tall," said Patrick critically.

Lord Randolph strode briskly toward them across the flattened grass of the yard. He was dressed much as Ted was, except that he had on his head something that caught the early light. As he came closer, and smiled at them, Ted saw that it was a circlet of silver set with three of the blue stones.

"Good morrow," called Randolph.

"Good . . ." said Ted, and stopped.

Randolph and Patrick were staring at one another. Randolph looked taken aback and caught, somehow, between anger and amusement. Patrick stood where he was; he looked as if he were waiting to be executed.

Randolph came right up to Patrick, disregarding Ted, and took hold of the sleeve of Patrick's T-shirt as if to make sure it was there. He looked at Patrick's jeans and raised his eyebrows.

"So," he said, "these are the garments which so galled Benjamin."

Patrick did not seem disposed to reply, so Ted did. "Yes, sir."

"Whence came they?"

"We were in the West Tower," said Ted, truthfully.

"Where else?" said Randolph. "But what hath preserved them? They are not old, yet it must be that none hath worn them since before the West Tower tapestries were woven."

His speech was harder to understand than it had been at the council, and Ted had not followed the second part at all, but he answered the question. "We don't know, sir," he said.

"And wherefore did they gall Benjamin?" said Randolph, letting go of Patrick, who still looked stunned. Randolph stepped back from him a pace and looked him over with a gaze which would have made Ted squirm if it had been directed at him. Patrick just stood there. He began to look a little less stunned, and to examine Randolph in his turn. Ted, afraid of what Patrick might say, spoke himself.

"The only ones he really saw were mine, and they were much dirtier."

Randolph laughed, not looking away from Patrick. "What is that to Benjamin?" he said. "No, it is, I think, that this one knoweth more than a telleth."

A cardinal hooted in the fir trees that bordered the yard. Ted and Patrick both jumped. The cardinal settled into a series of whistles. Randolph put one hand to his circlet; he looked a little sheepish, like someone caught stealing the cookie dough.

"Thou too?" he said to Patrick, who nodded gravely at

him. Randolph waved his hand with its silver ring at the fir tree. "I cry you mercy," he called, and the cardinal shut up instantly. Randolph turned to Ted.

"Well, then," he said, "shall we begin?"

Ted's stomach clenched itself, but he nodded.

"Mark us well, young Patrick," said Randolph, reaching for the racks of swords. "The day cometh when I shall require these things of thee."

"Is he that good?" Ted asked Randolph, stalling for time. If he could see how Randolph chose a sword, perhaps he could avoid at least one of the mistakes awaiting him.

"Think'st thou he is not?" said Randolph, rattling a sword out of its housing as if it were an umbrella he did not think he needed. Ted, craning his neck, saw that although it did not have the plastic button on the tip, it did not look very sharp. "He is very nearly thy height," said Randolph, "though I had not noticed till today, and he is no less quick than thee."

He tried the grip of the sword and seemed displeased. "Hast been at these in thy play hours?" he demanded.

"No, sir," said Ted, meekly, and then reconsidered. Randolph had not treated him like a child at the council, and Ted had liked that better than he liked this.

"And if I had?" he added.

Randolph cocked an eyebrow at him, but answered readily enough. "Why, then I should know what this sinister grip does among the right ones," he said, and tossed the sword to Ted. Ted caught it clumsily, by the guard, but Randolph had already turned and was rummaging among the swords again.

Ted tried the grip in his hand. It did not seem to fit. And then, as Randolph turned around, sword in hand, smiling, Ted remembered what *sinister* could mean. He took hold of the sword with his left hand, and it fit very well. Ted tried to remember his dream, and almost groaned aloud. He remembered perfectly that he had held the sword in his right hand.

"Pat, come here," he called. He had the beginnings of an idea.

Patrick trudged over to them. He still looked a little glazed.

"Where did I hit you?" Ted asked him.

Patrick, looking surprised, put a hand up to the left side of his face.

"What's this?" said Randolph. He put a hand on Patrick's shoulder and looked at his face. "A pretty bruise," he said, frowning, and wheeled on Ted. "Faugh," he said, "to strike from behind."

"He didn't," said Patrick.

"I used my right hand," said Ted, the idea settling into his mind.

Randolph looked the way Ted's mother had when Ted told her that the cat had had five kittens in the linen closet, on the Christmas tablecloth.

"Faugh," he said again, "practice on thine own face."

"No, no!" said Ted. "He woke me out of a bad dream, and I hit him without thinking. See, Randolph, I'm trying to learn to use my right hand as well as the left, and—"

"I have told thee, to use the left is great advantage," said Randolph.

"But to use both—" said Ted.

"Thy ambition leadeth thee astray," said Randolph. "One day, perhaps. But—"

"But can I show you?" said Ted, trying to sound like someone who is dying to show off, rather than like someone in a panic. He had never used his left hand much. He could not possibly fake a fencing match using his left hand, and the dream would not help him with a left-handed match. How could Prince Edward be left-handed?

Randolph was looking taken aback. After all, Prince Edward was meek and biddable.

"Do so quickly, then," said Randolph; he sounded half grudging and half pleased.

Ted got himself a right-handed foil from the rack. He did not bother to choose it carefully. He had no idea what he should look for, and Randolph wanted him to hurry. He wondered about masks and gloves, but Randolph was wearing neither.

He turned around with the sword, and Randolph saluted him with his. Ted copied the gesture, not too awkwardly. It had not been in the dream. His memory of the dream began when they were already in the middle of something. So Ted waited for Randolph to begin.

The moment Randolph moved, Ted knew what to do. The sword seemed to be the same weight as the dream sword. It did not fit his hand as well, but it fit well enough. Whatever Ted had done had made Randolph retreat. Ted, following him, realized that his feet were wrong and quickly arranged them correctly. Before he had finished this, Randolph's sword bounced into his shoulder. It came with surprising force; it actually hurt.

"One-love," said Patrick, perkily, from the edge of the yard. Ted would have liked to hit him.

"Hold thy tongue," said Randolph.

Then they had to stand apart and salute and begin again. Ted thought this was silly, but he did it. This time he had his feet right at the beginning, and he and Randolph fell quickly into the fight of the dream.

Ted could not find the names of his moves flickering in the back of his mind, but they worked well enough. He was getting much tireder than he had in the dream, and there was sweat in his eyes, and the grip of the sword was becoming slippery with it. Suddenly, he knew he had Randolph, and before he could remember that this part of the dream had not worked, he had slid Randolph's blade out of the way with his own and lunged straight at him.

He felt much more foolish this time. Randolph did not look disappointed; he rolled his eyes.

"Thou wilt do it," he said. "I am sorry thou art not so tall as would like thee, but an imagined height winneth no duels. I have told thee, learn to work close in. It discomposes many."

Ted, wobbly with relief and exertion, tried to get to his feet and sat down on the ground. Randolph, smiling, came across to him and helped him up. He froze, his hand suddenly hard on Ted's arm.

"What's this?" he said. "Prithee stand a moment."

He measured Ted against himself. The top of Ted's head came to a little below Randolph's shoulder. Randolph put Ted away from him, holding on to Ted's shoulder with the firm but delicate grip that Ted had been taught to use on small animals to keep them still without hurting them. Ted felt as perfectly trapped as a frog in a cupped hand.

"What sorcery is this?" said Randolph, so quietly that Ted could barely hear him. "Thou art precisely the height of my shoulder. Not a sennight ago we found 'twas so."

Ted felt the heaviness of panic spread through his chest. With it came, more sharply than before, the feeling of betrayal. He looked like Edward. He sounded like Edward. He knew, if he thought about it, how to act like Edward.

He could almost fight like Edward. He even, like Edward, wished to be taller. But Edward was left-handed, and Ted was shorter than Edward. What sorcery was this, indeed, thought Ted, and both panic and resentment were swallowed in a deeper fear.

He looked at Randolph, who was waiting patiently for his answer.

"Perhaps . . ." said Ted, creakily, and cleared his throat.

Randolph did not really look as if he thought the answer would be any great matter. Maybe people here said "What sorcery is this?" without meaning anything by it. Randolph looked patient, speculative, and a little amused.

"Perhaps I was wearing different shoes," said Ted, still creakily. He wondered if Randolph, who still held his arm, could feel his pulse pounding. He wanted to go home.

"Very different they must have been," said Randolph; he sounded as if he knew what Ted was going to say, as if he were trying to help out.

"You might as well tell him," said Patrick at Ted's other side. Ted, who had not heard him come up, jumped violently, and Randolph let go of him.

"You tell him," said Ted, with a sulkiness that was only half put on. Patrick was altogether too fond of taking over, so let him worry about it.

"Oh, yes, they were very different," said Patrick.

"The West Tower?" said Randolph to Ted.

"Uh," said Ted, who was discovering a disinclination to lie to Randolph, and finding it very inconvenient.

"They were enchanted—or at least they might have been," Patrick said hastily, "and they made him look taller."

"Not so much taller," said Randolph, dubiously, and Ted began to regret his vengeful impulse. He would have to remember that what got Patrick in trouble could get him in trouble too. "Had not Lord Andrew in what he was pleased to call a jest," Randolph was saying, "asked me when His Highness would be of a height to wear the armor the dwarves forged for him at his birth, I had not known Edward was the height of my shoulder."

"But that was enough," said Patrick, with an audacity that stunned Ted; it was far more likely that Edward had been discovered not to be tall enough for the armor.

"Aye," said Randolph, "and how, Edward, gotst thou wind of Andrew's intentions?"

This stumped Patrick, which made Ted so furious that he spoke immediately.

"I didn't," he said, trying to undo Patrick's damage. "I wanted shoes to make me much taller, but I thought I should work up to it, you know, get used to a little difference, then a bigger one, like that. It was just luck with Andrew."

Randolph shook his head. "The adage, my lord," he said, formally, "is, 'Be what you would seem to be'; it is not 'Seem to be what you would be.' That is the way of Andrew; that was the way of Shan. I beg you," he said, quite seriously, and as if he were addressing another grown-up, "let it not be your way."

Ted was too astonished to reply.

"Dost thou understand the difference," said Randolph after a moment, "between this matter of thy shoes, and this matter of learning to fence with thy right hand?"

Ted, thinking frantically, was a little surprised to realize that he did. "The matter of the shoes is the way of Andrew," he said, "but the matter of the hands is the way of the adage." He saw Patrick wince, and thought that it was too easy to pick up the way Randolph spoke.

"Remember it, then," said Randolph.

"So what about the right hand?" said Ted hopefully.

"Thou hast the right of me," said Randolph. "I had no conception that that hand could serve thee so well. Not so quick, not so elegant, but serviceable. Thou dost repeat thy earlier blunders; have a care. But 'twas well done."

Ted, wiping a sweaty hand across his sweatier forehead, grinned and was silent.

"Patrick," said Randolph, "what surprises hast thou in store?"

"None, my lord, save that I have not practiced," said Patrick. Ted could tell by his tone that this was one of his lines; somewhere, sometime, they must have played a lesson in which Randolph asked Prince Patrick that question.

"Do so now, then," said Randolph, a little grimly, and tossed Patrick a sword.

Patrick caught it neatly and then stood at a loss. Randolph went toward him. Ted stood where he was, equally at a loss. Their masquerade would not survive Patrick's failure any better than it would have survived Ted's. Patrick was beginning to look a little sick; perhaps he could use that as an excuse. Or perhaps Ruth could wriggle out of an accusation of sorcery better than Patrick could explain a display of ignorance. Ted was not even sure that a sorcerer of the Green Caves could make anyone forget something. He should have asked Patrick instead of arbitrarily dismissing the suggestion. Now that the dream had done its job, he realized that he had expected too much of it. It had solved his problem; it had not solved theirs.

Randolph's sword achieved a whistle as he saluted Patrick.

"Well?" said Randolph.

And the cardinal whistled yet again from the fir trees.

"Oh, come on!" said Ted, involuntarily, as if Laura or Ellen had suggested this way out and he thought it was too easy.

Randolph merely rolled his eyes again. "I knew 'twas folly to allow rival magics in this castle," he said. "Patrick—"

"I didn't ask them to!"

"Canst ask them not to?"

The cardinal sang shrilly.

"Next time maybe?" said Patrick. He looked half unbelieving and half smug.

Randolph fixed him with a look not at all angry, but worse than a glare. "There will be war in this kingdom," he said, "long ere thou canst so much as call the winds. And if thou spendest thy time on learning to call the winds, thou wilt have neither sorcery nor swordsmanship that shall survive that war. If thou canst forget thy sorcery, thy sword may be good enough."

"When?" said Patrick. "By when?"

"September at the latest," said Randolph.

"How do you know?" said Ted.

"Thou'lt know that when thy father does."

"Does he know this much?"

"Oh, aye," said Randolph; he sounded as if he would have liked to add, "For all the good that does."

"Well," said Patrick, "I'll remember that, but for today I think—"

"Go thy ways," said Randolph.

Patrick put the sword back. Randolph stopped Ted as he went to do the same.

"For the next lesson, pray, the left hand," said Randolph. Ted stared at him, formulating wild plans for spraining his left wrist, and Randolph added, "Thou canst no more spare time for the right than thy brother for his sorcery."

"What about *your* sorcery?" asked Ted, who was immensely curious about why Randolph had worn the circlet to a fencing lesson but not to a king's council. The circlet meant that he was a journeyman wizard; in High Castle, that meant he was of Fence's party. Wearing the circlet to the council would have been another way of defending Fence, but wearing it to a fencing lesson would only, as far as Ted could see, make it harder to fight.

Randolph's eyebrows rose. "Mine," he said, "may be of some use to me. I have been at it these five years. And how long hath young Patrick studied thus?"

"My lord, I don't know," said Ted, not altogether truthfully. He was quite sure that Patrick had never studied magic at all. He could not remember whether Prince Patrick had done so, but he doubted it. It would not be like him. Patrick and Prince Patrick had a lot in common.

"That is why the Green Caves mislike me," said Randolph, rattling his sword into the rack. "A great huggermugger of secrecy, and for what?" He turned to Ted, and the rising sun struck gleams from the stones in his circlet. He looked very tired and a little desperate, and Ted was afraid again.

"I don't know," he said, with entire truthfulness.

They left the yard together, and caught up with Patrick in the hall before the kitchen door.

CHAPTER 10

L AURA missed Ellen that night. Their room was too big for one person. The dark was much darker than it would have been in a normal house: There were no street-lights outside, no yard lights, no car lights. The air of the room moved and rustled. Laura remembered unhappily that there was no glass in the windows. She had noticed all these things the night before, but with Ellen there they had not mattered.

It took her a long time to get to sleep, and when she did sleep, she dreamed. She dreamed that she stood in the shallows of a lake and spoke to something she could not quite see. The whole outside was damp and misty, but the mist was not the problem. No matter how she turned her head, no matter how she squinted, she could glimpse the thing to which she spoke only out of the corner of her eye.

She could hear it much better than she could see it. It had a clear and piercing voice, like the sound of a flute. But Laura could not understand a word it said. It was very im-portant that she tell it something and have its answer. When she spoke to it it seemed to take no notice.

While she struggled with these things, the mist slowly brightened, until suddenly the sun sprang red before Laura and a freezing wind whipped the mist away.

The lake stretched like a bloody mirror before her, and

where it met the sun at the burning horizon, she saw, for the barest instant, fleet white shapes that might have been horses, bounding into the sun.

She stood there, hoping they had not been horses, until the wind rose to a howl and drove lake water into her face. She put her hands up to stop it, and woke up shivering.

The window was a pale square in the moving dark, birds were muttering outside, and Ellen had not come back.

Laura flung herself out of bed, charged over to the window, and leaned upon the broad sill. Cold shot through her from stone sill and stone floor. The outside air of early morning was warmer than her room. She did not like to think about what High Castle would be like in the winter. Perhaps they would not have to be here in the winter. The story they knew ended in September. She did not like to think about its ending, either.

The outside was like her dream. The grasses were dull with dew, the lake scummed with mist. The western sky was gray, the mountains almost lost in cloud. But watch though she would, no things almost seen plied the misty air, no voices piped. Even the birds were silent now. Nothing moved in earth or sky. And the only sun she would ever see from this window would be setting. Laura began to shiver again. Almost anything could have happened to Ruth and Ellen in a place that had such dreams and such mornings.

The bedroom door opened heavily behind her. Laura jumped, banging a hipbone and an elbow on the stone, and craned her head over her shoulder. Agatha, immensely irritating in her reality and her wrongness, stood there. She had a tray in her hands.

"An thou hangst out a window in thy nightgown," said Agatha, "thou'lt catch thy death."

"Better than it catching me," said Laura, and was immediately ashamed of herself. This was what she had thought up, after years of exasperation, to say to her grandmother, who had used to tell her that doing anything Laura particularly wanted to do would make her catch her death. She had hoped she could make her grandmother laugh and give up saying it. But her grandmother had died just after Laura had thought of the answer.

"It matters not who shall start that duel," said Agatha, putting the tray on the bed, "'Tis thou wilt lose it. Drink thy chocolate. And dress thyself."

She had gone and shut the door before Laura had finished turning around.

Laura took an enormous mouthful of the hot chocolate, sputtered, and spewed it all down the front of her white nightgown. It was dreadfully bitter. Laura stared at the cup, aghast. Someone must be trying to poison Princess Laura. She bolted for the bathroom, whimpering, and rinsed her mouth, finding time to hope that, whatever Lord Randolph gave King William, it would taste better than this. When she showed no immediate signs of dying, she drank water till her stomach sloshed; she had some vague memory that this was what you were supposed to make babies do if they swallowed poison.

After this she put her clothes on, muttering fiercely at the unfamiliar buttons and laces, and went to find Ted and Patrick.

They were not in their room. Laura noticed that they had already managed to make it into a mess, and headed downstairs. She had no very clear idea of where she was going, but she wanted to find Ted and Patrick and tell them about the poison and ask about Ruth and Ellen.

She turned corners and pushed through doors at random; she had no idea where they would practice fencing. People kept saying good morning to her, men-at-arms, people hurrying past her carrying things. She would have liked to ignore them, but princesses were more polite than that. She knew that it was polite to courtesy to people, but it seemed that there was too little room, and that they were all in a hurry. So she grinned at them and went faster. The water sloshing in her stomach was beginning to make her feel sick. She wondered whom she should tell if she were poisoned. At home you called an ambulance.

The more Laura thought about this and the more strangers she had to grin at, the unhappier she got, and the faster she went, until she ran smack into a man in gray, and burst into tears.

"Heaven and earth!" exclaimed this person, dropping to his knees in the passageway and taking her by the shoulders. "Hast thou fallen, then?"

He sounded as if he were talking to a five-year-old, and to her fury Laura found herself behaving like one and wailing, as her grandmother used to say when Laura was really five, as if someone were burning her alive.

The man in gray evidently did not see it that way. "An thou canst caterwaul so, thou'rt hale enough," he said, sitting down on the floor and taking her in his arms. "Now what tempest of the spirit is this? Hush, thou'lt crack the stones w' that noise. And though I've no doubt thou'lt argue that the castle be hideous and its people fools, yet wouldst destroy all my work as well? I taught thee thy letters; wilt not spare mine, then?"

Laura pulled her head out of his shoulder and looked at him; yes, he had red hair. The pleasure of discovery made her stop crying.

"You're Matthew!" she said.

Oddly, he looked a little hurt, but he nodded.

"Now what's the matter, Princess?" he said. A woman with an armful of bright red cloth came by and gave them a curious look, but Matthew paid no attention.

Laura, casting about her for a plausible lie, looked at his kind face and interested eyes and gave up. "I can't find Ted and Patrick," she said.

Matthew cocked his head at her; he looked unconvinced. But all he said was, "That's easily remedied. They will be either at their fencing or at their breakfasts, and knowing how late Randolph and I sat over our wine last night, I'll wager he has let 'em off easy. Come, let's go to breakfast; have you had yours?"

Laura shook her head. He stood up, and helped her up, and stood looking at her.

"If you will, permit me," he said, and handed her a handkerchief. It was very large and very white and felt more like a festive gown, Laura thought, than like a handkerchief. She scrubbed her face on it, but it seemed wrong to blow her nose with it. She handed it back to Matthew, forgetting to say thank you. He took her by the hand, which, now that she was recovered, she was not sure she liked, and led her along the passage.

The men-at-arms and passersby gave them indulgent looks; Laura began to feel embarrassed. She could not remember how old Princess Laura was; she could do a lot of things very well for her age, but what the age was was another question. It occupied her until Matthew led her into a high hall wherein five or six people were clustered at one end of a long table, eating and laughing. Laura saw that Ted and Patrick were there, looking very still and alert, but managing to eat a great deal nevertheless, if they themselves had emptied all the empty dishes in front of them.

Then she saw the man between them, and if Matthew had not gone on walking, and had not held her hand, she would have stood still with her mouth open. The rushes on the floor slid and crunched under her feet. A dog yelped as she trod on its tail, and a cat butted its head against her ankle. She paid them no attention.

It was not that he looked like Ruth and Ellen, although that was startling. It was not that he had about him a settled wariness, like that of a cat asleep in a forbidden place, although that was intriguing. It was that she knew him. She had figured out Benjamin, Agatha, and Matthew, but she knew Randolph.

"Good morrow," said Matthew, to the group generally; then he looked at Randolph, who was buttering a slice of bread with a dagger.

Laura's gaze rested on the dagger and froze there. The hilt was set with blue stones. Randolph, spreading the butter with the care it deserved, but which grown-ups so often did not give it, moved his hand through a shaft of sunlight, and the colors it struck from the stones made Laura blink.

In the space of that blink she saw, very quickly and very clearly, the woman with the broom from the secret house. The woman sat peering with great seriousness into a mirror which did not reflect her. Laura, having opened her eyes before what she had seen registered, promptly closed them again, and saw only darkness with red pinpricks.

"Aren't you awake yet?" Patrick's voice said querulously.

Laura gave up and opened her eyes.

"Thou wouldst not be awake thyself, hadst thou thy way," said Randolph, biting into his bread. "Make room for thy cousin," he added with his mouth full.

Ted slid over on the bench, and Laura went around the table and sat between him and Patrick. Matthew had found room across from them.

Laura looked dubiously at the food on the table. None of it looked like breakfast to her.

"You're early," said Matthew to Randolph.

"My students are handy today," said Randolph, not shortly at all, but Matthew looked at him and changed the subject.

"I have been translating the journals of Shan," he said, helping himself to what looked like a chicken drumstick.

Randolph's head came up. "Which of them?"

"Those dealing with his travels in the south."

"What say they? Aught to the purpose?"

"Perhaps," said Matthew. The two young men on either side of him looked at each other over his head, drained their mugs, and stood up. Laura did not recognize either of them, but they looked as if they were good-tempered.

"We are not speaking secrets," said Matthew to them.

"Nor are you speaking aught to keep us awake," said the one to Matthew's right.

"It may yet keep you alive," said Randolph. The two young men gave each other the kind of look that Laura and Ellen would give each other about Patrick, bowed, said, "Our duties to Your Highness," in the general direction of the children, and went out.

"The meat pies are all right," said Patrick in Laura's ear. "The ale is awful."

"Well, could you pass the bread?"

"Not speaking secrets?" said Randolph to Matthew.

"Those men are none of Andrew's."

"They are none of ours."

"Sits the wind in that quarter, then?" said Matthew, with

a glance at Ted, Patrick, and Laura. Laura saw that Patrick was steadily eating bread and honey, and that Ted held a forgotten slice halfway to his mouth. The honey was running down his arm.

Laura saw Randolph's look slide over Patrick and herself and rest behind her, on Ted. "Art thou any of mine, Edward?"

"Sir," said Ted, with no discernible hesitation, "all I know you have taught me."

Something made Laura look at Matthew, and she surprised on his face the same faintly hurt look that had been there when she told him who he was. She remembered that he had tutored the royal children when they were younger. That would account for his not liking what Ted had said. But that did not explain why he should have been hurt when she said, "You're Matthew."

"Maybe," said Randolph. "But the disciple has ever left the master before the master thought him ready."

This gave Ted pause, but not for long. "As you have left Fence?" he said. He sounded as if he were joking, but there was something a little odd in his voice, and Laura saw Patrick stop chewing. Randolph frowned.

"Randolph, is that not answer enough?" said Matthew.

"The question was thine," Randolph told him, reasonably.

"I say all here are ours, then," said Matthew, flushing a little. "My lords and lady, I ask your pardon," he added.

Laura blinked, Patrick said, "Sure," and Ted nodded.

"So," said Randolph, "what of these journals?"

Matthew picked up the heavy pitcher and poured himself a mug of ale. "'Tis the group with the doubtful handwriting," he said, clearly enjoying himself.

"Your handwriting would be doubtful also, had you spent four years in the service of the Dragon King," said Randolph.

"That is my view," said Matthew. "But there are those who hold that Melanie, not Shan, wrote these journals; in which case one cannot trust 'em."

"But if she wrote them for her own use?" said Ted. He sounded terrifyingly grown-up, but the honey was still running down his arm.

Matthew shrugged. "If she had, why write them after the style of Shan?"

"What other teacher had she?" said Ted.

"What," said Randolph to Matthew, "of the journals?"

"Shan's order of sorcerers wielded no arms save their magic," said Matthew. "Not until he entered the service of the Dragon King, whose minions would as soon kill one another as eat their dinner, did he need true weapons. His magic was less than theirs, you will understand, for his came by craft and theirs by nature. And because he needed to battle such creatures as the Dragon King uses, he learned what weapons vanquish them."

"That were a boon indeed," said Randolph, slowly. "Is the translation complete?"

"So much as I can do," said Matthew, looking rueful. "There are passages that need the wisdom of Fence."

Randolph's brows drew together. "Is there help in them in their present state?"

"I would have you look at them, if you will."

"Gladly," said Randolph, rising and thrusting the buttery dagger into his belt. "And as soon as may be. Have you eaten enough?"

"As much as I have stomach for," said Matthew, rising too. "My duty to Your Highness," he said to the children, and moved for the door.

"Edward, if you would eat with the proper hand," said Randolph. He stopped, and sighed. "I will impart to you what we discover," he said, pulled Laura's hair, and followed Matthew.

Patrick looked at Ted, and snickered. "You might as well have been eating with your left hand, the mess you've made," he said.

"Do you know a good way to sprain a hand?" Ted asked him.

"Where's Ruth?" Laura demanded of Ted.

"I wish I could get a look at those manuscripts," said Ted, gazing into the depths of his mug as if it were a crystal ball. He picked it up, took a large swallow, and made a face.

"You could have asked," said Patrick.

"Where's Ruth and Ellen?" said Laura.

"If you've finished eating, we can check the stables and Ruth's room," said Patrick.

"Let's go," said Laura. The water was still sloshing in her stomach. She got up. "Agatha tried to poison my cocoa," she said as they went out the door.

"*What?*" said Ted, pleasing Laura immensely. She did not really think that it had been Agatha, but she had wanted to get Ted's attention.

"How do you know?" said Patrick. Laura told him. Patrick leaned on the passage wall and howled. "You crazy kid," he said when he was finished laughing. "It's bitter because they don't put sugar in it, that's all."

"Why not?"

"Same reason people don't put it in tea and coffee, I guess."

"That's stupid," said Laura, knowing full well that Patrick thought it was she who was stupid.

Ruth and Ellen were not in Ruth's room nor in Ellen and Laura's, and they were not in the stable. It was a sunny day, cooler than the weather had been since they had arrived, and still a little misty. After some discussion the three of them decided to sit on the outer wall of the moat on the west side of High Castle, where they could watch for Ruth and Ellen's approach and feed the swans at the same time. High Castle was situated on rising ground, so that from the moat's wall they could see quite easily over the high pink outer wall.

They went back to the hall where they had eaten. There were several lords and ladies, dressed in what looked like hunting garments, eating there, but nobody remarked on Patrick's taking a loaf of bread. They crossed the drawbridge, being greeted by name and with apparent affection by both the guards there, and settled themselves on the sun-warmed wall of the moat.

"At least nobody's missed them," said Patrick.

They had fed the swans perhaps a quarter of the loaf of bread, and begun an argument about what Matthew had meant when he had said, "Sits the wind in that quarter?" when they saw the distant figures of horses plodding over the plain. They scrambled from the wall and ran through the front gate to greet them.

Ruth would not say a word until they had turned the horses over to a groom, and then she would say only that she wanted some breakfast. She and Ellen seated themselves in the rose garden, and Ted and Patrick and Laura all went back to the breakfast hall once again. It did not need three of them to bring Ruth and Ellen breakfast, but none of them felt able to stay in the garden with Ruth and Ellen while Ruth and Ellen were not talking.

A flurry of cats leaped from the table when they came in, and some of the dishes had already been cleared away. So they bundled bread and drumsticks and a lump of butter and a honey pot into a tablecloth, and hurried back to the garden. It was starting to get hot.

"Did it work?" asked Ted.

"We had the most awful time," said Ellen. Her hair was full of leaves and her face scratched, but she sounded complacent.

"Did it work?"

"Our sword does so work on your hedge," said Ellen to Laura.

Patrick yelped. "It can't!"

"It was probably Shan's Ring that let it," said Ted. "Did it work, Ruth?"

"Why should Shan's Ring let it?" bristled Patrick.

"Shut up and let her talk. Ruth, did Shan's Ring work? Did you change the time?"

"Yes," said Ruth.

Ted and Patrick immediately looked happier. Laura's stomach contracted. She had hoped that, if it did not work, they would have to go home. Now they were stuck. And what did Ted look so pleased about, anyway? He was the one who'd been so upset, and hollering that nobody understood. Laura felt deserted.

"So how?" said Patrick.

"Not the way we thought," said Ruth. She was cleaner than Ellen, but she still looked draggled. She picked a yellow rose and sniffed it thoughtfully. "We tried the Ring at the bottle trees and not a darn thing happened. So we finally thought we might as well at least look at the hedge. It was on the way home anyway, and we thought the horses could drink at the stream."

"They wouldn't, though," said Ellen.

"So we tried to get through the hedge into the yard, and it worked," said Ruth. "There were streetlights on the other side of the hedge, instead of the stream, and cars parked. So then I tried all the things I'd tried by the bottle trees."

"Did you throw the ring in the air and say the verse?" asked Patrick. "I thought of that when it was too late."

"Didn't work," said Ellen.

"I tried everything," said Ruth. "So finally I thought I should throw it over the hedge. So I tried standing in the stream and doing that, and Ellie stood in the yard to catch it."

"You could've lost it!" said Patrick, furiously.

"Well, we didn't," said Ruth, with the kind of patience usually reserved for very small children. "So then I stood in the street and Ellie stood in the yard."

"I didn't like that," said Ellen. "There was a light in the attic window, a purple one."

"And I threw the ring over the hedge and said the verse." Ruth paused.

Laura could see that Ted would not give her the satisfaction of being prompted, but Patrick was too wild to care about that. "Well?" he said.

"There was a very bright flash of purple light," said Ruth, "and a big space opened in the hedge, and I could see the Secret Country in it. Ellen had the sword, so I thought I should go on through. I did, and I was back here, but Ellie wasn't. I'd just been looking around for a moment, when I heard a splash in the stream."

The three members of the audience looked at Ellen.

"I saw the purple light too," she said. "It hurt my eyes, and I couldn't see where the ring fell. And while I was waiting for the spots to go away, I looked at the house, because the whole hedge was lit up. All the lights in the house went on, and the front door burst open and there was a lady with a broom just screaming her head off."

Ted and Laura looked at each other.

"What'd she say?" asked Ted.

"'Aroint thee,'" said Ellen. "And she called us something

like 'onions,' but it can't have been. I wish all these people didn't talk so weird." She pushed her hair away from her eyes. "So I wanted to get out of there, and I ran for the hedge and the hedge went out—I mean it wasn't glowing anymore—and the sword pulled me and I fell down."

"How pulled?" said Patrick.

"It pulled," said Ellen. "It made me lose my balance. So I fell down and right in front of my nose was the ring, shining."

"Shining how?"

"Shining," said Ellen. "Anybody'd think you don't speak English. The gold was all yellow—"

"It's brass," said Patrick.

"—yellow, like sunshine, okay? So I grabbed it, and the sword let me up."

"What do you mean, let you up?"

"It stopped pulling," said Ellen, dangerously, and waited for her brother to say more, but he was silent. Laura thought he looked like somebody doing mental arithmetic in front of a crowd of parents.

"So," said Ellen, "I got up and got through the hedge and fell in the water."

"Now I thought," said Ruth, "that what Ellie said happened with the lady took more time than the time between when I got back here and when I heard Ellie fall in the water. But I wanted to make sure."

"And I wasn't going back in there," said Ellen.

"So I did," said Ruth. She paused again, twirling the yellow rose.

"Come on," said Patrick. He snatched the rose from her.

"I took the ring," said Ruth, "but not the sword. Just to see what happened."

"Well?" said Ted.

"I wasn't back in your town, because the streetlights and cars weren't there."

"*Well?*"

"But I wasn't just in the Secret Country, either. Ellie wasn't on the other side of the hedge. It was daytime, and there was an army all over the plain."

"Camped?" said Ted.

"Moving."

"What'd it look like?"

"Well, it looked like the Secret Country, more or less. I mean, the Well of the White Witch was there, and there was a cardinal singing like mad in the yard. I got out of there fast."

"Why?" said Patrick.

"It felt wrong."

"Wrong how?"

"The air was like a sheet of glass," said Ruth, helplessly. "And I felt too small and the sky was the wrong color. I don't know, Patrick. It just was."

"I'm going to have to check this out," said Patrick. "Go on."

"I came back and got the sword from Ellie," said Ruth, "and ended up in the right place when I used the ring and the sword to get through. The lady had gone in, there was just the light in the attic again. So I just sat and waited for a few minutes. I got chomped by mosquitoes, and there was a cat in the yard that hissed at me."

"She must be a witch," said Laura to Ellen. "She's got a broom and a mean cat."

"Too young," said Ellen.

"What then, Ruthie?" said Patrick.

"So when I got tired of the mosquitoes, maybe in five

minutes, I came back here," said Ruth, "and Ellen fell all over me."

"She'd been gone, for hours," said Ellen a little reproachfully.

"So we figure we changed the time," said Ruth.

"Did you go back to the bottle trees and check out Australia?" asked Patrick.

"We certainly did not," said Ruth. "We were late."

"Ellie, didn't you have a watch?" said Patrick.

"You know I lost it."

"But we don't know the conversion factor, if you don't know how long you waited for Ruth!"

Ellen shrugged. "It was dark when I started waiting, and the sun came up and had *been* up for *ages* when she got back."

"Do you remember anything about that army?" Ted asked Ruth. "How big was it? Infantry or cavalry?"

"It covered the whole plain," said Ruth, submitting to this interrogation with more of her usual meekness than she had shown for some time. "There were men and horses and other things. Maybe a dragon, probably ogres. I didn't look long."

"Which way was it going?"

"Toward High Castle," said Ruth. "What's wrong? It wasn't our Secret Country."

"Sounds like the Dragon King's army," said Ted. "So that's why everything looked wrong. The Border Magic."

"It didn't look that wrong," said Ruth. "The grass wasn't burned, it wasn't turned into a desert. The birds weren't gone; I heard the cardinal."

"Well, who's to say the Border Magic works the way we thought it would?" said Ted. Laura looked at him in surprise. He sounded pleased.

"Who's to say the Border Magic works?" murmured Patrick.

"Cut it out," said Ruth. She stretched luxuriously, and almost fell off the wall. "Everything's going to be all right now, so stop making trouble."

"How do you figure that?" demanded Patrick. He had finished with the leaves of Ruth's rose and began methodically pulling the petals off and holding them up to the light.

"How do you figure anything else?" said Ruth smugly. Lady Ruth had spoken so when the emissary of the dwarves had asked her to tell them how to grow trees underground. It was the demand of tribute they had the right to make every ten years, and it had been a plot on their part to ask for something she could not do. Then she would have had to reveal the magic of the Green Caves to them. But she had said, "How not?" to them, in just that tone, and taught them to make trees grow underground. Laura began to feel a little better.

Patrick clearly felt worse. "You talk to her," he said to Ted. "You believe this stuff."

"I think she might be right," said Ted; he did not sound as smug as Ruth had, but he sounded hopeful.

Patrick flung his hands up in the air, scattering rose petals and bread crumbs in all directions. Three pigeons came out of nowhere and began squabbling over the crumbs.

"I think we can change things if we work at it," said Ted. "If we changed the time, why not other things? We just have to do it by the rules inside the Secret Country."

"What makes you so optimistic all of a sudden?"

"Changing the time," said Ted. "I never thought it'd work."

"You went to an awful lot of trouble for something that wouldn't work."

"Well, but if it didn't work, then we could go home. But it seems like if that worked, anything will. I think we'll be all right."

"You do still think this is real?"

"Really real," said Ted. "We can do things with it."

"Well, what did you think it was before, then?"

"Well, real, but magically real. I thought we might be stuck with the story, and it wasn't even quite the story we knew, so we couldn't play it right, even if we'd wanted to. But this is just wide open, so it's all right."

"So what do we do?" asked Patrick. He was not giving in; he was waiting for Ted to say something stupid so he could argue some more.

"Keep Randolph from poisoning the King," said Ted, promptly.

"How?"

"Convince the King that he's fighting dragons and monsters," said Ted, "or convince Randolph that no matter what happens it won't do any good to kill the King, or just keep him from doing it by letting him know we know, or watching him all the time, or something."

"If Randolph can't convince the King," said Patrick, "what makes you think we can?"

"And it *will* do good to kill him, so how do we convince Randolph not to?" said Ruth.

"I'll tell him I believe the King, that there's no magic."

"Great," said Ruth. "Then he'll kill you."

"He will not!"

"Why shouldn't he?" cried Ruth.

"He . . ." said Ted, and the word stuck in his throat. He looked sick.

"But . . ." said Laura.

"He's going to kill King William," Ruth said to both of

them. "And as far as I know, he's known the King a lot longer and likes him a lot better than Ted."

"He might think he can control Ted," said Patrick, thoughtfully.

"He does think so," said Ruth. "That's why he kills the King; he figures he can push Edward around, because he's weak. But if Ted doesn't act weak, which it looks like he already isn't, and tells Randolph that he doesn't believe in magic, then I think Ted's had it."

"What should Randolph do?" demanded Ted.

There was silence.

"Fence says," said Ellen, slowly, "I mean, in the game, doesn't he, that Randolph should obey the King and go to war, and if he dies, and if the Secret Country gets burned up, then so what."

"But what do we think?" said Ted, with an intensity that made Laura glad that he was not addressing her.

"Hey," said Patrick, absently, shaking what was left of his rose. "There are insects here after all. Here's an ant on this rose."

"Patrick," said Ted.

"Look," said Patrick, suddenly furious, "I didn't write this story. I didn't make things so that all the choices are stupid."

"I think we'd better think about what we think," said Ted, and no one laughed at the way he put it.

CHAPTER 11

THEY had little time to think, and none to resolve anything so complicated. Preparations for the Banquet of Midsummer Eve began days before the event, and no one was exempt from work. No matter where Laura went, to the rose garden, to the moat, to the clove-scented fastness of the West Tower, some harried grown-up would hail her with glad cries and send her on some incomprehensible errand. Burrowing in the cellar among piles of sheepskins, she wondered why any banquet should need thirteen black ones; picking all the white roses in the garden, and sucking her pricked fingers, she racked her memory for what was wrong with the red and yellow.

She met Ellen carrying an armful of indignant kittens. She found Ruth scattering sand in the halls. She watched Ted grimly sort through colored ribbons; she giggled to see Patrick make ferns and wildflowers into garlands, scowling as fiercely as if he were reading poetry.

This flurry was not without its benefits. Ted and Patrick had no more fencing lessons. Randolph told them to practice and left them alone. Laura learned her way around the innermost part of High Castle; Ellen was spared the ordeal of geography lessons. Ruth, rummaging in the library for a recipe which one of the undercooks had disgraced himself by forgetting, discovered a collection of damp and unpleasantly stained volumes about the sorcery of the Green Caves. She sat up late reading them every night and was grumpy every day from then on.

They had little time to argue and barely time to eat. "If it's this bad before this banquet," said Patrick, one evening when they sat in the dining hall painfully picking the seeds out of millions of raisins, "what will it be like before the Unicorn Hunt?"

"That's outside," said Ellen, crunching an unseeded raisin.

"So what?" said Patrick. "We'll probably have to weed the whole forest." He flung a handful of seeded raisins into a wooden bowl and looked balefully at Ted. "Quit using your right hand," he said.

"You'll make him stutter," said Ruth.

Ted was awakened on the morning of the banquet by the faint but persistent sound of bells. He sat up, and saw Patrick leaning out the window. He was wearing one of the nightshirts they both hated. It was too cold in High Castle at night not to wear them.

"What's that racket?" demanded Ted.

"Dunno," said Patrick, absently, to the outside.

"How's the weather?"

Patrick shrugged. Ted got reluctantly out of bed and joined him at the window. Like most early mornings in the Secret Country, this one was damp and blurry, like a botched and abandoned watercolor. The bells pealed on. Ted thought the sound might be coming from the North Tower.

He looked at his cousin. Patrick was preoccupied, which was not unusual, but he was also unsettled.

"I didn't dream anything last night," said Ted. "It was a nice change."

Patrick, uncharacteristically, did not look at him as he spoke. "Maybe I got your dream too."

Ted waited.

"I dreamed about the Crystal of Earth again."

Ted was exasperated. "We forgot to ask Ruth about that!"

"Yeah."

"So what'd you dream?"

"Nothing clear, really," said Patrick, still not looking at him. "Somebody was trying to smash it, to prove there wasn't any magic, and everybody thought that that would destroy the Secret Country. Things got pretty nasty, people killing each other all over."

"Is the Crystal of Earth like the Border Magic, then?" said Ted, who preferred not to be reminded of killing people.

"Worse," said Patrick, leaning further out and appearing to address the paving stones of the inner courtyard. One of the more feathery of the hunting dogs trotted across it, barking desultorily.

"It doesn't just get the Secret Country," said Patrick. "It gets this whole place, whatever it's called: Fence's Country and the Dubious Hills and those Outer Isles of Ellie's— everything."

"I sure don't remember anything like that."

"No," said Patrick.

"What's it look like?"

"Oh, one of those tacky paperweights with the snow-storms in it, only bigger."

There was nothing specific to object to in this answer, but Ted found it objectionable just the same. "We'll ask Ruth," he said. "But what'd you dream that I should have dreamed?"

Patrick straightened up and looked at him. He looked as if someone were taking a splinter out of his finger. "You dream it," he said, and went into their bathing room.

Ted began to get dressed, absently. It seemed to him high time to do something about his left hand. He could not use it at a formal banquet without receiving severe comments on his sloppiness. A week's practice at eating left-handed had provided great amusement to his companions, but little improvement in his skill. He would be chided for disobedience as well if the seating arrangements put him and Randolph at the same table. And after the Banquet, he and Randolph would resume their fencing practice.

He had already decided that he could not pretend to have hurt his hand; Benjamin or Agatha would be sure to insist on looking at it. Besides, he had an obscure feeling that this would be cheating. He looked after Patrick. Patrick was in a foul mood. He might enjoy disabling Ted's hand. Ted crouched down beside the bed, reached under it with both hands for the sheathed sword, and was rewarded with a stinging pain in the left one. He jerked back and watched the blood drip onto the stone floor.

"Pat!"

Patrick came out, trailing his towel. "Good God," he said. "Here, take this." He crumpled the towel against the cut and jabbed his thumb onto the pressure point.

"Ease up; I haven't severed an artery," said Ted.

"I thought you'd settled for spraining your wrist."

"Reach under there carefully," said Ted, jerking his head at the bed.

Patrick looked first, and pulled the sword out by the hilt.

"Where's the sheath?" asked Ted.

Patrick looked again. "Other side," he said. "Didn't you take the sword out of it?"

"No."

"Neither did I." Patrick paused. "Unless I did it in my sleep," he said. "I dreamed I was using a sword to—" He looked secretive.

"Well," said Ted, knowing better than to prompt him, "it certainly solves the handedness problem." He stood up. "I'd better take this to Agatha."

"You can't. She'll put cobwebs or dung or something on it, and it'll get infected. Besides, I bet it needs stitches."

"I just grazed the blade. And how can it get infected if it's not a real—"

"You think it's real."

"So I also think it won't get infected."

Agatha, when applied to, provided a lecture, a handful of goldenrod, an odd-smelling salve, a clean rag, and great expertise in bestowing the first on Ted and Patrick and the rest on Ted's hand.

"Feel better?" said Ted to Patrick as they left.

"No," said Patrick. "I'm wondering if somebody else was messing with that sword."

Laura thought she was looking for something. She trudged through the crackling leaves, throwing up the scents of cinnamon and dust and dampness. The trees were huge and the woods dim, and the air had the sharpness of frost. It smelled like Halloween.

Noticing all this had made her forget what she was looking for. She blinked and pushed the hair out of her eyes. She must have been doing this for some time: The hair was very tangled, and full of twigs and leaves. Her hands were filthy.

"Now what," said Laura aloud, "would I be looking for in the middle of the woods?"

The sound of her own voice made her remember that she was not looking, but listening. It also woke her up.

She opened her eyes painfully. It was gray early morning, and she felt dizzy and unrested. Ellen was not in bed, but Laura could hear her splashing and singing. Laura wished she would stop; the singing sounded wrong.

She got out of bed and bounded across the bare floor to the window—not because she felt suddenly awake but because the floor was so cold—and looked out. It was misty again.

"It's a rotten morning," said Ellen cheerfully, behind her.

"It always is," said Laura.

"It must be the lake," said Ellen, rubbing vigorously at her hair with a square of linen. "I hate these towels, they don't soak anything up."

"The lake at the farm never did this," Laura said to the misty outside. The trees looked as distant as mountains. The mountains and the lake itself were hidden. Shivers ran up and down her spine, perhaps from the cold floor.

"There's more water in this lake," said Ellen, wandering away from the window. "What shall we wear today?"

"I think it's the unicorns," said Laura. "It's their lake."

"Well, it's their *forest*," said Ellen, doubtfully. "Get dressed, I'm hungry."

Two pages pounced on them at the door to the dining hall and crowned them with garlands. They found that half the tables had been usurped by a lot of girls about Ruth's age, all wearing white lacy dresses and all sewing on enormous masses of red and blue and black silk.

"Do *we* have to dress like that?" demanded Laura. She hated lace. And white just got dirty.

"Gosh, I hope so," said Ellen.

"They sure are noisy," said Laura, helping herself to bread and honey.

"So would you be if there were that many of you. Where's the drumsticks?"

"You sound like Agatha."

"Agatha hates drumsticks."

Laura sighed, and sat down on the corner of a bench. It was unusually crowded in here today, even if you made allowance for all those sewing girls.

Ellen came back empty-handed and glaring. "There's nothing to eat here!" she said.

A young man grinned across the table at them. Laura thought he was one of those who had left the table, on their first morning in High Castle, when Randolph began talking about Shan's manuscripts. "You don't want breakfast, Your Highness," he said to Ellen. "Save your hunger for the banquet."

"Have some bread," said Laura, afraid Ellen would be rude to him.

Ellen thumped down next to her and bit morosely into a hunk of bread. "I want cornflakes," she said.

"Gah," said Laura.

They wandered aimlessly about after they had eaten, resigned to being caught and put to work. But no one heeded them.

"I know," said Ellen as they dawdled past the kitchen. They had discovered very early in their stay that no children were allowed in the kitchen on the grounds that anyone under sixteen would eat more than he helped. "Let's go to Fence's tower."

"With that beast?"

"I liked it," said Ellen. "And it won't be nearly so bad in the daytime."

The corridor to the foot of Fence's tower was not much improved by what little daylight was coming into it when they got there. The fog had not lifted as it usually did, and the corridor was still dim and cobwebby. The purple torch still burned before the shut door. There was no beast.

"Well," said Laura gratefully, "so much for that."

Ellen put her hand on the heavy door and pushed, and it swung inward without a sound. Another purple torch glared across the darkness at their feet, where the stairs went down, not up. They looked at each other. A cold air came up the staircase and stirred their hair.

"*Well,*" said Ellen. She stared into the darkness earnestly, as if she were trying to read a street sign. Laura wondered if there was anything anywhere that Ellen was afraid of.

"Let's get a light and try these stairs," said Ellen.

"*No.*"

"Oh, come on. This is Fence's tower, it must be all right."

"If this is Fence's tower maybe I don't like Fence," said Laura grimly. Everything else had come out funny, why should not Fence be, after all, the kind of magician who lived in a cold cellar and kept gurgling purple beasts? She hunched her shoulders, shivering. She had not realized how much hope she had been putting in Fence's return.

"Huh," said Ellen. "I guess it's not much like Fence. He's all cheerful and fiery, now that I think about it. I wonder if this isn't his tower after all?"

"Whoever's it is I don't want to meet him," said Laura, doggedly. Now there was a nasty thought. Maybe there was no Fence at all, but some utterly unknown person.

"Maybe something's wrong," said Ellen. "If this is Fence's tower, maybe some of his enchantments have gotten loose while he's gone and are lying in wait for him." She shut the door firmly and leaned on it, tracing its intricate carving with her thumb. "We should tell someone."

"Who?" said Laura, watching her cousin's grimy thumb move over carved leaves and branches and strange small animals like cats or rabbits. "Maybe it's not Fence's enchantments. I think he's too good for that to happen—he's the best wizard in the Secret Country. Maybe it's a plot. Maybe Andrew did it."

"But there's something *magical* wrong here, and Andrew doesn't believe in magic," said Ellen. She rubbed a forefinger along the carved wing of an eagle, scowling.

"Lots of people don't like Fence," said Laura. "And we don't know what's going on. I don't feel like trusting anybody."

"We should tell Ruth and Ted anyway."

"Well, yes," said Laura. Ellen's aimless finger thumped suddenly into a shapeless indentation in the door's carving, and Laura's mouth fell open. "Ellie, look! The door's like that tapestry!"

Ellen looked, and jerked her hand away. "Let's find Ted and Ruth," she said.

They did not find either of them, nor did they find Patrick. They were quickly caught up in last-minute bizarre preparations of the Banquet. They found themselves back in their room at six in the evening under orders to bathe and dress, and with no idea where their companions were.

They did not have to wear white. Agatha had told them to wear "the green," and they determined after some debate that this must mean either the green velvet or the green muslin. Ellen said that it must be the muslin because you didn't wear velvet in the summertime. Laura said they should wear the velvet because it was cold. The fog had still not lifted, and Laura had felt everywhere she went as if the air from Fence's stairway were blowing down her neck.

They went and knocked on Ted and Patrick's door, Ellen in muslin and Laura in velvet. Patrick let them in, scowling. He was wearing a dark blue tunic with what looked like a fox embroidered on its chest, and he held a crumpled mass of dark blue in one hand.

"What's that?" said Ellen.

Patrick slammed the door, and Laura jumped. *"Stockings!"* he spat.

"Hose," said Ted, wearily. He was sitting on the bed unlacing his sandals.

"They look warm," said Laura wistfully.

"If I want to be warm I'll wear jeans."

"I'd a lot rather wear your clothes than mine," said Laura.

"I don't see what you're upset about," said Ted. He picked another mass of dark blue off the bed and went into the bathing room.

"They look ridiculous," Patrick snarled after him, "and they're uncomfortable."

"Why should you care?" demanded Ellen. "You don't think it's real anyway."

Laura wondered if Patrick would forget this if they didn't keep reminding him.

He had rounded on Ellen as if he were going to hit her, but he only let his breath out in a snort. "Even if I'm only dreaming," he told her, "I don't like nightmares."

"Yeah," said Laura, remembering the purple beast and the cold stairs.

Patrick looked at her. "What happened to *you* today?"

"There's something wrong with Fence's tower," said Ellen. Patrick shrugged. "There's something wrong with everything else. Why shouldn't there be something wrong with Fence's tower?" Ellen told him about the staircase, and Laura watched interest creep over his face. "Heh," was all he said.

Then Ted came out and they had to tell it again. Ted was dressed for the banquet, and he looked frighteningly grown-up when he came out. But when Ellen had finished, he just looked frightened. Laura was not sure which was worse.

"I think we should tell Randolph," he said. "Let's go on downstairs. He's bound to be at the banquet."

"Patrick's not dressed," said Ellen.

Ted looked at him. "You could wear your jeans under your tunic and look like a college student," he said.

Patrick picked up his hose and headed for the bathing room. Laura thought he looked as if he preferred revenge to argument.

The Banquet was held in a hall none of them had been in before. They found it by following the groups of wonderfully dressed people they met almost as soon as they got out the door. The hall was enormous, full of torch- and candlelight and even fuller of people. Laura felt as if she were lost in a department store at Christmas. She had never imagined the Banquet as having so many strangers in attendance. Neither the sight of other people in velvet nor the sound of musicians hooting and burbling upon odd instruments made her feel any better. She wanted her mother.

They could not find Randolph, and they could not find Ruth. The strain of being among so many people so much bigger began to tell even on Ted after a while, and he found them a spot where they could observe untrampled. They were between the tables and the door to the kitchens, so they stood and watched young people in white carry plates and bowls and platters past them, and smelled the rich smells from the kitchen.

The hooting of the instruments began to settle into something resembling a rhythm. The glittering crowd began to separate and order itself.

"I hope they sound better than that when they get going," said Patrick.

"I think the dancing's starting," said Ted.

"And who'll dance with us?" said Ellen.

"Gah," said Laura.

"Let's get out of here," said Patrick. The people moving back to make space for the dancing were crowding all four of them into the wall.

They squirmed their way along to the other end of the hall. Laura looked hopefully at the tables spread with food, but they were guarded by more young people, Ruth's age maybe. One of them caught her looking and stuck his tongue out at her. Laura showed her teeth at him and turned away, bumping her shoulder on the jeweled hilt of someone's dagger. In her confusion and irritation, she expected him to notice her and draw it, but he did not.

They came at last to an empty alcove. "Is that all they wanted those sheepskins for?" demanded Laura. The skins were spread on the stone bench and on the floor.

"Maybe we shouldn't sit there," said Ted, and jumped as a hand came down on his shoulder.

They looked up into Benjamin's face. He seemed displeased.

"Thy father wants thee," he said to Ted, and began to maneuver him through the crowd. Ted cast a despairing glance over his shoulder and disappeared behind somebody's billowy sleeves.

The other three stood abandoned, and the musicians' hooting and burbling settled into a melody. Laura jerked her head up. She knew that music. She had been listening for it in her dream.

"What are those weird instruments anyway?" said Patrick.

"Be quiet," said Laura quickly. Far in the back of her mind the music made her remember places she had never been and things she had never seen.

Patrick was so astonished that he was quiet. Ellen moved closer and stared at Laura, but she was quiet too. Laura pulled her braids and scowled. "What *is* that song?"

"Is that all?" said Ellen. "It's 'The Minstrel Boy,' don't you remember? Your mother used to sing it to us when we were little."

"No," said Laura. That was the tune, but that was not what she was trying to remember.

"What are all those instruments?" repeated Patrick.

"And where are they?" said Ellen.

Patrick pointed to a balcony at the end of the hall from which they had come. It was dim so high up. "I can see the harp," he said, "but what's all that other stuff?"

"Why do you care?" said Ellen, dodging an old man in red who carried a cushion.

"The J-shaped ones," said Laura hastily, "are crumhorns. That's what hoots. And they've got recorders and a dulcimer, because I can hear them." She stopped, dumbfounded. She did not know how she knew these things.

"What's that thing on the left?"

Laura squinted at it, and felt the shock of a different and more normal sort of recognition. It did not come from the back of her mind as the names of the other instruments had. "That's a zootibar."

"A what?"

"It's from a story Ruth read us," said Laura, "but *I* decided what it looked like, and it does."

"Huh," said Patrick. He looked at her for a moment. "What's it supposed to sound like?"

"The story didn't say," said Laura. "I thought, like a glass with a lot of safety pins in it, only it could play real tunes, of course."

"Jesus," said Patrick.

"Don't *swear*," said Ellen.

"I wasn't."

"Why aren't they dancing?" said Ellen, looking back to the center of the hall. People had cleared a wide space, and were standing around it.

"You don't dance to that song," said Laura.

"Well, the words are a little sad," said Ellen, dubiously, "but the music's okay."

That was not what Laura had meant. Not knowing what she did mean, she was silent. Concentrating on the knowledge in the back of her mind only made it recede further.

The musicians began another song, and this time people did start to dance. They overflowed the space cleared for them and pushed the rest of the crowd back toward Laura and Ellen and Patrick. It began to get hot, and Laura almost regretted her velvet.

"Come on," said Patrick, "let's get closer to the door."

They edged along the wall, being elbowed, and stepping on people's feet with a certain vengeful satisfaction. Nobody paid the slightest attention to them.

This hall had double doors which opened onto a paved place, which in turn led to either the stables or the rose garden. The doors looked west. They were open. No guards stood in the doorway, which Laura thought odd. Any door in High Castle which opened on outside air, even those to the inner courtyard, always seemed to have a guard or two on it.

They struggled out of the last of the crowd and stood breathing the cool air from the doorway. In the gray light just inside it, three children were playing something which looked like jacks, but probably wasn't. It involved two balls and a number of wooden pieces.

Laura stopped dead when she saw the strange children. Patrick and Ellen did not seem to want to get any closer to them either. Laura was sure they were dangerous; they would be able to find out far faster than any grown-up how little she and the others really knew.

"There aren't many children in High Castle, are there?" said Patrick.

"Well, a lot of the servants are just kids," said Ellen.

"We don't have to talk to them."

"We don't have to talk to these either."

"I wonder if we're supposed to know them," said Patrick.

Laura went back a way and settled herself onto a bench in an alcove where she could see out the doorway. Patrick and Ellen stayed where they were, arguing in low voices. Outside, suddenly, the sun came out and fell in a block over the strange children. They all had yellow hair, and the sun made them look exactly as children in a fairy tale should look.

They seemed to think the sun had spoiled their game. They craned their necks at the sky outside, shook their heads at one another, and began packing up their pieces in a wooden box. Patrick and Ellen, noticing this, moved off to one side and went on arguing. The strange children went by them without paying them any heed. Laura shrank back as they went past her, but they paid no attention to her either. She noticed that all of them looked a little like Matthew, and wondered if they were his.

She looked back at the doorway. She was beginning to get bored.

Ellen and Patrick came over to her.

"Who were those kids?" asked Ellen.

"Is Matthew married?" Laura asked her.

Patrick looked over their heads back into the noisy hall. "Hey, here comes—" he said, and stared.

Laura and Ellen turned around. Lord Randolph was coming toward them with a woman. She was a snaky lady with black hair. She wore a dress of deep red which showed exactly how snaky she was. She had her hands folded around Randolph's arm, and against the blue of his sleeve the ruby in the ring she wore gleamed as a cat's eye will when the light hits it just so. She was beautiful.

"Who's *that*?" said Laura.

They came up to the three children, and Randolph bowed as well as he could with the woman on his arm. She looked at them measuringly, not as if she were greeting them, but as if they were something she might want to hang on the wall.

"Good festival to you," said Randolph. He wore his circlet and his ring, and the jewels on the silver hilt of his dagger were those same blue ones. Laura wondered if he ever got tired of them.

"And to you," said Patrick.

Ellen was staring at the woman, not in a friendly way.

"Where is thy angry cousin?" Randolph asked Patrick.

"Benjamin said . . ." said Patrick, and stopped. Laura could almost see him remembering that Ted, however angry, was not his cousin here, but his brother.

"Should any of you see her," said Randolph, "tell her to ware Lord Andrew."

"She always does," said Patrick. Randolph laughed, but

the woman in red looked at Patrick as if she would have liked to step on him.

"Tell her to ware her temper, then," said Randolph. "He is baiting every magician in the place with his vain philosophy, hoping one will break the ban and disgrace the calling. Thy cousin hath a hasty temper. Let her look to't."

"Yes, my lord," said Patrick.

"And have a care thyself," Randolph added thoughtfully. The woman looked at him and at Patrick, surprised. "Forgo thy accustomed tricks," added Randolph, with a meaningful look Laura was at a loss to interpret.

Patrick seemed to understand it. He bowed. "I shall," he said.

Randolph smiled at all of them as the woman steered him away. "'Tis but a jest," she said in his ear, and the sound of her voice made the fine hairs stand up on the backs of their necks. Then she and Randolph were too far away to be heard.

Ellen sat down heavily on the bench. "Gah!" she said.

"He likes her," said Laura, staring after them.

"Well," said Patrick, "she is awfully pretty."

"Not really," said Ellen. "Not healthy pretty. She's like Spanish moss."

"Just because she hangs all over him," said Laura. She and Ellen looked at each other and laughed.

"But who *is* she?" said Laura again. "If she's with Randolph, she must be important, and I sure don't remember her."

"Wait until we can find out her name," said Patrick. "That might bring it back to you."

"I thought I recognized her voice," said Ellen.

"It sounded like Ruth doing the Demon Queen," said Patrick.

"Well, sort of. You don't suppose she is?"

"I doubt it."

Laura looked back at the doorway. The late sunlight still poured through it. Laura felt a desire to do something sensible, like swimming in the moat or playing with the dogs. Evenings always made her restless.

A shadow fell into the middle of the block of sunshine, and a man came slowly into the hall. He was rather short, and he wore a long blue cape. It was patched and stained and dusty. His boots were caked with dust. His hair was so dusty it looked gray. He wore a pack, as dusty as the rest of him. His back was bowed, his head down. Laura hoped he would go on by, but he paused just inside the hall, lifting his head and rubbing at his eyes.

Laura jerked upright, gaping. A shock went through her as if someone had put an ice cube down her back.

"Fence!" she shrieked, leaped up, bowled Ellen aside, and ran at him.

He laughed at her out of his filthy face and went down on one knee to meet her. "Gently, gently," he said, as she cannoned into him and a cloud of dust rose up. "I am a dusty carpet indeed, and moth-eaten too. You will ruin your dress and I shall topple." He hugged her anyway, and then pushed her back and looked at her. His smile vanished. "What hast thou been up to?"

Laura looked at the patched knee of his hose, disappointed almost to tears. She knew him as she had not known anyone else here, and he could take one look at her and see that she was not what she should be.

"Hey!" shouted a girl's voice behind her. "Mark! Fence is back! John!"

Boots clattered on the floor behind her, and the three children who had been playing in the doorway flung themselves upon Fence. Laura backed hastily out of the tangle to where Ellen and Patrick stood looking embarrassed.

"Nice work," said Patrick to Laura. "I didn't know you had it in you."

"You forgot to ask him if he'd brought you any presents," said Ellen, "but you were very good."

"Where's Randolph?" said Laura, looking back at the crowd. She found him by the color of his companion's dress. They were standing a little apart from the main crowd, holding each other's hand. Randolph had his back to Laura.

Laura began to jump up and down and wave. The woman in red shot her the meanest look Laura had ever seen. Randolph had not seen Laura jumping and waving, but he saw that look, and turned around. He looked as if he expected a dragon; his hand was on his dagger.

Laura pointed at Fence. Randolph stood quite still while all the expression went out of his face. Then he disengaged his other hand from the lady's and took a step. She caught his arm and spoke to him urgently. He shook his head, shook off her hand, and came running. Laura got out of his way.

Fence rose out of the strange children's embraces just in time. Randolph hurtled into him and swung him right around. They hugged each other briefly, hard. Laura, seeing Randolph's face over Fence's shoulder, was reminded of her mother's face when Ted finally arrived home three hours late, in the middle of the worst storm in eighteen years.

"My friend," said Randolph, letting go of Fence and regarding him soberly, "I had not thought to see thee again."

"Am I so late as that?"

"This is Midsummer's Eve."

Fence put a hand on his arm, but said nothing.

"Fence," said the strange girl, who still stood there with her companions, "what did you bring us?"

"Precious little," said Fence, ruefully. "I have been in the Dubious Hills." But he smiled at her.

"You could have brought a rock."

"Peace," said Randolph to the children. "He is weary. Plague him tomorrow."

They scowled briefly and then made off through the crowd.

"Come on," said Patrick to Laura and Ellen.

Fence looked around. "Not you," he said to the three of them. "I hope that you and Lord Randolph will sup with me."

"Thank you," said Patrick.

Laura poked him. "What about that snake woman?"

"Snake woman nothing," said Patrick. "Sir," he said to Fence, "what about Ruth?"

"Has she forsaken her calling, then?"

"What?"

"I hope you do not propose to wait your meal until midnight."

"He forgot," said Ellen. Patrick just looked glazed.

"Well," said Fence, "if the bolder of you would oblige us by telling the kitchen what we require, we will go before you and dust the dishes." He looked at Patrick and Laura as he said this.

"They won't pay any attention to us," said Laura. "They'll just think we want our dinner early."

"I'll go with them, Fence," said Randolph.

Fence looked at Ellen. Laura suddenly understood what was going on. She and Patrick were the bolder ones. Princess Ellen was shy, so Fence was sparing her the ordeal of going to the kitchen. Princess Ellen was shy for much the same reason that Prince Edward was: Ellen, like Ted, had had too much else to do to properly attend to her namesake.

Laura pulled a braid over her shoulder so she could chew on the ribbon. This would be awful, if Fence was going to be so considerate all the time. Ellen would hate being left out of things, and Laura would hate being put in them.

Ellen must have decided much the same thing, because she turned to Randolph. "Laurie's bruised her arm," she said, which was true, "and she shouldn't be carrying things," which was not.

"Patrick and I will do well enough," said Randolph.

So Laura and Ellen went off with Fence. It was not until they came to the corridor before Fence's tower, which now had sunlight pouring into it and looked nothing worse than dusty, that they remembered that there was something wrong with the stairs.

CHAPTER 12

FENCE produced a key and a cloud of dust from his sleeve.

"The door's not locked," said Ellen.

Fence was instantly still. "When was it not locked?"

"This morning."

Fence handed her the key. Laura saw that it, too, was silver, with a blue stone on the shaft. Fence bent and peered through the keyhole. "Did you go through the door, then?"

"Not very far," said Ellen. "The stairs went the wrong way."

Fence froze again; then he grinned. "I wonder. Hath Randolph played the fool again?"

"It didn't feel like Randolph," said Laura, and immediately felt foolish. But Fence seemed disposed to take her seriously.

"Was it cold?" he asked her, and she nodded. "Dear heaven," said Fence. He looked through the keyhole again. Then he took the key from Ellen and turned it in the lock. Then he tried the door, which, since he had just locked it, did not open. Then he unlocked it and pushed it open.

On the third step up, the beast gurgled at them. Laura leaped backward, squeaking. Fence laughed, but not at her.

"Is that yours?" Ellen asked him.

"No," said Fence.

"Told you," said Laura.

Fence looked at her over his shoulder. "You would know," he said, puzzling her.

"Whose is it if it's not yours?" said Ellen.

"This," said Fence, "is the best outcome of trying to reconcile rival magics."

"What's the worst?" said Ellen.

"You'll know soon enough," said Fence, shortly. He gurgled at the beast, and it coiled in upon itself, shrank to a trickle, and was gone.

Laura felt a little better about the beasts now that Fence had laughed at one, but much worse about the stairs having gone the wrong way this morning now that Fence had looked sober about it.

Fence put the key back in his sleeve and began to climb the steps, leaving drifts of dust in his wake. The steps themselves were quite clean, and there were no cobwebs. The walls were stained amber by the sunlight coming through the arrow slits. It was very warm, almost like summer. Laura and Ellen followed Fence.

Fence had the three top rooms of the tower. He lived in the third from the top, and slept in the second from the top, and did his stargazing and his magic at the very top. Fence was a white magician, but Laura had never liked to think about his magic. She and Ellen had discovered several years ago that reading old spells, which they had tried in order to give themselves an idea of what Fence actually did, made them nervous, and they had had to give it up. Laura and Ellen had, therefore, only the vaguest notion of what Fence did in the top room, but its presence brooded on them as they scrambled behind its owner.

They soon had something more tangible to worry them. Ellen had asked that there be two hundred and eight steps to

Fence's rooms, that being the number of steps, she said, to Merlyn's tower at Camelot. Patrick said that he was not sure you could build a tower that high without modern methods, but he had been overruled. It seemed that he had also been wrong. If there were not two hundred and eight steps to Fence's rooms, Laura thought, wiping sweat from her forehead onto the green velvet of her sleeve and looking at Ellen's sweat-damp muslin back ahead of her, it was only because there were three hundred, or five hundred. She started counting steps after they had gone around a few curves and it had become evident that they were nowhere near the end. She gave up at one hundred and nine; it was enough trouble just breathing.

She was almost desperate enough to say something when Fence stopped and turned around to wait for them.

"I cry you mercy," he said. "I am very weary. You may take the key on ahead." He looked at them and grinned. "I see," he said, and sat down on a step next to an arrow slit.

"You've been gone a *long* time," Ellen told him, testily "And there aren't this many steps anywhere else." Ellen prided herself on being able to keep up with Ted or Ruth even though they were bigger; Fence's grin must have irked her.

Her speech did not seem to irk Fence, but it certainly startled him. "Hast learned courage, then?" he asked her.

Laura's stomach sank. She had been gladder to see Fence than she had ever been to see anyone. He might as well have been the person she loved best in the world. And now he looked to be more trouble than all the rest of them put together.

"Well," said Ellen, "you've been gone a long time."

"Longer for me than for you," said Fence. He leaned his head on the stone wall and shut his eyes. Laura looked at him, and wondered if he was supposed to be that thin, and how old he was. She had thought he was older than Randolph, but he looked more like a young person who has had a hard time. She looked at Ellen, who shook her head and grinned.

"Two hundred and eight steps," said Ellen.

Fence's eyes jerked open. They were green, like Ellen's. Laura wondered whether, under all the dust, his hair was like Ellen's too. She had not thought that Fence was related to anyone in High Castle. He came from outside.

"How know'st thou that number?" Fence demanded of Ellen.

Ellen looked at Laura, who stared helplessly back. "I counted them?" said Ellen as if she were proposing the idea for consideration.

"How many times?"

"Isn't once enough?"

Fence laughed, as if in spite of himself. "Hast been studying sorcery?"

"No," said Ellen.

"Thou?" said Fence to Laura.

"No."

"Perhaps you ought," said Fence, and stood up. Laura sneezed.

The door to Fence's living chamber was carved like the door to the tower stairs, except that in the place of the jagged hole there was a perfectly round piece, surrounded with rays, like a sun. Laura and Ellen looked at each other. Fence unlocked the door with a plain key.

Fence's living room had seven narrow windows, a bearskin on the floor, tapestries on the walls, a few carved chests and a plain table and chairs, all of dark wood, and a fireplace across from the door. It was disappointingly normal. Laura supposed that the interesting things were in the top room, and once she thought of it its weight settled over her spirits again.

Fence stood in the middle of the room with his head tilted, as if he were sniffing or listening for something.

"All seems well here," he said, and made a sign in the air with his hand. The logs in the fireplace sprang into flame, and three lamps sputtered and burned bright. Laura jumped. This was much more startling than the blazing of their magic swords, because Fence had made so little fuss about it.

"You may set the table, if you will," he said to them, and unlocking yet another door, a plain one this time, he took another flight of stairs up. Dust drifted through the air where he had stood, and Laura sneezed again.

"You'd think," said Ellen grumpily, "that if he can light a fire just like that, he could keep the dust off," and Laura knew that she had been startled too.

Only one of the chests opened, and the dishes were in it. They were thick, glazed, and white, with a colored border of great intricacy. Laura squinted at the border of a plate as she carried it to the table; they were too heavy to carry more than one at a time.

"Ellie!" she said, caught her foot on the edge of the bearskin, and let go of the plate. It landed on the stone floor with an enormous musical crack and broke into six pieces.

"Hell," said Laura.

"What made you do that?"

"I was looking at the border."

"While you were carrying it?"

"I *noticed*," said Laura, upon the verge of tears, "that it's like that tapestry again."

"Huh," said Ellen. "Does it have the sun or the hole?"

"The sun," said Laura. "Fence'll kill me."

"I bet he can fix it."

Ellen was finishing the table, and Laura was still crouched over the broken plate to see whether it might be mended, when Fence came back.

He did not look like Ellen after all. He had the same coloring, but his face was rounder, his nose shorter, and his hair both shorter and much straighter. It was still damp, and it looked as if he had cut it himself in the dark.

Laura gaped at him, however, not because of how he looked but because of what he was wearing. He had put on black robes embroidered with stars and comets and constellations and galaxies and universes. They were every color you could think of, and they drew your eye into themselves until you had forgotten what you were looking at and wandered lost in glory.

Laura, who was nervous enough when she did know what she was looking at, jerked suddenly back from these marvels and discovered that she had cut her finger on the broken plate.

"Dear heaven," said Fence. "What an omen. Clear we it up, child, before Randolph sees it. He will conceive that it spells his doom and commit some rash act."

It was impossible to tell from his tone if he was joking. Laura put the cut finger in her mouth and gingerly began to stack the jagged pieces. "Can't we fix it?"

Fence, moving in a swirl of fire and darkness, came across the room to look, and Ellen blinked and dropped a cup onto the bearskin.

Laura glared at her. "How come you're so lucky?"

"Clean living," said Ellen, staring at Fence.

Fence knelt beside Laura, gathering his robes out of the way, and inspected the remains of the plate. He smelled faintly of burning leaves. Laura wondered if it was the robes.

"I think not," said Fence after a moment. "The pattern is broken here, you see." He put a finger on a cracked border, where the stylized sun from which the animals fled was split across its center. He took the pieces upstairs with him and came back with a broom for Laura.

She knocked two mugs from the table with its handle, but neither of them broke. Fence favored her with precisely the same look Patrick had given her when she tripped on the bridge. That Fence had far more right to give it did not make it any easier to stand up under.

Fence gave them some mulled wine. Laura did not think it tasted as good as it had smelled when he was heating it, but it was better than cold wine. Ellen gulped it as if it were hot chocolate, and grinned at Laura. The firelight made her look a little wild.

When they heard footsteps on the stairs, Fence stood up from the hearth like a flurry of fireworks, and there was a dagger in his hand. It was silver, with the blue stones. He did not put it away until Randolph and Patrick had come in, set down their burdens, and closed the door behind them.

"*You,*" said Patrick to Ellen and Laura, "can carry what's left back down." He sat on the floor and breathed.

"You need not have brought so much," said Fence.

"Children have great appetites, and thou art half starved," Randolph told him.

"Not starved," said Fence. "Say rather, burnt away."

Their eyes met across the sparkling table, and held. Laura stared at them, fascinated. Randolph looked like a cat which is seeing things that aren't there. Fence looked like someone who has been sick for a long time.

"Didst thou lock the stairway door?" Fence asked Randolph.

"Aye."

"Hath any other the key to't?"

"What?"

"'Twas unlocked when I came to't. These say 'twas so this morning."

"Three demons," said Randolph, abstractedly. He pushed a hand through his hair, righted the circlet again, and scowled. "Well, sit we down regardless. Our wits will not suffer from food, and thine of a certainty suffer for its lack—nay, say not again. I know the look of magic, and I know the look of hunger."

He began pulling things from the hampers and thumping them down upon the table. He seemed nervous to the edge of irritation. Fence came around the table and sat down at the end of it.

"Fence," said Randolph, "I prithee, set not thy back to the door."

"There speaks the warrior," said Fence, and smiled at him.

"Oh, no," said Randolph, "here speaketh the wizard. I never feared what might come through a door till thou hadst me in thy keeping."

Fence smiled again, and stayed where he was. Randolph jerked his head at the children and sat down at the other end of the table. Laura sat on Fence's right, Ellen on his left. Patrick sat between Laura and Randolph.

Laura, as usual, found one or two things she liked and one or two she could stand, and ate a great deal of them. She noticed that Fence ate steadily, but not as if he were interested, and that Randolph ate almost nothing. His gaze slid about the room, always returning to the door behind

Fence. Patrick and Ellen ate a great deal of everything and got very sticky.

About halfway through the meal, Fence spoke over the crackle of the fire and the sound of crunching.

"What is the temper of the court?" he asked.

"Uncertain," said Randolph.

Fence looked at Laura, who said what she had been wanting to say for some time. "Who was that snake lady?"

Randolph laughed. "Well put," he said. "She is the Lady Claudia, sister to Lord Andrew. I had thought thou knew'st her."

"Well, I've seen her," said Laura.

Fence looked at Randolph. "What did she want with thee?"

Randolph looked back at him amused.

"Apart from the obvious," said Fence.

Laura nearly dropped her knife. She wondered when one of them would say, "Not in front of the children." This was clearly one of the conversations in which that would be said just as you began to understand what they were talking about.

"Well," said Randolph, "she wants that, when the time comes, I should vote with her brother on the matter of dragons."

Laura, seeing the conversation drift of itself away from intriguing subjects, leaned over to Patrick and whispered, "Do you remember any Lady Claudia?"

"Shut up," said Patrick, quietly but forcefully.

"Vote!" said Fence, scornfully. "The council is an advisory body, no more. What needs the King thy vote, or any man's? A wilt do as a wilt."

"So I told Claudia."

"And?"

"Still she stayed."

Fence grinned, and Laura's ears pricked up.

"No," said Randolph. "Do not flatter me. Still she seeks to persuade me that her brother hath the right of it; not for my vote, but for that she thinks I have the King's ear."

"Doesn't he?" said Laura to Patrick.

"She?" said Fence. "She? She knows better than any the power of magic."

"She knows nothing of it," said Randolph, staring; "she thinks it a matter for fools and children."

"And so she should," said Fence, "if thou, a magician, hast believed she thinketh so."

"What?"

Fence stood up, staring in his turn. "Do you not know?" he said. "She was my apprentice, and she failed."

Nobody moved, and the fire hissed. Randolph was looking at Fence as if he thought Fence was crazy. "No," he said, as if Fence had given him the wrong answer to a problem in arithmetic. Fence looked at him. "When?" said Randolph.

"Four summers ago."

"And where was I?"

"Feren," said Fence. Laura had never heard the name before, but it seemed to satisfy Randolph.

"Why did not the court buzz with it on my return?"

"Claudia is a secretive child," said Fence. Laura blinked; Fence looked closer to being a child than Claudia had.

"Well," said Randolph.

Fence pushed his chair back and went to the hearth for more wine. Randolph looked into his own cup, shook his head, and put his hand to his forehead. The stone in his ring caught the firelight and dazzled Laura's eyes. Vague shapes fled across her vision, purple and white and green. Looming over them all like a monstrous setting sun was the face of

Claudia. Laura realized that it was the same face she had seen in the sword when they roasted marshmallows by the Well of the White Witch. She blinked, and the sight was gone. Fence was sitting down again, and Randolph had picked up his cup.

"Perhaps we should speak of this later," said Fence to Randolph, and Laura sighed.

"No doubt," said Randolph. "Matthew hath manuscripts of Shan which need thy skill, and thou hast not yet spoken to thy spies."

He smiled at Laura, who felt a qualm. Across the table she saw Ellen's eyes get big.

"I thought to feed them first," said Fence. He looked at their empty plates, and Laura stifled an urge to grab the nearest food and start gnawing. She was afraid she knew what was coming.

"Who shall begin?" said Fence. "Ellen?"

There was a pounding on the door.

"Oh, come *on*," said Ellen. Laura jumped. Patrick picked up his knife and looked grim. Randolph leaped up, jarring the table and spilling his wine exactly as Laura would have if she had jumped up. His dagger was in his hand.

Fence stood up slowly and went to the door, holding his hands a little out from his sides as if he were doing a balancing act. "Who goes there?"

"The King commands your presence," said a voice, loud but a little breathless.

Fence's hands fell to his sides. He shrugged. Then he opened the door. Lord Andrew stood there. He was flushed from his climb, but he seemed pleased. What *now,* thought Laura.

"When do lords run errands?" Fence asked him. Laura knew that this was half of a proverb, or riddle, or something of the sort, but Andrew did not seem to know it. It would be just like Andrew not to.

"I do the King's will," he said.

Andrew looked over Fence's shoulder at Ellen, and at Laura, and at Patrick. Laura felt like a spilled ashtray. Then Andrew looked at Randolph. "Strange company, my lord," he said.

" 'Tis strange to thee," said Randolph.

"Where doth the King await me?" Fence asked Andrew.

Andrew looked at him as if he had forgotten who he was. Then he smiled. "In the Council Chamber," he said.

"I will attend him with what dispatch I may command," said Fence.

"Thou wilt come with me."

"I will not come with you," said Fence, and shut the door on him. Laura giggled.

"This is not a jest," said Randolph. "Fence, let me come with you. It is far more likely that there is a trap on the stairs than that the King awaits you in the Council Chamber."

"He doesn't even know you're here," added Ellen. "Those kids could've told—" said Patrick

"Or Claudia," said Randolph. "Marjorie and her brothers will not speak to the King at banquet, but Claudia—"

"They'll have told their father," said Fence.

"Matthew will let you announce yourself when you will."

"True," said Fence. He picked up his mug and finished his wine. "Have we a look, then."

He went to one of the chests Laura and Ellen had not been able to open, and took out of it a round mirror. The wooden frame was carved with a scene that Laura expected even before she recognized it. Fence came to where Randolph still stood with his dagger drawn, and each of them took a side of the mirror. They looked into it, frowning a little.

Laura, with no compunction, came around behind them and peered between them at the mirror. It did not reflect them, or her. It held an empty stone staircase dimly lit with purple light. Fence tilted the mirror a bit. The scene in it swirled in on itself as the purple beast had done, and then swirled out again. It looked the same, except that there was an arrow slit in the wall. It had grown dark outside, and one star shone through the arrow slit.

Fence and Randolph followed the stairs down to the bottom and back up again. Laura grew bored. Ellen put her head on the table and fell asleep. Patrick watched Randolph.

"So," said Fence, and laid the mirror on Randolph's chair. "Better you stay here with these."

"Fence," said Randolph, shifting his grip upon his dagger, "I beg you to do me the honor of remembering that I am not a fool. Then consider that this Claudia has been by me night and day these three months, and I never divined what she was. Then consider that Andrew is her brother."

Fence let his breath out. "And what of my spies?"

Laura backed away a few steps.

"They will be safest here," said Randolph.

Fence rounded on Laura. "Lock the door behind us," he said to her, fiercely, "and abide till I come, or Randolph, or Benjamin."

Fence went to the door, Randolph right behind him. Fence looked at him, and shrugged, and stepped aside. Randolph, still holding the dagger, went down the stairs, Fence behind him. Laura, hurrying to shut and bar the door, saw that Fence was not holding up the skirts of his robe; they seemed to be getting out of his way by themselves. Laura pushed the door closed and slid the bolt home.

"Wake Ellen up," said Patrick as she came back to the table. "I want to know what's going on."

They heard a faint sound from the stairway, perhaps the echo of the echo of a voice, and then the clash of metal. Patrick and Laura flung themselves at the door, dragged the bolt free, and pushed the door open.

Laura ducked under Patrick's arm and ran down the stairs. She got safely around two turns of the spiral, but then she tripped and went rolling around the next. She cracked an elbow on the wall as she went by, scraped both hands in an effort to stop herself, and brought herself up suddenly and painfully against Randolph's legs. Randolph plucked her off the step as if she were a wet sock, turned them both around, and sat her down at his feet. He still had his dagger out.

Fence was standing two steps down from Laura and Randolph, with his back to them. Both hands were buried in the folds of his robe, end his head was bent. Facing him, two more steps lower, was Claudia. She had a knife in her hand, but she had let the hand fall to her side, and she stared at Fence with eyes so wide and empty that she did not seem to be there at all.

Patrick came clattering around the turn with Ellen behind him. Randolph put his dagger back into its sheath and thrust his arm in front of them to keep them from falling over Laura. Laura risked a glance at his face; the look he gave them was eloquent of many things, all of them unpleasant.

"Randolph," said Fence, without turning around.

"Well?" said Randolph.

"This is a most powerful sorcerer."

Laura felt Randolph stiffen. "If she failed with thee," he said, "who hath taught her?"

"She herself," said Fence.

Randolph said something explosive and unintelligible.

"Keep thy dagger to hand," said Fence, and took hold of Claudia's wrist.

She did not move. Fence pried the knife out of her hand and held it up to Randolph without looking around. Laura's eyes winced away from it. It was twisted. The hilt held two red stones and one blue. The colors were quite clear in the dim light.

"And she hath fashioned this," said Randolph, holding it as if it were sticky.

"We will hope so," said Fence. "If another did so then we have two of them to deal with."

Laura knew she should keep quiet, but she was too curious. "What'd you do to her?"

"I entranced her," said Fence, shortly, in what Laura recognized as an adult I-dare-you-to-make-a-joke-out-of-that voice. She could not think what the joke would be anyway.

It seemed that Randolph could. "And will it endure so long as the spell she held me under?"

"No," said Fence. "I think we must have Ruth."

"*Ruth?*" said Laura, appalled.

"'Twill wait on the ending of her ceremony," said Randolph, luckily misunderstanding her. Fence, however, finally turned around, and looked at her sharply, as if he wondered what she knew.

"That is still two hours off," was all he said.

"The interim is ours," said Randolph.

Fence's mouth quirked, and then he grinned. "Wherein," he said, "we may finish the wine, and I may hear from my spies." Laura and Ellen looked at each other. "And thou, my apprentice," said Fence to Randolph, "shalt tell me all strange wonders that befell thee."

"And swear," said Laura and Ellen, looking at each other and taking the dare, "nowhere lives a woman true, and fair."

"Go along with you," said Randolph, pulling Laura's braids.

"Are we going to *leave* her there?" asked Laura.

"She will be safe," said Fence. "She has taken the road back, but 'tis a long way out of the simplest of these spells, and I have put that in her way which will make her wonder if 'twere not better she stay where she is." He sounded a little grim, and quite pleased. Laura looked at his pleasant round face, and shivered.

Randolph looked at him, too, but he did not shiver. "Thou art better suited to these matters than I had thought," he said.

"Never doubt it," said Fence. "Now come your ways," he said to all of them.

They trooped upstairs, laughing. But Laura could not help looking over her shoulder at where the stiff form of Claudia stared. The red stone of her ring caught the purple torchlight and made a color which almost hurt. Laura turned from it and hurried after the others.

CHAPTER 13

TED did not have a pleasant evening. He trailed around after the King, who seemed to be pursuing some plan. The King would look around the bewildering shift of gold and velvet and jeweled daggers and laughing faces and flying hair, until he spotted someone he wanted. Then he would pounce.

He talked to some people about their children, to some about their dogs. He talked to one, whom Ted would dearly have loved to talk to himself, about a sword he was making, and to some about why the falcons were not eating. He asked where the six dozen nails he had ordered from the dwarves had gotten to, and why it would be as bad to oil the hinges of the Old South Door as it would have been to mend the break.

If these had been random conversations Ted might have enjoyed them. But the King so clearly had a list in his mind of what he had to do. Three or four times Ted saw him avoid someone whom he later sought out. Ted tried to amuse himself by deciding why it was important to discuss the goats in the north pasture before one found out about the dwarfish nails, but the music was giving him a headache. He liked loud music, but this was so hollow and shrill that it hurt.

He was also disturbed because they saw nobody he knew. Not only had his sister and his cousins vanished, but Benjamin, having delivered him to the King, disappeared as well, and he could not see Randolph or Matthew or anyone else he recognized. He also felt that he should keep an eye out for Fence and warn him about that staircase.

He was much too harried to be hungry, but it was a relief to sit down and be quiet. The music stopped for dinner. He had to sit on the King's right, and the King, having finished whatever he had been doing earlier, paid Ted more attention than Ted liked.

Lord Andrew sat on the King's left, and Matthew sat next to Andrew, and Conrad next to Ted; they all courteously refrained from interrupting the King's conversation with his son. Andrew was plainly listening to it, but Ted was not sure that an interruption from Andrew would have been much relief anyway. Conrad was arguing about recorder music with the man beside him, and Matthew talked earnestly to a thin young woman with yellow braids and a scarred forehead. There was no help there.

Having remarked on all the earlier conversations and asked after Ted's studies, and noticed that Ted was not eating, the King looked as if something had dawned on him.

"Thy duties sit ill on thee at festival," he said. "But I release thee now. Thou shalt dance as thou wilt after dinner."

"Dance?" said Ted, horrified. That was no escape.

"Thou wilt not?"

"No, sir; thank you, but no."

The King raised his eyebrows in a way that made Ted wish he were elsewhere. "I wager thou'lt dance after midnight."

"Sir?"

"Not then neither?"

"Sir, I'd rather not at all." Surely shy Edward didn't like dancing. He was probably terrified of girls.

The King put a finger on the tip of Ted's nose; this was so bizarre that it was not even embarrassing. "Spite not thy face," said the King, lightly enough, but Ted felt sure that he had been given a warning, without having the remotest idea of what he had been warned against.

The King turned to Andrew and asked after his sister, and Ted tried to figure out the silverware so he could eat. Normally in High Castle you used your dagger and your fingers, and there were wooden spoons for soup or porridge. But this table was set with enough silver for a family of four at each plate. That the handles of the utensils were all made in the shapes of animals' heads did not make up for there being so many utensils.

He managed to feed himself fairly well by watching what Matthew served himself and how he ate it, and doing likewise. He had begun by copying the yellow-haired woman, but she kept serving herself things he didn't like.

Ted was watching Matthew dismember some complicated shellfish and talk to Conrad at the same time, when Matthew dropped his fork with a clatter and straightened, looking with some alarm down toward the other end of the table. As Ted looked that way, he caught with the corner of his eye the expression on the face of the yellow-haired woman. It was ferocious.

The cause of all this was a dark and slender woman in a red dress. She came rapidly up Ted's side of the table; Ted thought she moved like an otter. She was beautiful, but she looked murderous. The closer she got, the less Ted liked her. She looked important, but he did not recognize her. She passed behind Ted's chair with a flurry that lifted the damp hair on his neck, and stood at the King's elbow.

"Sire," she said. Ted wondered if she had a sore throat.

The King looked at her as if he had not expected her and didn't want her. "Lady Claudia?" he said.

"Sire, Fence has returned."

Ted shot out of his chair, jarring the table and spilling his wine. Matthew had half risen, his face exultant, but when Ted's wine slopped into his plate he sat down abruptly. The yellow-haired woman said something quiet but urgent into his ear, and Matthew tried to give Ted a quelling frown. Ted beamed at him. He could not help it. If Fence had come home on schedule, maybe everything would still be all right.

The King, too, looked as if he thought everything would be all right. He got carefully to his feet, and his look at Claudia became more gracious. "I thank you, child," he said. "Where is he? He shall not face this crowd; I will go to meet him."

Claudia appeared distressed and reluctant, but Ted thought that she did not mean it. She was not much like an otter after all; she was grim, not playful.

"Sire," she said, "Fence and my lord Randolph have gone to Fence's chambers."

Ted hated the way she said "my lord Randolph." She sounded as if he belonged to her and as if he had somehow done her an injury. If she had the right to talk about Randolph like that, thought Ted, I'd know who she was.

The King frowned. "Sent he greetings, then?"

"Sire, he did not speak to me nor I to him. I did see him enter and greet Randolph and depart." She shrugged.

So how'd you know where they were going? thought Ted. The yellow-haired woman still looked ferocious, and Ted was beginning to feel the same way.

The King's brows drew together. Before he could speak, Andrew appeared at his other elbow. Ted had not even seen him get up, and was startled.

"Shall I fetch him out, my lord?" said Andrew.

"He's not a weasel!" burst out Ted. He had no idea what was going on, but Claudia and Andrew seemed to be getting away with something, and Ted saw no reason to let them. This was the worst departure from the Secret story yet, and it seemed to be Claudia's doing. Ted felt as if she had insulted him.

"Edward," said the King, gently, and turned back to Andrew.

"He is long overdue," said Andrew, "and his tidings are most needful. Should not we call a council at once?"

"In the middle of a *banquet?*" said Ted.

"Edward," said the King, less gently. He added, with a sort of icy indulgence, "Thou needst not attend."

Ted's face grew hot. Now he really had been insulted. "Of course I'll come, but what's the *point?*"

"Ted," said Matthew, not loudly.

"I won't be quiet!" cried Ted. The disappointment of his earlier exultance made him reckless. He was determined to shove this story back on its proper course. "*He*," said Ted, scowling in the direction of Andrew, who was regarding him with an amusement that Ted might have found disquieting if he had been in any state to think about it, "is just trying to make trouble, anybody can see that. You know Fence always has a good reason for what he does, you know it, Father. He'd have come to you in his own time. Who's *she*," and he scowled at Claudia, who did not look at all amused, "to come sneaking to tell you he's here before he's ready to see you?"

"Does the King serve Fence, or Fence the King?" said Claudia, more huskily than ever. Ted hoped she had strep.

"Who are *you* to say?" he demanded.

"Edward, I pray you be quiet," said Matthew. He sounded as if he were really saying something else, which Ted should be able to figure out.

"Let him shriek," said Andrew pleasantly. "His is the visage of a prince on the soul of a beggar."

Ted, in an excess of temper even worse than that in which he had once thrown an egg at Laura, launched himself across the table at Lord Andrew. Andrew was either unprepared for this or a slow thinker, for he was knocked sprawling. Ted had the breath struck out of him by the edge of the table, and he slid sideways to the floor at Matthew's feet, soaked with wine and gravy, plastered with squashed shellfish and burst pasties, the echo of broken glass jarring his ears.

There was dead silence. Ted could not believe what he had done. Andrew picked himself up, drew his dagger, and advanced on Ted, all with a calm deliberation that was worse than anger would have been.

"Andrew," said Matthew, "put up thy knife."

Ted sat up against his knees. He was still breathless, still dizzy, and still furious. Andrew took another step. "You would!" said Ted, trying to stand up. He had started this and he saw no way out of it, so he might as well go on. Matthew slid both hands under his arms and picked him up. Ted had to lean on him.

"Young fool," breathed Matthew in his ear. "Where's thy dagger?"

He thrust Ted to one side and put a hand to his own knife. The yellow-haired woman got to her feet with one quiet motion, pushing her chair back onto Ted's feet. He got out of her way; she still looked ferocious and she had a knife too.

Andrew stopped. "Do you not know a jest?" he said to Matthew. He smiled a smile that made Ted shiver and Matthew stiffen. Andrew looked as if he had gotten what he wanted.

Ted had enough breath and wit back now to remember the King. The King held out his hand to Andrew, who lifted his chin with a defiant glance, and handed the King his dagger.

"Here's mine, my lord," said Matthew.

"Thou didst not draw," said the King.

"I so intended."

"Thou didst not," said the King. He looked at Ted, who immediately felt sticky inside as well as out. "Nor," said the King, "didst thou."

There did not seem to be much to say to this, especially when Ted was not sure if drawing was a good thing or a bad. He settled for bowing his head. The King waited. Ted did not think that explaining that he had no dagger to draw would improve matters. There was still dead silence in the hall. It was eerie that so many people who had been so noisy could be made so quiet so quickly. The King waited. Ted found himself lifting his chin in a gesture much like Andrew's.

"I'll speak to thee later," said the King, saving him from whatever he might have found to say. The King looked around, and Ted realized that all the serving people had vanished. "Lord Andrew," said the King, "summon Fence to the Council Chamber. Lord Matthew, be so good as to find my other counselors. Lady Claudia, we thank you for your trouble and would that you attend also."

Andrew bowed and departed. Matthew squeezed Ted's shoulder, said, "As you will, my lord," and went out after him. The King, without a glance at Ted, moved slowly for the door. Ted, sinking gratefully into Matthew's chair, found time to wonder where Benjamin was. He shoved his matted hair out of his eyes. Conversation was starting again at the other end of the hall, and he preferred to escape quietly after people's attention was elsewhere.

That did leave the attention of the people at his end of the table to deal with. They could hardly pretend to eat their dinner: He had squashed it. The table before him was a crazy quilt of broken glass, puddles of wine, and flattened food. He had ruined his own place, Matthew's, the King's, Conrad's, and the yellow-haired woman's. Well, things could be worse. At least no one was saying, "Move down, I want a clean plate." Ted saw that some of the serving people were creeping out again, and he waved a hand at one of them and held his breath.

The young man came over to him promptly enough. He looked, not frightened at all, but as if he were trying not to laugh. Ted gestured at the mess on the table and raised his eyebrows as the King did. This seemed to be enough. The young man said, "Yes, my prince," and beckoned to several other people, to whom he gave orders.

"Well," said Ted. "I regret very much having subjected you to all this." His mother had once said that to someone whose tulips Laura had fallen into. He hoped that it would sound sorry but not too abject, and would somehow imply that he had had no choice in the matter. "Is anyone's dress damaged?"

Conrad, to his grateful astonishment, grinned at him. "Ah, lad, I'll give myself more wine splashings than thou couldst, didst thou crack a bottle o'er my head."

Several people sitting nearby laughed as if this were an

old joke, so Ted smiled too. He looked at the yellow-haired woman. "My lady?"

"Never fear," she said. She spoke as if she knew him well. He wondered who she was.

"I'll take my leave of you, then," said Ted, and fled the hall. The musicians began hooting and burbling on their instruments as he went, and he felt that his own story was laughing at him.

He went up to his room and washed off the gravy.

He did not care to think about what he had done, or its possible consequences, just yet, so he worried about Claudia instead. Who in the world was she and what was she doing here? She was messing things up more than all the other differences put together. You'd almost think she was doing it on purpose. If she hadn't opened her big mouth, Fence would have presented himself properly in the morning, and the council would have been held that afternoon. Ted knew what to say in it, but he did not like having things upset this way.

Besides, in the game he and Fence had been supposed to have a long conversation after this banquet, and he had hoped, somewhere in the course of it, to find a way of warning Fence about Randolph, or at least of finding out what Fence would do if the King persisted in disbelieving in dragons. Ted was sure Fence could think of something more sensible than killing the King if he had more warning than the original story provided. If Ted could then tell Randolph this more sensible idea, then maybe things would be all right.

"You're as bad as Claudia," Ted said to himself, dropping his damp towel on the bed so Patrick could complain about it later. "Running around changing a perfectly good story."

He wandered over to the window and looked out. The

night was clear and warm for the first time since they had been here. He craned out the window. The stars were enormous, and in no patterns that he recognized. Far around the sound of bells still trembled.

"Except," said Ted, pulling his head in, "she wants to make trouble, and I don't."

He went down to the Council Chamber in a frame of mind only a little more cautious than that in which he had attacked Andrew; he took his dagger with him.

CHAPTER 14

L AURA last, they trooped back up to Fence's living room—
or maybe, thought Laura, it was a parlor—and sat down
again.

"Fence," said Randolph.

"Wait," said Fence. He looked at Laura until she dropped
her gaze to the cluttered table. She could feel him looking at
Ellen and Patrick, and she sneaked a glance sideways in time
to see Patrick drop his eyes too. So somebody somewhere
could stare Patrick down. Laura wished she could be gladder about it.

"Did I or did I not," said Fence, "tell you to stay here
with the door bolted? Do I or do I not know whereof I
speak touching sorcery? Did you or did you not all three
disobey?"

"But Fence," said Ellen, "we heard *metal!* It was fighting,
not sorcery."

Laura dared to look at him. He had a way of quirking one
corner of his mouth when most people would raise an eyebrow, and he was doing it now.

"And dost thou know more than I of fighting?" he said.

"In fighting, numbers matter," said Patrick.

"On the narrow stair?"

"Fence," said Randolph. Fence glared at him irritably
and then smiled. "Consider," said Randolph, "that it is I

who do teach Patrick to fight. Thou chastiseth the impulse when 'tis the judgment at fault."

Fence's mouth quirked. "Well, then, my lord," he said to Patrick, "come not so precipitate that thou overturnst thy friends. And thou," he said to Laura, "where was thy weapon wherewith thou couldst save me?"

"I bet I'd have scared her," said Laura, wanting to cry and forbidding herself to do so.

"And me," said Fence.

"*Fence,*" said Randolph.

Fence sighed. "I commend you all for your courage," he said. "But I most earnestly urge you to consider what help or hindrance you may be before you disobey me. An you disobey me in a matter of sorcery, we will all die miserably."

They all nodded. Fence got up and poured them more wine. When he got to Randolph, Randolph put a hand on his wrist and bore the jug down to the table. "Thou and I have work before us this night."

Fence looked at him.

"That Andrew summoned you and Claudia's knife awaited may not signify."

Fence frowned.

"If she had means to fashion that knife, could she not use the mirrors as well?"

Fence blanched. "No doubt. And as evilly as she made the knife."

"Fence, there was skill there."

"Oh, aye; there is skill also in slaying the unicorn."

"Well, then."

" 'Twere best to discover if the King indeed awaits me." Fence turned his wrist under Randolph's, moved his hand under Randolph's hand, and gripped it. "I would it were not so. I am very weary, and these"—he nodded at the children—"have not yet oped their coffers."

"Tell us quickly," said Randolph to Laura, who went cold all over and stammered.

"The worst is the staircase and the beast. There was a beast in the West Tower too."

"What besides sorcery?" said Fence.

In the horrible silence that followed, they heard the distant echo of footsteps. It drew nearer, and stopped suddenly, and a man's voice boomed up the stairwell. "Suffering stars!"

Randolph let go of Fence and stood up. The footsteps came rapidly up to the door and someone pounded on it. "Fence!"

"Who goes there?"

"Matthew."

Fence went and unbolted and opened the door. Matthew came in, breathing hard and staggering a little, and saw Randolph. "You are wanted at the King's council, and not by and by." He leaned on the wall and breathed for a moment. Then he took Fence by the shoulders and did not quite shake him. "My lord, you are most heartily welcome. For the mercy of Shan, what doth Claudia on your stair with such strange mien?"

"Fear not," said Fence, absently. "Randolph."

"More harm will be done by thy absence than by thy ignorance," said Randolph.

"Wait," said Matthew. "Randolph, thou at least must know that Edward hath—"

"Tell us as we go down," said Randolph, coming around the table.

He and Matthew started down the stairs. Fence looked

back at Ellen and Patrick and Laura. "Forgive this disarray," he said to them. "I pray you, stay here or leave word where I may find you. Find Ruth if you can." He turned in a swirl of stars and shut the door behind him.

Ellen and Patrick and Laura looked at one another. The dying fire murmured, and a mouse shot across the floor and vanished. Nobody even jumped.

"Talk about the nick of time," said Patrick.

"I wonder what Ted did," said Laura.

"Was he supposed to do anything?"

"Sometimes," said Ellen, "we've had him have a nasty scene with Randolph over Ruth. But Randolph was with us, and it looks like Ruth wasn't around anyway. Does anybody remember any ceremony of the Green Caves at this banquet? I think it's a dumb idea."

"I hope she's doing okay," said Laura, thinking what her own sensations would be if she were trapped into a strange ceremony.

"She's been reading all those books," said Ellen.

"Well," said Patrick, "what's important right now is to figure out what we're going to tell Fence. Who the hell decided we were his spies, anyway?"

"It's a good idea," said Ellen calmly. "Nobody notices kids. Look at all we've overheard tonight. We weren't *using* Princess Ellen and Laura hardly at all, or Patrick either. It seemed like a waste. I mean, you were Fence and I was pages and messengers and Laurie had to do the animal voices. So I made them—us—Fence's spies."

"Well," said Patrick, "what'll we tell Fence? We don't know anything, really."

"Well," said Ellen, "since it worked out all right—I said we were Fence's spies and sure enough we *are*—we should just tell him what I made up for us to tell him. It should be all right."

"Yeah, and what if it's not? Tell him we didn't find out anything. I think it would be refreshing to tell the truth for a change."

"No!" said Laura, surprising herself.

"Why not?"

Laura sloshed the wine around in her cup. Its faint sour smell came up to her, altered a little by the spices. She wished for a cup of cocoa.

"Fence'll be disappointed," she said.

"Who the hell cares?"

"Besides," said Laura, trying to think like Patrick, "what if he needs to know something Ellen made up?"

"If pigs had wings," said Patrick, bitterly, "they'd be pigeons."

"Come on," said Laura to Ellen. "Tell us what we should tell Fence."

Ted came breathlessly into the Council Chamber and was relieved to see that it was only half full. Benjamin was lighting torches. Claudia and Andrew stood together, speaking quietly. Matthew slumped in his chair, glowering at Claudia. The King sat straight. He wore the dark blue robe of the council. Ted, in his workaday tunic, felt the heart-stopping panic that usually came of forgetting his homework, until he realized that neither Benjamin nor Matthew had put on a council robe.

He made his way to his own chair and thumped into it gratefully. There was no telling what was going to happen, and the thought of all the things that might was making his knees uncertain.

Matthew looked over at him expectantly.

"I want to thank you," said Ted, realizing only as he said it just what he owed Matthew. "And I regret . . ." he added, and stopped. He was not sure what he regretted or whether he ought to admit it.

Matthew shook his head. "They say the ass is known by his ears."

That sounded insulting, but before Ted had decided what to do about it, Matthew added, "He who cannot keep a temper must temper a knife to keep him. Where have you kept so hot an anger these seventeen years?"

Ted, closing his mouth on his reaction to being seventeen, shook his head. He still wondered what was going on. The fault seemed to lie not in his having jumped at Andrew and broken a lot of valuable glassware, or even in disrupting a banquet, but in what he had not done with a knife he did not have. Surely they hadn't expected him to kill Andrew in the middle of a feast? Andrew had had to give his knife to the King, so drawing during a feast must be frowned upon. But the King had also seemed to frown upon Ted's not drawing. You the artistic type, Ted thought, and not drawing. Tsk. He almost giggled, and began to wonder seriously what was wrong with him tonight.

"For all our sakes," said Matthew, "curb thyself or find the means to curb others."

"Did I get you in trouble too?" What he means, thought Ted, is that you'd better decide whether you're Ted or Edward.

"By the letter, aye," said Matthew. "By the spirit, thou hast done me some good. Thy father is of too many minds to be altogether displeased by aught that may happen."

Benjamin passed behind them with his taper, and bent down to Ted. "What is this they babble of thee?"

"I lost my temper with Andrew," said Ted.

"Well and good. What is this mouthing of knives?"

"I didn't have one."

"Dear heaven," said Benjamin. "Thou unweaned whelp. Where have thy ears been?"

"I didn't expect to need it!"

Benjamin and Matthew exchanged a glance that made Ted apprehensive.

"And thou?" said Benjamin to Matthew.

Matthew shrugged. "A hand on the dagger suffices with Andrew."

Benjamin looked as if he had heard as much as he could take. "So he would have thee think. One day thou wilt so think and 'twill not be so. Shan's mercy, are we all children here?"

Matthew turned red. Benjamin, grumbling, went on lighting torches. The room had filled and quieted as they talked. Ted looked to see where they had put Claudia. She was in Randolph's place, on the King's right. Randolph was not to be seen.

"Hey!" said Ted, outraged, and turned to Matthew, who had jerked open a drawer in the table and was pulling out his pen and ink and parchment. Matthew looked up and froze.

"Where *is* Randolph?" said Ted.

Matthew slammed the drawer, and the King looked inquiringly in their direction.

"Off on some fool's errand," said Matthew, furiously. "This is a very midsummer madness upon all of us."

"Where's Fence?"

"Aiding Randolph in what he needs no aid to do."

Ted worked this out silently, and could not help grinning. The King rang a bell, and everyone still talking shut up.

"My lords," said the King. "We are met with ye this twenty-first day of June, in the forty-sixth year of our reign, the four hundred and ninetieth year since King John vanquished the Dragon King, that ye may hear the report of our most honored lord and sorcerer Fence and advise me touching it."

There was a pause, during which Ted leaned over to Matthew and whispered, "What's the use of starting a council because Fence is back, without Fence?"

The door to the room swung open, and Randolph strode in, followed by a shorter man in black robes. The robes were dotted with galaxies and nebulae, and in the dim light of the torches they drew Ted's eye like a hypnotist's crystal.

"That he might be late to't," said Matthew in Ted's ear.

Ted hardly heard him. The short man had moved so that Randolph could shut the door, and stood under a torch. He looked down the table and caught Ted's eye. Ted gasped and sat up. He felt as if he had gone from a stuffy room into subzero sunny weather. Neither was comfortable, but the outside was cleaner. If this were Fence, maybe he *could* make everything all right.

Randolph came to stand on the King's right, with Fence behind him like a shadow. Randolph, too, had not put on his counselor's robe.

"I crave pardon for my lateness," he said, and stopped. He had seen Claudia in his chair. She smiled at him, which made Ted shiver, and Randolph smiled back, which made Ted want to be somewhere else. Fence blanched, and then he scowled, and then he smiled too. He looked like someone who does not understand something but is very pleased by it anyway.

"My lord Benjamin," said Randolph, very gently, "I beg

to point out that there is an insufficiency of chairs in this chamber."

"My lord, there is," said Benjamin. "I was told that some would be absent and the visitors accommodated thereby." His glance at Andrew was withering. Andrew wore the "Who, me?" look of a cat asleep by a broken milk bottle.

Randolph bowed to Benjamin.

Benjamin said to the King, "By your leave, Sire."

The King nodded at Benjamin, who stood up and went out. As he passed the short man, he put a hand on his shoulder in a gesture that might have been to welcome or to move him aside. Fence took two steps out of his way, and the corner of his mouth quirked.

Then he looked at the King. "Will his Majesty receive my greeting?"

The King turned in his chair and held out a hand. Fence knelt and kissed it. Ted admired them both. He would have looked and felt foolish in either position, but they did it as a matter of course, the King elegantly and Fence simply; they did it as if they meant it, although it was clear that the King was angry with Fence and Fence with the King.

Randolph moved suddenly to open the door, and Benjamin came through it with a heavy wooden chair, like the others in the room, in each hand. He held them as if they were wine bottles. Randolph and Fence got out of his way. Benjamin, with no hesitation, set one chair on either side of the King, a little back from the table, and looked at Claudia. Randolph slid behind Fence and caught Benjamin's sleeve.

"My thanks to you," he said, and sat on the King's right, between Claudia and the King. Fence's mouth quirked again, and he came around Benjamin and behind the King to sit on the King's left. Benjamin rolled his eyes to the ceiling as if he were giving up on two children, and took his own seat.

"Randolph," said the King, "wherefore art thou late?"

Ted saw Fence turn his head and stare at the King. Randolph merely looked resigned. "Sire, I was but arranging to hold harmless Lady Claudia," and he bowed in her direction, "who tried to stab Fence on the stairs."

Ted almost fell out of his chair. The King simply became very still, as if he were listening for something. Andrew slammed his hand down on the table. "You're mad!"

The King looked toward Claudia, who sat very straight in Randolph's chair with her hands relaxed on its arms. She looked back at him gravely. Ted saw the way her hair fell over her neck, and found himself blaming Randolph a little less, even if she had tried to stab Fence on the stairs.

When she did not speak, the King looked back at Randolph. "Thou hast not succeeded?"

"It appears not, Your Majesty."

"Is this business more urgent than that which called us here?"

"Only," said Randolph dryly, "in that it puts the Lady Claudia's presence under most grave doubt."

The King hesitated. "Who brings the accusation?"

"I do," said Fence, so quietly that Ted could barely hear him. Everyone else's voice carried well. Ted wondered if Fence was unaccustomed to speaking in council. Fence puzzled him. Nobody who looked and acted so ordinary should be able to make one feel so—so effervescent.

"Who are thy witnesses?" said the King.

"Lord Randolph," said Fence. He paused, and just as Andrew's hand moved on the table he added, "Prince Patrick, Princess Laura, Princess Ellen."

Ted jerked upright and banged his knee on the table leg. How had they managed *that?* He saw Benjamin cover his eyes with one hand in a gesture of despair, and grinned. Four of the five of them had been in some sort of trouble this evening. He wondered where Ruth was.

"Children," said the King.

"Children have eyes, my lord," said Fence, rather sharply.

The King's eyebrows went up. "I said not otherwise, my lord."

"Your pardon," said Fence, tranquilly.

"Lady Claudia," said the King.

"Sire?" Ted hoped she had strep and pneumonia. "Answer you this accusation?"

"Not presently," said Claudia.

"Leave you then our council. Your honor hath been questioned. The witnesses thereto were better in their beds. Therefore, until you challenge and prove trusty, you are barred from our council and our person."

Ted was taken aback by the harshness of this speech. Claudia did not seem upset about it, which was only to be expected. No one else seemed surprised by it either, so perhaps the words were just a formality.

"Our lord Jerome," said the King.

A large, blond, gloomy man whom Ted did not recognize stood up. Claudia stood up too, and they both came to stand at the door.

"Take your privilege," said the King to Fence.

"My lord, I humbly thank you," said Fence, "but naught I can conceive may bind her. She must go whither she will."

Benjamin and Randolph grimaced at each other. The King looked mildly surprised, and fumed in his chair to speak to Jerome. "The South Tower, then," he said.

"Your Majesty," said Jerome. He took Claudia's arm. The door boomed shut behind them.

There was an extended silence, during which the King stared over Ted's left shoulder in a way that made Ted itch to look behind him, and nobody fidgeted. Ted saw that Fence kept his eyes on the King, in the manner of one who is watching the sky, waiting for a falling star. Randolph sat on the edge of his chair as if he were impatient to be out of it.

When the King stirred, it was to look at Randolph's empty seat. "Take thy place, Randolph," he said.

Fence's mouth quirked. Randolph did as he was told. The King turned to Fence.

"My lord, this council hath swollen since last you sat on't. For the present, you may take Jerome's seat."

Fence did so. This put him on Ted's left, two spots away. Matthew grinned at him, and he shook his head.

The King repeated the opening speech, and looked at Fence. "Will't please you to make your report."

"Good my lord, it will."

Fence stood up, somehow managing not to scrape his chair on the floor. He leaned the palms of his hands on the table and stood there, looking unconcerned.

"My lords, the Outside Powers are rising again," said he.

Ted grew cold. Their story had no Outside Powers in it; but the Riddle of Shan's Ring did. What if they had read it all wrong in their ignorance, and made this happen?

He had no idea what the announcement meant to the others, but nobody looked pleased. Their expressions filled the range between Benjamin, who looked as if he were going to faint, and Andrew, who looked as if the waiter had brought him the wrong order for the third time. To Ted's dismay, the King's expression was much closer to Andrew's than to Benjamin's.

"The scouts' reports you have already," said Fence. "Seeing with different eyes and a greater knowledge, I have found worse than they. The further south, the sharper the country; on our borders the Dragon King hath set a sword in every blade of grass. Many wizards I sought have vanished from the land. Those I found told me that all signs in heaven and earth spell disaster."

He pushed a piece of ill-cut hair off his forehead and continued. He was still speaking quietly, and a little dreamily, as if he were talking to himself. "There is a most precise correspondence between events in the south and what King John's Book tells us of the signs which foretold the coming of the Dragon King. Now the Dragon King is the yeast of the Outside Powers. But other signs I saw in the south, and in other books than John's are written tales of the greater powers and the signs that come before them."

Fence looked around the room and seemed displeased at the effect he was having. When he spoke again, it was in a language which, in the ten minutes he spoke it, drove Ted almost to distraction. Ted almost understood it. It was like trying to go to sleep while people were talking neither quite quietly nor quite loudly enough in the next room. All the words seemed slurred sideways. Ted had gotten used to the way people talked here, even Benjamin. This was worse than that, and different.

Several people, Andrew among them, seemed to be having trouble understanding Fence, but nobody looked as thoroughly baffled as Ted was. Randolph seemed delighted, and Benjamin recovered from his shock. The King was alert, but seemed to have no opinion.

Whatever Fence said just before he sat down seemed to please neither Benjamin nor Andrew nor the King. Both Benjamin and Andrew had their hands on the table. Fence bowed to the King, jangling Ted's eyes with stars, and sat down. The King looked from Andrew to Benjamin to Andrew.

"Our Lord Benjamin," he said.

"Your Majesty," said Benjamin, "break we up this council on the instant. What time was to lose we have lost already. We will need both soldier and sorcerer ere this is done. They will seek to break the Border Magic. They made it; if any can break it, 'tis they."

"My lord," said the King. "Our Lord Andrew."

"His Majesty knows my views."

Randolph put his hand down.

"Randolph?" said the King.

"Fence hath not heard these views," said Randolph, "and they concern him closely."

The King looked at Andrew, who nodded.

"We spoke then," said Andrew, "of the renegade wizards of the reign of King Nathan. It is my view that those were not villains, but honest men endeavoring to show forth the trickery of their fellows. It is my view that all wizardry is but trickery, and all spells but illusion. Of a certainty we have enemies to the south, but they are weak and mortal as we, and may be dealt with as such."

Ted watched Fence, who sat perfectly still and grew white. When Andrew had done, Fence stood up.

"Fence," said the King.

"Andrew," said Fence, "do you surmise, then, that these weak and mortal enemies to the south have plotted four hundred years that they might cozen us with this at last?"

"I do not."

"How, then, is it that their illusory spells match so precisely both King John's Book and other writings of sorcery which have never been out of wizards' hands?"

"One who knew such things," said Andrew, "had only to tell them."

Fence did not even blink. Randolph was looking at him as if awaiting a signal, but Fence still looked at Andrew. "Where is your proof?" he said at last.

"Of what?"

"I see," said Fence. He looked at the King.

"Andrew," said the King. "Will you not repeat that accusation you made a sennight ago?"

"I was o'er hasty," said Andrew. "Many could have given lore to the southerners."

"Many could not," said Fence, without permission. The King let him go on, as he had let Andrew earlier. "Many could have brought them the book of King John. But most few could have told these other things. I, and Belaparthalion, and Chryse. Hath Belaparthalion visited High Castle, Andrew? Hath Chryse lightened your doors?"

Ted had never heard either name, but the rest of the council seemed to find this funny. Only Randolph and Benjamin still looked grim. Andrew looked as if something were dawning on him and he was not sure he liked it.

"So," said Fence. "They have not come hither for King John's Book, and none other knoweth the other writings. Stands now your accusation in better state?"

"There is yet no proof save reason."

"Reason may prove aught," said Fence.

Andrew shrugged. "My opinion, my lord," he said, looking straight at Fence, "is that you are a fraud and a traitor. I have no proof thereof."

Ted found himself standing up.

"Edward," said the King. This could have been either a recognition or a warning. Ted chose to take it as the former.

"Isn't it written," he said, "that he who makes an accusation without proof makes himself what he accused his enemy of? Is it not treacherous of Andrew to tie us so in doubt that we can neither prove nor disprove him and thus neither take nor spurn his advice?"

There was a profound silence. Benjamin had his hands over his eyes again. Fence was shaking his head slowly, but did not seem displeased. Randolph was astonished. Ted wondered if he had stolen Randolph's speech, and whether Randolph would have delivered it better. Matthew tugged gently on Ted's sleeve and made him sit down. The King was furious; he looked as if he were counting to ten and finding it insufficient. Andrew looked blank. Ted thought that the King should have been blank and Andrew furious. He still felt a tiny prick of outrage at this, as if his cousins had played their parts wrong.

The King opened his mouth, and Fence stood up again. The King said, "Fence," as if he were not sure how to pronounce it.

Fence looked from Ted to Andrew, and grinned. His grin was not infectious like Randolph's, but it was reassuring. "My lord," he said to the King, "will you have both of us, or neither?"

The King cocked his head. "Send you to join Claudia, or have you wrangling at my every council and have no peace withal?"

"Nor no wisdom neither?" said Fence.

"I protest!" said Randolph, slapping the table; he was laughing.

So were others. Ted turned and stared at Matthew, who was chuckling as he wrote. The entire council had turned benign, as if it were a snarling cat upon which Fence and Randolph had dumped catnip. Ted wondered how they had done it. He looked at the King, who was smiling faintly, and gave up.

"We will hear no more accusations," said the King. "But we will hear all your philosophy now, our Lord Andrew, for Fence is here to answer you."

Matthew eased the drawer open and got himself a new pen, and Ted tried to settle comfortably into his chair. A cold wind sifted through the chamber, and the argument began.

CHAPTER 15

IN Fence's living room the fire had burned low, and none of them could find the wood to build it up. It was past midnight, and growing cold again. Laura and Ellen and Patrick sat at the far end of the table, keeping a wary eye on the door, and rehearsed their parts.

"*Why,*" demanded Laura, "should Fence care that Prudence has been hiding bread in the West Tower? And who's Prudence?"

"Oh, he doesn't," said Ellen, poking her finger into a dish of jam and then licking the finger. "But it's not our job to decide what's important. We just tell him things." She reached for the jam again.

"Don't put your finger in there after you've licked it," Patrick told her.

Ellen stuck her thumb in and licked that.

"You'll get fatter than me," said Laura.

"You're not fat."

"Claudia makes me feel fat."

"Claudia's a weasel."

"Ellie," said Patrick, "did you really not make her up?"

"Nobody could," said Ellen. "She changes the story too much."

Patrick got up to poke at the fire, which glowed sullenly for a moment and then collapsed into gray lumps.

"*Now* look what you've done," said Ellen.

One of the lamps flickered red and went out. The shadows in the corners shifted and gnarled, and a cold air came from the dead fireplace.

"I wish Fence would get back," said Laura.

"It's after midnight now," said Ellen. "We could go find Ruth."

"But how do we leave word of where we may be found?"

"You go get Ruth," said Patrick, "and I'll stay here. It shouldn't take long. If she has any sense she's gone to bed."

"What if they have a cast party after the ceremony?" said Ellen.

"What'll she do with Claudia when she gets here, is what I want to know," said Laura.

"The sooner you get her here the longer she'll have to think about it," said Patrick. He herded them along to the door and bolted it loudly behind them.

It was freezing in the stairwell; Laura expected to see frost and icicles on all the stones. They went down cautiously, steeling themselves for the sight of Claudia as they came around the third turn.

The steps were empty.

"Where is she?" said Ellen.

"Maybe we didn't count right," said Laura.

They went down a few more steps, and a glint on the step caught Laura's eye. For the barest fraction of an instant she saw Ted's face, with blood on it, and then there was only the twisted silver knife, its jewels burning hurtfully. Laura would not have touched it for the world.

"This is the right place," said Ellen. They looked at each other in the shivery light.

"We should tell Fence," said Laura.

"We should find Ruth."

They ran down the echoing stairs.

The guard at the door to the Council Chamber was not inclined either to speak to them or to let them in.

"It's very important," Ellen told him. "If we can't go in, can't you get Randolph or Fence to come out?"

The guard looked skeptical.

"Can you give one of them a message?" persisted Ellen.

The guard, a solid young man with big eyes, shook his head.

"If we *write* them a message," said Laura, "could you give it to them?"

The guard nodded with no more hesitation than he had shown in shaking his head before. He did not look likely to have paper or pen, so they trudged back to their room. Laura felt that she had never properly appreciated elevators.

Ellen wrote the message, telling Fence that Claudia was gone, but had left her knife, and that Ellen and Laura were looking for Ruth and would try to bring her to Fence's tower. She signed it "the Princesses Ellen and Laura," and they grinned at each other.

Ellen insisted on sealing the note with sealing wax. There was a heavy ring in the drawer with the wax. The signet of the royal family appeared to be a fox. Laura was not sure she approved of this.

"Well, it's not my fault," said Ellen, shaking the folded letter in the air to dry the wax. "I wanted our sign to be a unicorn."

"I don't know if the unicorns would like that."

They bounced out of their door and clattered along the corridor, making echoes.

"Let's get Ruth now, as long as we're here," said Ellen.

They went along the passageway to its end, turned right, went up some steps and around another corner, and pounded on Ruth's door. Laura took great comfort in the plain yellow torches, but she wished it were warmer.

Ruth did not answer, so they tried the door. It swung silently open into darkness. They padded in, and Laura tripped on a rug and fell down with a thump.

"Who goes there?" said a voice so imperious that Laura did not recognize it at once. She rubbed her elbow.

"It's us," said Ellen crossly, "and we don't know how to unfold ourselves, so there."

"You just did," said Ruth, sounding more like herself. Laura heard the bed creak, and Ruth make an exasperated noise. "I wish this place had electricity."

"You can't have proper adventures with electricity," said Ellen.

Ruth snorted, and got out of bed, a dim white shape. She came around the bed's end and tripped on Laura, who said "Hey!"

Ruth picked her up with one swift motion, made sure she would stay up, and went on out. When she came back in she had the candle lighted. She put it on a table, and they all crowded around it. The shadows in Ruth's room were less crawly than the ones in Fence's.

"Fence wants you," said Laura.

"Why weren't you at the banquet?" said Ellen.

Ruth made them shut up. Then she made Ellen tell the story, with the provision that Laura could interrupt if Ellen made a terrible mistake. Ellen did not, although Laura thought that she made too much fuss about their being Fence's spies.

"So," finished Ellen, "you'd better come back up with us and wait for Fence."

"That is *not* a good idea," said Ruth. "I got through this ceremony tonight, which nobody told me about because I was supposed to know, by the skin of my teeth, because I'm only a student and I could copy the other students. I couldn't go talk with a real magician like Fence without giving us away."

"Won't you give us away if you won't talk to him?" said Laura.

"I don't think he knows anything about what you're supposed to know," said Ellen. "It's two different kinds of magic."

"So why does he want me then?"

"Well, he doesn't know about *Claudia's* magic, but you might."

"Well, I don't. I never even heard of Claudia."

"Well, it can't hurt to say so."

"But what if Claudia's magic is Green Caves magic?" said Laura uneasily. If they were Fence's spies, as Ellen had made up, it was probably all right to tell Fence what she had made up to tell him. But knowing nothing about Claudia, how could they tell what they were supposed to know?

"You better get dressed," said Ellen to Ruth.

When they got to the door of Fence's tower, there was a beast on the steps. Laura liked the beasts less each time she saw them, even if Fence did think they were funny. This one was sloshing steadily, like the shore of a lake. It lapped a few inches up the wall, and a few inches back from the wall, over and over.

"We need to get by, please," Ellen told it.

The beast sucked itself into a tighter pool and made a number of rapid splats.

"Great," said Ruth.

"Let's wait for Fence here," said Laura. "He can talk to them."

"Patrick'll get worried," said Ellen. "Go away, beast."

The beast bubbled. Laura wished she had not eaten so much dinner.

There was a clatter of boots and voices in the passageway. Laura grabbed at Ruth. The beast snorted. Ted, Fence, and Randolph came down the darkness in sober discussion.

"Did you get our note?" cried Ellen.

Fence gave her an absent pat on the shoulder, nodding, and looked at Ruth. In the purple dimness of the stair torch, the stars on his robe seemed to grow and swarm.

"My lady, I thank you most heartily for your trouble," he said. "Will it please you to examine the knife?"

Ruth looked as if it would have pleased her to go away quickly, but she nodded. "If your beast will let us by," she said.

"It is not mine," said Fence, and addressed it in burbles.

It shifted and seemed to swell, and from it came a hissing like water droplets on a hot griddle. It was not a loud or particularly menacing sound, but Laura's hair prickled and Fence looked astonished. He hissed back. The beast slurped and squelched, and overflowed onto a lower step.

"You had better remind it of its place," said Randolph, at Fence's shoulder.

Fence gave him much the same kind of pat he had given Ellen, and shook his head. Then he looked at Ruth, who was standing at his other side with Laura hanging on to her hand. She was gripping Laura's hand with more force than that necessary to be comforting. Ellen was cramped between Laura and the wall, looking as if she wanted to pet the beast. Laura, who did not even want to see it, looked over her shoulder and saw that Ted stood behind them all, seeming bored.

"Can you do aught with it?" Fence asked Ruth.

Laura felt her tense, but she sounded quite composed. "I can call on water," she said.

"You and Randolph are both too precipitate," said Fence.

Laura glanced up in time to see Randolph look at Ruth over Fence's head. He rolled his eyes at the ceiling and grinned. Ruth smiled back.

"Well," she said to him, "we could call on the mountains, then."

"Nonsense," said Fence, "this is rival waters."

"And that rivals all nonsense," said Randolph.

Laura looked to see if Ruth was as bewildered as she was. Ruth looked outraged, but she said nothing.

"What are you talking about?" demanded Ellen.

Ruth looked at Fence, took a deep breath, and answered her sister. "When the power of the Green Caves, which is over earth and water, meddles with matters of the Blue Sorcery, which is of fire and air, then these beasts are made, which are air and water." She sounded as if she were quoting.

"Who's been meddling?" asked Ellen.

"Claudia, no doubt," said Fence.

The beast sucked and bubbled like someone trying to pull the last drops of a milkshake through a straw—a loud and unmistakably rude noise. Fence laughed at it. "Thou art a guardian, not a warrior," he said. "Begone."

The beast rose up like a geyser, swirled, and vanished. Fence and Randolph stared at each other. Then Randolph shrugged and Fence started up the steps. The others followed, one by one.

Laura hung back to walk with Ted, who still looked bored. "What did you do at the banquet?" she asked.

"Ate."

"No, what did you do *wrong?*"

"Thanks a lot."

"Well, Matthew told Fence you did."

"Great," said Ted, climbing faster.

"Well, what?"

She expected him to shut her up, but he told her. Laura was awed. "Prince Edward would *never* do that!"

"Well, I'm not Prince Edward."

"Shhh!"

"Sorry."

"Why can't you play Edward the way we're all playing?" Laura was breathless just from asking questions, and it was hard to climb stairs and pay proper attention to Ted's answers. But who knew when she might find him in this mood again?

"Because it's not a game. It's important. Maybe if Edward wasn't such a milksop Randolph wouldn't have to kill the King. Maybe if the King respected Edward he'd listen to him about sorcery."

"He doesn't respect you for hitting Andrew, does he? Didn't you say he was mad?"

"Sure he was, but he might respect me for it anyway."

Laura gave up and climbed in silence. The closer they got to the top, the colder it became. As she came around the last corner before Claudia's knife and bumped into Ted, she realized that she could see her breath in the purple air.

"You see," said Fence to Ruth.

"Uh," said Ruth.

She knelt on the step and looked at the knife. Laura, regarding the cold gleam of the jewels, felt a picture begin to form in them and looked away quickly, right at Fence's robe. The stars exploded at her so that she blinked, and the flat red and green afterimages wavered into a vast field where the tiny figures of men and beasts strove together.

Laura finally blinked again, and screwed both eyes tight shut, breaking the picture into meaningless dots. When she opened her eyes again, Ruth was talking.

"It's like she took one of yours and one of ours and put them together," she said.

Fence looked horrified. "And where is the desert she made in the combining?"

Ruth looked taken aback, but Fence did not seem to expect an answer.

"'Twas not made for you," he said to her. "Can you hold it harmless?"

"Well," said Ruth. She looked at the knife, and back up at Fence. "Why don't you get Meredith?"

Randolph made an incredulous noise and looked at Ruth as if she were crazy.

Fence shook his head. "Think, child," he said. "I did not say 'unmake,' but 'hold harmless.'"

"Oh," said Ruth. She looked at the knife again.

"Ruth," said Ellen, "you want to slow it down, right?"

Laura looked at her with admiration. She had forgotten all about Shan's Ring, but it was certainly the only thing they had that might keep Claudia out of the way.

"Oh," said Ruth.

"Hey," said Ted, sounding alarmed. Laura wondered what was the matter with him.

Ruth put her hand in the pocket of her skirt and furrowed her brow.

"I am a trinket," said Ellen.

"Hush," said Ruth.

"Ruth," said Ted.

"Shut *up,*" said Ruth, fiercely. She shut her eyes and put out her other hand for the knife.

"Ruthie, *don't*," said Ted, putting his hand out too. Randolph caught his wrist, and looked at him as if he too were crazy. Ted seemed about to try to wrench his arm away, but then he gave up and stood glowering.

Ruth's hand came down on the knife. There was not a sound in the stairwell. Ruth's lips moved briefly and she opened her eyes. "Blow time awry for this!" she said, and the jewels in the knife hilt went dark. Laura was impressed. At least things were working properly for Ruth.

"Well!" said Ruth, pleased. She handed the knife to Fence, who flinched but took it and bowed to her, in the narrow stairway, without knocking anybody over. Randolph let go of Ted and they all began to climb again.

Patrick was standing in the open door to Fence's living room with a rug over his shoulders and a sword in his hand. Both were too big for him.

When he had looked everybody over, he moved to let them in and put the sword on the mantelpiece. It was warmer inside, but it was not warm. Fence gestured at the fireplace, and flames leaped up again.

"It was a warm day for so cold a night," he said.

"There is nothing amiss with the night," said Randolph, sitting down where he had sat for dinner.

Fence brought another chair to the table for Ruth, between Randolph and Patrick. Everyone else sat in his old place. Fence put both hands around the wine jug, and when he poured the wine, it steamed.

"Before anyone else pounds upon my door with urgent summons," he said, "I will have my spies' reports."

So Laura and Patrick and Ellen recited their parts, while Ted and Ruth sat with their mouths falling open. Fence made Ellen repeat one thing twice, and Laura two things.

During Patrick's recitation of how the kitchen staff would not let an undercook magic the soup to make up for having left out the saffron, Laura saw Randolph look over at Fence, who grimaced at him. But that was all the reaction they got, and the whole thing was quickly over.

"Well done," Fence said to them. "You have earned your rest, and 'twere best you go to't. Agatha will have my head on a pole if she discovers how late I have kept you."

Ellen jerked herself up from where she had been falling asleep in Ruth's lap. "But what happened at the council?"

"And where's Claudia?" said Laura.

"What do you mean, where's Claudia?" said Patrick, coming suddenly out of his slouch.

"Naught happened," said Randolph. "Fence and Andrew aired their philosophies."

"Who *won?*" said Ellen.

"None wins in the airing of philosophies," said Fence, patiently.

"What did the King think?" persisted Ellen.

"He said not," said Fence.

"Ellie," said Ted, "go to bed." She looked at him, outraged, and he mouthed, "I'll tell you later," at her. Ellen shrugged. Fence's mouth quirked.

"Where's Claudia?" repeated Laura. She felt that it was necessary to keep track of Claudia, much as it was necessary to keep track of a large puppy. They both made trouble when you weren't looking.

"Claudia came to the council," said Fence.

"What about your *spell?*" said Ellen.

"She broke it," said Fence, shortly. "She came to the council and I made accusation of her, which she chose not to answer. She was taken to the South Tower. If she chooses to stay there and be tried, which she well may if 't amuses her, all of us save Ruth may be called as witnesses. If she hath not chosen to stay she is no doubt wherever it pleases her to be. I could discover her with some effort. Without her knife she is, I think, less menace than nuisance. Randolph and I will make shift to deal with her, with Lady Ruth's help." Ruth looked nonplussed.

"How does she do all this?" said Ellen.

"Peace," said Fence.

"I'm sorry," said Ellen to Fence. "Only nobody knows anything, and anything can happen."

Randolph reached out and patted her head. Ellen glowered but sat still under it, like a well-trained cat. "Anything may usually happen," he said to her. "Get thee to bed—and thee, and thee."

Laura and Ellen got up, reluctantly, and came around to Fence, Patrick on their heels. "Thank you for dinner," they said, almost in chorus. Ellen burst out laughing, and Patrick looked disgusted.

Fence smiled. "And for thy aid," he said. He kissed Laura. Laura, looking back over her shoulder as he kissed Ellen, saw Patrick's eyes grow wary. He took Fence's kiss as Ellen had taken the pat on the head, and came quickly away, hunching his shoulders.

Randolph came to bar the door behind them, but he stood in the doorway watching them go down, and under even his imagined gaze they were quite silent. It was deathly cold in the stairwell, and every shadow looked like a beast about to appear.

CHAPTER 16

WHEN the younger ones had disappeared down the steps, Ted began to say something to Fence, and saw with dismay that Fence had put his head into his hands. Ted and Ruth looked at one another. When Randolph shut the door behind Patrick and came to stand by Fence's chair, Fence still did not move.

"Let it wait upon the morning," Randolph said, and his look was anxious.

"Claudia waiteth not," said Fence into his hands.

Randolph was silent, and the four of them sat listening to the fire. Ted was very sleepy. Even with the fire, a cold crept out of the corners that made him expect to hear the wind howling outside. He looked at Ruth. He had to warn her about using Shan's Ring. He wondered what else she might have been using it for.

Fence took his head out of his hands, and Randolph moved to sit on the edge of the table.

"Three matters," said Fence. "This cold, Claudia, and Edward's performance at dinner."

Ruth looked a question at Ted, who scowled at her.

"I had not thought the cold was Claudia's doing," said Randolph. "I had thought it one of the workings of the Dragon King. And proof of thy observations, if any heeded. But when thou didst arrive, the cold was lessened."

"And lessened also," said Fence, "for that short time she held in my spell."

"To make the cold," said Randolph, slowly, "is neither Green nor Blue sorcery, but yellow. Her studies have been wide. Heaven grant they have not been deep also."

"Claudia, then," said Fence, and he looked at Ruth. "I am in your hands."

Ted admired Ruth; she hardly blanched. "Well," she said, "I can do to her what I did to the knife."

"How long does such an enchantment endure?" Randolph asked her.

Ruth did not even hesitate. "A year and a day," said she.

Fence whistled, and Ted jumped.

"I wonder if I have missed my calling," said Fence.

Randolph laughed. "Each magic hath his benefits."

"After all," said Ruth, "I can stop Claudia, but you have to find her for me first."

Both Randolph and Fence looked astonished, and Ted wished he knew more about the magics of the Secret Country. If Ruth were winging it, she ought to stop.

"I'm only a student," said Ruth, so crossly that Ted knew that she had been winging it.

"Randolph," said Fence, "how is thy searching eye?"

"Sharp enough," said Randolph. He went to one of the carved chests, took a mirror from it, and left the room.

"Ruth," said Ted.

"Edward," said Fence, "have a care."

"I just want to say," said Ted, "that she shouldn't do to Claudia what she did to the knife."

"It won't hurt her," said Ruth.

"It might hurt *us*."

Randolph came briskly in, laying the mirror on the table before Fence.

"Is that she?" he asked. He sounded put out.

Ted and Ruth craned to see into the mirror. It showed a tower room much like the one they were in, except that it had a bed and fewer tapestries. There was a shadow on the floor, but no figure to cast it.

Fence put both hands through his hair, but he could not make it look much worse. Ted wondered who had cut it that way, and why. Fence turned the mirror around, tilting it, and sighed. "Of a certainty," he said. "Is that the South Tower?"

Randolph nodded.

"Go we there," said Fence to Ruth. He looked at Randolph. "Canst deal with this miscreant?"

"Better than thou," said Randolph, with an emphasis Ted did not care for.

Fence gripped the edge of the table and started to stand up, and Randolph moved quickly and almost lifted him out of his chair. Fence looked at him reproachfully. Randolph shook his head, and Fence laughed.

"Thou wilt be my greatest comfort in mine old age," he said, "if only thou dost not tire of cosseting me sooner. My lady," he said to Ruth. Ruth stood up.

"Wait!" said Ted.

"Be quick," said Fence.

"Ruthie," said Ted, using the pet name and trying to catch her eye and strengthen his speech with significant gestures so she would know that it was he, Ted, and not a besotted Edward worried for her safety, who was talking. "You can't use that spell on Claudia."

"Why?" said Ruth, warily, in her sorcerer voice.

"It's very dangerous!"

All three of them stared at him. Their expressions were

exactly alike: the condescending and slightly impatient look of an expert faced with a wrongheaded amateur. Ted felt as if he had told his French teacher that *oeuf* meant *ear*.

"I know what I'm doing," Ruth told him, making faces so that he would know that it was she, not Lady Ruth, who spoke. She seemed quite irritated and a little frightened, and Ted was not reassured. She was probably just afraid that he would give her away, or make her give herself away, to Fence and Randolph.

"I know what I'm doing too," he said.

"Time arrays itself against us," said Fence to Ruth.

"Calm down," said Ruth to Ted.

Ted felt desperate, and decided to beat her at their own game. "I command you not to do this thing!"

Ruth burst out laughing. Fence's mouth quirked.

Randolph, looking acutely unhappy, said in a constrained tone, "I beg to remind Your Highness that no worker of magic is at your command."

"You stop them, then!"

Randolph's face set in formidable lines, but his voice was very gentle. "I am an apprentice," he said. "In all earthly matters I obey you, my lord, but in the matter of magic even I am no servant of yours. I earnestly regret it."

Fence by this time looked actually sick. "And I," he said.

"Go," said Randolph, and opened the door for them. When they had gone and he had bolted it, he swung on Ted like a cat pouncing.

"Are you mad?"

Ted opened his mouth to reply, and a hot tear slid into the corner of it, startling him. He had been aware of no emotion save wrath. He swallowed, felt his face crumpling up, and turned around hastily. Standing up to Andrew, who was a villain, or even to the King, who was wrongheaded, was one thing. But he hated fighting with Fence and Randolph. He hated losing to them even more.

He wrapped both arms around himself and stared at the watery rug. His vision cleared gradually, and he saw that the rug really was watery. It depicted a fountain crowded about with animals. Ted wanted to be intrigued by it, but that would have been an excuse. He had to face Randolph sooner or later.

He turned slowly, still hugging himself. Randolph stood just where Ted had left him, his grave and troubled gaze bent steadily on Ted. Ted refrained from backing away.

"Now, Edward, what's the matter?" said Randolph.

"What isn't?" said Ted, stalling.

Randolph sat down on the edge of the table and reached for his cup. "Art thou still my rival, then?"

"No, it's not that," said Ted, so miserably that he could tell at once how very unconvincing Randolph found this assertion.

He wondered if he should simply tell Randolph the truth, but all his instincts rebelled. In the first place, the others should approve such a drastic step: It was their game, or their adventure, or their necks too. After all, if Shan's Ring did what he thought it might, they would all be in terrible trouble for using it. And if they were not really the royal children, there was nothing to stop everyone from deciding that they were spies. They might be just the people Andrew was looking for.

"My God," said Ted.

"I beg your pardon?" said Randolph.

"Sorry," said Ted. "Nothing."

His knees were so shaky that he sat down across from Randolph. He felt as if someone had just hit him in the stomach. He could not imagine why none of them had thought of this sooner. If the Secret Country were real, then where were the real princes and princesses? Back with the Barretts, wreaking havoc? No, of course not, or the Barretts would have had something to say about it when he and Laura got back. Where, then?

Ted felt suffocated. He had to talk to the others immediately. But Randolph still regarded him gravely, and would have to have some sort of explanation.

"Andrew bothers me," Ted told him. "I don't like the way he's disrupting everything. How did he get the King to pay so much attention to him anyway?"

Randolph put his cup down. "Perhaps because thou hast paid so little to the King?"

Ted was confounded, and said nothing. He supposed that if Prince Edward were as shy and bookish as they had made him in the Secret, he would have been too scared and too absorbed to pay much attention to the King.

"Not thou alone," said Randolph. "He is a warrior, and his favorites wizards all: Benjamin, Conrad, and even I. Thou art no wizard, but thou preferrest thy books to thy sword. No man likes a wizard, who hath not some magic himself, and William hath none. 'Tis said it passeth from grandsire to grandchild, missing the son." He had sounded more and more as if he were thinking aloud; now he shrugged and smiled. "Thou seest," he said.

Ted was not sure either that he saw or that he did not. "Anyway, that's not the point," he said. "You know he'll do it Andrew's way, and you know what'll happen if he does. What are we going to do to make him change his mind?"

"It may be that we cannot," said Randolph. "But if we can, the answer lies in just such things as I have said. Reason hath little power here. If thou wouldst thy father thought well of wizards, 'twere well thou see to't that he thinks well of thee."

"So maybe it was a good idea to jump on Andrew?" said Ted.

"Didst not know when thou didst it?" demanded Randolph.

"Know what?" said Ted, confused.

Randolph pulled the circlet from his head, turned it in his fingers, and jammed it back onto his head as if he were slamming a door he knew would pop open again. "When you flung yourself upon Andrew," he said carefully, "did you not think it was wise to do so?"

"I didn't think it was anything to do so," said Ted, irritated. Part of him still itched to go after Ruth and stop her from using Shan's Ring, and this conversation no longer had anything in it to make up for wasting that opportunity.

"Angels and ministers of grace defend us," said Randolph, and something in the quality of his voice told Ted that he was quoting Benjamin.

"He made me angry," said Ted.

"What hath come over thee?" Randolph asked him. "Time was when neither taunts nor blows could make thee angry."

"Isn't it better this way?" said Ted.

"Not if thou must show it thus. Answer Andrew with worse words—draw and challenge and be done with it—but this starting what thou wilt not finish is madness. Besides, 'twere better not to quarrel with Andrew, who has thy father's ear, and is useful in his fashion. And furthermore," said Randolph, gesturing with both hands as if he would have liked to take Ted and shake him, "if thou must flout what hath been taught thee, I prithee flout not what I have taught thee so that thy father cast an angry eye on me as well."

"Oh," said Ted. "Sorry."

"Flouting what I taught thee," added Randolph, "in defense of a wizard. Oh, Edward, when follies come they come not single spies but in battalions."

Ted wished he had not mentioned spies, even in a figure of speech. "But what are we going to do about Andrew?" he said. "It's a bit late for me to start being a model son."

"How late?" said Randolph.

"Well, Benjamin said—"

"Ah," said Randolph. "To win quickly, cleanly, easily, and with small loss, far from our borders, we must indeed do as Benjamin says. To win a bloodier battle perilously close, we have yet a few months."

"Well," said Ted, "I'll do what I can." He hesitated. "I'm really sorry, Randolph, but everything's just falling apart."

Randolph frowned, but his voice was kinder. "Make shift to gather the pieces together, then, and kick them not asunder like a child with a frozen puddle," he said.

"May I go now, please?" said Ted.

Randolph nodded. "And ease thy mind," he said. "All may yet be very well."

As Ted left he saw Randolph settling himself by the fire to wait for Fence.

Fence's living room had not been warm, but the stairwell was like stepping into cold water. Ted's breath steamed away from him and made an eerie mist in the purple light. It seemed to be growing warmer as he went on down. Ted was not sure that this made sense, because warm air rises. He was pondering this problem and wondering if the knowledge he could gain would be worth the trouble of asking Patrick for it, when quite abruptly the stairwell became warm.

Ted almost fell down the steps. He was not sure he liked the change. Presumably it was better for a castle to be warm in the middle of the summer, but it could hardly be natural for it to change so fast from being cold. He wondered if using Shan's Ring could do that.

"Claudia," he said aloud. If Claudia had been making the cold, and Ruth had used Shan's Ring on her, Claudia would not be able to make the cold anymore, and things would go back to normal.

Ted almost fell down the steps again, as the tower shook itself and made grinding noises. Ted moved faster. He had half thought of waiting for Fence in the stairwell, but now he wanted nothing to do with it.

"Why would Claudia make it cold anyway?" he asked the gray walls. He found it hard to think without the others clamoring at him. They were a nuisance, but at least they asked the right questions.

The tower shook again, more gently. Ted burst through the door at the bottom and ran along the passage. He stopped at the next door and looked back. He knew that in an earthquake one was supposed to go outside, but he was not sure that there had been an earthquake. The torches still burned in their sockets, and now all was quiet. If he went outside he might miss Fence returning.

He perched himself on the sill of one of the windows that looked upon the inner courtyard. The stone was cold, but in the new heat of the air this was pleasant. A green smell came through the window, and behind it a faint scent of lilac. It seemed to go well with the purple torches.

Ted was almost asleep when Fence came trudging along the passage. Nobody looked his best in that light, but Ted, knuckling his eyes and shaking the blood back into the foot he had been sitting on, thought that Fence looked as though he were sleepwalking.

"Sir?" said Ted.

Fence blinked, and focused on him. "Where is Randolph?"

"He's upstairs," said Ted. "I wanted to speak with you alone."

Fence came and sat next to Ted. "Well, then?"

"Did Ruth take care of Claudia?"

"Oh, aye." Fence fixed him with a glare. "Hast forgotten all thy courtesy?"

Ted, who could make no sense of this remark, suppressed the desire to ask whether Shan's Ring was part of the Green Caves magic. In the first place, Fence might think that rude too; in the second, it might give everything away.

"Is there aught else, my lord?" Fence asked him. Ted could not tell whether he was being polite to soften the fact that he wanted to get away, or whether he was angry and therefore being formal.

"Yes," said Ted, recklessly.

Fence nodded at him.

"I fear me," said Ted, "that if we do not convince the King that Andrew is wrong, that he must make sorcerous preparations, then Randolph will kill the King to keep us all from being destroyed."

Fence did not move for what seemed a very long time. Ted became aware of the singing of summer insects in the courtyard, and of the autumnal smell that hung about Fence.

"Are you mad?" said Fence at last. Randolph, asking the same question, had sounded furious; Fence sounded stricken.

"No," said Ted, wondering how Patrick would answer that.

"Hath he spoken of this, then?"

"Well, no. I tried to bring up the subject, but he put me off."

"So," said Fence.

"He did say we probably *couldn't* convince the King."

"Probably we cannot."

"But Fence, if we can't, what else is there to do but kill him?"

"What is the matter with you? We will do our best in the battle, and live or die as it falls to us. There was never kingdom that did not end at last, and to hear you, one would think this one's ending delayed o'er long." His look at Ted, even in the uncertain light, was formidable.

"But—"

"Why Randolph?" asked Fence.

"Claudia," said Ted.

"Well, you are not so mad as you might be," said Fence. "She hath no doubt embittered him and may have dulled his wits, but none could so change him that he would do what you accuse him of planning. Lords of darkness," said Fence, vehemently, "I am weary of accusations." He put out a hand, suddenly, and took hold of Ted's chin to make Ted look at him. "Why Randolph?" he repeated.

"He's my regent, isn't he?" said Ted, feeling on firmer ground. "He'd have the power to do what he wants done, then. He's my teacher—he knows I'm safe—and not a match for him," said Ted, grumpily. More and more he chafed under the restraints of Edward's personality.

"Any man in council knows thy mind, and Randolph's," said Fence.

"But if anybody else killed the King, Randolph would get him," explained Ted.

Fence put a hand to Ted's forehead, and dropped it with a sigh. "I had hoped you were feverish," he said. "Does not the fact that Randolph will deal with any man who does the deed show that he would not do't himself?"

"He'll get himself too," said Ted, a little desperately. "He'll admit it after the battle."

"None of this," said Fence, as if in spite of himself, "regards the fact that Randolph is not of the temper which does such things."

Ted felt a sort of gleeful shock; just so had he sounded himself when his sister and his cousins used to draw him into heated discussions of the ridiculous.

"You've been gone a long time," he said. "Maybe he's changed."

"You have been by him," said Fence. "What think you is the instrument of such a change?"

"Claudia," said Ted, with considerable force. Claudia certainly was an instrument of change, and even though she was providing a convenient excuse at the moment, he hated her.

"We have had that already," said Fence. "Nohow save by sorcery could she force him to such an unnatural deed as kill a king, and there is no sorcery at work in him. Besides, as Ruth has disposed her, she cannot reach him now."

"Can't you ask him?" said Ted. "He'll have to tell you the truth, and then you'll know, and that might stop him. Or you could stop him."

Fence's hand came down on the stone they sat on. "Why didst thou not ask him thyself?"

Ted considered, while Fence's eyes caught a gleam of light from somewhere and seemed to bore into him. Ted tried to distract himself by wondering how anyone could smell like burning leaves, but it did not work. He was forced to the dismal conclusion that he had not asked Randolph himself, first because he was afraid to, and second because he had not decided beforehand what he was going to do, but had acted without thinking.

He did not much want to tell these reasons to Fence. But the recklessness which had possessed him for some time was still working, and he recognized now that part of it was a spirit of experimentation. For all his belief that the Secret Country was real, still he felt the impulse to see how far he could push in how many directions, and what would happen if he did. The thought of the sword sat in the back of his mind like a refuge: Even if it were all real, they could go home if it got too bad, and he could not see that they would have made things any worse.

He answered Fence's question.

"Ministers of grace defend us," said Fence. Ted thought that things could not be too bad if Fence did not call on the angels too. He found that he had to choke back a giggle at this piece of wit.

"Thou?" said Fence. "Thou! Thou whose main fault is that of thinking so precisely on the event that thou dost it not?"

"See?" cried Ted. "See! I've changed. Maybe Randolph has too."

Fence was silent a moment. "I will go so far with thee," he said, "as to watch for some change in him. The question is not one to be asked by friend of friend, or even by master of pupil. But I will watch for any change—the more so," he added, chuckling, "for that I see already how he watches for any in me."

"Thank you," said Ted.

"Get thee to bed," said Fence.

CHAPTER 17

Fence had brought presents for each of his spies, and he gave them out the next day. He gave Ellen a leather pouch full of packets of seeds from all the strange plants he had seen in his travels. Ellen was intrigued but nervous. ("He'll expect me to plant them," she said to Laura, "and I don't know how." "Isn't it the wrong time of year for that?" said Laura. "Depends on what they are," said Ellen, "and that's what I don't know.")

He gave Patrick a bronze knife with bats and snakes on its greeny hilt. Patrick was fascinated but wary. Laura caught him practicing with it several times, but he became sullen when discovered.

He gave Laura an ivory unicorn that fit in the palm of her hand, with beryls for eyes. ("Which is not according to nature," he told her, "for the eyes of the unicorn are violet. But there is more virtue in the beryl than in the amethyst." Laura was enchanted. "I'll lose it," she said. "So you will not, then," said Fence, "for I have put on it a spell of finding and returning.")

Ted and Ruth, to Laura's great amusement, were irked that Fence had brought them nothing. Ruth seemed merely to want something exotic; Ted was hurt that Fence did not think enough of him to bring him something. Patrick pointed out that none of the gifts would survive the return trip anyway, a remark which reduced Laura to tears and re-opened the discussion of whether Ted's flashlight had really turned into a lantern.

"If it did," said Patrick, testily, "then Ellie'll end up with a bag of petunia seeds, and Laurie'll have a plastic horse, and I'll have a Swiss Army knife or something. But it won't work that way, actually, because these aren't real objects. The flashlight was; it came from the other side, you see."

"Like your watch, I suppose," said Ruth.

This occasioned an argument which got them nowhere but shortened tempers considerably. None of them seemed to be feeling well after the rigors of the night before. Laura was sleepy. She thought Ted looked as if he had a headache. Ellen looked sick to her stomach. Ruth and Patrick merely looked grouchy. The weather was grouchy as well. The morning had dawned clear, but by noon the sky was the color of the water used for a long session of painting with watercolors, and little bouts of wind blew the dust from the dry paths into every corner of the rose garden.

Then Ted brought up the matter of Shan's Ring and the Outside Powers. Nobody seemed to find his theory convinc-ing. Ruth was furious with him for, as she put it, trying to ruin her position as a sorcerer by preventing her from doing the only thing she had been able to think of doing. Ted ac-cused her of wanting to show off no matter what happened. This occasioned another argument which got them nowhere but made them thoroughly sick of each other's company.

Sick though they might be, they had still to hear Ellen and Laura tell them about the door to Fence's tower, and Fence's dishes. Nobody had any idea what the original tapestry meant or why it was duplicated all over Fence's possessions.

Ted made the mistake of using this fact to reopen the argument with Patrick over whether what was happening to them was real. He elicited only the theory that they were making it up as they went along, as if they were dreaming it. Patrick sounded a little desperate as he propounded this idea, but he stuck to it stubbornly.

After that it was still necessary for Ted and Ruth to explain all the things they had been doing. Nobody but Laura approved of anything Ted had done. All the others felt that they should have been consulted. Ted's explanation that he would have told Randolph the whole truth if he hadn't wanted to consult them did not make them any happier. When he explained his idea that they would be treated as spies if they tried to tell the truth, everyone (except Laura) was even madder.

Then Patrick asked them about the Crystal of Earth, and they all looked at him as if he were crazy. Laura did not like the sound of the Crystal of Earth. She did not like to think that someone could break it like a cereal bowl and the Secret Country would disappear. Being wrought up and tired, she began to cry again.

Ruth said emphatically, "There is no such thing. It's just a product of Patrick's perverted mind. Did you look for it, Pat?"

Patrick looked secretive, hesitated, and nodded. "Yeah," he said. "It's not where I dreamed it was."

"I wonder what's with these dreams," said Ted. "Has anybody else had any?"

"Not like that," said Laura. "But I see things in—"

"Hey, that's weird," said Patrick. "If this is a dream, should we dream that we're dreaming?"

"Oh, for heaven's sake," said Ruth. "I've had about enough of this."

They left one another with relief and wandered about desolately on their own, brooding.

Ted and Patrick expected their fencing lessons to begin again two days after the banquet. They had not practiced. Ted had kept hoping for more dreams, and Patrick affected, at least, not to care what might happen.

They both overslept that morning, and hurried down to the practice yard assuring each other that Randolph would have overslept, too. Castle gossip had him and Fence closeted in the North Tower day and night, either making battle plans or concocting arcane spells, depending on whom you listened to.

In fact he was not in the yard when they arrived. There were several other people off at the far end of the yard practicing exotic-looking maneuvers with short curved swords. Ted got from them the information that Randolph had not been there since they began, at dawn.

"He'll be here any minute, then," said Ted. "Let's practice what we can."

"I've been wondering what would happen if we didn't," said Patrick, picking up a sword and putting it down again. "Whether the cardinal would rescue us again."

"Randolph'll have a fit even if the cardinal does rescue us," said Ted. "He'll probably go ask its owner what he thinks he's doing, and then he'll find out we don't have anything to do with the cardinals and we'll be in for it. Come on."

"What makes you think we don't have anything to do with the cardinals?"

"What makes you think we do?"

Patrick acquired his secretive expression. Ted had never seen it until they came to the Secret Country, but he was already as tired of it as he had ever been of Patrick's other habits. A natural desire to make Patrick as tired of him caused him to remember something.

"You know what," he said. "It was a cardinal that got us into this. If Laurie hadn't heard one singing, she wouldn't have dived into that hedge."

Patrick looked intrigued.

"Did you hear a cardinal when you were fooling around in the bottle-tree thicket?"

"There aren't any cardinals in Australia," said Patrick, in his most patient scholarly tones. "They're a North American bird."

"Come on," said Ted, defeated.

Ted's dream had remained clear in his mind—clearer, in fact, than he really liked to have it. Although the fencing moves were useful, he hated remembering Randolph's face. But he was able to show Patrick a few things, of the when-I-do-this-you-do-that variety; by assuming a stance without thinking about it and then looking at what he had done, he was able to show Patrick how to salute, stand, move, and hold his sword.

He thought Patrick did very well for someone who had never liked any activity except that required to get him from one place to another.

They worked for an hour, and Randolph did not come.

"I don't like this sword," said Patrick suddenly.

"I don't like mine either," said Ted, dropping its point to the ground. "But that's because I dreamed about a better one. Did you?"

"I also," said Patrick, "don't like the way those people are looking at us."

Ted considered them. "They don't look threatening to me."

"No, just curious. What if they come over to see what Randolph's so proud of teaching you?"

"Well, we could quit."

"What I want to do," said Patrick, "is go get our swords and find somewhere private to practice."

"Our—?"

"The ones we got here with!"

"Are those for fighting?" said Ted, uneasily.

"Why not?"

"Well, they're magical."

"They sure are. They make these look like sticks of wood."

"That's all we used to have," said Ted.

Patrick squinted at him in the sunlight. "Come on."

They ended up in the rose garden. Nowhere else seemed free of people. Ted was not altogether pleased with this. He saw laid over the brilliant sun and precise red and green of daylight the silver garden of his dream, like something in a double exposure.

The magic sword did feel better in his hand than the practice sword had. To his considerable relief, it did not fit like the dream sword.

"Pat, I don't think this is a good idea," he said. "These are sharp. We could hurt each other."

"We don't have to do the whole sequence," said Patrick. "Just the initial stuff. I think we should get used to handling these swords. We should have them with us all the time, really; they're our way home."

Ted reluctantly fell in with this plan. There was no wind. On the thick moss of the garden their feet were soundless. A great silence hung from tree to sky. The swords burned in the sunlight, throwing back blue and green so sharp that the garden seemed to pale and shrivel. They left great shining swaths in the clear air, like fireworks but unfading. Ted caught at the names of their motions as they fled under his mind: bind, double bind, circle parry, riposte.

"Cease!" said a voice, at an enormous distance.

Cold seized Ted's fingers, and the sword drooped slowly and slid to the moss. The sword paths dimmed and tattered like smoke in a wind, and as they went out the color came back to moss and rose and stone. Ted saw Patrick standing stock-still, his pale brown hair brilliant, his white tunic dazzling. His face was horrified; he was looking at something over Ted's right shoulder.

Ted found that he could move, and swung around. Randolph stood a few yards away, lowering his arms. He came and took Ted by the shoulders. "What in heaven's name!" he said, and his voice shook. He was very pale.

"We were practicing," said Ted. "You didn't show up."

Randolph stooped for Ted's sword, and a flash of blue light pained their eyes as he touched it. Randolph said something Ted did not catch, and the light dwindled.

"Patrick," said Randolph, "bring me thine."

Patrick's face acquired a stubborn set, but he obeyed. Randolph held one sword in each hand and stared at them for some time. Ted looked at Patrick, who shook his head ruefully. He was very pale and sweaty. Ted felt pale himself.

"How did you come by these?" Randolph asked them.

I found mine under a hedge," said Ted, and saw Patrick close his mouth and look annoyed. "Patrick found his under a clump of trees."

Randolph's gaze sharpened and pinned him. "Where?"

"Near the Well of the White Witch," said Ted.

"Do you know their nature?"

"They make it easier to practice," said Ted. Wishing to tell the whole truth and afraid of the consequences, he told as much of it as he could, which for some reason made him feel better. "They seem to make it easier to learn things."

"They give a headache to every sorcerer, every wizard, and every apprentice for leagues around," said Randolph. "And what price the two of you have paid for their use I do not like to think."

"We're all right," said Patrick, edgily.

"I think they were meant for us," said Ted.

"If they are what I think they are, woe to anyone for whom they were meant," said Randolph. He frowned, and gave the swords back to them. "I think we must see Fence," he said.

He herded them along the paths to the castle.

Fence's room was flooded with sunlight. Fence was on his knees before one of the carved chests, rummaging briskly and whistling a tune that Ted almost recognized. He looked up as they came in, and the cheer and energy of his aspect were almost shocking. Ted thought that he must have needed a few nights' sleep very badly indeed to look so much better than he had. He still was not impressive.

Fence's mouth quirked when he saw Ted and Patrick. "These?" he said.

"Show him," said Randolph.

Ted pulled his sword from the sheath and held it out.

"Shan's blade," said Fence. Ted thought he was merely being emphatic, but when Randolph nodded slowly, Ted realized that Fence had meant it.

"Show him, Patrick," said Randolph.

"This is *mine*," said Patrick, but he drew it out.

"That is Melanie's," said Fence. He was very still for a moment. "How came they to your hands?"

"Found where you might expect," said Randolph, when neither Ted nor Patrick answered.

"How long ago?"

Randolph looked at Ted in such a way that Ted thought it better to answer. "A few weeks."

"And," said Fence to Randolph, "is't so long he hath not been himself?"

"It is."

"I think," said Fence, "that we had better have them."

Ted handed his over promptly, although doing so gave him a sinking sensation in the stomach. The less fuss he and Patrick made about losing the swords, the easier it would be to get them back again.

Patrick must have had other ideas. He put his sword back into its sheath, and his expression was not pleasant.

"Patrick?" said Fence.

"This is mine," said Patrick. "You can't know it's Melanie's without testing it."

"You have tested it for us," said Fence, dryly.

"Pat!" said Ted.

"Thy training is not in this," said Randolph. "It will serve thee ill."

He took a step toward Patrick and held out his hand, as if he were trying to make friends with a dog of uncertain temper.

Patrick leaped back against the wall and whipped out the sword. Ted's had done nothing when he took it out to give to Fence, but Patrick's blazed green.

"Patrick!" said Ted, and moved toward him. Randolph caught his shoulder and held him still.

"My lord," said Randolph to Patrick, with the sudden assumption of icy formality that the Secret Country people did so well. "Will you be pleased to hand over the sword, or must I take it?"

"You must take it," said Patrick.

The sword Patrick had held the night before when they all came back upstairs after the council was leaning against the mantel. Randolph took it, jerked it from its sheath, tossed the sheath behind him, and went at Patrick so fast that even if Ted had known what to do he would not have had time to do it. There was a clash of metal and a flare of green, and Patrick's sword thumped to the rug. Patrick stood backed against the wall, furious, Randolph's sword at his throat.

"Fence," said Randolph, but Fence had already stooped for the blazing sword. It dimmed as he touched it.

Randolph drew back and put his sword into its sheath again, and leaned it against the mantel. Patrick stayed where he was, his eyes steady on Randolph. Ted was glad that Patrick was not in the habit of carrying a dagger.

"Thank you, Edward," said Randolph.

This was a dismissal. Ted moved for the door, trying to signal Patrick to come along quietly.

Patrick would not look at him. He pushed himself away from the wall as if he wanted to knock it over, and addressed himself to Fence.

"You'll be sorry," he said. He was still wrathful, but there was a tinge of satisfaction in his tone that made Ted anxious.

Fence nodded. "The more you say," he said, "the less sorry I shall be. It is high time these were taken from you both. They work great ill. Edward, I think thou seest now the force behind that which we spoke of last night."

Ted was too eager to get out to argue. He nodded and pulled at Patrick's arm as he went by. Patrick yanked away from him, but came along.

"What the hell got into you?" Ted demanded, when they were several turns down.

"Me?" said Patrick, in such a low tone that Ted could hardly hear him over the stony echo of their feet, but with considerable force. "Me? I'm not the one who turned traitor and gave up our only way out of here!"

"What'd you expect me to do, kill them both?"

Patrick went faster, passing Ted and disappearing around the next curve. Ted's legs still hurt from the climb up, but he tried to hurry too.

"Where are you going?"

No answer.

He trailed Patrick back to their own room, where his cousin flung open a wooden chest, banging its lid on the wall behind it. He pulled out a sword, thumping the hilt on the side of the trunk, and whipped past the astonished Ted, the sword held in front of him like a hockey stick.

Ted, panting and incredulous, caught up with him in the stairwell and grabbed the collar of his tunic. Patrick just stood there, waiting for Ted to go away.

"What's that sword?"

"It's nothing special," said Patrick, "but it'll do what I want."

"I suppose it'll kill Fence and Randolph for you?" said Ted, trying for sarcasm and achieving what sounded to him like fright.

"Yes and no."

"You can't beat Randolph fencing. You'll just get yourself in trouble and feel stupid."

"Come on and see," said Patrick, twitching out of Ted's grip. He rounded a corner in the wrong direction for Fence's tower. Ted, hoping that he had gotten confused, said nothing. It soon became obvious that they were headed for the

North Tower. Ted tried to remember what was there, and could not.

The corridor to the North Tower was dim at this time of day, and the dust raised by their hurried passage made it worse. Ted began to wonder how much of High Castle was unused.

The door to the stairs was carved very oddly, and Patrick did not give Ted time to figure it out. He banged through it as if it were any door in a supermarket, and bounded up the stairs.

The door to the first tower room was plain wood. Patrick pushed it open and waited for Ted. Ted, panting, looked into a round bare room. In the middle of the room was a round wooden table. In the middle of the table was a dazzling globe. It might have been full of bits of colored glass, or the color might all have been the rainbows made by the sunlight shining through the crystal. It was bigger than Ted's head. It made the tears come to his eyes, and when he had blinked them away, Patrick was standing over the globe with the sword raised.

"This is another way out," he said to Ted.

"What the hell are you doing?"

"This is the Crystal of Earth. And when I break it, all this will vanish and we'll all be back home."

He gripped the sword with both hands.

"Patrick," said Ted, in an agonized squeak; then, when Patrick ignored him, he shouted. "Don't!"

Patrick raised the sword above his head and brought it down.

There was a tremendous flash, as the crystal of the Secret Country exploded into a billion colored shards, and a ringing, terrible, sustained crash as the land, from end to end, from the Mountains of the North to the Dubious Hills, from the Wide West Waste to the Sunrise Sea, cities of men and manners, climates, councils, governments, the boast of heraldry and pomp of power, all that heart heard of or mind expressed, trees, flowers, cottages, and wells, the unicorn, the cardinal, the dragon, and the owl, sun, moon, stars, clouds, the loving detail of High Castle, the barely imagined cities of the Dwarves, the fabulous mines whence came Lord Randolph's ring, the Green Caves and the Magic Wood, King John's solemn tomb, Laura and Ellen downstairs, the stones beneath them and their very bones, shook, rang, shattered, and seemed to collapse in dust.

CHAPTER 18

TED breathed for one moment a dustier and thicker air, and saw in a flash the drooping leaves of the hedge and the bulk of the secret house, looking shabbier than he remembered it. A car horn honked behind him, he jumped, and the scene was gone.

Ted and Patrick stood still. Sunlight streamed through the flawless windows. Out of the windows, far away across the green plain, they saw sheep grazing the slopes. Above the sheep the clouds sailed, high and white. A bird went in a red streak by the window. Patrick's sword was stuck six inches into the solid oak of the table, and on the table was a scattering of broken glass and bits of color, brighter than the bands of sunlight on wall and floor.

"Criminy," said Ted, whispering. "What will they do to us?"

"What will *we* do?" said Patrick.

"Get a broom," said Ted. He thought he should be angry, but he was much too tired.

"How are we going to get *out* of this?"

Ted looked at him. Patrick went out, and came back with a broom. He tried to sweep up the glass, but he knocked the wooden handle of the broom, which was taller than he was, into all the chairs until Ted, who felt he could not stand any noise that he was not making himself, took the broom away from him and began sweeping.

Patrick put both hands over his face as if he were going to cry—which Ted had never seen him do—and said, matter-of-factly, "When does this stop?"

"When it's over," said Ted, wishing he had the strength to say, "I told you so."

"Are you going to kill Lord Randolph?"

"No," said Ted.

"What makes you think you have a choice?"

Ted unbent himself from under the table, where he was pursuing elusive splashes of glass, and said, "Why shouldn't I?"

"Everything else we've tried to stop it hasn't worked."

"We haven't really tried much," said Ted. "And anyway, this is *me*. I have a sword, and I can use it, or not, and I won't."

"That's what *I* thought," said Patrick, looking at the scarred table.

"But you were trying to do something, and it didn't happen to work. I choose not to do something. How can that not work?"

Patrick shrugged. "Maybe you'll stab him through the arras because you think he's Andrew."

Ted shivered. Then he thought about it. "Well," he said, "even that would be better than killing him in the rose garden."

"Why?" demanded Patrick. "As long as we're stuck in this story we might as well . . . stick to it. Deviating only causes trouble, as far as I can see. I bet if you hadn't been acting so weird, Randolph wouldn't have taken the swords away."

"Me?" said Ted, stung. "Me? If you'd been satisfied with normal practice swords and not wanted to play with the magic ones—"

"Okay, okay," said Patrick.

"And did you hear what Fence said to me? He thinks my suspicions of Randolph were caused by the sword, and now he'll never believe them."

"Yes, all right. But see? Deviating causes trouble, that's all. I wish I'd thought of this sooner."

Ted sat down, feeling resigned. "Thought of what?"

Patrick said patiently, "I think a random element enters the plot whenever it's necessary to keep us from changing the final outcome."

"What random elements?"

"Shan's Ring," said Patrick. "That Lady Claudia. And now this."

"But how—"

"We never found out the riddle of Shan's Ring before, but we had to do it this time or we couldn't have stayed at all. And this crystal didn't work the way it should have, so we'd have to stay."

"How did you expect it to work?"

"Well," said Patrick, "I thought that just this once, my mind might be able to overpower all the rest of your minds, because the other three don't believe anything about the Crystal of Earth because we didn't make it up and they haven't seen it. And you weren't sure what you thought about it, and you hadn't seen it either. I figured that, whatever is really going on, if I destroyed this place or seemed to, by its own rules, you know, we'd have to end up back where we came from."

Ted, about to yell at him for being stupid and risking all

their lives on his pet theory, remembered the brief glimpse of their own world he had had, and bit his lip. "You know," he said, "it almost seemed to work. Did you notice—"

"Yes," said Patrick, a little smugly. "For just a minute I saw the bottle trees and the dog. But something kept it from working. So now I'm not sure what's going on, but I think something's trying to keep the story going."

"And what about that Claudia?"

"Now there's a really random element," said Patrick. "Telling the King about Fence too soon, getting that council called too early, trying to ambush Fence on the stairs—and bewitching Randolph."

"But she hasn't really managed to *do* anything," said Ted. "Well, unless you count making such a fuss that Ruthie used Shan's Ring on her, which I think could have had a nasty effect."

"That's what I mean," said Patrick. "I think she wants the story to come out right, and since we're different from the characters in the story and it might not, she has to do things differently to balance that."

"You think she kept the crystal from working, then?"

"Well . . ."

"I don't see how she could have," said Ted.

"With Shan's Ring holding her, you mean. Well, maybe she's working for somebody else. Say for the cardinals. We never had any cardinal interrupt our practice before."

"And they also had her bewitch Randolph?"

"So he wouldn't be reasonable about killing the King. That's what I think."

"But look," said Ted, grappling rebelliously with this theory, which seemed even mistier than Patrick's other theories, "in the first place, I don't think she did bewitch Randolph."

"He said she did."

"That was just a figure of speech," said Ted.

Patrick looked scornful.

"Why should she have to, anyway?" said Ted.

He was beginning to get a headache, and his cheek hurt suddenly. He put a hand up to it and came away with a smear of blood.

"I mean," he said, "Randolph was going to be unreasonable, in the original story, so she shouldn't have had to mess with him." He thought some more. "I mean," he said, "*if* she did it, she bewitched him before we got here, right? Now if she'd bewitched him after we'd done something to make him change his mind, that would make sense."

Patrick screwed up his forehead. "Wait a minute," he said. "Let me think. This just came to me, you know. Okay. What if she knew we were coming and so she got him ready just in case."

"How could she know?"

"Maybe she brought us."

Ted felt a cold creep up his backbone. "Patrick," he said. "We got so mad at each other, when we were all talking yesterday, I forgot to mention something. It hit me—if we're not the right kids for this story, then where are they?"

"I think they ought to be back home," said Patrick. "That would at least be tidy."

"But then we wouldn't have been missed all those times we were gone."

Patrick shrugged.

"So what else did Claudia do?"

"Tried to kill Fence, and got the King mad at Fence, and got that council moved."

Ted frowned. "That doesn't make sense. If she *had* killed

Fence, that wouldn't have helped the story. I can see getting him in trouble by telling the King he was here before he was ready to see him. And maybe ruining his performance at the council by calling it before he was ready."

Patrick sat down on the table. "Well," he said, "if you're right about Shan's Ring being dangerous, maybe she never really meant to kill Fence; she knew he could beat her in a fight and then he'd call Ruth and Ruth'd use Shan's Ring."

"How would she know it's dangerous?"

Patrick shrugged again. "If she could bring us here, she probably knows a lot." He shook his head violently. "Why am I arguing with you? Who cares what the mechanism is if it isn't real?"

Ted said sourly, "You want it to be tidy, whether it's real or not."

Patrick got up on his knees on the table and tried to pull the sword out of it. "I wonder how I got it in so deep?" he said.

"You were pretty worked up."

"Well, how are we going to get out of here?"

"When the time comes, we'll steal the swords."

"Easy, huh?" Patrick, having begun scornfully, looked suddenly thoughtful and then secretive.

Ted tried to disregard this. "Well, we've got lots of time to find out where they keep them. And we don't have to be sneaky about it. I figure that when we get desperate enough to steal the swords, we won't want to come back."

It probably wouldn't really be that easy, but Ted felt even tireder by now, and another discussion with Patrick would be too much.

"And just when will that be?"

Ted shrugged. "Well, either before the battle if we don't want to have anything to do with that, or before I'm supposed to kill Lord Randolph, because I certainly don't want to have anything to do with *that*."

"Last time we mentioned it you didn't want to have anything to do with the battle."

"I guess I still don't," said Ted, slowly. "But if you're right about something working to make the story come out, then there's really nothing to be afraid of, is there?" Even as he asked the question, he remembered Laura's ideas about waiting for the worms to come. He put the thought away.

"Only killing Lord Randolph," said Patrick, with a nasty grin. "In for a penny, in for a pound."

"Stop sounding like Agatha."

"You know what I mean."

"Well," said Ted, "why shouldn't we be able to fight this thing, whatever it is? Especially now that its—its secret agent—is out of the way."

"If you fight it," said Patrick, "what's to keep it from getting fed up and letting us all get killed after all?"

"I still think you're crazy," said Ted, whose patience was wearing thin. He did what was almost always a mistake, and told Patrick what he really thought. "This is real, and I think we can do things to make it different."

"Explain how it fits in with the game, then."

"Well," said Ted, "we've all been acting as if we put this here, out of our heads. What if it put itself into our heads somehow?"

Feet pounded up the stairs.

"Here it comes," said Patrick, and sprang off the table.

Ted was expecting guards. But it was Ruth, Ellen, and

Laura who burst into the room. They all looked absolutely wild; windblown somehow, Ted thought, and furious.

Ruth opened her mouth, and Patrick spoke first. "How'd you find us?" he said mildly.

Ruth clamped her mouth shut; she was clearly fighting to keep from either shrieking at him or slugging him.

"The noise came from here," said Ellen, "and it just pulled us along."

"Did you think you were home?" asked Ted.

"Maybe for a minute," said Laura. "Ellen thought so, but I don't see how anybody could tell anything with all that noise."

"I thought so too," said Ruth, very quietly.

She had been looking around the room while the others talked, and now she stooped under the table and picked up a shard of colored glass. She held it up to the light, and behind her on the bare wall sprang the figures of an old man in wizard's garb with a young man at his feet. They were wavery, as if they were under water, but the colors were brilliant and the scene easy to recognize. It was one of the earlier scenes from the tapestry in the West Tower.

"*Again!*" said Ellen, almost in a wail. "I'm not even sure I blame you for smashing it. Did it have the hole or the sun, Patrick?"

"What did you smash?" demanded Ruth.

Patrick looked straight at her, and Ted, who had been trying to think of a plausible lie to save them much anger and more argument, saw that Patrick wanted to tell her the truth, and was relishing the moment.

"The Crystal of Earth," said Patrick.

Ruth flew at him and shook him. "You idiot! You are so stupid! You are so stupid I could kill you!"

She smacked him across the face. Laura burst into tears. Ellen, crying, "Cut it out, Ruthie!" flung herself at them, fell over a chair, and knocked them both over.

Ruth stood up. "You are so stupid I don't have to kill you, you'll do it yourself," she said, calmly.

"I'll tell you who's stupid," said Patrick from the floor. "You didn't even bother to find out why I did it."

There was a bright red mark on his cheek, and he was considerably ruffled, but he managed to exude great dignity. Ted was not sure whether to cheer for him or kick him. Probably it would make no difference to Patrick.

Ruth tossed her head. Ted had never seen her do anything like that, even when she was Lady Ruth.

"Well, why did you?" Ellen asked Patrick. She was still on the floor herself.

"Because Fence and Randolph have the swords," said Patrick. He looked so pleased that Ted would not have minded smacking him too.

Ruth looked up from patting Laura. "And how did they get them?"

Patrick told the story with aplomb, but it did not help his case with Ruth.

"I said you were stupid," she remarked. She looked at Ted. "And so are you. Don't you have any better sense than to play with magic swords?"

"Don't you have any better sense than to play with magic rings?" Ted said bitterly.

"That's different. It was necessary. You just got those swords out of laziness because you didn't want to learn fencing."

"You just used the ring out of laziness because you didn't want to learn sorcery," said Patrick.

"That's not true!" cried Ellen. "She had an emergency. You were just practicing."

Patrick shrugged and stood up. "What's the matter with Laura?"

"I want to go home," said Laura.

"Don't we all," said Patrick.

"No," said Ruth.

"It occurs to me," said Patrick, "that we ought to get out of here. Why didn't the guards come running when I broke that thing?"

"You made me forget, screaming and fighting," said Ellen, "but everybody was frozen, like somebody stopped the movie. We couldn't stop to look at them because the noise was bringing us here, but they were just stopped in the middle of what they were doing."

"Lucky for us," said Patrick. He looked at Ted. "Add another one to your list."

"What list?" said Ruth irritably.

"Not now," said Ted. "It's another one of his theories. If he tells you now you'll probably kill him."

"All right, later," said Ruth. "But look, Patrick. You've got to stop doing things like this on your own. You could've killed us all. And it's not fair."

"I don't care about fair," said Patrick. "I just want us to stay in one piece."

"We won't if you run around doing things without thinking."

"It wasn't without thinking. I thought about it for days. I just didn't expect to need it."

"You're missing the point."

"Not *now*," said Ted.

"All right," said Patrick. "Let's discuss something easier,

like how to keep Laura from breaking her neck on the Unicorn Hunt."

"I'm not going," said Laura.

"It's not just Laura," said Ruth. "Ellie and I can't—what?"

"Not going."

"It'll be fun," said Ellen, sounding outraged.

"Banquet of Midsummer Eve was supposed to be fun."

"Didn't you like it?" said Ellen, surprised.

Laura was silent.

"Anyway," said Ruth, "Ellie and I can't ride that well, either, Pat. Rocks and hills and trees, and galloping."

"I think," said Ellen, frowning, "that Agatha and servants and old people walk on behind with picnic baskets or something. Maybe we could go with them?"

"I don't think any of us should ride," said Patrick.

"Well, maybe we could all go with the walkers, then," said Ruth.

"I can ask Agatha," said Ellen.

"And now can we get out of here?" said Patrick. "I suppose the guards will have to unfreeze sometime, and they might remember that something odd happened."

"Well, don't leave the evidence lying around like that," said Ruth.

She supervised Ted's sweeping the shards of the Crystal of Earth into one pile. They all stood around looking at it. Ted felt the sadness of having broken something beautiful, and wondered whether Laura felt like that all the time.

"They're bound to find out about this sooner or later," he said. "I wonder why it wasn't guarded."

"I wonder why it didn't work," said Patrick.

After some halfhearted argument, Ruth was allowed to bundle up the pieces of the Crystal of Earth in Ellen's pinafore and bear them away to her room. Patrick wanted to bury or hide them somewhere, but Ruth said shortly that she would feel better being able to keep an eye on them.

Ted and Patrick went back to the practice swords, and had little to say to one another.

CHAPTER 19

ON the day of the Unicorn Hunt Laura woke up at dawn with her ivory unicorn clutched in one hand. Ellen had objected to Laura's sleeping with it, maintaining that she, Laura, would certainly let go of it in her sleep and she, Ellen, roll over on it and be gouged. But Laura had been stubborn. Now, wriggling her hand to get rid of the lines and creases left by the statue, she decided that Fence really had put a spell of finding and returning on it.

She climbed out of bed and went over to the window. She tried to be quiet. If she couldn't sneak out and hide herself before Ellen woke up, Ellen would make her go to the Unicorn Hunt. The floor was chilly, but no more than you would expect of a stone floor in the early morning. She put her head out into the pale air.

The sky was faint and pure. The long thin sunlight of early morning spread like a blanket over the treetops, but the roots of the Enchanted Forest were blue with shadow, and High Castle reared its massive height over the lake so that the lake too was dark. Or was it? Laura almost fell out of the window. There were hundreds of them, a sea of cloudy manes and spiral horns, and they shed about them a substantial light. The trees in the sunshine were more ephemeral than they. Laura jumped down from the window seat and made for the door.

"Ellen!" she yelled. "Wake up!" She jerked open the door and ran in her nightgown down the passage, down the back stairs, and out into the light.

"Good morrow, Child of Man," said the unicorn.

"Good morning," said Laura, staring.

"What do you wish?"

"I only wanted to watch," said Laura, and bit her tongue, wondering if this was an admission that she had never seen a unicorn. "And to greet you," she said.

"That was gracious," said the unicorn.

Laura was embarrassed, and said nothing.

The unicorn too was silent. The others had drifted away, elusive as the things that crowd the edges of your vision. This last one slid farther into the lake, and Laura grabbed handfuls of her nightgown and waded into the water. It was shockingly cold.

The unicorn said, "We do not regard the Children of Men with such awe as you give to us, and you are only a child, who will grow only to a woman. But you seem to me full of some power, as if we were the transient thing and you the lasting. But this is not so. What power is in you?"

I made you up, thought Laura. But looking at the unicorn, she could not believe that she had. It was enormous and solid. Its breath was warm on the top of her head. It had whiskers on the sides of its nose. The long horn with its spiral of violet gleamed and slanted, cold and dangerous, as the animal moved its head. Laura, sinking slowly into gravelly mud, looked up into its inquiring eye—violet, as Fence had said, and with an upright pupil like a cat's—and felt herself a slight and wavering thing. She remembered the exasperating line from *Hamlet* that Ted quoted at her when she could not understand his explanations, and she shook her head.

"No," she said, "I never dreamed you in *my* philosophy."

The unicorn took two paces backward, drenching Laura to the waist.

"Certainly you did not," it said, but it sounded startled.

"Oh, don't go away," pleaded Laura.

"You will see me again," said the unicorn. "Today is the hunt." It wheeled around like a leaf in a whirlpool and fled after the rest of the herd.

Laura, backing away slowly, as if she were retreating from an audience with a king, tripped over her nightgown and sat down with a tremendous splash in the shallows of the lake.

She trudged back upstairs, leaving a trail of sand and water, and dripped into their bedroom. Ellen sat in the middle of the unmade bed with a very red face, trying to braid her hair. "Shan's mercy!" she said fiercely as Laura entered.

"Don't swear," said Laura.

"That's not swearing," said Ellen crossly as she looked up and stared. "What happened to *you?*"

"I talked to the unicorns!"

"In the water?"

"I tried to wake you up."

"Well, you did, but you were already gone."

"And I have to talk to Patrick."

"You'd better dry off first," said Ellen. "He won't be very pleased if you go dripping cold water on him. Did you go swimming?"

"No. I just talked to one of them for a minute. Oh, Ellie, you should have seen."

"Was it like the Secret?"

"Much better," said Laura. "We didn't know anything about it at all. *Those* are *real* unicorns."

"Are you going to start arguing with Patrick?" demanded Ellen.

"I'm just going to tell him."

"Well, let's get dressed first."

"What in?" asked Laura, stopping in the act of untying the bow at the neck of her nightgown. "I refuse to go in the woods in one of those dresses."

Ellen bounded out of bed and went over to the wardrobe.

"They're special festive clothes," she said, "like the ones for the banquet. So if we can find two more outfits that look alike, I'll bet that's it. No, don't you come over here, you'll get everything all wet. Why don't you go dry off."

Laura dripped obediently into their bathing room. Today, for some reason, the towels were black, but they were still linen. Laura wrapped herself up in one and wished for a mirror. Agatha had a hand mirror which she used to show Ellen and Laura what she had done to their hair, although Laura did not think that a protest on their part would make her change the hair. Ruth had a hand mirror in her room. The only other one Laura had seen was Fence's, which was probably not a mirror at all. There was a room called the Mirror Room, but in fact its walls were covered with tapestries.

Laura stalked out of the bathing room, intoning, "I am the Demon Queen."

Ellen, who had her arms full of green stuff, favored her with the remark, "You don't have any warts." She dumped the clothes on the bed. "These must be the right ones," she said. "See, they've got short skirts and no lace, and they're all loose. This one is bigger, it must be mine. Here." She threw the other dress across the bed to Laura and began climbing out of her nightgown. "Did you hang up that wet nightgown?" she added.

"Claudia doesn't have any warts," said Laura, dropping the towel in a heap on the floor and pulling the dress over her head. "And she's a demon queen."

"She's somebody awful," said Ellen.

"I want my tennis shoes," said Laura.

"They're in Agatha's mending basket," said Ellen. "And the cat ate one of the laces. They'd look funny with that dress anyway." She went over to the wardrobe again. "Here. Green boots. Or moccasins. Or something."

"Too heavy," said Laura.

"There are brambles out there," said Ellen. "Agatha said if we tried to wear our sandals like we did last year, she'd leave us behind with bread and water."

"Oh, well." Laura sat down and took the boots. "*Did* we wear sandals last year?"

They put the boots on, with some trouble, as the laces were complex. "Let the cat eat these," mumbled Laura. Then they went to find Patrick.

He was sitting in the middle of his bedroom floor, lacing his boots up with a sort of pleasurable concentration on his face. He was wearing a tunic of the same color and material as their dresses, and his boots were green too.

"Agatha says both Ted and Ruth can't come with her party," said Ellen.

Patrick looked startled. "Oh," he said. "I should have thought of that. But will she let Laurie go?"

"Sure. Everybody except Ted, or except Ruth. So one of them has to ride."

Patrick finished his boots and frowned. "Who rides better, Ted or Ruth?"

"Ruth," said Ellen, loyally.

Patrick shrugged. "I think Ted should go with the main hunt. He's the prince, after all."

"I'll tell Ruth to come with us, then," said Ellen. "Agatha says if we're late we'll be left behind."

Patrick shrugged again.

"Where's Ted?" asked Ellen.

Patrick pointed to a lump in their wildly untidy bed. "He won't get up. He had bad dreams last night, and spent hours walking the battlements, or something."

"Well, tell him he has to ride today."

Laura, who had been fidgeting around, said, "Patrick, we didn't make up those unicorns."

"No, of course we didn't. The Greeks did," he said. "Or was it the Middle Ages?"

"But you said—"

"*We* didn't," said Patrick. "Not the way we made up Lord Randolph. Not the idea of unicorns. But we put them here. It doesn't make them any realer, Laurie, just because somebody else made them up, does it?"

"You don't make any sense at all!" said Laura, crossly, and bolted into the hall. She was not sure, now, that she could describe her early morning experience to anyone. She certainly could not describe it to Patrick. She wondered what he would say if she told him that the unicorn had seemed to think that she had made it up.

"I hope," said Ellen, joining her, "that you're not going to be nasty all day."

"Who's nasty?" said Laura, astonished.

"Never mind," said Ellen, eyeing her sideways as they went down the stairs. "Sometimes you act *just* like Princess Laura."

Laura considered this all the way down to the dining hall, and became pleased with herself. She thought that High Castle must be rubbing off on her somehow. She thought about riding horses, and liked the idea no better than she ever had. The rubbing off must be slow.

There was nobody in the dining hall, but there was even more food than usual on the sideboard; some empty plates and cups on the table showed that other people were up too. They inspected the sideboard.

"Hey!" said Laura. "Oatmeal."

"Gah," said Ellen. "I'm getting tired of pork chops for breakfast."

They took their food and dishes and sat down at one end of a long table. The high roof of the hall arched above them, full of shadows. It was very quiet. Outside two birds argued. Laura buttered her bread lavishly, licked her knife, and blanched. She kept forgetting that there was no salt in the butter. There was none in the oatmeal either, or perhaps something else was wrong with it. Whatever was wrong, she didn't like it.

"How long," she asked Ellen, "are we going to be here?"

"Well," said Ellen, laying a bare chop bone on her plate, "I guess it depends on how many stories we've made up. We never did use them all, you know. By the time Ted comes back to life and is king—"

"But wait," said Laura. "Those other stories came before now. We didn't want them to happen afterward because we didn't like having stories without Lord Randolph."

"*I* never thought Lord Randolph was so much," said Ellen, scowling. "Who wants murderers around anyway?"

"But he wasn't a murderer before."

"He was thinking about it."

"Well, you agreed," said Laura.

"Huh," said Ellen. She picked up her plate, letting the

bone fall to the table, and examined the pattern. "Hey," she said. "It's that darn pattern again."

"Has it got the sun or the hole?"

Ellen turned the plate, examining it. "Well!" she said. "It doesn't have that scene at all."

"I wonder what's going on," said Laura, sadly.

There was a sudden commotion at the door as Ted, Ruth, and Patrick all struggled to get through it at once. It was just barely too narrow for all of them, and none of them would give way. Ruth and Ted were laughing, but Patrick, who was stuck in the middle, kept repeating calmly, "I won this race."

"Ha!" said Ruth, dropping to her knees and scooting between their legs and across the floor to the sideboard. "Ha!" she repeated, standing up. "You said, I'll race you to breakfast. *This* is breakfast. I win."

Ellen and Laura looked at one another.

"Maybe she's forgotten about being a sorcerer," whispered Ellen.

Laura doubted it. She knew of no rule that sorcerers could not occasionally be silly.

Patrick picked himself up off the floor and came sedately over to join her. Ted followed. Before they had finished choosing their breakfasts, Randolph, Fence, and Matthew came in and made for the sideboard.

"Listen, you guys," said Ruth, holding a ladleful of oatmeal over the iron pot and watching it dubiously, "do you really think Ted can keep up with the hunt? I've been riding longer, and—"

"Shut up!" said Ellen, making odd movements with her eyebrows at the two lords and the magician.

Ruth did not see her, but they did. Fence and Matthew simply stopped walking and looked receptive, but Randolph, to the everlasting astonishment of Laura, came quietly up behind Ted, who was carefully spooning honey onto a plate, and tickled him. Ellen burst out laughing. Laura dropped her cup of mead into her lap.

Ted gave an unnerved shriek and leaped backward, his hand going to his belt. Laura saw that he had there a dagger in a leather sheath, and any impulse to laughter she might have felt was stilled.

Randolph was smiling at Ted, but he looked a little anxious. Ted stared at him for a moment and then giggled, possibly in relief. Patrick rolled his eyes at the ceiling, which made Laura giggle too. Ruth placidly served herself some oatmeal. Fence and Matthew, exchanging glances Laura would have given a great deal to know the meaning of, came and got their own breakfasts.

Fence sat across from Ellen and Laura as Ellen was trying to mop the mead off Laura's dress.

"Stupid napkins," she muttered. "They're as bad as the towels."

"Never mind," said Laura, trying to squirm away from her. Fence looked suspicious again. She had not seen him since he gave her the ivory unicorn, and her reaction to that seemed to have been what he expected. Apparently spilling mead in her lap was not what he expected of her. Laura cursed Princess Laura and pushed Ellen's hand away.

"Seek out the old napkins," said Matthew to Ellen, sitting down beside Fence. "They grow more pliable with age."

"Unlike men," said Randolph, and slid himself in next to Ellen.

"This is not a day for such remarks," said Fence severely.

Randolph looked at him, and Laura expected him to shrug. He looked remarkably like Patrick for a moment. Then he smiled. "I cry you mercy," he said, and bit into his bread.

"I have been thinking," he added, with his mouth full, a

thing for which he had chided Laura at dinner the night before, "that we require a new riddle for the ceremony for the hunt, if that which we commonly ask the unicorns hath been answered by another. Am I not right, lady," he said to Ruth, "to say that you have solved the riddle of Shan's Ring?"

Ruth choked on her oatmeal and turned red, whether from the choking or from embarrassment Laura did not know. The rest of them sat very still; Laura looked at Ted and saw that he was afraid.

"What?" said Fence, dropping his knife.

"Well," said Ruth, and cleared her throat.

"Oh, well done!" said Fence, beaming at her. Ruth was too nonplussed to say anything.

"It's what I used on Claudia," she told him, cautiously.

Fence nodded. "I had wondered," he said, "but—ah, well, 'tis not for me to pry into your secrets. So Shan's Ring goes now to be an heirloom of the Green Caves."

Ruth shrugged; Laura suspected her of being confused.

"I would we had known this sooner," said Fence, looking reproachfully from Ruth to Randolph.

"Well," said Ruth, "I thought we'd ask the riddle again and check the unicorn's answer this year, just to be sure. I mean, the Ring could do what it's done so far because of a lot more theories than mine."

Laura felt Patrick, who had sat down on her other side, move jerkily. She glanced at him. He looked outraged. She supposed that he disliked Ruth's taking credit for his ideas.

"Cautious, prudent, sober," said Fence. "Not according to the Unicorn Hunt, methinks."

"What instead, then?" said Randolph.

"There is our present distress," ventured Matthew, but both Fence and Randolph shook their heads at him.

"Not so close to battle as we are," said Randolph.

"Indeed not," said Fence. "The answer would raise more dispute than it could answer; each man would bend it to his own need. The unicorns speak not straightly. We would be more muddled than we are, and what little strategy we have would be undone. Besides, some things it is better not to know."

"Isn't that pretty cautious and prudent too?" said Patrick.

"Very well," said Matthew, patiently. "Then let us ask the unicorns what is the nature of Claudia?"

Everyone turned toward him with exclamations of surprise and pleasure. He looked smug.

"Excellent," said Fence.

"Oh, good," said Laura. "We can find out who she is and what she's up to and—"

Ellen bumped her.

"Why do you ask who she is?" said Randolph. "She has lived here longer than you have. She and I were from our childhood days brought up here."

"She was a goodly child," said Fence, thoughtfully. "When, I wonder, did—"

"*I* keep wondering," said Laura, who had just thought of it, "if she could have put a spell on us to make us think she'd been here and was Andrew's sister and was nice, but—"

"That would be a considerable spell," said Fence.

Laura began to feel irritated with him. Obviously he did not like to admit that someone he had not taught could do anything right.

"In the same league," said Randolph, suddenly, "as covering the Southlands with monsters that seem as trees?"

Fence stared at him. "I had thought she furthered her own ends. A spy of the Dragon King?"

315

"No, *no!*" cried Laura, unbearably exasperated. "Lord Andrew is the spy of the Dragon King!"

"*Laurie!*" said Ted.

"*Laura!*" said Randolph a bare second behind him, and much more severely.

But Fence brought his hand down on the table with a crash that rattled the bones on the plates and spilled what remained of Laura's mead. "Why not?" said he.

"Why?" said Randolph.

"Consider his beliefs touching magic," said Matthew.

"All the better," said Fence. "The deluded mind is the easier to deceive."

"Fie on this," said Randolph, "where is the evidence?"

"Laura?" said Fence, and looked at her much too intently for comfort.

Laura was unbearably frustrated and extremely frightened. None of the others seemed inclined to help her. Or perhaps they could not; they looked frightened too. She swallowed.

"I just thought so," she said. "Because he hangs around the King all the time and you can *tell* he doesn't like him." This was a restatement of something Ted had said when he was reporting the second council to them.

Randolph shrugged. "Andrew likes no one, save perhaps himself."

"Well, he doesn't hang around anybody else," said Laura, gaining a little confidence from the mere fact that someone had bothered to answer her.

"Maybe he wants to be King," said Ellen, a little shakily. Laura looked at her with gratitude.

Fence had an expression on his face that Laura was not sure she liked; he looked as if he were about to pounce.

"How could he become King?" said Ruth to Ellen, a little irritably.

"He's related," said Ellen, bristling.

Randolph, looking at Fence, said, "It is but distantly."

"So," said Fence, "who stands in his way? Ted, Patrick. Who next?"

"Siblings," said Randolph, with a sort of glee that Laura did not understand at all. "Patrick the Elder. Anna. Children of siblings. Justin the Younger. Angus. Laura, Ellen. Children of the grandsires' siblings."

Ellen began to giggle.

"William's father, John V, had one brother, Edward," said Fence, frowning as if he were doing mental arithmetic. "His children were James and Elaine."

"Elaine," said Matthew, with the air of one entering a game, "is High Sorceress, and has forfeited her claim."

"James," said Fence, "is a hermit in the Dubious Hills."

"John also," said Fence, "had one sister, Celia, who had five sons and two daughters. None is dead and all have children."

Laura had not the remotest idea what they were all doing, but they were so obviously having a joke that she, too, began to giggle.

"We may see by this," said Fence, raising his voice over their chortles, "that the other heirs to the throne are far too numerous to be disposed of by assassination or by any other means that Andrew might effect on his own. His alliance with the Dragon King lies therefore within the borders of the probable. Granting the premise," he added, nodding in Ellen's direction. She snorted, and began to laugh again.

"There is a much simpler premise," said Randolph. "Andrew wants, not the throne, but rather that considerable degree of power that comes from being in the King's favor and in his confidence, both of which he hopes to gain by speaking what he views as hard sense, when every other counselor who is his own man is babbling children's stories."

"In which case," said Matthew, "Andrew must himself believe what he says touching magic?"

Randolph shrugged. "It's like him," he said, scornfully. "He can see inward to the minds of men, but never outward to anything that is not Man."

" 'The proper study of Mankind is Man,' " mumbled Ruth.

"And a more foolish teaching I've seldom heard," exclaimed Randolph. "Had King John studied Man we would all be slaves in the mines of the Dragon King and all our gardens would be a wilderness of snakes."

"Laura," said Fence, "why did you say that Andrew was a spy?"

Ruth said to Randolph, "If the Dragon King had studied man, he'd only be a man now, and we wouldn't have to worry about Andrew's loyalties."

"If pigs had wings," said Fence, laughing, "they would be pigeons."

"No matter the circumstances, we needs must concern ourselves with Andrew's loyalties," said Randolph, "for that they lie always with himself whether that be right or wrong."

"Randolph," said Fence.

"Have a care for thine own tongue," said Randolph, smiling; there was an edge to his words.

Fence looked thoughtfully at him, and nodded. "A very palpable hit," he said. "This is a day neither for politics nor for philosophy, save what twisted and uncertain bits of't come our way in the Riddle Game. But once more, before we turn our tongues to merrier things. Laura?"

"I already told you," said Laura, a little sullenly; she had thought the danger was over.

Fence dropped his hand to the table. "You may be a child," he said, "which I can see you hope will excuse you, but you are not stupid, nor malicious, nor fanciful. I will have this out of you ere the next council. Let it be for now."

With one accord they stood and made for the door.

I knew I shouldn't have come, thought Laura, but she could not dread Fence's questions when the Unicorn Hunt lay before her. She felt that seeing a unicorn again was all that anyone could ask for.

"Not malicious or fanciful, maybe," said Ted in Laura's ear, "but you're certainly stupid. What made you do that?"

"They need to know!"

"Not unless you can back it up."

"Well, you told Fence about Randolph!" said Laura, and then stared at him. Had he told Fence as she had, without thinking, because he was exasperated? She tripped on the doorsill, and Ted picked her up. Laura was relieved that Fence had not seen.

"Keep an eye out for Agatha," said Patrick, on the other side of Laura. "We don't want you breaking your neck."

"Agatha's right there," said Laura, waving as they came out into the courtyard. "Where are the horses for Ted and everybody?"

"There's Benjamin," said Ellen, behind her.

All four of them stopped and stared. Benjamin was on foot, and he was not dressed for riding. He led one white horse, without a saddle. With him came the King and the other counselors. They were all on foot, and they were not dressed for riding either.

"What now!" said Ted. "Claudia again?"

"Where?" said Ellen.

"No, I mean she did this."

"How could she?" said Laura. "She's locked up."

"Be quiet a minute," said Ted, watching the rest of their breakfast party merge with the King's. Randolph kissed the King's hand and spoke to him earnestly. Several counselors made for Fence. Matthew stood looking amused, and Ruth hovered nervously near him. A cardinal whistled out of the fir trees.

"I know perfectly well," said Ted, "that this hunt goes on horseback. Now what's she done?"

"Well, it saves a lot of trouble," said Ellen.

"That's unusual for Claudia," said Ted. He caught Patrick by the sleeve. "Name me those random factors again," he said.

Patrick blinked at him. "Solving Shan's Ring. And it looks like you were wrong about that too; it's not dangerous. Let's see. Getting Fence in trouble a couple of different ways. Claudia definitely did that. And the Crystal of Earth not working."

"And no horses on the hunt?"

Patrick strode across the courtyard, followed by Ted, and tapped Matthew's elbow. "Sir."

"My lord?"

"Were we not to ride upon this hunt?"

"The Unicorn Hunt?" said Matthew, astonished. "It was never so. You know that."

"He's just being troublesome," said Ted, dragging at Patrick, who had acquired his stubborn look.

"Don't be an idiot," Ted said to him. "If she can make them believe she's been at court all her life, if she did, or get out of Fence's spell, which he says she did anyway, she can make them think they've never used horses for the hunt, can't she?"

"I want to know what's going on."

"Still at Claudia?" said Matthew.

Patrick looked up at him. "I remember as well as I remember anything that we ride to this hunt."

"And I," said Matthew, "remember better than anything that we do not."

"You're bewitched!"

"Or you are," said Matthew, sounding mildly interested.

"*Me!*" said Patrick, outraged.

Ted felt cold all over. "Why not?" he said. "How could you tell? Maybe that's how they put all this into our heads."

Behind them there came a tumult of horns, a blare and blast of enormous melody that shook the bones in them and seemed likely to accomplish what Patrick had wanted when he broke the Crystal of Earth. Their ears rang, the ground trembled, a cloud of pigeons shot away from the towers of High Castle, and Ted saw the cardinal go like a red arrow out of the fir trees.

CHAPTER 20

THE hunters came in a crowd of hounds. They were tall men, with intent faces and large eyes. They were dressed in red and green, and they had caps with feathers. Some of them carried horns, but most of them had long spears. Their eyes stared over or around or through the assembled lords and ladies and servants and children. They seemed to contemplate, with infinite patience, something enormously remote, farther than the mountains, past the shores of evening, west of the west.

The King stepped from among his counselors to greet these men, and he bowed to them.

"You are welcome, my lords," he said. His voice carried as well in the courtyard as it had in the Council Chamber. "You do us great honor, to come so far for so brief a time that we who cannot even track the hart may be overbold and merry with the unicorn. Is all well with you?"

"My lord," said one of the hunters, "one who was ever of our company goes missing."

Ted was quite sure who this was, and he looked at Patrick. Patrick seemed poised between fury and fascination.

"My lord, it grieves me to hear it," said the King. "Who?"

"The Lady Claudia does not ride with us."

"How did he know that so fast?" Ted whispered to Patrick.

Matthew glared at them, and Patrick did not reply; he did manage to look eloquently disgusted.

"My lord," said the King, "I deeply regret that you were not informed, and that we sought not to replace her. We are hedged about with troubles, and our minds set on things other than festival. I crave your indulgence; this shall be remedied."

He looked away from the hunter, and his eye fell on Ruth, who stood between Matthew and Patrick, looking at the ground.

"Milady Ruth," said the King.

Ruth looked at him warily. "Sire."

"I prithee take Claudia's place in this game, that all be not cheated of their celebration. Thy hand dispatched her to the dungeon; come then and fill the gap thou'st made."

"Sir," said Ruth, in a voice so low that Ted, just the other side of Patrick, could barely hear her. He saw Laura and Ellen, across the courtyard with Agatha, staring in bewilderment. "I did not dispatch Claudia to the dungeon on a whim," Ruth went on, looking straight at the King and growing red, "but because it was needful. And I will never, in jest or in earnest, ask me who will, my lord, play such a part as she played yearly here. Do not ask me to."

The King seemed to have had no trouble hearing her; he turned red, too, and began to speak.

"*Ruth!*" said Patrick, overriding the King. "*It's only a game!*"

Ruth stepped clear of Matthew, who had tried to take her arm. She glared at her brother; this time her voice carried to everyone.

"It is a base treachery," she said, not with the shrillness of Ruth when she was excited, but with the impressive deepness of Lady Ruth in a temper, "and I would not act such a part in the meanest theater in Telma!"

Patrick closed his mouth, despair in his face. Ted, crazily, wondered what Telma was.

Into the awful silence came Ellen's voice.

"I'll do it," she said.

Ted jumped and looked at her. Laura was gaping at her; Agatha was regarding her with the kind of proprietary pleasure Ted had seen exhibited by mothers at school concerts. She had startled other people too.

Patrick elbowed Ted. "Who did the maiden in the game?"

"Ellen," said Ted, wearily.

"Yes, I know, but was she *Princess* Ellen or just—"

The King cocked an eyebrow at Ellen, and gestured. She came across the cobblestones to him, looking defiant. The King looked down at her for a moment, and nobody breathed.

"That was well done," said the King. He turned to the hunter. "Will you take this maid to be of your company this day, that all things may be as they were first done and written?"

"Will she be faithful?"

"I pledge it," said the King.

"Ouch," said Patrick in Ted's ear. "If she should break it now."

"Shush!" said Ted violently; this entire ritual was new to him and he did not want to miss any of it.

"Let her come, then," said the hunter, beckoning, and Ellen went to stand with his tall grave men.

"Here begins the Hunt of the Unicorn," said the hunter.

Three of his men put horns to their lips. Ted braced himself, but they blew more gently this time. Then they all began walking down the hill, through the terraces and gardens below High Castle, making for the Enchanted Forest. The inhabitants of High Castle fell in behind them in a babble of voices which sounded, to Ted, more strident than merry.

"Ruthie's going to get it," said Patrick, on Ted's right.

"You shut the hell up," Ruth said over Ted's head to him.

"No doubt she is," said Matthew behind them, to Ted's relief. "But must you talk about it here and now? For shame, all of you. If you cannot be merry together, have at least the grace to sulk separately. This is festival."

"I don't care if I do get it," said Ruth to Patrick, heatedly. "It's a dirty rotten trick to call the animal when you know it has to show up because you're all pure and innocent, and then let the hunters—who could never catch it on their own—come and kill it. They can cut my head off before I'll do it."

"Ruthie," said Ted, with sudden hope, "listen, okay—that's how I feel about what I have to do."

"Claudia," said Patrick, loudly, "doesn't look very innocent to me."

"Do not slander the absent," said Matthew, peaceably.

"It's not the same at *all*," said Ruth to Ted.

"I didn't say it was, I said I felt the same."

Matthew, staring at them, opened his mouth.

"My lord," said Patrick to him, desperately, "are those wild strawberries?"

"Where?" said Matthew.

Patrick pointed ahead of them. Ted looked too, and saw that the grass beyond the last terrace was thick with flowers, as thick as the needlepoint his grandmother did. Among them he saw trails and clumps of the sharp-edged leaflets and pale yellow stars of the strawberry.

"Indeed they are," said Matthew.

"We'll have to come and pick them when they're ripe!" said Patrick, with an exuberance foreign to Ted's experience of his moods. He bounded down the last steps ahead of them and went knee-deep into bluebells.

"Think again," said Matthew. "Where even you lose the path, my prince, the strawberries in that field are perilous. This is the border of the Enchanted Forest."

"Where *is* the path?" said Ted. "Where's the hunt?"

They looked at him, and they looked ahead and behind. Up the hill among the terraces and fountains, no one walked. The bright meadow before them was empty of all but butterflies, and the eaves of the forest were full only of shadows. They heard the wind, and one lone cardinal, and their own breathing: no step, no laugh, no cry of hound or horn.

"This is the first spell of the Enchanted Forest," said Matthew. "Mayhap we are set for our own adventure." He looked at Ruth. "My lady, you may yet play that part you refused. The Hunt of the Unicorn goes not always to the hunters."

"It doesn't?" said Patrick. Ted winced, thinking that Patrick should know this already, but Matthew did not seem to think so.

"One year when I was very young, it went to two of the king's counselors and a village child," said Matthew. He chuckled. "Oh, and the murmuring and whispering among the other ten of the counselors, and the dark looks and hints! My father was a counselor then, and he brooded over it in the evenings until the feast of Shan."

"Why did it go to them?" asked Ted. They had all stopped walking.

"Why does the wind blow?" said Matthew.

"Do you really think, my lord, that this time it could go to us?"

"I won't do it," said Ruth. "I'll throw rocks at it first."

"Even if you should accept the part," said Matthew, "which among the rest of us would draw his sword?"

"Not I," said Ted.

"Nor I," said Patrick.

Ruth, disgracefully, giggled. "You sound like the bad animals in the *Little Red Hen*."

Patrick grimaced at her, and Ted, whose parents did not like the traditional children's stories, simply stared, but Matthew smiled.

"Do *you* know the story?" demanded Patrick.

"How old are you?" said Ted at the same time.

Matthew looked at them in mild surprise. "Certainly I know it, and I am seven-and-twenty," he said. Ted caught himself goggling, and looked at Ruth and Patrick, who were staring at Matthew as if he had tongues of flame above his head.

"How long have you been a counselor?" Ruth asked.

"Five years," said Matthew.

They went on staring at him.

"Is there aught else you would know?" said Matthew, not unkindly. "If there is not, we had best be on our way. A show of effort likes the unicorns."

"But do they like it?" murmured Ruth, who, thought Ted, knew perfectly well that *likes* once meant *pleases,* and that Matthew was so using it. Ted poked her, and she grinned at him.

"Keep thy distance from the maid," said Matthew to Ted.

"Oh, for heaven's sake," said Ruth.

"I had not thought," said Matthew; he was beginning to look grim.

"Neither had we," said Ted.

"Let's go," said Patrick. "Where's the path?"

Matthew stepped down into the grass, and, following

him, they saw that there was indeed a path hidden in the flowers, barely wide enough for one person to stand on with his feet together.

"Look," said Ruth. "Periwinkles. But what are those? I wish we had Ellie with us."

"I've never seen so many flowers in my life," said Ted, and could have bitten his tongue; he ought to be acting as if he had seen them every year since he could walk. He looked out of the corner of his eye at Matthew, but that young man only smiled at him.

"There are none anywhere like these," he said.

"More bluebells," said Ruth.

They plowed on through the waist-high grass. The scent of flowers and greenness and grass baking rose to Ted. He felt as if he had the soul of summer almost in his grasp.

"Watch it!" called Ruth.

"*Ow!*" said Patrick.

"Brambles," said Ruth, ruefully, looking at her brother as he tried to pull them out of his tunic.

Ted and Matthew came panting up.

"You don't want to come this way," said Ruth.

Ted, blinking, saw that they had come some considerable distance into the forest.

"Nor do we," said Matthew. "Here, hold still." He caught hold of Patrick and began unwinding him. "Can you get out, my lady?"

"Wait a moment, I think I see something," said Ruth. "There's a clearing on the other side of these bushes. I think. The sun's coming in, anyway."

"You can't get there from here," said Ted, gloomily. He had liked the meadow better.

"We can go around these things."

"That is the stream, not a clearing," said Matthew.

Patrick yelped.

"I cry you mercy," said Matthew.

"It's all right," said Patrick, "as long as I'm out." He sucked at a scratch on his wrist and looked over his hand at his sister. "Are you coming out of there?"

"The path—" began Matthew.

"Hush up a minute," said Ruth, as if he were one of her siblings.

They hushed. Thin and far they heard what might have been the crying of hounds, and then thin but clear the notes of the hunters' horns.

"Ah," said Matthew. On his flushed and sweaty face was an enormous pleasure. "At least we shall not miss't altogether."

Ruth crashed her way out onto the other side of the brambles and looked back at them. She was covered with scratches and her hair was coming down, but she looked as pleased as Matthew.

"A little water clears us of this deed," she said gaily, and plunged on into the underbrush.

Matthew flung his hair back from his forehead and went after her. Ted and Patrick stood looking at each other.

"They're crazy," said Patrick.

"I guess," said Ted. He thought he knew how they felt, and wondered why they had kept the feeling when he had lost it.

He and Patrick plowed through the bushes, trying to steer around the worst of the brambles. Ted hit himself in the forehead with a tree branch.

"God damn it!" he said, reeling back.

"Hey," said Patrick, "hey, Ted. Look at this tree."

Ted was dizzy, and he felt that sense of enormous outrage peculiar to people who have been hurt unexpectedly. "How the hell can I look at it when I've practically killed myself on it?"

"Look at the fruit."

Ted, rubbing an aching and gritty forehead with a grimier hand, squinted at the vexatious tree. "Huh," he said.

Patrick held a fruit out to him. It was perfectly round and dull red, with a thick rind.

"What's that?"

"I think it's a pomegranate."

Ted stared at it, and an idea crept into his mind. "Patrick," he said.

"What?" said Patrick, warily.

"Let's see if two can play this game."

"What?"

"Claudia's changing things. Let's change something ourselves."

"What the hell do you think I was trying to do with the Crystal of Earth?"

"Not like that. Let's try to add something new."

"We did that back at the beginning, when Ruth tried that story about Green Cave ceremonies on Benjamin."

"Not like that. Let's decide, the way we used to, that something new is true."

Patrick looked skeptical.

"Let's say," said Ted, deliberately, "that for every pomegranate seed we eat, any of the five of us, we all have to spend one month out of every year in the Secret Country."

"You can say it," said Patrick, "but I won't eat it. Besides, we've eaten them before; we've probably eaten ten years' worth. Do you want ten years here for every one at home?"

"Not just any pomegranate, then," said Ted, dismissing the notion that there was something wrong with Patrick's arithmetic. "Only the ones here. This *is* the Enchanted Forest."

"What do you want to come back for?" said Patrick. "What I want is to get out."

"I want out, too, so I don't have to kill Randolph. But—but once I'm out of that I want to be able to get back in—I want to know if this is real, I want to know what's going on."

"You're crazy," said Patrick, "if you think you can get out of killing Randolph if you come back. How do you know you just won't come back right where you left off? What makes you think they'll let you off so easy?"

"Who?"

Patrick shrugged.

"Let's say," said Ted, "that while we are gone, then, time goes on here as it does at home with us, but that while we are here, the spell of Shan's Ring holds."

The wind died among the leaves; the birds were still. Ted looked at the strange pointed leaves of the pomegranate tree. For a moment he was acutely conscious of his tangled hair, his torn tunic, his scratched legs. Then he felt full of confidence and power. The tangled ground sent a prickle through him, as the swords had done. He could do as he said. He dug with his thumbs at the fruit, unsuccessfully, and above his head a mockingbird began to sing. The breeze picked up again.

Ted felt grimy but determined. "I can't get it open."

Patrick put a hand to his knife. "One month a year for the rest of our lives? What if we get tired of it?"

"Don't you think we'll get tired of *that?*" demanded Ted, waving his arm in what he thought was the direction of the well, the house, and the hedge.

"But the rest of our *lives?* Look, why not one seed for one month, period? Every time we come back we can eat another if we want to."

"That's risky."

"Your way's worse."

Ted felt his certainty draining away, but he still wanted to do something, and still thought he had the power. "Well."

"And shouldn't we ask the girls?"

"Well—"

"I've got a knife to cut it open with, but I want you to know what you're doing."

Ted was shocked. Patrick had never acted this way before. Ted wondered if the Enchanted Forest was having an effect on both of them. But at the same time he felt that Patrick was behaving properly, however uncharacteristic of him the behavior was. Ted thought, suddenly, that many of Patrick's most exasperating habits might always have been caused by his wanting the rest of them to know what they were doing. He grinned at his cousin. The feeling of power steadied in him.

"Never mind the pomegranates," he said. "But stick around when I'm king, will you?"

Patrick did not seem surprised. "Let's go find the hunt," he said.

They made their way around the brambles and down a slight slope tumbled with stones and logs, and stood considering the stream.

"Looks deep to me," said Patrick.

"Ruthie's got longer legs."

There was a sudden clamor of hounds and a discordant bleat from one horn, and right out of the bushes across the stream from them leaped a unicorn. They sat down hastily, and the unicorn cleared the water, themselves, and the whole bramble patch with one leap. The hunters crashed through the bushes a bare five seconds behind it, made a tremendous noise of splashing and trampling, gained the opposite bank, and began plunging their way around the brambles. Behind the hunters crowded the hounds, and then Ellen, and then all the inhabitants of High Castle, flushed and gleeful.

Ted and Patrick scrambled to their feet and turned around, and the scornful remark Ted had planned for the hunters and their clumsiness died in his throat. The unicorn had stopped just before the brambles, and stood waiting for the hunters under the pomegranate tree.

Ted saw the animal framed in trees: plum, holly, hazelnut, hawthorn. When he had hit himself in the head with the pomegranate tree and proposed his plan to Patrick, he had seen nothing on the ground but sticks and stones, nondescript greenery and the offensive bramble. Now the ground blazed with the crowded blooms of daisy, marigold, primrose, yellow flag: incredible gold, but it was not so bright as that horn; there was flaming and jubilant white, but a mere field and moonlight color beside the coat of the unicorn.

Ted had never paid any attention to the names of trees and flowers. He knew these because their names ran along under his mind as the names of the fencing moves had in his dream.

A spear whished between Ted and Patrick and hit the ground with two thuds, to be swallowed up in flowers. A second one hit the pomegranate tree, shook there for a moment, and flopped meekly down. But a third grazed the neck of the unicorn. Hunters and hounds pushed past Ted and Patrick, who stood staring, to close on the unicorn, which shook itself like a man interrupted in his daydreams, whipped itself around, and kicked vigorously. Two hunters

333

fell back onto several hounds. The dogs yelped and everyone who had not fallen laughed. The unicorn cleared them all again and went, with a shower of water that caught almost everyone, into the middle of the stream.

Ted and Patrick turned around again and craned their necks to see over the crowd. Behind the unicorn on the banks of the stream and far up the thinly wooded slopes grew feverfew, love-in-a-mist, and forget-me-nots; down into the water crowded cattails and plantain and water soldiers. Water lilies covered the stream from bank to bank.

"What happened to the trees?" demanded Patrick in a whisper. "It was dark over there before, they were so thick."

Two hounds bolted into the midst of the water lilies, snapping at the flanks of the unicorn. It put its head down, graciously, and touched the throat of one and the side of the other with its horn. The touch did not even ruffle their fur, but both of them yelped, much more loudly than they had when the hunters fell on them. They backed out of the stream in a flurry of water and fell over onto their sides, neatly and identically.

The unicorn looked at the hunters, daring them to move. One of them stepped to the water's edge and raised his spear; the unicorn moved its head the barest distance, as if it had heard something far off, and knocked the spear aside with its horn. The hunter leaped backward, shaking his hand and gasping. Two more hunters moved forward. The unicorn slid out of the stream like a wisp of morning fog and was gone up the opposite slope. Two spears crashed into the underbrush far behind it, and several people groaned.

"This is worse than usual," said one of the counselors; Ted thought a minute and remembered that this was Conrad.

"Remember that this is the unicorn's sport as well as ours," said Matthew, whom Ted had not noticed before.

"Even so, it could choose less brambly ways."

The master huntsman looked around at the company and raised his eyebrows. "Beaten so soon?" he said.

"Early, but not easily," said Randolph.

Ted wondered what had been happening to them while he and the others looked at the flowers, and while he and Patrick debated over the pomegranate.

"Well, if you choose to begin your feasting at noon and not at sunset, what is that to me?" The huntsman looked them over again. "Ellen," he said.

Ted followed his gaze and saw Ellen standing between Ruth and Agatha. She was bedraggled, and had lost her boots.

"Sir?" she said.

"Make thy garden."

Ellen came forward slowly, her great cloud of hair standing out in all directions and her eyes like a cat's. She went by Ted and Patrick as if they were two more trees and strode barelegged into the brambles.

Ted, watching her progress, saw that as flowers had grown wherever the unicorn stood, all around Ellen the brambles were covered with roses. It was not that they sprang suddenly into being. They were not gone one minute and there the next. It was like looking at a tree and thinking that it was a bear, and then suddenly realizing that it was only a stump after all. Roots and lumps and oddities you had ignored when you thought it a bear, because they did not fit the bear shape, suddenly assumed their proper importance, so that you wondered now how you could have ever thought the stump was a bear.

In the same way, as the change in the mind from stump to bear takes no time, so, suddenly but not unnaturally or magically, for it was his eyes changing, not the forest, the tangled sprawl of brambles became a hedge of roses.

There was an arched opening in the hedge, and through it Ted saw a garden and a fountain.

"Well," said Patrick in Ted's ear, "she always was good with the garden."

A rabbit hopped over Ted's foot, and another, and two more. He watched them lollop through the arch in the hedge, and then he saw two pheasants balancing on the rim of the fountain. A wanking and a flapping from behind made him wince, and two mallards landed noisily in the stream. Two white ducks came more sedately after them.

"Criminy," said Ted as Patrick's fingers dug into his arm. He wondered if Patrick realized he was doing this: It was a most uncharacteristic gesture. Finding it more comforting than otherwise, he did nothing to disturb it.

Two lions came drifting through masses of violets and cornflowers and the three shadings of the periwinkle. Behind them, treading delicately in the path they had made, was a stag. Caught in its antlers were trailing ribbons of green leaves. A hissing made Ted look from the stag back to the stream, where two ruffled swans and a serene heron now paddled and sailed. Ted looked at Patrick.

"There must be a forest fire somewhere," said Patrick, but he did not sound as if he believed it.

The heron came out of the water right next to Ted and began to preen itself. Ted jumped, and hit his elbow: He was standing under a peach tree. He had thought it just another brambly bush, and a danger only to the shins.

"Come along in," said Matthew behind him. Ted was holding up the procession.

Ted obeyed him. The fountain had several intriguing but not pleasant stone heads, of no clear family. They spat torrents of water back into the stream, which had suddenly developed a branch of itself in the garden. The smooth lawn around it was aswarm with animals. Ted saw foxes, and squirrels, and one lynx, staring down one of the hounds from a nest of pimpernel and ground cherries.

The crowd of people was quite silent, and the animals were so still that Ted wondered if they were illusory. Then the breeze shifted, and he caught a whiff of lion. He was not sure whether he recognized it from trips to the zoo, or whether the back of his mind was telling him things again.

Ellen stood under an apple tree just beyond the fountain. She looked bemused. The unicorn turned its head one way and then the other, surveying its serene animals and its sweaty pursuers. Then it knelt and dipped its horn into the stream. The bowl of the fountain was hidden in roses. In the silence Ted could hear water trickling. Ellen sat down in the grass and held out her hand to the unicorn.

"Please come," she said. She did not speak very loudly, but in that quiet she did not have to.

The unicorn stood up and looked at her. It reminded Ted of a cat deciding whether to obey you. Then it lowered its head and went to her. It slid to its knees with a movement very like a cat's, certainly more like a cat's than a horse's, and laid its great head on her knee. Ellen was as pale as the unicorn. She put a hand on its ear and burst into tears.

A cluster of hounds bowled over the rabbits and birds and swarmed upon the unicorn. The birds squawked, the hounds barked, and Ellen shouted, "Get away!" Two hunters picked her up from under the unicorn's head and put her down in a cloud of milk thistle.

The master huntsman put his spear to the breast of the

unicorn. The unicorn flung itself into the air with a terrible cry, its horn flashing, but the hounds fastened themselves on its flanks and bore it down. The unicorn seemed to hover a moment, its shadow a dark stain on the green lawn. Then it dropped to earth with a force that shook the forest from end to end.

Birds flew shrieking from the trees. The animals vanished into the brush and flowers. The bowl of the fountain burst and soaked everyone's feet. People put their heads in one another's shoulders, cringing. The sunlight darkened and went gray.

In the silence that followed, they looked at the unicorn. It lay in the dimness, shining with its own light. The hounds, the only moving things in all the landscape, stood four feet away from it and extended their long heads, sniffing cautiously. The master huntsman, his bright colors quenched, stood like a figure in a tapestry, staring not at the unicorn but at his fallen spear.

After a long time one of the hounds whined, and the huntsman moved. He looked over the fallen unicorn at his group of men, and gestured with his hand. Two hunters carrying long horns pushed through the group of rigid hounds to stand before the unicorn. They blew their horns, and in a blare and flash of gold the sun came back. The unicorn stood up like a flower opening and bowed its head to the hunters. People shook themselves and began to murmur, and all the animals crept out of the bushes, twining and rubbing on people's ankles as they went, and fawned upon the unicorn.

Patrick let go of Ted's arm. "I'd hate to see a real hunt," he said.

One of the hunters crossed to where Ellen still sat in the milk thistles, and bowed to her. She stood up with a rebellious air and looked at him. He held out to her a gold collar. Ellen took it and looked at the unicorn.

Ted watched her across the broken fountain, which still gurgled cheerfully to wet all their feet. He had been observing Ellen's expressions ever since she had been old enough to play with him, and he recognized this one. He knew, with a dreadful certainty which threatened to turn to laughter, that Ellen was going to throw the collar right into the stream. Beside him Patrick drew in his breath.

Ellen, with a wild grin, lifted her arm, and froze as the unicorn came toward her and bowed its head for the collar.

"That's right," said Patrick, under his breath. "The unicorn wouldn't like it."

Ellen put the collar around the unicorn's neck, fumbled, and fastened it with a distinct and final-sounding click.

"Not for them," she said, in a voice that could probably be heard back at the castle, "but for you."

The unicorn said something in her ear, but Ted could not hear it. They turned together, Ellen's hand hooked in the collar, and sloshed peacefully past the fountain and across the garden, followed by the hunting party and an exaltation of animals.

In the middle of the garden was a peculiar tree with a fence around it. It was another pomegranate. Ellen led the unicorn inside the fence, came back outside, and shut the gate on it. The unicorn lay down neatly, its forelegs stretched out before it like a cat's and its plumy tail draped over the fence. It looked smug.

Ted and Patrick, by dint of pushing and elbowing, managed to find themselves places at the front of the throng. There were a fox and a lion in front of them, but the fox was not in the way and Ted did not feel like disputing with the lion. Patrick did not seem to like being so close to it.

"You can't trust them even when you think they're tame," he informed Ted.

The lion turned around and yawned at him.

Ted's stomach quivered, but he also wanted to laugh. "You should be more polite, then," he said.

The master huntsman made his way through all the live things and stood near the fence. "Let the First Riddler come forth," he said.

"I hope," said Patrick, "that somebody told the King about Shan's Ring."

King William came gravely out of the crowd with a cardinal on each shoulder, and stood outside the fence before the unicorn. He did not bow, probably because of the cardinals, but he inclined his head.

"Who are these who come from the south
On the eagle's wing with the lion's mouth?"

"What?" said Patrick.

The King had taken his counselors by surprise too. Ted, by craning his neck, could see that Andrew was pleased, Matthew astonished, and Randolph furious. He could not see Fence.

The unicorn's head came up a little, and it fixed the King with its great eye as if it hoped to make him back down. The King stood patiently. The cardinals, against his white hair, looked as if they had been cut out of cardboard.

At last the unicorn spoke. Its voice was clear and piercing, like the sound of a flute. It said,

"These are the stuff of foolish dreams;
these are far more than they seem."

Ted looked as if by compulsion at Randolph, who smote his forehead in exasperation. A lynx leaped at the swinging tassel of his sleeve. It missed and landed upon two squirrels. They scolded. It spat at them. The unicorn looked at them and they quieted down like guilty children. Randolph was bright red, and Ted felt a treacherous laugh welling up in him. He began to wonder if he could get through this ceremony without disgracing himself. The crowd was remarkably quiet. Many people were grinning, but no one laughed or spoke.

The King retired back into the crowd, grinning himself, and the master huntsman said, "Let the Second Riddler come forth."

"All the riddles on the same day?" whispered Patrick.

"Put it on your list," said Ted.

Conrad came forward, followed by a number of ducks that muttered behind him like a gossipy chorus.

"I thought of a great way to put this one," said Patrick into Ted's ear. " 'Is King John/Putting us on?' "

Ted quelled him with a glare and managed not to giggle.

Conrad said,

"Did King John write in earnest or in jest?
Are those who shun his works the worst or best?"

"You know," said Patrick, "they're doing just what Randolph and Fence thought they shouldn't."

The unicorn said,

"King John wrote as he thought he knew.
His readers are as mixed as you."

"You know," said Ted, answering Patrick a little obliquely, "I don't think the unicorns take this very seriously."

"They don't take anything seriously, if you look at their history," said Patrick. "Ellie and her weird ideas."

The lion turned its head and yawned at them, and Patrick was silent.

"Let the Third Riddler come forth," said the huntsman.

Ruth came forward. No animals came with her. She did the unicorn a courtesy, and it inclined its head to her with a little chink of its collar. This pleased Ted immensely, and he saw that Patrick looked briefly smug.

"Who is Claudia, what is she?" said Ruth, and Patrick made a muffled snort. "Does your high court commend her?" finished Ruth, and sent Patrick a look almost as alarming as the lion's.

The unicorn paused, flicking an ear. "Subtle, fair, and wise is she," it said, and although its voice had no expression as human voices do, Ted could have sworn that somewhere in its answer there was a touch of delighted malice. "But none of ours did send her."

A murmur rose from the crowd, and a number of animals snarled, whether to shut the people up or because they too found the answer odd, Ted did not know. He looked at Randolph. Fence had appeared beside him, and the two of them were carrying on a conversation with grimace and gesture. They both looked put out.

"'Subtle, fair, and wise'?" demanded Ted of Patrick.

"Fair is foul, and foul is fair," said Patrick, gloomily.

"Hover through the fog and filthy air," said Ted, completing the quotation.

They stared at one another, and the gaze of the lion did not stop them this time.

"You know," said Ted, "there was an awful lot of fog and filthy air around before we locked her up."

"Yes," said Patrick, intently, and then shrugged. "Whatever that means."

Ruth had made another courtesy and backed off. The unicorn stood up, shook itself and chinked its collar, and cast an indecipherable look upon the crowd. It leaped the fence, and was gone through the woods like a shaft of sunlight between cloud and drifting cloud. Ted looked around in some alarm, but the lion had disappeared.

CHAPTER 21

THE huntsman inclined his head to the crowd with a gesture like that of the unicorn. "Go to your feasting, then," he said to them. "Meet we again next year?"

"Meet we again," said the King.

The huntsman beckoned to his men. They moved into the thick of the forest. They went south, while the unicorn had gone north, but were gone almost as quickly as the unicorn. With their passing the quality of the light changed. It was still that of a clear summer day, just past noon, but it felt, at least to Laura, ordinary, as if it might have been in Illinois or Australia as well as in the Secret Country.

People began to chatter and laugh, and to move down an avenue of trees that had not been there before. They went in the direction the hunters had taken.

Laura had lost Ruth and Agatha in the crowd, so she hung back to wait for Ellen. But the hunt, it seemed, had not done with Ellen yet. Benjamin came up to where she stood by the empty circle of fence around the pomegranate tree. He led the white horse they had seen at the beginning of the hunt. Laura thought that, as horses went, it was beautiful, but after the unicorn it looked like a bad drawing.

Ellen seemed to think so too; she scowled at Benjamin and started to walk away. Laura hurried to intersect her path, tripped over a rabbit, and fell face first into a clump of brilliant red flowers. She sneezed.

"It is the honor due thee," Benjamin said.

"For what?" demanded Ellen.

Laura sat up and watched them.

"Thou hast tamed the unicorn."

Ellen opened her mouth, and shut it again. She looked as if she were remembering something, and the look stabbed Laura with jealousy as sharp as a splinter. Laura had hoped that the hunt would be even better than that morning, but she had barely seen the unicorn, let alone spoken to it. Knowing that she was a coward, she had admired equally Ruth's refusal to be the hunt's bait, and Ellen's offer. But suddenly she thought that, if she herself had offered to be the bait, then she would be sitting there with that look of secret delight. Tears burned her eyes, but they were not the easy tears that turned to howls. Laura forced a swallow down her aching throat and stood up, grimly.

Benjamin made a stirrup of his hand, and Ellen stepped into it and swung herself astride the white horse. She petted its ear. "You poor thing," she said.

Laura knew what she meant, but she was surprised when Benjamin did.

"She would not be as the unicorn," said Benjamin.

He turned to lead the mare after the last of the hunting party, and Laura ducked behind a peach tree. She watched them out of sight, and set off to follow the unicorn.

Once she got out of the immediate area of the hunt, this was easy. The unicorn had left, in the brambly and branch-littered forest, a clean trail of flowers. Laura felt so fierce that she did not even mind stepping on them. Their trampled scent rose about her and made her dizzy. Even in the shade it grew hot, and sweat stung all her scratches.

It was extremely quiet except for the crackle and thud of her footsteps. All the animals in the forest seemed to have come to the Unicorn Hunt and stayed for the feast. After a time that probably seemed much longer than it was, she came to a real path, brown and beaten. The unicorn's flowers grew on either side of it, so she followed it.

She was getting tired, and plodded along with her head down. It had certainly been a long time now. A wind began among the branches, swooped down, and blew a flurry of leaves past Laura, drying the sweat and blowing her hair into her eyes. She swiped it out of the way and looked up.

"Shan's mercy!" she said. There was a sudden stillness in the forest, but she was too stunned to mind it.

All around her it was autumn. She did not know the names of the flowers that still bordered the path, but they were rust- and flame-colored, and so were the trees. The floor of the forest between them was piled with red and yellow and brown. Many trees already held bare black branches against a watery blue sky. The wind came back, a chill puff, and Laura shivered.

She looked along the brightly bordered path. Ahead, almost on the edge of her vision, rose a green hill topped with a wall or fence; the path led up the hill.

"Well," said Laura, "it's shorter to go on than to go back." This was something Agatha often said to her and Ellen when they were tired of doing something and wanted to leave it unfinished.

The path led to an iron gate in a stone wall. The gate was heavy, but it opened outward. After she had tugged it the first few inches it swung wide suddenly, and she fell down the hill. The grass was soggy.

She trudged back up and went through the gate. Inside, making her blink after the thorny tangle of the forest, was a vast flat green space full of gravestones amid a riot of flowers. Some stones stood up, and some lay flat on the ground. Some were brilliant white, and some were gray, and some were green with moss.

Laura paused just inside the gate, biting her lip. This did not look like a place for unicorns. But it would be silly to go back without looking around. She trod sturdily across the close green turf. There were no walks here, no trees or bushes. Flowers were planted thick around each gravestone, but otherwise there was only the flat grass. Laura felt as if she were in the middle of a mosaic.

The first stone she came to had raw earth around it, and its flowers were less thick than those of its neighbors. It must be newer. Laura bent to look at the letters on the stone. She did not even recognize the alphabet, but a shiver crept up her backbone just the same. She turned away, and two rabbits shot across the grass.

Laura felt better; where there were animals, there might be unicorns. She methodically quartered the whole place, but nothing else moved, and the only marks on the grass were hers. She knew the letters on some of the stones, but the words they spelled made no sense to her.

Laura stood in the middle of the graveyard and thought. All she could decide was that she had gone the wrong way when she came to the path. She went back out through the gate and hauled at it unsuccessfully for a little while. She barked three knuckles, but she could not push it closed against the slope of the hill. Leaving it open made her feel that she was letting something soggy and unpleasant in from the forest, but there was nothing to be done about it.

Laura went back through the forest, faster than she had come. The wind was colder. She did not realize until she came to where the trail of flowers met the path how much she had expected it to be summer here. It was still autumn. The path did indeed run on both sides of the flower trail: Laura had turned right the first time, so now she took the other way.

After a few windings the path settled down beside the stream. Laura threw a few pebbles in, startling a school of silver fish, and tried whistling "The Minstrel Boy." She still had not remembered why it was so familiar.

Nothing happened. Laura, with a vague idea of seeing farther, climbed a willow tree. Once there, she sat stolidly. The water mumbled along below her, the yellowing willow leaves hissed and fluttered. But not a bird, not a squirrel, not a rabbit moved or spoke anywhere. The wind died and the air sat like a damp blanket on her head.

She looked in all directions, but saw no white elusive shapes. She found that she was exasperated, and was pleased not to be afraid. A certain amount of thought produced the conclusion that, if she could not find the unicorns, she would have to make them find her. She had thought that the "Minstrel Boy" tune should do this. But as long as she was whistling . . . she imitated, as best she could, the song of a cardinal, and almost fell out of the tree as something landed pricklingly on her shoulder.

"Please," she said to the cardinal, feeling not at all foolish for sitting in a tree in the middle of a wet woods and talking to a bird, "I'm looking for the unicorns."

The cardinal rose from her shoulder and flew away. When she started to climb down to follow it, it came back and scolded her severely, so she stayed where she was. The cardinal darted off and returned in a very little time, not with a unicorn, but with Lady Claudia.

Ruth had said that Shan's Ring would keep Claudia out of the way for a year and a day, but here she was. Laura found herself more resigned than surprised. It was just like Claudia. Then she scowled. Maybe it was not this fall, but next fall.

Claudia was collecting plants from the waterside and noticed neither the cardinal nor Laura. Laura was just as happy not to be noticed, but she felt she should trust the cardinal.

"Good afternoon," she called, feeling foolish.

Claudia, with no evidence of surprise, gave Laura a smile that made her feel like a mirror Claudia was looking into, and came gracefully along the stony path. She was not dressed for walking, and wore slippers, not boots, but she seemed perfectly comfortable. Laura, whose hunting clothes were not elegant at their best and had suffered from the hunt and her subsequent ramblings, stopped feeling like an adventurer and began to feel rude and rumpled.

"Art thou stuck?" Claudia asked her, increasing the feeling.

"No," said Laura, "I can see more from up here." Claudia's husky and insinuating voice, so strange in the wet and prickly forest, was familiar to her, but she did not know why. Ellen, she remembered, had recognized it, too, at the banquet.

"What wishest thou to see?" asked Claudia, looking straight up at her and sounding so like a fortune-teller that Laura shivered unexpectedly and again almost fell out of the tree.

"I was hoping to see a unicorn," she said.

Claudia seemed amused. "It is too late in the year, mild autumn though this is," she said. "They are all gone south for the winter."

Laura was both disappointed and appalled. Unicorns should not migrate like robins; they should not have to pay attention to the weather. Claudia's voice still nagged at her, but she could not place it. I must be going crazy, she thought, I keep recognizing things I can't remember.

"Well, I was hoping," she said.

Claudia shrugged. "I must be going on before the forest dries more," she said. Her voice was not as eerie in its familiarity as the tune of "The Minstrel Boy," but Laura had had enough of it.

"I'll just sit here awhile longer," she said.

Claudia nodded and went on her way.

Laura looked up and saw the cardinal a few branches above her, looking smug.

"Thanks a lot," she said.

The cardinal beeped at her.

She looked down, and there was a unicorn standing in the water and drinking, with no more noise than the stream made going over the mossy rocks.

Laura's first feeling was not relief or pleasure, but an outrage directed at Claudia for lying to her. Then she sat and watched the unicorn. It was browsing in the plants that Claudia had been gathering. The water where it stood was flashing with fish. Rabbits stood up along the banks, five squirrels ran down Laura's tree, and hundreds of birds sat above her, singing. She looked over the heads of the rabbits and saw two stags standing among the trees. She looked back to the unicorn. Six butterflies shot out of the bushes and made a dance around its horn. Laura stared; it was too late for butterflies.

The unicorn raised its head. Laura, fearful of losing it, climbed down the tree and walked straight into the chilly water. The unicorn nuzzled her as a horse would; its whiskers were wet. Laura thought perhaps she would think more kindly of horses in the future.

"Well, Child of Man," it said.

"Claudia said you had all gone south."

The unicorn snorted. "We are always here," it said. "Claudia is a tale-weaver. What did you desire of us?"

"The answer to a riddle," said Laura. It occurred to her for the first time that she had not invented a rhyme. Well, it was too late now.

"That must be decided in council," said the unicorn. "It is not the season for riddles."

"Can you take a message to the council, then?"

"No," said the unicorn.

Laura was relieved. She had seen and spoken to the unicorn. It would have been fun to have returned in triumph with the answers to all the riddles the hunt had been too stupid to ask, but that had not been what she wanted most.

"But I can take you," said the unicorn.

Laura was taken aback. But the thought of being left alone in the woods in the wrong season and with only Claudia for company was worse than the thought of riding even a horse, and this ought to be better than riding a horse.

"All right," she said.

The unicorn knelt in the water, and Laura climbed onto its back. It felt like satin, and it was much warmer than the water. She took a double handful of cobwebby mane, wondered how many bones she would break, and said, "I'm ready."

The unicorn went in one bound out of the stream and over an enormous stretch of underbrush. Laura's hair unbraided and tangled itself behind her. The trees went by like a flurry of fallen leaves. The sky streaked to gray. The unicorn stopped, and Laura promptly fell off into a pile of leaves.

A dozen other unicorns moved away to give Laura room

to stand up, but she could not see where she was. They were warm and spicy smelling. The one she had ridden spoke to the others in a most peculiar language. Laura could not help expecting them to sound like horses; they looked more like horses than like anything else. But the one she had spoken to in the lake, and the one at the hunt, and the one she had ridden, all sounded like flutes when they spoke human languages. When they spoke their own, they sounded deeper, but still like some strange horn.

The others did not answer the one Laura had ridden; when it had finished speaking to them, it said to her in human language, "Speak your riddle, Child of Man."

Laura took a breath. It had been hard to think while riding the unicorn, but she had come up with something that sounded formal, if not rhymed.

"How can a world be and not be? How can a play be a world? How can a sword be a gate?"

The unicorns moved like a flash of sun on water and made odd noises, like a group of recorders being warmed up.

"The form is not proper," the one she had ridden informed her.

"I haven't had much practice," said Laura, at random, and a little sulkily.

The unicorns became discordant. Laura lay back on the crackling ground and watched the leaves whirling against the clean-washed sky. She breathed in the cinnamon-or-ginger smell of the unicorns and discovered that it was impossible to worry.

"That is nonsense," the one she had ridden said. "You have walked out of your own time, you have played the Flute of Cedric, and you have found one of our number outside all feasts and customs."

"I didn't mean to walk out of my own time!" protested Laura. "And I never even heard of the Flute of Cedric, and I asked the cardinal to find me a unicorn."

The unicorns became even more discordant, like a very badly played brass band. They moved uneasily, and Laura suddenly found it hard to see them when she looked straight at them.

"What hast thou seen that thou hast not told?" demanded one of them.

Laura, who was by now thoroughly bewildered, felt as if she were in the middle of a mystery novel. She had never read one herself, but Ruth had read dozens of them one summer in a rebellion against Shakespeare, and had told the stories to the rest of them. Patrick had said that Shakespeare did it better, which had enraged Ruth. It was true, though, that none of those mystery stories had become parts of the Secret Country.

Unless, of course, she was in one now. Maybe Ruth, while being mad, had made up a mystery story for the Secret Country without telling anyone. In that case, Laura could not possibly know what she had seen and not told. She sat up thoughtfully. Thinking of things happening to her that had not happened in the game . . .

"Oh," she said. "You mean the pictures I see in the swords, and the lamps, and the jewels, and all that?"

"No doubt," said the unicorn, dryly. It sounded, despite the airy and inhuman quality of its speech, like Fence. Laura wondered if he often talked to unicorns.

"Why," the one she had ridden asked her, "did you see so much and tell nothing?"

"They don't listen," said Laura, quite sulkily.

The wind stopped, and the leaves fell straight down,

showering the unicorns and making Laura sneeze. The unicorns hooted like the musicians at the Banquet of Midsummer Eve, but more melodiously.

"The seasons listened," said the one she had ridden. "The path of flowers listened. The cardinal listened. Those others are but men. Wherefore could one such as you not make them listen?"

"Particularly," added the other one who had spoken, "to such things as these must be. Why, look you, Child of Man, how the not telling hath turned you awry."

"Is that why I'm out of my proper time?"

"We do not answer why," said the one she had ridden. "But that is how."

"How do I get back, then?"

"Tell what you have seen."

"But how can I unless I get back?"

"A pretty problem," said the other one who had spoken. The rest of them made burbling sounds that Laura was sure were chuckles. Being laughed at by unicorns was unnerving. They looked serene, austere, unearthly, and more beautiful than anything she had ever seen. They did not look as if they could laugh. She did not like to think of what kinds of things must make them laugh.

And it's not as if they're laughing because I'm me, or even because I'm a Child of Man, she thought, or they would have done it earlier. They're laughing at the way things are. I want to go home.

"Wait," she said. "If I went to High Castle now and told them *then,* could I go back? Do I have to go back? Could I stay in the fall?" After all, everything bad should be over by then.

"Things should be told as they are seen," said the one she had ridden.

"But I already didn't," said Laura, ready to cry.

"Tell as close to the occurrence as you may, then."

"But you said I couldn't get back until I did tell them!"

The unicorns were quite silent.

"Didn't you?" said Laura.

A flurry of wind rustled the drying leaves, and a rabbit streaked into the underbrush. Laura picked up a handful of leaves, stirring up a rich smell that reminded her of Fence. The thought of him was comforting. She looked up at the circle of pale sleek faces and violet eyes. She was not good at puzzles and riddles, but she recognized the quality of this silence. The older children had a certain type of joke that produced this same smug, expectant, and gleeful quiet. Laura thought carefully.

"You didn't say I had to tell *them* before I could go home!" she cried. "You just said I had to tell!"

This was greeted with a chorus of whistling and piping. They were pleased with her, which was more than Ted and the others had ever been on the rare occasions when she figured out their jokes.

"If I tell you will you take me back to summer?"

"If you tell us you will return to summer."

"Do I still have to tell people too?"

"It would be wise," said the unicorn she had ridden. "Although we might find mirth in your not telling."

Laura resolved to tell anyone she could find everything she could remember as soon as she possibly could.

"Well," she said, "I have to think."

The unicorns murmured, and several of them lay down with the abrupt motion of a cat that wants to play. Laura thought. She was surprised to realize how long they had been in the Secret Country. Finding the sword seemed like something that happened in another year. Of course, from where she was now, it *had* happened in another year. Laura wondered if she was having trouble remembering through that much time even though she hadn't lived through it yet. Magic was certainly confusing.

"Okay," she said at last, slowly. "The first time the swords lit up, I just saw a lot of faces, and more swords shining, and something like a horse, only . . . I bet it was one of you."

"No doubt," said one who had not spoken before. Laura wondered if Fence had taught them English, or whatever it was she was speaking with them.

"After that," said Laura, "at breakfast, the first day, I saw something. In the jewels on Randolph's dagger. It was that lady in the secret house. She was looking in a mirror, but she wasn't *in* the mirror." She stopped, fearful that she had given too much away, or that the unicorns would want to know why she had said the "first day." They gave her a grave and attentive silence.

"It seems like something else happened that day too," said Laura, "but I can't think what." She looked at the unicorn she had ridden. "Can I go back even if I forget?"

"Perhaps."

The unicorn sounded uncompromising. Laura thought harder. The unicorns around her were perfectly still. As she thought, they faded and slipped sideways into the periphery of her vision, and the things she had seen and not told crowded the leafy clearing.

"On Midsummer's Eve," said Laura, "at supper, in Fence's room, I looked at Randolph's ring, and I saw a lot of shapes, all misty, but up in the sky was Claudia's face. And it was the same as one of the faces I saw in the sword, before. It was big, bigger than the sun would be."

The silence held.

"And later Ellie and I found the knife Claudia made, and I saw Ted's face in it, all bloody. Hey!" said Laura, sitting up and trying to address a unicorn through the shifting shadows. "When Patrick broke—I mean, later, I did see Ted with blood on his face! Really. Except . . ." She frowned. "I think," she said, slowly, staring straight before her to where a ghost of Claudia's dagger winked, "I think when I saw him in the dagger his face was a lot dirtier. It's hard to be sure."

"Certainty is a trap," said a unicorn.

"Well," said Laura, "and that same night I looked at Fence's robe and I saw a lot of people and beasts all running around on a flat place. And I think," she ended, "that that's all." A great gust of wind swept through the trees, and the unicorns filtered back into view. Laura blinked. How had they done that?

"Well, Child of Man," said the unicorn she had ridden, "I think it is time we had your name."

"Laura," said Laura. In the silence after she had spoken, a kind of resinous fragrance wafted by, prickling but sweet; on the very edge of hearing a horn blew happily.

The unicorns drew back a little.

Laura wondered if she had been rude. "May I have yours?" she asked.

The one she had ridden came forward again. "Chryse," it said. Laura, gazing upward, saw for the first time that its eyes were not violet like the others', but a brilliant gold. The wind and the light sweetened suddenly into summer again, and the grass was full of dandelions.

"That's pretty," said Laura, before she thought, but Chryse did not seem to take it amiss.

"My thanks to you," it said, graciously. Then its ears went back. "Yours," it said, "is much more than pretty."

Chryse did not sound precisely pleased, so Laura changed the subject. "I guess you can't answer my riddles?"

"When you change time of your own power," said Chryse, "when you have played the Flute of Cedric and found the unicorn in winter, bereft of the cardinal, then we will answer your riddles."

"Thank you," said Laura, glumly. Ruth could change time of her own power, and she could play the flute, too, though she probably didn't know who Cedric was; Laura saw no possibility of doing any of these things herself.

"I think," she said, "since it's summer again and they might start to miss me, I'd better go back now."

"This is not your summer," said Chryse. The other unicorns were slipping sideways again, sliding into sunbeams and not emerging on the other side. "But I will take you to it." It knelt, and Laura climbed onto its back again.

Chryse leaped, and things became a blur of green and blue and gold, and Laura fell off suddenly, flat into the middle of the abandoned fence from the hunt.

"Thank you," she said.

"Due payment duly paid," said Chryse, with a remote amusement, and it shot over the fence and disappeared.

Laura picked herself up, brushed herself off, climbed over the fence, and followed the trampled trail of the others to the feast.

CHAPTER 22

I T seemed that Laura had not been gone very long. She caught up to Ellen, Benjamin, and the white horse before they had come to the feast. She trudged along behind them, looking at the wild tangle of Ellen's hair, and found that she was still jealous, but that she no longer had to do anything about it. She was sure, without knowing why, that Ellen had not felt the harder edge of the unicorns' character, the almost malicious mirth and the inhuman laughter. Ellen had behaved in accordance with custom, and the unicorns had been kind to her. Laura had not, and though they had not been unkind, they had been difficult. Laura tried to think of this as a superior adventure, but it felt more like a breach of manners. She shrugged and ran.

"Wait for me!"

The white horse shied and Benjamin spun around, but Ellen looked over her shoulder and grinned. "There you are," she said. "Did you get to see everything?"

"Yes," said Laura.

"Now I know what you meant about the lake," said Ellen confidentially.

"You were braver," said Laura, with an effort, and felt a little better.

"But you were first," said Ellen.

Laura looked at Benjamin, but he seemed to be busy leading the horse. He was a little grim, but Benjamin had never, either in the game or in the reality, been a very cheerful man.

The avenue of trees ended and they came out into a wide sunlit space crowded with people. There were three pavilions of dark blue with banners flying from them. The banners all bore a running fox, like the one on the tunic Ted had worn for Midsummer's Eve—or, come to think of it, like the one on the seal Ellen had used for the note they had sent to Fence.

Laura turned to Ellen as Benjamin helped her off the horse.

"You see why it couldn't be a unicorn on the banner," she said.

"What?" said Ellen, rubbing the horse's neck. "Will it have a feast too?" she asked Benjamin.

"Of a certainty," said Benjamin, and took the horse away.

"You see why it couldn't be a unicorn on the banner," repeated Laura.

"Oh," said Ellen. "No, I suppose it couldn't. It would be wrong."

"It would be asking for trouble," muttered Laura.

"Let's eat," said Ellen.

"I have to tell you something," said Laura, following her through the crowd. "The unicorn said I had to tell you."

"At the hunt?"

"No."

"Oh," said Ellen, "the one this morning, in the lake."

Laura blessed her for the mistake. "I see things in things," she said.

"What?"

Laura explained.

"That's weird," said Ellen, stopping in the middle of the crowd, so that a young woman carrying a tray of pasties had to dodge her, and two pasties flew off the tray. The young woman looked as if she would have liked to swear, but a small boy caught one pasty and a large dog the other, and she smiled and went on.

"What all have you seen?"

Laura told her. Ellen was unconvinced by Laura's feeling that Ted's face had been too dirty, in her vision, for the vision to have been of Ted in the tower after Patrick broke the Crystal of Earth. She became very excited.

"You're a fortune-teller!" she said.

"I am not," said Laura. "What's the use of telling people they're going to have blood on their faces sometime?"

"I wonder what it meant about Claudia," said Ellen.

"Well," said Laura, "when I saw her looking in the mirror but she wasn't *in* the mirror, that means that Randolph is right and she can use those mirrors he and Fence use to see other places. But I don't know what her face in the sky means."

Ellen's gleeful expression vanished. *"Brr,"* she said. "You know, if we were what she was looking at in the mirror, and we could see *her,* wouldn't her face look huge?"

Laura's stomach jerked. "I guess it would," she said. "But I don't know if she *was* looking at us, then," she added hopefully. "She was looking at a battle, I think."

"Well, we're going to be in a battle," said Ellen.

"Oh."

"I don't think I'm so hungry after all," said Ellen.

"I was wondering if I should tell Fence that Claudia can really use those mirrors," said Laura. She thought Fence might make her feel better.

"You sure should," said Ellen. "Let's find him." She began to push through the crowd, and Laura followed her.

"Why," Ellen demanded over her shoulder as they stood

waiting for a cart full of bread to pass by, "didn't you tell anybody sooner?"

Laura was indignant. "They don't listen, you know they don't."

"*I* do."

"You do not. You were right there when I tried to say things, and you didn't pay any attention either."

"Everybody's so *loud*," said Ellen, more thoughtful than defensive. This being true, Laura could not say anything to it.

"There's Fence," said Ellen.

Laura looked to where she pointed. Fence, distinguishable mainly by his shortness, stood between the King and Randolph. They were all laughing. The sight of the King laughing made Laura very uncomfortable. He was going to be poisoned soon; this might be his last feast. It would not seem so bad if he were unhappy anyway.

"You know," said Ellen, "I don't know if we're allowed to be serious today."

"Fence didn't like it at breakfast," said Laura, grateful for any excuse for staying away from King William.

"We'll tell him first thing tomorrow, all right?"

"Sure."

One of the undercooks, dressed in motley, came by and popped a sticky confection into each of their mouths.

"Well," said Ellen around it, indistinctly, "maybe I could eat after all."

Laura laughed. "And you have to tell me about the unicorn."

They helped themselves to the more portable sorts of food, shook their heads at the long tables full of potential eavesdroppers, and went and sat under an oak tree at the edge of the clearing.

Ellen had many things to say about the unicorn, but only two of them, Laura thought, were important. The first was that the unicorn had, Ellen thought, found the entire hunt, including the most solemn and formal portions of it, enormously funny. Laura had suspected this herself. The second important thing was what the unicorn had said in response to Ellen's, "Not for them, but for you." It had said, "For such a sentiment, my house owes a debt to yours."

"Did it think *that* was funny?" asked Laura.

"Well, I don't think so," said Ellen. "It's hard to tell what they think. It said it quite seriously."

Laura chewed thoughtfully on a piece of marzipan. When it was gone, she said, "I didn't tell you everything." Then she did.

Ellen kindly overlooked all mention of jealousy, an emotion Laura had often thought her to know nothing about. She was excited all over again by what the unicorns had told Laura.

"Do you *remember* any of it?" Laura asked her anxiously. "Did you make it up? Do you know anything about Cedric?"

"Not a thing," said Ellen, with every evidence of satisfaction. "It's all new. Isn't it great?"

Laura gave up on her, and ate in silence. They were about two-thirds of the way through their collection of food, and considering whether they had perhaps taken too much, when Ruth, Ted, and Patrick joined them.

"Laura has something to tell you," said Ellen, by way of greeting.

Ted sat down next to her. "I have something to tell you." Laura stared at him, almost forgetting her own news. He no longer reminded her of Lord Randolph.

"No, you don't," said Ellen. "Laura first. She's been in terrible trouble for not telling you already."

Laura thought this an exaggeration; the unicorns had been discomforting, certainly, but as terrible trouble they had nothing on Aunt Kathy in a responsible rage.

"Who's been yelling at you?" asked Ruth, showing that her ideas of terrible trouble were like Laura's.

"Unicorns," said Laura, with some pleasure.

She had expected a babble of comment after her explanation, but they received it in a profound silence.

"I wish you'd seen something more *definite*," said Ruth at last.

Laura, suddenly knowing how Patrick felt at times, just shrugged.

None of them knew how she might change time of her own power, none of them remembered anything about Cedric, let alone his flute, none of them knew what it might signify to find the unicorn in winter.

"Does that mean we'll *be* here in winter?" inquired Ellen. "I thought we were going to leave so Ted wouldn't kill Randolph."

"That's what I wanted to talk about," said Ted. "When we lost the hunt—after you and Matthew disappeared, Ruthie—Pat and I found a pomegranate tree."

"Pomegranate trees don't grow in this climate," pronounced Ellen.

"Well, all right. It was a tree with pomegranates growing on it, I promise you. And we were talking about trying to change the game, by saying that for every seed we ate of a pomegranate from the Enchanted Forest, we would get to spend one month out of every year in the Secret Country. We *didn't* try it," he said hastily, stilling several furious

364

protests. "We thought we should consult you. But listen. We could have done it. You know how the magic swords make your hand fall asleep? The ground in the Enchanted Forest feels the same way. We could stand on it and change anything. I could tell."

"Anything?" said Ruth. "Make it that Randolph and Fence didn't take the swords away? Make it that Randolph doesn't kill the King, and the King sees reason?"

"I think so," said Ted.

"That's cheating," said Ellen.

"Ellen Jennifer Carroll," said Ruth, "for the millionth time, this is not a game."

"It is," said Ellen, turning red, "if you can change it just like that."

Laura, who had been waiting for some time for Patrick or Ellen to say a particular thing, decided that she had better say it herself. "How do you know you can change anything if you didn't try it?"

"I could tell," said Ted, stubbornly.

"Let's go try it," said Ellen, standing up and showering them with crumbs. "Right now."

They looked around. The clearing was still crowded with people, and the sun was still high. They could probably go and return with no one the wiser—except, Laura hoped, themselves.

They shouldered through the crowd and walked in their best unconcerned manner down the avenue of trees, back toward the clearing where the unicorn had allowed Ellen to tame it. Once she had put the matter to herself that way, Laura found it hard to behave unconcernedly.

The avenue of trees ended abruptly at the bank of the stream. The clearing and the circle of fence were gone.

Laura, after a little effort, found the hedge of roses. It looked as if it had been planted a hundred years ago and left to itself ever since.

"The ground doesn't feel magical," said Ellen.

"Can you see the pomegranate tree?" Ted asked Patrick.

"It'd be on the other side of the stream."

"That stream's much deeper than it was," said Ruth.

"The forest is reverting," said Patrick, looking at Ted. "What if it can change things only when the unicorns are in it?"

Ted wore a very Patrick-like expression, an I'm-miles-ahead-of-you expression. "The ground didn't prickle until after I'd said what I wanted to do."

"Well, what, then?" said Ruth.

"Let's say that Patrick and I didn't practice with the magic swords, and therefore Fence and Randolph didn't take them away from us."

The mild breeze went on moving the leaves, and the remains of the rose hedge blurred and wilted a little before Laura's eyes.

"Ted," said Patrick, forestalling a scornful remark by Ellen, "the last time you wanted to change something, it was something that hadn't happened yet."

"But we need a test," said Ruth. "We need to see a change *now*."

"Let's say," said Laura, their ritual phrase giving her courage, "that Prince Patrick broke not the Crystal of Earth."

She yelped and sat down suddenly, as both arms and legs fell thoroughly asleep and then very slowly began coming awake again. The others stood over her in attitudes varying from exasperation to alarm.

"Did a bee sting you?" asked Ruth.

"No! The ground put me to sleep."

"You!" said Ted.

"I can't help it," said Laura, hurt. He had the grace to look sorry.

"Let's go see!" said Ellen.

"No, wait," said Ted. "Laura, if it's you who can do it, we might as well try everything, okay?"

"Tell me what to say," said Laura, who was beginning to feel frightened.

"Let's say Randolph and Fence didn't take the magic swords away from Patrick and me."

Laura repeated this.

"Did you feel anything?" asked Ted.

Laura was still prickling and tingling too much to know how to answer this. After considering for a moment, she said, "Nothing special, I think. Not *another* prickle."

"Maybe the first one's still working," said Ted. "Say, 'Let's say that Randolph will convince the King to see reason about the strategy for the battle, and Randolph won't have to poison the King.'"

Laura said it, with no great conviction. She felt more normal and less magical every minute. Despite the seriousness of the situation, she could not help being relieved at this.

"Anything else?" Ted asked the assembly in general.

"Do you suppose we could keep your aunt and uncle and our mother and father from noticing we were gone, when we get back?" asked Ellen.

"Better not," said Ruth, to Laura's great relief. "They're outside the Secret Country. I think that really *would* be cheating."

"I know," said Ted. "Let's say, please, Laura, that, no matter what else happens, I don't kill Lord Randolph."

Laura said this, resignedly. She would have been willing to bet a great deal that, somewhere, the unicorns were laughing at them.

"*Now* let's go see," said Ellen.

Ruth picked Laura up, and after a few most unpleasant moments, she was able to walk. They found the avenue of trees narrower and the ground of it rockier and beginning to be overgrown. Laura supposed the unicorns thought that this was funny too. She felt desolated. She wished she had not come back to see the forest in its everyday dress.

People were still feasting when they returned to the clearing, but there were fewer of them. The five children accordingly went back to High Castle as fast as they could go, nodding at guards and muttering to one another.

Ruth, by refusing to listen to anyone, got them all to her room first, and pulled from a chest the linen towel in which she had wrapped what Patrick had left of the Crystal of Earth. It did not clink or rattle. Ruth laid it on her bed and unfolded it with considerably more care than any of the rest of them thought necessary.

There was nothing inside the towel. Ruth shook it in the air a few times, looking pensive, and consented to go to the North Tower. Patrick, who had disappeared without anyone's noticing, met them at the foot of its stairs with the announcement that his sword, at least, had not returned to the place he used to keep it.

"Maybe we can only change things we did," suggested Ted. "So we should have said, 'Let's say Patrick and I didn't practice with the magic swords.'"

"Well, at least you did say that you wouldn't kill Lord Randolph," said Ruth, and they started up the stairs.

The North Tower was already dim at this time of day. It was perhaps for this reason that the light spilling out of its first-floor room seemed so vivid. Laura, trudging in the rear as usual, thought that the door must be open. But when she peered under Ted's elbow, she saw that the door was firmly shut, the light welling all around and through it and showing up a myriad of tiny cracks and holes. It was like sunlight, but a deeper gold. It was much less discouraging than the purple light Laura had seen at other times, but it still made her uneasy.

Ruth and Ted looked at one another, and simultaneously put a hand to the door. The door opened quietly.

"Good Lord!" said Ruth, walking in nonetheless.

Nobody else found anything to say. Laura followed them into the room and understood why. Poised in the middle of the air was a globe the diameter of a wading pool. It painted the bare stone room with gold light, but inside itself it had shifting and sparkling points of all colors.

"Good *Lord,* Patrick!" said Ruth. "How did you bring yourself to break that?"

"I didn't," said Patrick. Even with the gold light on his face, Laura thought, he looked pale.

Laura moved closer to the globe, and cracked her chest against something hard. The globe was sitting on a table.

"Be careful, Laurie," said Ted, grabbing her. "That's not what he broke, Ruthie. What we saw was much smaller, and it didn't glow."

"You know what, though," said Patrick. "*This* is the one I dreamed about. It's not where it was in the dream, but this is what it looked like."

"You mean somebody knew you were going to try to break it and put a false one here for you to find?"

"Claudia, I bet," said Patrick.

"Well, maybe she put the false one here, but who put this one back?"

"The unicorns," said Laura. "They'd think it was funny."

"I suppose that's *your* fault," said Patrick to Ellen.

"They'd be boring without a sense of humor."

"Some sense of humor," said Ted.

"Well," said Patrick. "I bet if we broke *this* one, it would be all over for the Secret Country, and we wouldn't have to put up with their sense of humor."

"Don't you dare," said Ruth.

"I'll save it for more desperate times," said Patrick, only a little reluctantly.

"Maybe we won't have more desperate times," said Ted.

"I guess this means we aren't going home?" said Laura, half wishing that she had never made her first wish about the Crystal of Earth.

"Do you still want to?"

"Well—all the things that were supposed to be nice are over, that you didn't want to miss. All that's left are the awful ones."

"Well, we think we've prevented the awful ones."

"So all that's left are boring ones, then. Councils and battles."

"Now look," said Ted, cajolingly. "You have an important mission. You have to change time of your own power, and play the flute of Cedric, and find the unicorn in winter, so the unicorns will answer your riddles and we can find out just what the hell is going on around here."

"Don't swear," said Ellen.

"You shut up. Okay, Laurie?"

Laura wished very much that it were Ted, or Ellen, who must do all these things. Either of them would delight in it. She herself hated the very thought of being important. But she would have to be important later; if she declined

her mission, they would laugh at her and scorn her courage now.

"Okay," she said.

They looked at the Crystal of Earth for a long time, but its colors made no shapes or pictures, and no answers.